CU00747036

BEST SUPPORTING ACTOR

CREATIVE TYPES

BOOK THREE

JOANNA CHAMBERS

SALLY MALCOLM

Best Supporting Actor

Copyright © 2023 Joanna Chambers & Sally Malcolm

Cover art: Natasha Snow

Published by Joanna Chambers

ISBN: 978-1-914305-07-8

All rights reserved.

No part of this book may be reproduced in any form or by any electronic or mechanical means, including information storage and retrieval systems, without written permission from the author, except for the use of brief quotations in a book review.

This is a work of fiction. All characters, places and events in this book are fictitious. Any resemblance to actual persons, living or dead, or business establishments or organisations is completely coincidental.

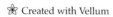 Created with Vellum

Best Supporting Actor

Lights, camera…attraction!

When Tag O'Rourke, struggling actor-slash-barista, meets Jay Warren, son of acting royalty, it's loathing at first sight. Loathing…and lust.

Tag's dream is to act, but it's a dream that's crumbling beneath the weight of student debt and his family's financial problems. If his career doesn't take off soon, he's going to have to get a real job. After all, feeding his family is more important than feeding his soul.

Luckily, Tag's about to get his big break…

Jay never had to dream about acting; he was always destined to follow in his famous mother's footsteps. But fame has its price and a traumatic experience early in Jay's career has left him with paralysing stage fright, which is why he sticks to the safety of TV work—and avoids relationships with co-stars at all costs.

Unfortunately, Jay's safe world is about to be rocked…

After an ill-judged yet mind-blowing night together, Jay and Tag part acrimoniously. So it's a nasty shock when they discover that they've been cast in a two-man play that could launch Tag's career and finally get Jay back onto the stage where he belongs.

Sure, it's not ideal, but how bad can working with your arch-nemesis be?

All they have to do is survive six weeks rehearsing together and navigate a cast of smarmy festival directors, terrible landladies, and vengeful journalists. Oh, and try not to fall in love before the curtain rises...

Break a leg!

This book is dedicated to everyone engaged in creative work, and especially to the screen writers and actors who, at the time of publication of this book, are striking for fair pay and AI protections.

PROLOGUE

TAG

Hallowe'en

Tag O'Rourke was thoroughly enjoying the Reclined Pigeon Productions Hallowe'en party. He was mildly drunk, had just spent the last hour dancing like no one was watching —although quite a lot of people *had* been watching, thanks to his eye-catching costume, which consisted of tight, silver lamé shorts, lots of body paint, and very little else—and now he was heading to the bar to get a couple of cold beers for himself and his friend Aaron.

The RPP lot were a pretty nice bunch, it turned out. He'd met loads of new people tonight, both actors like himself and behind-the-camera types.

Tag liked meeting new people. He was naturally gregarious, and besides that, he'd come along tonight determined to make the effort to network with industry people. Like it or not, opportunity was all about who you knew in this business. Talent could only get you somewhere once you were through the door, and for a guy like Tag, with no connections in show business, getting through the door was the hardest

1

part. In fact, since he'd left drama school a few years ago, he'd mostly come up against firmly closed ones.

But maybe his luck was finally beginning to turn. After getting to know Aaron a few months back, he'd discovered that his new friend worked at RPP and was one of the writers of a new TV pilot called *Bow Street*. It was Aaron who had encouraged Tag to audition for the show, and he'd actually landed a role—a small one, but still. They started filming in the new year, and while it wouldn't earn Tag much, it would certainly help flesh out the television credentials on his CV, which currently consisted of one toothpaste commercial.

As Tag approached the bar, an older guy he'd met earlier waved at him, beckoning him over. *Len*, Tag recalled, head of the RPP lighting crew. He'd turned out to be from Tag's neck of the woods and had worked on construction sites with Tag's dad back in the day.

Tag began to make his way over, eyeing a younger guy standing with Len who wore a t-shirt splattered with fake blood and a headpiece that made him look like he had an axe buried in his skull.

"Enjoying yourself?" Len asked cheerfully when Tag reached them.

"I am, yeah. It's a great party!"

"Yeah, the RPP Hallowe'en bash is legendary," Len said, grinning. He jerked a thumb at the younger guy and added, "This is my nephew, Liam. He reckons he went to the same school as you."

"Yeah?" Tag said, turning to the younger guy. "Woodville Secondary?"

"Yup," Liam said, grinning. "You were two years above me, in my sister's year. You remember Jodie Fleming?"

"Oh my God, Jodie's your sister? How is she?"

Liam began filling Tag in on what Jodie had been doing since their schooldays. They were so deep in conversation that Tag barely noticed when someone else greeted Len and started talking to him. It was only when the new arrival laughed—a warm, inviting, deeply attractive laugh—that Tag glanced his way, at which point his jaw practically hit the floor. Because Len was talking to *Jay Warren*, the male lead in RPP's flagship show, *Leeches*.

Jay Warren was standing right there, right next to Tag!

"Oh my God," he said, before he could stop himself. "You're Jay Warren." Then he felt himself flush, heat flooding his cheeks.

Jay's gaze flickered over him, a quick up-and-down that was somehow friendly, distant, and heated all at once. And Tag was suddenly more aware than he had been at any other point this evening that he was wearing nothing but a very small pair of silver lamé shorts. And that Jay Warren was probably even hotter in real life than he was on TV, if that was even fucking possible. Christ, those eyes. Storm-grey and intense.

Fuck, was he getting a hard-on?

Tag shifted uncomfortably.

"Hey," Jay said. "Nice to meet you...?" He trailed off, a faint question in his voice. An unspoken invitation for Tag to offer his name. Luckily, Len leapt in at that point, since Tag wasn't sure he could have managed actual words.

"This is Tag," Len said. "He's going to be working on that new show, *Bow Street*." He nodded in Liam's direction then. "So's this one actually. He's my sister's lad. Just joined the crew, didn't you, Liam?"

Liam smiled proudly. "Yep, following in the family footsteps!"

"That's great," Jay said, smiling affably at Liam.

"Hey, funny thing," Len said, elbowing Jay. "Turns out that Tag and Liam here went to school together. Small world, innit?"

Jay managed to express a suitable level of surprise at this really rather unremarkable fact, to Len's obvious gratification.

"Tag was mates with my sister," Liam offered as further evidence of this cosmic coincidence, and Jay managed to look impressed, while Tag stood there thinking, *For fuck's sake, Tag, say something!* But he couldn't seem to dredge up a single word, and now Jay was asking Len how the family was, and Len was telling him all about his daughter starting university, while Jay smiled and nodded, adding polite little pleasantries at just the right gaps in the conversation, all posh and uber-confident and—*Christ*, he was sexy. Tall and dark with miles of golden skin, overlong messy hair that looked silky to the touch, and Skye Jäger's trademark heavy stubble that somehow accentuated the classical beauty of his features.

It was only when the conversation between Len and Jay wound up that Tag finally got a chance to say something.

"Great to meet you," he said eagerly before Jay could escape. "My mum'll be well impressed when I tell her you were here. We love *Leeches* in our house." He was suddenly, stupidly, aware of his accent. It didn't usually bother him—hell, he was proud of it!—but for some reason, as those words gushed out, he found himself noticing and cringing at each glottal stop and silent 'h'.

"Thanks," Jay said. "And, er, nice to meet you too." He glanced at Liam then, including him in his next comment. "You'll both love working on *Bow Street*, I'm sure. It sounds like it's going to be an awesome show." His attention slid back to Len then, and he clapped him on the arm. "Good to see you, Len. I'm going to grab a drink, but I'll catch you later, yeah?"

Len saluted his agreement with his beer bottle, and then Jay was walking away, towards the bar, and Tag hadn't even managed to say anything halfway sensible to him.

He sighed.

So much for networking.

~

It was some time later that Tag ran into Jay Warren again. Literally.

He'd been dancing with Aaron and his *Bow Street* colleagues for a while and, inevitably, the drinks had caught up with him.

"Just going for a quick slash," he half-shouted at Aaron over the pounding music. Aaron, who had to be sweltering in his long wizard robes, but still looked as cool as a cucumber, gave him a thumbs up and continued dancing.

After the heat of the dancefloor, it was a relief to slip out of the function room into the cool hotel corridor.

Despite how busy the party was, the toilets were empty, and Tag lingered after he washed his hands, spending a couple of minutes taming his rumpled hair before heading back out, whistling cheerfully.

Perhaps he pushed the door open a little too hard, or maybe he barrelled out a little too quickly. Whatever the reason, as he strode out of the bathroom, he crashed into another guy on his way in. A proper, full-on body slam.

"Bloody hell!" the other man exclaimed.

Tag's first thought was that the guy sounded posh. His second thought was, *That's Jay Warren*, and his third thought —which came as his gaze travelled downwards and he took in the bright smear of body paint now adorning Jay's expensive-looking black shirt—was the one he spoke aloud. "Oh my God, I'm so sorry! Some of my body paint's got on your shirt!"

Jay blinked and looked down at the streaks of silver and red on his chest.

"It should come out," Tag said hurriedly before Jay could respond. "It's meant to be water-soluble. Do you want to…?" He trailed off and pointed uncertainly at the bathroom door. "We could try and get it off just now."

As soon as the words were out of his mouth, they struck him as funny. He did a sort of giggle-snort, and Jay looked up from his shirt. Their gazes tangled, and somehow—Tag couldn't help himself sometimes; he really couldn't—he found himself raising a flirty eyebrow, poking his tongue into his cheek and adding, "Maybe we could get each other off while we're at it."

He grinned as soon as the words were out, to show it was a joke—though maybe it was only *sort of* a joke because, yeah, Jay Warren was *fucking* gorgeous—but Jay didn't grin back or laugh.

Instead, he gave a tight, awkward little smile and cleared his throat. "That's, um, a very nice offer, but I'm afraid I— well, I make it something of a rule not to get involved with the crew."

"Crew?" Tag's eyebrows surged up and he gave a bark of angry laughter, unsurprised by the man's blatant prejudice. Tag faced it all the time. "Clever of you to guess my job. What gave me away?" He pantomimed thinking. "Let me guess: was it my accent?"

Jay blinked then, his expression shifting into something uncertain. "You—you're Tag, aren't you? We met earlier. You work with Len and—"

Tag tilted his head to one side, smiling sarcastically. "Yes... and no. I'm Tag, yes, but I don't work with Len. Believe it or not, I'm an actor too. I've got a role in *Bow Street*, actually, which is why I was invited tonight." He offered a tight smile. "I might not be as successful as you yet, *Mr.* Warren, but we can't all have famous mums sending us to posh schools and giving us introductions to Hollywood producers, can we?"

Jay winced and closed his eyes. When he opened them again a moment later, he said wearily, "Look, I'm sorry. That came out wrong. It's not actually a crew thing. I wouldn't get involved with *anyone* at RPP—actors especially."

Tag gave another bark of laughter. "Oh my God," he said, almost speechless now. *This guy.* "Calm your tits," he said drily. "It was only a joke. I don't expect the famous Jay

Warren to be interested in a nobody like me—even though you *were* totally eye-fucking me when we met."

Jay flushed at that, pink staining his sharp cheekbones. "Well, excuse me," he said. "I didn't mean to knock the chip on your shoulder. I just thought you were coming on to me and—"

"Yeah," Tag said, brushing past him. "I got the message, thanks, loud and clear." Over his shoulder he added, without looking back, "You should really wash that paint off before it stains."

About an hour after his run-in with Jay Warren, Tag was waiting at the bar for a drinks order and chatting to a very hot male model called Mason who, it turned out, he'd been following on Instagram for a while. He was in the midst of posing for a selfie with the guy when his phone pinged with a message from Aaron.

Hey, I'm on my way home—sorry for not saying goodbye—totally knackered. Let's catch up next week? xoxo

Tag fired a quick message back while Mason posted their selfie to Instagram—*No worries, enjoy your lie-in tomorrow.* Briefly, he pondered whether he should head home himself, then decided not to. He'd met a lot of fun people tonight—Jay Warren *very* much excepted—and he was having a good time. Might as well enjoy the free bar a bit longer.

Lifting the tray of drinks, he grinned at Mason. "I'm just going to deliver these to my friends, but I'd love to chat more if you fancy grabbing a drink with me?"

Mason smiled an easy smile. "Sure, why not?"

"Great. See you back here in five, then."

After dropping off the drinks with the *Bow Street* crew, Tag headed back to the bar, where Mason had commandeered a couple of tall stools and ordered two of the hokey Hallowe'en cocktails the hotel had put on for the party. Green lurid stuff they'd mixed up in giant jugs festooned with fake cobwebs.

They chatted easily for a while, and then Mason revealed that he was Lewis Hunter's most recent ex—Lewis, who in addition to being the writer and creator of *Leeches*, was Aaron's former boss. Tag had encountered him earlier in the evening. He'd been staring at Aaron all night like a total psycho. When Tag had suggested to Aaron that Lewis seemed a tad obsessed with him, Aaron had waved him off as if he was being ridiculous.

But come to think of it, he hadn't seen Lewis since Aaron had left the party…

"I just can't *believe* it!" Mason exclaimed, interrupting Tag's train of thought. "I mean Lewis *hates* that kind of thing."

"Sorry," Tag said. "I missed that. What is it you can't believe?"

"It's bloody loud in here, isn't it?" Mason said, leaning closer. "I was just saying I can't believe that Lewis came as Skye bloody Jäger!"

Skye Jäger. Lewis's fictional creation and Jay Warren's character in *Leeches*. It made a sort of sense for Lewis to dress up as Skye, Tag supposed. The two men were quite similar, both tall and dark and very good-looking.

"Well, he'd probably be better at playing Skye than Jay Warren," Tag quipped. "Christ, that guy's wooden. Good job he's hot and has a famous mum, or he'd never have been cast."

"Oh, that's not true!" Mason said, and Tag blinked, surprised. Somehow he'd thought Mason would be the bitchy type, but now he was frowning at Tag. "Jay's fantastic in that role, and he's won loads of awards for it."

Which was, annoyingly, true. Not that Tag wanted to admit as much.

Before he could decide how to respond, a voice behind

them said smoothly, "Well, I suppose I should at least thank you for saying I'm *hot*."

Tag and Mason both turned in their seats to find Jay standing behind them, a small, supercilious smile on his face.

Tag's cheeks flamed with hot embarrassment.

"You're wrong about one thing, though," Jay said, arching a brow at Tag. "I also had a famous *father*. Though *you* probably wouldn't know about him." He smiled thinly. "He was a sculptor."

It was a subtle insult, and Tag didn't have time to think of a reply before Jay turned to Mason and said smoothly, "So, what were you two talking about before I arrived and made everything *horribly* awkward?"

Mason laughed. "Oh, I was just boring the pants off Tag here, going on about Lewis. Just like I was doing to you earlier."

The fond way Jay smiled at Mason made Tag want to gag. Gritting his teeth, he said belligerently, "And I was trying to persuade him to go out with me."

Jay's head whipped back to Tag. *Ha! That got his attention*!

"Oh, Tag, you know you're bloody gorgeous," Mason said, rolling his eyes. "But like I said, I'm really not up for another relationship right now."

It was an effort, but somehow, Tag managed to drag his gaze away from Jay and plaster a grin on his face for Mason. "That's okay. It doesn't have to be serious or even romantic. We could just go out together and have some fun." It was a spontaneous idea, but even as he suggested it, Tag realised it wasn't a bad one. Mason had a lot of followers, and Tag needed to raise his profile. Besides, it wouldn't be a hardship to spend time with Mason, who was easy to talk to and seemed to be a nice guy. "You know what they say about getting back on the horse," he continued. "Besides, don't you want to show all your 'gram followers that you're not heart-broken about Lewis?"

Mason had been smiling up to that point, but at the mention of Lewis, his face fell, then hardened. "You've got a point there," he admitted. "And I do need to keep up my content." He paused, then shrugged. "Okay, yeah, why not? That is, if you're fine with going on a sort of fake date? Just for fun?" He put his hand on Tag's knee. "I know my followers will *love* you."

Tag beamed at him, delighted by this turn of events—until bloody Jay Warren stuck his oar in.

"You know, Mason," Jay said, tapping his chin thoughtfully, "if it's your followers you're keen to impress, maybe you should be seen out and about with someone who's... more well-known?"

Tag's mouth fell open in shock. *What the hell?*

"In fact," Jay went on, as though inspiration had just struck, "weren't you telling me earlier that Lewis won't be going to the British Fashion Awards with you now? If so... how about I fill in?" His gaze flickered to Tag and back again as he added, almost apologetically, "I'm guessing you need a *celebrity* date for that kind of event? I'm sure Tag understands."

"Oh my God," Mason said, his eyes lighting up. "That would be amazing, Jay! I only got invited because of Lewis and was thinking about pulling out, but if you can come, I won't have to." His eyes slid to Tag, his expression awkwardly apologetic.

Well, Tag wasn't about to roll over and admit defeat so easily. Setting his jaw, he said brightly, determinedly, "You know what? This is perfect. Fake dating for likes! You should go on dates with *both* of us and see how your followers respond." He grinned his friendliest and most confident grin, leaning back on his bar stool. "I'm pretty sure you'll have way more fun on any date you go on with me *and* get more likes from your followers."

Mason laughed again, plainly relieved at Tag's reaction.

And maybe a bit tickled by his and Jay's competitiveness. "You know, this could actually be *fun*," he said, his green eyes dancing. "God knows I need a distraction, and my followers will love it. It'll certainly show them that I'm well and truly over Lewis bloody Hunter."

"That's the spirit," Tag said, grinning. But when his gaze flickered back to Jay Warren, the glint in those stormy grey depths was far from friendly.

ACT ONE

CHAPTER ONE

TAG

December - Six weeks later

No matter how gentle the alarm tone Tag set, he still woke up cursing when it went off at five-thirty in the morning. Especially at this time of year when it was pitch black. This particular alarm tone began as a distant, gently waking dawn chorus that gradually grew louder, but it might as well have been a pneumatic drill. It still made Tag roll over in despair and fumble blindly for his phone on the bedside cabinet to switch the bloody thing off.

It was too early. *Way* too fucking early. But he'd asked to swap shifts with Sarah this morning, opting to open up so that he could finish earlier and get over to the RPP studios in time for the afternoon's filming.

Filming. Just the thought made today's early rise worth it. This was it. The Holy Grail. A proper, paid acting job.

Today wouldn't be his first day of filming, but he hadn't featured much so far. Mostly, he'd just been standing in the background, speaking a few inconsequential lines here and there. But today, he'd be filming his character's pivotal scene, the one he'd spent weeks preparing for. His chance to shine. Okay, it was pretty small potatoes as far as the rest of the *Bow Street* cast and crew were concerned, but for Tag, it was the most important few minutes in the whole double-episode pilot, the moment when his character, Jude 'Bishop' Morton, went to Arthur Thorne of the Bow Street runners and betrayed the leader of the criminal gang that had been his surrogate family since he was a child.

Just one shift at City Beans coffee shop to get through first.

Throwing the bed covers back, Tag swung his legs over the side of his single bed and let the chilly morning air shock him awake before getting to his feet and heading for the bathroom. He tried to be quiet, since his dad was still sleeping. Downstairs, he could hear the faint sounds of his mum moving around in the kitchen. She'd been on the night shift at the care home, so she wouldn't have been back long. Probably having her habitual cuppa before heading off to bed, just as his dad was getting up.

"Ships that pass in the night, that's us," she always joked. And, yeah, it had been that way for quite a while. Money was always tight.

Tag started the shower, then loaded his toothbrush with paste while he waited for the water to warm up. When he was done brushing, he ran his tongue over the smooth surfaces of his teeth, examining them in the mirror. He'd made the mistake, back in the summer, of home-bleaching them ahead of the audition for the toothpaste ad. It had made them way too white, and his parents—being savage and merciless O'Rourkes—had laughed their arses off when they'd seen the result. Da was still calling him *Jaws* even now. Thankfully, the worst of it—when his smile had looked almost luminous—had worn off before the audition, and he'd got the job. His teeth had calmed down a lot more since then, but even now, he still worried they looked a little too bright. Overly bleached teeth didn't exactly scream 'serious actor', and they *definitely* didn't scream *Bow Street*, which was supposed to have a dark and grimy vibe. Bishop was meant to be a hard-worn and hungry street rat, ground down by life, not an Essex boy with waxed eyebrows and a dodgy tan.

Sighing, he turned away from the mirror, kicked off his underwear, and stepped inside the cubicle to get showered.

When he walked into the kitchen ten minutes later, it was to find his mum sitting at the table, still in her uniform and drinking tea from a 'World's Best Mum' mug Tag had got her for her birthday a few years ago, the words mostly faded now from repeated dishwasher cycles.

"Morning, love," she said tiredly. "You want a cuppa?" She pointed at the teapot on the table.

"Go on, then, since you've made a pot," Tag said. "I'll grab a quick one."

She crooked a smile at him as he grabbed another mug off the draining board and set it down on the table. "Don't you go getting used to it," she said. Her accent was strongly Irish even after all these years of living in England. "I only made a pot because I wanted to talk to you about something before I go and put me head down."

"Yeah?" Tag said, while he nabbed the milk out of the fridge. "Sounds serious." He sloshed a dash of milk into the mug.

His mum rolled her eyes, lifting the pot to pour the tea. "Nah," she said. "It's just about Christmas."

Tag groaned, even as he slid into the chair opposite her.

"What about it?"

"We're going over to Caitlin's on Boxing Day," she said. "And *no* wriggling out of it. You've only seen the baby twice since he was born, and he's five months. She's mentioned it. She thinks you're avoiding her."

"I'm not avoiding her," Tag grumbled.

"Why haven't you been over then?" His mother looked bewildered. Charlie was her first grandchild, and she was completely in love with him.

"It doesn't matter," Tag muttered, grabbing his tea and taking a big slurp.

"Don't give me that," his mum said, pointing a finger at him. "What's got you so you don't even visit your own sister and nephew for months on end?"

"Fine," Tag said, setting down his mug sharply on the table. "It was just—it was something Stevie said." Stevie was Caitlin's fiancé. He was a plumber and a lad's lad. Loved his footie and his beer. Got on famously with Tag's dad.

"What's up with Stevie?" his mum asked, frowning. Then her eyes widened. "Don't tell me he's one of them homophobes. I'm not having that!"

Tag let out a huff of helpless laughter and shook his head. "No, it's not that."

"Then what?"

Tag sighed. "I think he reckons I'm a bit of a waster. That I'm leeching off you and Da."

His mum frowned darkly. "He *said* that?"

He had actually. Not to Tag himself, but Tag had overheard him saying as much to Caitlin at Charlie's christening party.

"It's about bloody time your brother got a proper job and a place of his own. Let your mum and dad downsize and get that mortgage off their shoulders."

The worst of it was, Stevie was right. Tag's parents had been struggling with their overpriced mortgage for the last fifteen years, but with Tag living at home, they had no other options, even though he was paying as much as he could to help out.

Tag couldn't share what he'd overheard with his mum. She'd be pissed off at Stevie, and then there'd probably be an argument with Caitlin, who could be a bit of a hothead and was likely to leap to Stevie's defence the second their mother said anything critical.

"Nah," he said. "It's not anything Stevie said. It's just a feeling I get."

His mum's frown smoothed out. "Well, I think you're being a wee bit sensitive. Sure Stevie's a bit rough around the edges, but he's a nice lad. I can have a word with Caitlin, though? Just to be sure."

"No," Tag said, giving a rueful smile. "You're probably right. Besides, the next time I go over, I'll be able to say I'll be appearing in a real live TV show, won't I?"

She smiled at that, and her eyes—the same colour as his own, whisky-gold—were warm with affection. "It'd be even better if you could tell them they're making a proper series out of it that'll give you a regular paycheck!"

And just like that, Tag felt like a punctured balloon. This was just a pilot after all. The chance of *Bow Street* getting picked up wasn't that good, and Tag's chance of getting a recurring role in any potential full series was even worse.

In that moment, all the joy and anticipation he'd woken up with went out of him with a *whoosh*.

It wasn't even six a.m.

"Ah, Tag love—" his mum said, her voice regretful. His face must have betrayed him. Some actor he was.

He got to his feet and turned away, draining his mug, then opening up the dishwasher and stacking it inside. "I better get going," he said, his voice determinedly cheerful. "I'm not sure when I'll be home this evening. Don't bother making me any dinner."

And without waiting for a reply, he shouldered into his jacket and hurried out the front door.

Tag replayed the short conversation with his mum as he stacked the café's display fridges in readiness for opening up.

It wasn't that she wasn't proud of him. Tag knew that. Both his parents were incredibly proud of him. Hell, they'd spent half their lives chauffeuring him around to all his drama and theatre activities when he was a kid, and when he got into drama school, they couldn't have been more pleased for him. But he knew the thought of Tag living the life of a jobbing actor worried the hell out of them.

He understood their fears. They'd been stung badly when his dad's first business had failed. After that, they'd had to borrow heavily on the back of the house to start up again, extending the life of their mortgage by a decade. That was when his mum had started working full-time at the care home. So yeah, he got why they worried about money so much. He got why they'd always impressed upon him and Caitlin the need to be financially self-reliant.

But sometimes… sometimes it was like that was *all* they cared about.

Tag had only been out of drama school for a year when they'd tentatively raised the possibility of him joining his dad's business. But while Tag didn't mind labouring for his dad when an extra pair of hands was needed, he had absolutely no desire to become a builder. He wanted to *act*. And he'd told them that was what he was going to do. He was going to give it his best shot. Except somehow in the course of that discussion, that resolution had morphed into him giving it his best shot… for a few years. If, by then, he still wasn't getting anywhere, he'd promised to think again about working with his dad.

Two more years had passed since then, and the most he had to show for it was one TV commercial and his tiny role in *Bow Street*.

Tag sighed and reached into the box again, grabbing

another stack of breakfast paninis that he began sliding into the cabinet, next to the granola bowls.

He was almost finished when he heard a knock at the window. Looking up, he expected to see a customer. It was another fifteen minutes until the shop opened, but it wasn't uncommon for someone on their way to work to try to persuade him to open early. Tag straightened, pasting a regretful expression on his face that he dropped when he realised he knew the guy standing at the window. Grinning, he went to the door, pulled back the chain, and yanked it open.

"Mason," he said, beaming at his friend. "What are you doing here?"

"I'm on my way to a shoot near here," Mason said. "So I thought I'd swing past to see if you were working and if you had time for a quick coffee." He made a face. "But I see you're not actually open yet…"

"I'm always open for you, babe," Tag said, waggling his eyebrows. Then he laughed. "Seriously, it's good to see you. Come in." Ushering Mason inside, he locked the door behind them. "It's a bit dim in here, but I don't put the lights on properly till it's time to open up." He grabbed the box he'd been unloading and shoved the last two paninis onto the shelf, then began breaking up the cardboard as he headed for the coffee machine behind the counter. "Grab a seat. You want the usual?"

Mason slid into a chair. He sighed. "Yeah, black Americano."

"Mind if I have a cappuccino?"

"Why would I mind?" Mason looked surprised.

Tag grabbed two cups and grinned at him. "I've seen the way you eye my milk foam and chocolate sprinkles. You're practically green sometimes."

Mason laughed, his cheeks pinkening adorably. He really

was very cute. Not Tag's type, not really, but yeah, objectively, he was gorgeous.

"Okay, you've got me there," Mason admitted. "I love a cappuccino, but I can't afford the empty calories." He eyed his perfectly flat stomach glumly.

"I hear you," Tag said sympathetically. Like Mason, Tag viewed his body as a professional tool that needed to be taken care of. He went to the gym, ran, and did yoga to keep himself strong, fast, and flexible, and he ate pretty healthily. Even so, he knew he enjoyed quite a bit more dietary leeway than Mason did as a model. Which—thankfully—meant he could easily afford the breakfast panini he was planning on eating later. He'd wait till Mason was gone, though. No point torturing the poor guy with the smell of hot bacon.

The cappuccino, however, was non-negotiable.

While the espressos trickled out into the cups, Tag steamed the milk.

"You're looking very sexy this morning," he said, sending Mason a suggestive grin. "Have you done something different with your hair?"

Mason rolled his eyes. "Flirting at this time of the morning? Really?"

Tag chuckled. "There's never a bad time to flirt. Besides, you *are* looking sexy this morning. Not that you ever *don't* look sexy." He batted his lashes theatrically, and Mason gave a helpless sort of laugh.

"You really are incorrigible," he said, shaking his head, but he was smiling.

"It's a gift," Tag said lightly, sprinkling his cappuccino with chocolate, then carrying the cups over to the table and sliding into the seat opposite Mason, pushing the Americano towards him. "So, is there a reason you decided to pop by this morning?"

"Not really," Mason said, sipping his coffee. Then he

shrugged. "I suppose I wanted to see a friendly face before this shoot. Roger, the photographer, can be a real dick."

Tag made a sympathetic face. "Yeah? What's he like?"

Mason launched into an anecdote about his last shoot with Roger Mather. He'd kept calling Mason *Jason,* spent the whole day in a furious tantrum, and at one point had yelled at him to *"move his fat ass"* out of the way of one of the other models. Tag was suitably horrified. He immediately googled the guy and soon had Mason giggling over a series of unfortunate pap photos.

"Okay," he said at last, setting his phone down. "Enough of that loser. Let's think about something you can look forward to after the shoot. Have you got any fun stuff planned this week?"

Mason thought. Then he quirked a smile. "Well, I do have my next fake date with Jay later this week."

Tag frowned. "Wait, isn't it my turn next? Weren't you just at that perfume launch party with him the other night? I saw you got papped together—and your 'gram selfies were on point as usual." Mason and Jay had looked gorgeous together, their smiles so bright and genuine that Tag had sourly wondered if the fake dating might be turning into something real.

Mason looked a bit taken aback for some reason. "Oh, um…" he said awkwardly. "I didn't think that counted. Since it was, you know, an industry event."

An unwelcome wave of resentment washed over Tag. He tried to push the feeling aside. It was stupid to mind that Mason had taken Jay instead of him. Mason was free to go wherever he wanted, with whoever he wanted, and of course he'd choose someone famous for an event like that—someone who would attract the paps and get him all the press attention he needed to keep his Instagram audience growing. He'd hardly get that with Tag, an unknown actor with only one TV commercial and a few drama school productions to his name.

But even knowing he was being stupid, Tag couldn't help but feel resentful and a bit defeated. As much as he liked Mason as a friend, the main reason he was doing the fake dating stuff was to get his face out there and known. To try to create the same sort of buzz around himself that Mason had built so successfully around his own profile. The thing that *really* annoyed him, though, was that, while Tag would have loved to do that launch event, it probably meant nothing to Jay Warren. Jay had only elbowed in on the fake dating thing in the first place to piss Tag off. To put Tag in his place.

Well, Jay Warren could go and fuck himself.

Shoving his resentment down, Tag pasted a smile on his face. "So," he said cheerfully. "Where's Jay taking you on your next date?"

Mason had been eyeing him uncertainly, but now his smile returned. "Oh, I'm not actually sure. He said to wrap up warm, though, and that it's something festive."

"Hmm, I wonder what that could be?" Tag said, tapping his chin. "Christmas market maybe? Mulled wine under the stars?"

Mason grinned. "Well, it's a daytime date, so definitely no stars."

"Mysterious," Tag said, then yelped when he glanced at the clock on the wall. "Shit. I need to open up. Do you want another coffee? We can chat while I work."

"No, thanks," Mason said, getting to his feet. "I should get moving too. Don't want to rile up Roger unnecessarily."

Fourteen hours later, Tag found himself staring at his own pale face in the mirror. He was sitting under an unforgiving light in one of the production trailers while an assistant removed his make-up. His hair, which had been stuck under Bishop's distinctive bowler hat for the last few hours, was plastered to his head, and he had exhausted circles under his eyes… but Bishop's pivotal scene was in the can, and Tag thought it had gone pretty well.

God, he could sleep for a month, but tomorrow he had another early shift at City Beans, then a bar gig at a black tie event in the evening. The thought made him almost groan aloud.

Just then, the door to the trailer opened, and Pete Crowley, the director, stuck his head inside. He caught Tag's eye in the mirror.

"Come and see me when you're done here," he said, his voice clipped and business-like.

"Uh, sure," Tag replied, wondering what Pete wanted.

A few minutes later, face finally bare of make-up and back in his own clothes, he rapped the door of Pete's trailer, his heart hammering. Had Pete seemed annoyed, or was Tag being paranoid? He'd sounded brusque, but then Pete always did.

"Come in."

Tag warily opened the door of the trailer and stepped inside. Pete was sitting in his habitual spot, at the built-in eating area next to the tiny kitchen, his laptop open on the small table. He was a tall, spare man—a marathon runner in his free time—and he looked too big for the cosy booth, all elbows and knees. "Take a seat."

Tag obediently slid into the other side of the booth and waited.

"Your scene today," Pete began. "That was"—he paused— "it was good. Really fucking good."

Tag's heart, which had been pounding, seemed to entirely stop for a whole second, then start up again at a sprint. "Yeah?" he managed. His voice came out a bit strangled.

"There was stuff going on in your head through the whole scene—I could see it, behind your eyes. What were you thinking about?" Pete's brows were drawn together, his head cocked a little to the right in curiosity.

Tag swallowed. "Just, you know, the why of it."

"The why of what?"

Tag's stomach danced with nerves. He'd given this so much thought that it had become real to him, but perhaps Pete would think he was ridiculous.

"Why Bishop decided to inform on Jarvis."

Pete had been sitting forward, elbows bracketing his laptop on the table, but now he leaned back, eyes narrowing. "That's not in the script."

"I know. I just—I needed a way into the scene. What he must be thinking."

"And what was he thinking?" Pete's pale eyes were watchful.

Tag hesitated. "That he didn't want to betray Jarvis, but he had to. Had to sacrifice Jarvis to get closer to Thorne."

Pete's brows went up. "Interesting. You don't think it was just for the money then?"

"He doesn't ask for money in the script," Tag said. "There had to be another reason."

Pete smiled. After a moment, he said, "So why do you think he needs to get closer to Thorne?"

"Because he wants to destroy him."

Pete's eyebrows went up in surprise. "Really? Why?"

Tag felt a bolt of nervousness at that reaction. He'd made up his own backstory for Bishop since there was so little about him in the background notes he'd been given—which was hardly surprising given how minor the character was—but now he wondered if he'd been presumptuous. "I don't think it matters specifically why, for the scene," he mumbled. "I just needed an emotional anchor for how *I* was going to play it, and that's what I went with."

"Okay," Pete said slowly. "But there *was* something specific in your mind, wasn't there? I saw it in your eyes."

Tag flushed. "Well, yeah. I sort of made up a little extra bit of backstory for Bishop." He cleared his throat. "It's not inconsistent with the script or notes, and it helped me do the scene."

"I saw that," Pete said. "So what's the story?"

Christ, Pete really wasn't going to let this go. "I figured he thinks Thorne is his father. He blames him for his mother's death."

Pete said nothing, but he gave a mysterious sort of smile and looked up at the ceiling, seeming to consider that as he tapped on the table with his fingertips. "Yes," he said at last, his tone considering. "Yes, that's… I see that could work."

Tag wasn't sure how to reply to that, so he stayed silent. At last, Pete seemed to break out of his train of thought and returned his gaze to Tag.

"Well, I just wanted to say good job," Pete said, offering an uncharacteristic quirk of a smile. "And I really hope *Bow Street* gets picked up. If it does, maybe we can see about expanding Bishop's role."

Tag resisted the urge to jump up and punch the air in gleeful triumph, but he couldn't do anything about his grin, which was so wide it hurt. "Thanks," he said. "That means a lot."

Pete nodded, which Tag took as a dismissal. He began to get to his feet but paused when Pete held up his hand.

"Before you go," Pete said. "Look, this is a bit of a long shot, but… do you have any other work coming up next year? Late spring, summer?"

Tag sank back down. "Um, well, I have a regular gig in a coffee shop."

Pete chuckled. "Acting work, I mean."

"Oh." Tag's face heated. Feeling foolish, he quickly added, "No, nothing, um… just auditions, you know. When they come up." Shit. He sounded like a total loser.

"Okay, well, are you up for auditioning for a play?"

Tag sat up straighter, his heart pounding. "I—what?—*yes*. I mean, yes, I would absolutely love to—" He broke off. "Sorry, I'm—this is unexpected and—" He broke off again. Fuck, he sounded incoherent.

"I know," Pete said gently. "Look, here's the thing. The daughter of a good friend of mine has written a play that's going to run at a small arts festival in York this summer. It's about Siegfried Sassoon and Wilfred Owen." Tag probably looked puzzled because Pete paused and added, "The World War One poets?"

"Right," Tag said, flushing again and feeling like an idiot.

"They've got someone in mind for the Sassoon role, but they're going to be auditioning for the Owen part." He paused. "I think it might be right up your street. If you're interested, I could probably swing you an audition. I can't promise anything, but…"

"Oh my God," Tag breathed. "That would be—that would be fucking *amazing*, Pete!"

Pete chuckled again. "Okay, well, fair warning, the money isn't great, and you'll probably have to give up that coffee shop gig you mentioned, but the exposure could be great for you. Tim's pulling in some favours, and it looks like they've got a big-name lined up for the Sassoon role."

"Really? Who?"

"If you really want to know…"

"Yeah?" Tag said eagerly.

Pete grinned. "You'll have to land the role."

CHAPTER TWO

JAY

Two days later

Cold, crisp, and clear. Low winter sunshine glinting off the ice and the sounds of laughter and music rising into the unusually frosty London sky.

Jay Warren couldn't have asked for better weather for his skating date with Mason.

"Let's get a pic with the Christmas tree," Mason said, grabbing his arm and dragging him over to the forty-foot masterpiece set amid the glorious neoclassical courtyard of Somerset House, its lights sparkling even in broad daylight.

Happy to indulge him, Jay let himself be led towards the tree and pressed his face against Mason's while Mason fiddled with his phone, looking for the right angle to get the huge tree behind them into shot.

"Smile!"

Jay smiled, as directed, eyes hidden behind his sunglasses. That was another benefit of the cold, clear weather: he could keep his sunglasses on and his hat pulled low without looking like a loser. As much as Mason wanted to be seen, Jay preferred to avoid unwanted attention. Especially when he was on a date. Not that this was a *real* date, but it was still private time—not like when he went to industry events with Mason and did the whole red carpet thing. Those dates kept his agent on-side; she thought his relationship allergy damaged his castability as a 'sensitive leading man', so she was happy that he appeared to be involved with Mason. These private dates, though, were more about giving Mason content for his Instagram account, and, maybe, pissing off Tag O'Rourke, who was still being ridiculously competitive about scoring more likes than Jay.

To Jay's surprise, he had found he actually enjoyed these casual dates with Mason. Mason could be good company when he wasn't in one of his introspective moods, and today seemed to be a good day. He was happy, smiling, eyes bright and skin flushed from the cold.

Objectively, he was an extraordinarily beautiful man. It puzzled Jay that Mason didn't have a queue of men a mile long panting after him. Of course, Jay himself didn't feel any interest in pursuing anything with Mason beyond friendship, but then, Mason wasn't really his type. Mason was the sort of guy who wanted a proper, healthy relationship, and that absolutely wasn't Jay. No, Jay had tried the relationship path and realised he wasn't cut out for it. So, these days, he stuck to one-off hook-ups. That was why this arrangement with Mason was so handy—he had a perfect go-to plus-one for all the dinners and parties he got invited to with absolutely no risk of creating expectations.

"Can you skate?" Mason asked as they circled the rink, heading for the skate hire area.

"Yes, fairly well. My father had a house in Aspen. We'd spend a few weeks there every winter when I was growing up."

The corner of Mason's mouth lifted. "Wow, nice."

"It was, yes." His father, the eminent sculptor Ford

Warren, had been an American, and although he'd made London his home, they'd spent a lot of time in the States while Jay and his siblings were growing up—especially when their mother, Dame Cordelia, had been working over there. Which she'd done a lot. Jay had fond memories of the family Christmases they'd spent in Aspen, which was probably why he still loved this time of year so much. He nudged Mason's shoulder as they walked. "How about you? Can you skate?"

"Well, no house in Aspen so...expect me to look a bit like Bambi out there."

Jay laughed and glanced at the rink. It was crowded, which was never good if you were a beginner. "How about we fortify ourselves with a drink before we hit the ice?"

"Something to numb the pain?"

"I was thinking more about a hot chocolate," Jay said, nodding towards a cosy-looking faux Alpine chalet with a long wooden bar, twinkling fairy lights, and an enticing aroma of coffee.

"Sure," Mason said, agreeably. "I'll take an Americano, though." He made a regretful face. "I have a shoot this week."

Mason was always watching his weight. Jay counted himself lucky that he didn't need to be quite so careful, although he did have to keep in shape for *Leeches*. Nobody would be happy if he couldn't fit into his costume when filming started. Unlike Mason, though, Jay wasn't expected to strip down to his undies in front of the camera—and thank God for that.

They joined the end of the queue, which wasn't unreasonably long, and Jay was just debating whether to take off his sunglasses when Mason exclaimed, "No way. Look, it's Tag!"

Jay felt an uncomfortable lurch in his chest—heartburn, probably—as he searched the crowded tables. "Where? I don't see him."

"No, serving," Mason said. "Behind the bar."

And sure enough, there he was. Jay realised he'd been

unconsciously looking for a guy in silver shorts and body paint, which was possibly why he hadn't recognised Tag sooner. Today, he was wearing an outrageously tight-fitting black t-shirt bearing the coffee bar logo, the spectacular tattoos on his right arm on clear display, and his thick dark hair poking out from beneath a red bobble hat. It should have looked daft, but combined with his ridiculously cute, boyish face and cheeky grin, it provoked an inconvenient jolt of attraction in Jay. Mortified, he hid his reaction behind his professional smile. "So it is," he said smoothly, aware that his tone had stiffened but somehow unable to soften it. "That's a coincidence."

Bad bloody luck, more like.

"Tag works at City Beans," Mason said. "This must be one of their pop-ups."

"I thought he was an actor," Jay said, watching Tag flirt with a group of young women as he served them.

"He is." Mason sounded surprised. "You do realise that most actors have side gigs, right?"

Jay dragged his attention back to Mason, aware of the teasing in his words. "Of course I do," he said, flushing. "I just thought—Tag made a point of telling me he was an actor. That's all."

Mason hummed thoughtfully at that and then leaned forward over the bar and called Tag's name.

The grin that broke out on Tag's face when he saw Mason was… well, *spectacular* wasn't hyperbole. The way his face fell at the sight of Jay was equally dramatic, and Jay felt a beat of something ridiculous, like hurt or disappointment. He covered it quickly with a smile—a deliberately smug smile—and looped his arm around Mason's waist, making a point.

Tag's expression cooled further, not that those whisky-gold eyes of his could ever really look anything but molten. "Be with you in a sec!"

A few minutes later, they'd reached the front of the queue,

and Mason was saying, "I didn't know you were working here."

Tag grimaced. "Yeah, we're all rostered onto a few shifts down here at the moment. I drew the short straw today." His gaze slid to Jay. "This is your idea of a hot date, is it?"

"Nothing wrong with a bit of festive fun."

"Sure, if your idea of fun is staggering around an ice rink with crowds of tourists."

Jay offered his most charming smile. "We don't *all* stagger."

"Oh, you're an expert, I suppose?"

"He learned to skate in Aspen," Mason chipped in, teasing.

Tag's attention didn't leave Jay. "Of course he bloody did."

Jay held that glittering gaze for a moment too long, and then for another moment after that. Something inside him was fizzing up, escaping his control. He found himself saying, in a rather snooty tone, "One small hot chocolate with whipped cream and marshmallows, and a large Americano, please."

A flush darkened Tag's cheeks, the glint in his eyes turning fiery. "Coming right up, *sir*."

Taken aback by his own combativeness, as well as Tag's obvious embarrassment, Jay decided to retreat. Leaving Mason to wait for the drinks, Jay nabbed a table by the rink, and a few minutes later, Mason joined him, carrying their order.

"Don't let Tag bother you," he said as he sat down. "He just really wants to win this stupid dating-for-likes thing. I think he's actually keeping count of how many each of you get."

"Tag doesn't bother me," Jay said, uncomfortable with the idea. "Did I give the impression that he did?"

Mason shrugged, sipping his Americano, both hands

wrapped around the steaming mug. "A little? You seemed…" He shrugged. "A bit tense, maybe?"

Tense. Jay rolled his shoulders, trying to relax. "If I'm tense," he said, "it's nothing to do with Tag O'Rourke." He sighed and confessed, "I have to go to my mother's Christmas soirée this evening. It's an annual nightmare, to be honest. I'm dreading it."

"Christmas *soirée*?"

"It's exactly as awful as it sounds. Lots of theatre types braying about 'the craft' and congratulating each other on their performances. *Oh, darling*," he exclaimed, in his best approximation of his mother, "*your* Lear *was to die for!*"

Mason snorted into his coffee. "Do you have to go?"

"On pain of death, I'm afraid. Especially this year, because Ronnie is over from the States."

"Ronnie?"

"My older brother. He was christened Oberon, but everyone calls him Ronnie. He's a theatre director. My mother adores him."

"Sounds like the Warren siblings are all pretty talented."

Jay laughed. "Some more than others, I'm afraid."

"What do you mean?"

"Well…" He took a tentative sip of his hot chocolate, wondering briefly whether Tag might have done something untoward to it, but it tasted okay. "Ronnie is the director of the New York Durham Theatre, Portia is a poet and writer-in-residence at Cornell, Rosalind is a sculptor like our father, and I… play a vampire on TV. You see the difference?"

"Yeah," Mason agreed. "You're in a TV show beloved by millions, and a household name. Your brother directs plays that only a handful of people will ever see, and how many people can name a living poet or sculptor? Sounds like you're the successful one."

Jay shook his head, glancing back towards the bar where Tag was chatting with a group of three young boys. As Jay watched, Tag glanced in his direction, and their eyes met briefly, then moved away, like magnets instantly repelling each other. He looked back at Mason and said, "Thank you for saying so, but that's not how it's viewed in my family. Apparently, anyone can do television." He shrugged. "They've got a point."

Mason bristled. "First off," he said, "most people *can't* do television. Believe me, there are loads of us who'd love the chance. And secondly, there are great actors working in TV, and you've had fantastic reviews for *Leeches*. So why play that down?" He frowned. "To be honest, it makes you sound like a bit of a snob."

"I'm not a snob! You're right. There *are* some great actors working in television—but you'll usually find they're great stage actors, too." He smiled, to show Mason that it was fine. That *he* was fine. "I'm competent, Mason, but nobody would call me a *great* actor. And that's okay. I have *Leeches,* and I love it. I have a great life. I'm very happy."

Mason considered him for a moment, but all he said was, "Fine. Want to go and skate?"

Dame Cordelia's Christmas soirée had been a fixture in the social calendar of her theatrical circle for over two decades. She held it in her Mayfair flat on the second weekend of December, and entrance was strictly by invitation only.

Jay hated the whole thing, for many and varied reasons.

As children, they'd all been forced to learn a party piece with which to charm the guests—like a London version of the Von Trapp family. Frankly, Jay would have rather hiked across the Alps, pursued by Nazis, than sing a musical number under the professional gaze of thirty or so thespians.

One year, as a rebellious teen, he'd point-blank refused, and he hadn't heard the end of it for the next twelve months.

"Darling, an artiste never refuses an opportunity to share their talent!"

Thankfully, these days, no party piece was required. Although, at some point, his mother would no doubt wheel out the piano, which, naturally, she played like a pro. Ronnie, who never missed an opportunity to show off, would be only too keen to lead her other guests in an impromptu sing-song.

Jay would make himself scarce for that—he did *not* have a singing voice.

Right now, he was loitering near the extravagant buffet, nursing the bruises on his backside and knees courtesy of several unlikely run-ins with three unruly kids on the ice. Jay was sixty percent certain they were the same three boys he'd seen Tag talking to earlier. Mason had found it pretty hilarious, though, and no doubt a couple of pictures of them sprawled artfully together on the ice would find their way onto his Insta. Fabulous.

To take his mind off his humiliation, Jay had intended to make the most of his mother's excellent champagne but instead had been inveigled into conversation with an earnest young woman by the name of Tinsley De la Hay. For the last half hour, she'd been telling him all about the clothes-free production of *The Caucasian Chalk Circle* she was going to be directing at next year's Edinburgh Fringe.

"...and without costume of any sort masking the performance, Brecht's text becomes paramount. Do you see?"

"Of course," Jay said politely. "Nothing for the actors to hide behind." Poor buggers.

Tinsley nodded eagerly. "And thus the intimate connection with the audience will be intensified a hundredfold."

"Yes, I imagine they'll be paying *very* close attention."

"Ideally, the audience would be clothes-free too." She sighed dramatically, "But the venue refused—for hygiene reasons, of all things."

Stoically, Jay managed not to grimace at the thought of all those naked bums on seats. "A little chilly, too, perhaps?"

Tinsley blinked at him. "I'd hope they'd be too engrossed in the work to notice feeling *chilly*."

"Who's chilly?" Dame Cordelia Warren's thrilling contralto sailed into the conversation, entering boldly from stage right. "Are you sickening for something, Julius?"

Julius, because, yes, his mother really had named all her children for Shakespeare characters. Hence Jay deciding to professionally adopt his nickname from school. Jay turned to greet her with a smile. Her blue eyes were twinkling as she glided towards them, resplendent in a jewel-coloured kaftan, her short, silver hair entirely hidden by an extravagant matching turban.

"We were talking about Tinsley's production at the Fringe next year," Jay said. "It's to be played naked."

"Oh, Julius, your *face*!" Dame Cordelia hooted, amused. She turned to Tinsley and added, "Don't mind him. Julius can be dreadfully conventional. I *adore* naked theatre. Did I ever tell you about the *Lear* we did in Regent's Park? Poured with bloody rain. I was so cold my nipples looked like bullets. Nearly took dear Larry's eye out."

Tinsley laughed nervously, but Jay had long ago got used to his mother's outlandish frankness. "Are you enjoying yourself?" he asked her, changing the subject. "Everyone looks like they're having fun."

"Of course they are!" She narrowed her eyes at him. "Are you?"

"Naturally."

She regarded him a moment longer, then looped her arm through his and said, "Excuse us, Tinsley, darling, I want to have a little talk with my son."

Never a good sign. Jay resisted. "Now? Don't you have guests to entertain?"

"Oh, this lot can entertain themselves for hours just by looking in a mirror. Come along. I've got exciting news."

Worse and worse, but easier to get it over with now than drag it out. Whatever Dame Cordelia had in mind, there would be no escaping until she'd had her say. She led him through the large reception room, past Ronnie, who was holding forth before a small group of ardent admirers. Tall and commanding, Ronnie was a natural director, the centre of attention wherever he went. He caught Jay's eye as Dame Cordelia sailed past, Jay bobbing along in her wake, and winked in sibling solidarity. Jay lifted his hand in a resigned wave.

Dame Cordelia had a studio deep in her labyrinthine apartment, a place where she'd rehearse or run lines either alone or with others. Aside from the stage itself, Jay thought her studio was the place she was happiest, and he saw her visibly lift as they entered the quiet space. The floorboards were pale oak, golden and shining in the overhead light. During the day, they reflected the sunlight and turned the whole space mellow and warm. Jay rather liked it there too, and as he closed the door on the noise of the party, he felt tension ease from his chest.

His mother strode a few steps into the studio and took a deep breath, as if she were about to launch into an oration, before turning around to face him. "Now tell me," she said, looking at him shrewdly, "what's the matter?"

He frowned, taken aback. "Nothing. Why?"

"You look…fidgety in your skin."

Whatever that meant.

She drew closer, studying him. "An actor needs to stretch his wings, darling, or he gets cramped. And you've kept yours clipped for too long. It's time you flew, again."

For Dame Cordelia, it always came down to this. Acting was life.

"My wings are doing quite well, thank you," Jay said mildly. "We start shooting again soon and then—"

"*Leeches*," she said, waving her hand as if batting away a wasp. "Darling, how long has it been since you *trod the boards*?"

Jay gritted his teeth. "I appeared in that *Dracula* production a couple of years ago."

"Oh, I don't count that," she said dismissively. "It was only one night, and for a bit of fun."

One bloody awful night, actually. Not that he'd admit as much. "*Leeches* keeps me very busy," he said easily. "I enjoy it, I'm good at it, and—"

"Paint-by-numbers acting," his mother scoffed. "Darling, an actor like you needs the discipline of *The Work*." As always, she said those two words with heavy reverence. "And I've got a wonderful opportunity for you. Simply wonderful. You remember my dear friend, Timon, and his daughter, Bea? Of course you do. Well, Bea is a marvellous young playwright now —she's been working at the Young Vic, you know. Anyway, she's casting for a new play—her first full-length work—and she has the perfect role for you. It's a two-hander about Siegfried Sassoon and Wilfred Owen. You know, the war poets? You'll be Sassoon. Tall, handsome, and very gay! Right up your street."

"Mother…"

"Oh, don't be so coy. Oberon was saying just last night that you should lean into that harder."

"Lean into what?"

"Now you're being obtuse, darling. Your sexuality, of course. It's all the rage these days, isn't it? Which is marvellous. If only dear Johnny could be here to see it." She looked wistful for a moment, then briskly rallied. "Anyway, I've told Bea that you'll meet her in the new year to discuss the role."

Jay suppressed a groan. "Great."

Ignoring that, she said, "I've read the play, and it's very

good. And the poetry, of course, is sublime. You always had a knack for poetry."

That was news to Jay; she was probably mixing him up with Ronnie. Sighing, he said, "You know how I feel about theatre work—it's really not my forte."

"And how would you know? You've only done one play since RADA, and that was a disaster."

That was his mother. Never one to shrink from bluntly stating the truth.

"Which is exactly why I prefer television," he said, smiling determinedly. " I'm *good* at television."

Another dismissive wave of her hand. "Well, you have to at least meet with Bea; I've told her you will." She crossed the room to the tall cupboard where she kept her paperwork and fetched a script, walking back to him and holding it out. "In the meantime, promise me you'll read it."

Reluctantly, he took the script. It felt weighty, and his stomach lurched with a sickening twist of anxiety. No way would he accept the role, not a chance. There was no getting out of the meeting, though, so he'd have to go along and let poor Bea down gently. Not that he'd be any loss to her production. In fact, he'd be doing her a huge favour. There were plenty of actors better for the role than him. Frankly, any actor who could walk on stage without suffering a complete meltdown would be better for the role than him.

"Fine, I'll read the play," he promised his mother. "And I'll meet with Bea."

But no more than that.

"Wonderful." Dame Cordelia stepped closer and took his free hand, squeezing it tight. "That's all I ask, darling. And honestly, this will be good for you. I know it will. I have a sense about these things."

Since Jay knew she was entirely mistaken, he simply bent down to kiss her cheek and kept his thoughts to himself.

CHAPTER THREE

TAG

February - two months later

Tag rounded the corner into his road at a good clip, breathing hard, the muscles in his legs burning with a combination of cold air and exertion. Swerving around a dad and two small kids on scooters heading to school, he finished his run in a minute under his usual time. Not bad. Pleased, he pulled off one glove to rummage in his pocket for the front door key.

He usually ran earlier than this, but he'd managed to swap today's shift at City Beans for an early tomorrow. That wasn't ideal, because he was out tonight, but it did mean he'd been able to get a decent night's sleep and still have all morning to prepare for his audition.

His second audition, in fact, for the role of Wilfred Owen in Beatrice Lawson's play, *Let Us Go Back*. Tag had got the callback yesterday. It was between him and one other bloke, and Tag was up for the fight.

The house was silent when he let himself back in—his mum was working mid-shifts at the moment, and his dad always left by seven, which meant Tag had the place to himself. Perfect.

He took a few minutes in the hallway to catch his breath and strip off his hat and gloves. It wasn't that he loved running, but he did enjoy the endorphin rush afterwards, and he was feeling good as he took off his running shoes and worked through some basic yoga stretches. He felt great, in fact. Well-rested and excited about the day ahead. Determined.

Telling his family over Christmas that he might be up for a recurring role in *Bow Street* if it was picked up had been something, even if Stevie hadn't looked too impressed. This role, though, could be the break Tag had been waiting for. If it was true that they had a big name lined up to play Sassoon, then it could even be career-making—something that would get him in front of serious people in the industry. Who knew where it might lead?

Although he was sweaty from his run, Tag pulled on a hoodie and stuck his feet into his slipper boots so he didn't cool down too fast. The heating went off at eight and wouldn't come back on until six, and the house was already feeling chilly. Nothing that a cuppa wouldn't fix, though.

He headed into the kitchen, grateful for the silence. Tag was gregarious by nature, but before auditions he craved quiet and solitude, needing a bit of mental space to get himself into the right frame of mind, especially for something as important as this audition. He couldn't afford to mess it up —he *wouldn't* mess it up.

He smiled then, unsurprised to see a note propped up against the kettle.

Knock 'em dead, Tag! I'll be thinking of you today. Lots of love, Mum xxx

He folded the note and slipped it into his hoodie pocket. For luck.

Once he'd put the kettle on, he made himself a big bowl of

porridge. He needed something wholesome to fill his belly so he wouldn't be distracted by sugar crashes or hunger pangs while he was concentrating on nailing the audition. Then he sat down at the little table in the kitchen to eat while he leafed through the copious notes he'd made on the play and on Owen himself.

When Pete had first mentioned *Let Us Go Back* being about two First World War poets, Tag had imagined willowy young officers regretfully mourning their lost chums from the playing fields of Eton. How on earth, he'd thought, could someone like him find a way into a role like that? Once he'd done some research, though, his enthusiasm for the part began to grow beyond just its potential career benefits.

For a start, Owen had only been twenty-five when he'd died, right on the eve of the Armistice in 1918. That was practically the same age that Tag was now, which had given him pause when he'd worked it out. And yes, while Owen had been middle class, he'd not been wealthy enough to attend university. He'd had to work instead of swanning around Oxford like Sassoon. What had opened everything up for Tag, though, was discovering that Sassoon had once written that he found Owen's 'grammar school accent' embarrassing.

And suddenly, there was the character, fully formed in Tag's mind: a little awkward, extremely talented, probably gay, yearning to be taken seriously by a privileged literary elite whose gatekeepers, like his mentor and idol, Sassoon, couldn't see past Owen's gauche accent.

That's how Tag had approached Owen in the auditions, and it resonated deeply for him. The character felt genuine, the role meaningful.

In fact, it felt like Tag's to play, and nobody else's.

His thoughts and preparations were interrupted then by the ding of his phone. He'd turn it off soon, to avoid any distractions, but he smiled to see a WhatsApp notification from Aaron.

Break a leg!

Tag sent back a fingers crossed emoji.

RPP are springing for a limo tonight, Aaron messaged back. *Will pick you up at 7, okay?*

That made Tag grin. A limo? Hell yeah.

Lewis Hunter, now Aaron's boyfriend, had been nominated for Best Screenplay at the TV Best Awards, and, because of Tag's role in *Bow Street*, Aaron had invited him along to fill a spare seat on the RPP table at tonight's awards ceremony. Tag hadn't needed to be asked twice. Events like this were fantastic for making industry connections and impossible to get invited to. Of course, Mason might have taken him to a couple, if Jay bloody Warren hadn't muscled in on Tag's fake dating scheme. And *he* was the last person Tag should be thinking about right now…

He messaged Aaron back, *That'll get the neighbours talking!*

His mum would love it, too. His dad would take the piss, of course, but underneath all that, he'd be a little bit impressed. One day, if he ever made it big, Tag wanted to be the one rolling up in the limo to collect his parents and take *them* to an awards dinner—the BAFTAs, maybe—where he, obviously, would be winning Best Actor.

For a few moments, he lost himself in that fantasy before shaking it off irritably; he was losing focus and he had work to do. Switching off his phone, he turned back to his notes. Daydreams got you nowhere in this business. For actors like Tag, with few connections in the industry, the only way to succeed was through hard bloody graft.

And a little sprinkling of luck.

At 10:48, Tag found himself loitering outside the audition venue. It was a basement room beneath a quirky theatre bookshop, auspiciously located opposite the Young Vic.

His meeting was at eleven, but it always paid to be in plenty of time. Still, before he went in, he checked his reflection in the bookshop window. Today, he'd gone with khaki cargo pants tucked into his battered old DMs and a leather jacket. He thought it suggested 'soldier' without being too over the top. He'd slicked his hair back and let it part naturally in the middle, again approximating something from the 1920s. His messenger bag, with the script and his notes, was slung over one shoulder.

He took a breath, readied himself, and headed inside.

The rehearsal room was down a narrow flight of stairs, but there were a couple of chairs at the top where he could wait, and he took a seat. From the bottom of the steps, the sound of muffled voices floated through the closed door, but it sounded like talking rather than performance.

Tag sat straight, doing a couple of breathing exercises to keep him focused while he waited.

And then the door clicked open.

"...thanks, I appreciate your time," said a light, cultured voice. It reminded Tag, irritatingly, of Jay Warren's cultivated timbre.

Tag rose.

He recognised the guy heading up the stairs from the previous audition. He was about Tag's height, with dark hair and eyes. Rupert, or something else a bit posh, Tag thought.

Behind him came an older man wearing a shapeless knitted cardigan, a trilby hat, and a silver hoop in one ear. "Good luck, Rafe," he said, offering his hand to shake.

The other guy—Rafe—took it. "Great seeing you again, Henry. Grandy sends his best wishes."

Of course they bloody knew each other; somehow this lot always did. And, as always, it put Tag at a huge disadvantage in an industry that was rife with nepotism. He'd have to be twice as good as Rafe if he wanted to win the part, but win he bloody well would.

Henry inclined his head to Rafe, touching the brim of his hat with two fingers. "And the same to him."

Laughing, Rafe mirrored the gesture and turned to go, sharing a cool look with Tag as he passed.

"Tag O'Rourke?" He turned to find Henry scrutinising him from top to toe, pale grey eyes fierce and intelligent in his narrow, craggy face. "I'm Henry," he said. "Bea's ready for you. Come on down."

Tag followed him down and into the basement room. It was a cosy rectangular space, with a grey floor and walls and a large mirror on one wall. Beatrice Lawson, the playwright, sat on one of three plastic chairs, also grey, arranged in front of the wall opposite the mirror. She wore a long paisley skirt, combat boots, and a roll-neck green sweater, her cloud of red hair pulled back into a ponytail, freckled face shining, and eyes bright.

"Tag," she said, standing and offering both hands. "Thank you for coming back."

"My pleasure." He took her hands and performed the obligatory air kisses her sort went in for. "I'm really excited about the role. It's a wonderful play, and I feel a strong connection to Owen."

She smiled. "Good. Let's get to it, then, shall we? Henry's going to read the Sassoon part today."

Henry, who was just closing the door, lifted his hand in a wave and went to collect his script from a table set against the wall.

"Right," Beatrice said. "When you're ready, I'd like to begin with the argument scene in Act Two, Scene Three…"

Henry turned a smiling look on Tag. "Let's grab a chair for this, because Owen's going to be sitting down at the start…"

So they dragged one of the chairs into the rehearsal space, and Tag took a moment to set down his bag and pull out his script, getting himself into the mind of Wilfred Owen, a young soldier sitting in the officer's bar behind the front lines in France.

Quietly, Beatrice said, "When you're ready, take it from 'And this is where it all comes back to'."

Tag began to mime pouring himself a glass of wine, then turned to Henry.

"And this is where it all comes back to, Sassoon." He lifted his imaginary glass as if in salute. "For you—in the end."

"Meaning what?"

"*Meaning* that you think you should've bought it in '18." Tag raised a wry, unsympathetic brow. "You wish that bullet had killed you, don't you?"

"From time to time," Henry said airily. "Mostly when some half-witted bloody newspaper man asks me about *you*. Owen: the lost genius. And his eternal spokesman, Sassoon, the washed-up has-been."

Tag glared at him angrily. "My God, are you *jealous* of my death?" He gave a bitter laugh. "You needn't be. It was—"

"Okay," Beatrice interrupted. "That's great, Tag, but can you take the aggression down a notch? It's not really an argument, you see. Owen's revealing a truth to Sassoon. It's kindly meant."

Tag nodded gamely, but in his opinion it *was* an argument —or it should be. Here was Sassoon, at the end of his long and privileged life, envying Owen's pitiful legacy as a dead young poet. Why would Owen be *kind* about that? Sassoon was acting like a spoiled prick, and, in Tag's opinion, Owen would call him on it. Still, this was Beatrice's play, her vision, and if she wanted him to play Owen differently, then that's what he'd do. She was the boss.

Across the rehearsal space, he felt Henry's eyes on him again, watching with that intense assessing scrutiny Tag had noticed earlier.

"When you're ready," Beatrice said once more. And off they went again.

When they finally finished, Beatrice's smile was unreadable, but Henry's eyes glittered with obvious approval. Tag's heart raced—and not only with the usual performance high. It had gone well. He could feel it.

Beatrice and Henry exchanged a few quiet words at the other end of the room while Tag put his script away in his bag. He slid a couple of quick glances in their direction but couldn't hear what they were saying, although Henry looked quite animated. Then the conversation broke up, and Tag turned quickly back to closing his bag and slipping on his jacket.

"Great to meet you today!" Henry called then, and when Tag looked over again, he saw that Henry stood at the door, a heavy coat over one arm. "I've got to run, but good luck, Tag. You're a promising young actor. I'm sure you've got a big future ahead of you."

"Thanks," Tag called back. "And thanks for, um, reading in today. I appreciate it."

Henry nodded, touched the brim of his hat, and was gone, the door closing with a bang behind him. The little room seemed to deflate in his absence, as if he'd taken half the air with him.

"Come and grab a seat," Beatrice said. "Let's chat."

Was that a good sign? It felt like a good sign. Rafe hadn't had a chat afterwards, had he? Or maybe he had. God, Tag hoped this was a good sign.

"Henry—that is, *we*—really enjoyed your work today," Beatrice said as Tag sat down. "You're bringing a really, um, fresh flavour to the role of Owen. Very authentic. Henry called it 'chippy'. He loved it."

"Cool," Tag said, trying not to sound too pathetically eager. "And Henry...? Will he be involved in the production?"

Beatrice's eyebrows went up as though his comment surprised her. "Well, it's not official yet, but he'll be directing.

I mean, I was going to direct myself, but my—" She cleared her throat. "The financier wanted someone with more experience involved before he'd bankroll the production, so he called in a favour, and, well, enter Henry Walker, stage left." Hurriedly she added, "I'll still be involved in the direction. Sort of a co-director, I suppose."

Tag stared at her. "Henry Walker? Was that…?" He laughed, because it was impossible. "That wasn't *the* Henry Walker, was it?"

"Of course," Beatrice said, looking amused now. "I'm sorry. I assumed you'd recognise him."

"Right." Tag nodded and tried not to feel like a total idiot for failing to recognise one of the most respected theatre directors in the country. "Absolutely."

"So, a couple of things," Beatrice said, folding her hands in her lap. "First, *I* love how you're portraying Owen, too. I'm getting a real sense of his creative frustration, his social and sexual longing. It's *fantastic*."

Tag grinned at that, tried to hide his pleasure, but then decided not to bother. "Thanks," he said. "He was right on the edge of that world, wasn't he? And from what I've read, it seems like lots of people think he was more talented than Sassoon. Had he lived…?" Tag shrugged. "I suppose that's the point. Owen's early death gave him a sort of unearned immortality that Sassoon envied for the rest of his life."

Beatrice's gaze warmed with appreciation. "Envied, but regretted. I think Sassoon would have preferred Owen to survive."

"Or that they'd both died."

She conceded that point with a nod, smiling. After a brief pause, she said, "Well, Tag, as you've probably guessed, the role is yours, if you'd like it. Henry wants you for the role, and I concur. I think you'll make a wonderful Owen, and I'd love to have you in the production."

The punch of relief, of gratitude, of pure triumph robbed

Tag of words. He hardly had enough breath to say, "Yes. Oh my God, *yes*! Thank you."

"We've got a fantastic space lined up in York, and we'll be in rehearsal for six weeks before the two-week run. I'm afraid we don't have the budget to cover accommodation costs, though. Will you be able to manage that?"

"Oh." Tag's stomach gave a startled lurch, but he kept the reaction off his face. He'd known going in that, if he was offered the part, he'd have to take a huge financial risk. "Yes, that's fine."

It was *not* fine, but he'd make it work. He had to. He'd sleep on a fucking park bench if necessary. He *had* to have this role. Bloody hell, he was going to be in a play directed by *Henry Walker*!

"Wonderful," Beatrice said, smiling again.

"So, um, can you tell me who's going to be playing Sassoon?" Tag tried to sound casual, but the profile of the production, and consequently its impact on Tag's career, depended on this casting. He was desperate to know whose star he'd be hitching his wagon to.

Beatrice made a face, though. "I wish I could tell you right now, but we haven't signed anything yet, and until then…" She spread her hands. "What I can tell you is that I'm meeting with him tomorrow, *finally*, to make it official and—oh! Are you available? I'm sure he'd love to meet his co-star. He's that kind of actor, you know? Sensitive, talented, giving—an actor's actor. I *love* his work. So does Henry, and I think you'll have great chemistry together. I'm sure you'll agree, when you meet."

"Wow, okay," Tag said, failing to appear even slightly cool about the prospect. "I'd love to come along."

She smiled broadly. "Excellent. I'm taking him to lunch at the Camden Dining Room. One o'clock."

Which was when Tag remembered he had an early shift at City Beans tomorrow. "Shit," he said. "I'm working in the morning and don't get off until half one. I could be there by two, though?"

"Perfect," Beatrice said. "That'll give me time to ensure he's fully on board before you meet."

Tag's eyebrows rose, his heart misstepping. "Is there a chance he *won't* be on board?"

Fuck, would the whole production be derailed without this mystery star?

"Oh no." Beatrice waved off the idea. "It's just a matter of agreeing terms, you know? Besides, he's… sort of a family friend. I'm as sure as I can be that he'll do it. Lunch is just to let him know how excited we are." She winked. "A little flattery goes a long way."

Tag smiled, although he didn't really think it was funny. He'd been slogging his guts out for years to get this opportunity while this other guy, this *family friend*, was being wined and dined and offered the part on a silver platter. No audition for him, by the sound of it.

Still, only children expected life to be fair. "I'll be there," he said. "And thank you. Thank you so much for this opportunity. I can't tell you how excited I am."

Beatrice beamed. "Thank *you*, Tag. I'm excited to be working with you. I *am* going to ask you to keep the details under your hat for now, though. Just until we've dotted all the i's and crossed all the t's. You know?"

"Of course," Tag said, although it wouldn't be easy to keep this news to himself. He reckoned he could at least tell his mum and dad, though. Not that he could hide anything from them, anyway; they'd know as soon as they saw his face. For now, he strove to look serious and professional. "I understand."

"Good. There are a few more things I'd like to go through with you, if you have time?"

Tag laughed. "For you, I have all the time in the world."

Half an hour later, Tag floated up the steps from the little basement with a huge, irrepressible grin on his face. Even the terrifying prospect of having to quit his job at the coffee shop and live on air for eight weeks in York couldn't bring him down.

This was it. This was the opportunity that would change everything.

He *knew* it.

CHAPTER FOUR

JAY

The TV Best Awards dinner was proving to be tortuous. Even more so than usual. Partly, it was because Mason, Jay's convenient plus-one for the evening, was in one of his introspective ruminating moods, and partly because Jay was seated next to Misty Watson-King, a daytime TV producer at RPP, who'd been braying on about herself and her show all evening, but mostly, it was because, on the opposite side of the table, sat Tag O'Rourke.

When Tag wasn't glowering in Jay's direction, he was laughing and flirting, deliberately directing his ridiculously gorgeous smile at everyone but Jay. Fine, whatever.

And then things got worse.

"Hello, old thing!"

Jay froze at the familiar tone, an unpleasantly nasal whine he remembered all too well from his school days. Austin Coburn: writer, critic, and all-round shit. Stocky and rather nondescript with scruffy brown hair, a rumpled tux, and fashionably large glasses, Austin looked innocuous enough, but, as Jay well knew, he was the sort who took delight in other people's failures. Jay's in particular. Maybe because of Jay's success at school.

Thankfully, Austin's greeting had been directed at Misty, not Jay. Misty carolled a delighted reply. "Oh my God, Austin! Bloody hell, I might have known I'd see *you* here!"

Jay tried to ignore them both, taking a sip of the warm and rather average white wine they'd been served a few minutes earlier. He felt eyes on him, though, and when he glanced across the table, it was to find Tag watching him curiously. Their gazes tangled for a moment, Tag's eyebrows rose, and Jay looked away, feeling his cheeks heat. Why, he couldn't really say.

"Imagine seeing Austin here!" Misty gushed a little later, after Austin had slithered back to his own table. "I can't believe it!"

What she really meant, of course, was that she couldn't believe Austin had deigned to single her out, and now she was hoping he'd spare a couple of inches for her show in his bloody awful column. Jay frowned at the table; one of the worst things about this business was the way everyone sucked up to talentless shits like Coburn who had the power to make or break a career with a single fucking tweet.

"*You* were very quiet," Misty observed, interrupting his dark musings. "I thought you and Austin knew each other?"

Jay gave a slight shrug and said, in a tone that didn't invite further questions, "We went to the same school."

If he sounded curt, he didn't care; he had reason to dislike Austin Coburn, and that was nobody's business but his own. Luckily, Misty either took the hint or didn't really care. She turned to her PA, who was sitting on her other side, and began badgering her about inviting Austin to lunch.

Tuning her out, Jay stared down at his half-eaten bread roll. It pissed him off that he reacted so strongly to Austin. He wanted to be indifferent to him, to forget every supercilious, spiteful word he'd ever written. To rise above it, the way his mother would. The fact that he still hated Austin with the heat of a thousand fiery suns was so… unprofessional. So *demeaning*.

From across the table, Tag said, his tone biting, "I suppose he's beneath your notice now that you're so famous?"

Jay stiffened, surprised by Tag's sudden assault. Looking up, he met Tag's glare. "We're not friends," he said defensively. "Do you keep up with everyone *you* went to school with?"

"No," Tag shot back. "But I'd say fucking hello to them if they were standing right next to me."

Jay bristled, angry and stupidly… hurt by the unprovoked attack. "Well, you do have *such* a sunny disposition," he snapped. "I'm sure you make friends everywhere you go."

"I do, yeah. But apparently *you* don't need to bother."

"I only bother with people worth knowing." And that certainly wasn't Austin fucking Coburn.

Tag snorted. "Yeah? And what makes people worth knowing? Right friends? Right accent? Right social club?"

Oh, for God's sake. If they hadn't been sitting at an awards dinner, with a dozen journalists within earshot, Jay might have challenged that ridiculous accusation. As it was, he bit his tongue, set his napkin on the table, and rose. "Excuse me," he said. "I'm going to go and say hello to my agent."

He caught a flash of frustration on Tag's face as he turned away and felt a stab of savage satisfaction. Good. If Tag was spoiling for a fight, Jay was happy to disappoint. Unlike Tag, he knew better than to make a scene in public.

Steering clear of Austin's table, Jay made his way out of the ballroom and into the bar—he had no intention of seeking out his agent, who would no doubt tell him to get back to his seat. It was a relief to escape the noise, and to get away from Tag's hot glare. Hot in every sense, unfortunately. The man was insanely attractive despite his prickly personality. Or, possibly, because of it? There was something about Tag's spiky belligerence that Jay enjoyed, even when it was completely misdirected. Sometimes Jay found himself wishing that he could get Tag alone and just...well, *talk* to him. Tag seemed friendly enough with everyone else, after all, and Jay couldn't help feeling that they might get along if Tag would only pull in his bloody spikes.

That didn't seem likely, though, and certainly not tonight. The starter hadn't even been served, and already Jay's mood was ruined for the evening.

He was perusing the bar's top shelf when a kerfuffle at the entrance drew his eye. A phalanx of people strode in, heading through the bar towards the ballroom. Jay recognised it as an entourage of the sort his mother attracted at events like this—security, publicists, and various hangers-on. He was about to turn away when he caught sight of the tall, charismatic figure striding along at the centre of the group, and his heart dropped through the floor.

Sebastian Talbot was one of the country's most lauded theatre actors and a Hollywood star besides. He was also—though this was known to very few people—Jay's ex.

Seb's chilly blue eyes met his own, glittering in that handsome face beneath a crop of shining silver hair. His mouth curled into a smile, and he slowed. "Julius Warren, how wonderful to see you."

Mouth dry, Jay nodded but managed to say coolly, "You too, Seb." *That* was a lie. "And please, it's Jay."

Seb's smile broadened as he lifted a hand to halt his entourage and walked over. "Jay. Of course," he said, a note of indulgence in his voice, as though he was magnanimously agreeing to some ridiculous demand. "How *are* you, dear boy? Still doing that little television programme?"

"It's hardly little," Jay said. "They're about to launch a US version, actually." As soon as the words left his mouth, he wanted to call them back. What the fuck was he doing? Trying to win Seb's approval? *Still*?

"Oh, well, in *that* case…" Seb gave a condescending laugh, then turned to the gorgeous young—very young—man hovering behind him. "Niccolò, darling, this is Jay Warren— an old, er, friend. Jay, allow me introduce you to my beloved husband, Niccy."

Niccolò was a very pretty package made up of large doe eyes, a mop of angelic dark curls, and a slender, twinky body. Exactly Sebastian's type. "Pleased to meet you," Niccolò said softly, though his black-coffee gaze was disconcertingly direct.

Jay had seen their nauseating wedding exclusive plastered all over one of the celebrity rags and wanted to tell the poor boy to run for the hills.

Instead, he murmured agreement, then turned back to Seb. "I'm surprised to see you here. I didn't think you bothered with television."

"Oh I don't," Seb said, "but Niccy wanted to come, and I'm nothing if not his devoted slave."

He laughed, looking around for the plaudits from his entourage. They all laughed obligingly. Seb had been deep in the closet when he'd been with Jay, but he'd finally come out a couple of years ago and now never missed an opportunity to flaunt his sexuality.

Seb's attention returned to Jay, and he said, "What else have you been up to? I don't recall seeing your name attached to *anything*."

Jay gritted his teeth. "*Leeches* takes up most of my time these days."

"Well… Obviously, I'm talking about the theatre. Still nothing?" Seb shook his head sadly. "Cordelia must be at her wits' end."

That was uncomfortably close to the truth, which of course Seb would know. He was extremely talented at slipping the knife in at exactly the right angle to cause maximum hurt.

Just then, a man in a dark suit and an earpiece leaned over and murmured something to Seb, who nodded. "Duty calls," he said. "They've got me handing out some gong or other. But it's been delightful to see you again, Julius—sorry, *Jay*. Do give my love to your mother—that is, all the love I can spare from my darling Niccy."

With that, he and his entourage swept off towards the ballroom, leaving Jay behind with his heart thumping angrily in his chest.

After that, he *really* needed a drink and spent a good while salving his bruised ego by letting the handsome guy behind the bar—Will, apparently—chat him up. He was even pondering the notion of inviting Will up to his suite later on when a burst of applause erupted from the ballroom, and Jay realised that the award presentations had already begun.

Shit.

Making a hasty apology, he hurried back into the ballroom and only just managed to slip into his seat in time to see Lewis Hunter receive his best screenplay award for *Leeches*. Jay didn't think he'd been missed, at least not by anyone but Tag, who shot him another of those outraged glares just as the cameras and lights turned on their table.

Plastering on his most professional smile, Jay rose, applauding with everyone else. He even managed to cajole Lewis into posing for a couple of photographs with his boyfriend, Aaron, which was a miracle. Lewis was touchingly pleased to win, despite his curmudgeonly protests, and Jay was glad—for Lewis, and for the show. His show. Whatever Sebastian Talbot thought, Jay was immensely proud of *Leeches*.

That was the high point for the RPP table, though. Misty Watson-King didn't win her award, which started her off on a rant about the prejudice against daytime programming. Luckily, Leo Nowacki, one of *Leeches*' Executive Producers, came to the rescue. His teenage daughter, Sarcia, was a big fan of Skye Jäger, and Leo wanted Jay to come over to their table and say hello. Seizing the lifeline, Jay extricated himself from Misty and spent about twenty minutes chatting with the star-struck girl and posing for about a million selfies.

Jay always enjoyed talking to fans; it gave him real pleasure to see how important his show was to people. Whatever his family, and the likes of Seb Talbot, thought about his work in *Leeches*, Jay knew that the show and his character had a genuine place in peoples' hearts.

Somewhat buoyed by his chat with Sarcia, Jay glanced back at the RPP table. He should probably check in with Mason, make sure he'd got all the content he wanted for his socials, but right now, Mason was in deep conversation with Lewis's brother, Owen, and Misty Watson-King. And the last thing Jay wanted was more conversation with Misty.

Or more unsettlingly hot glares from Tag O'Rourke, who now appeared to be having a heated discussion with Aaron, one arm gesturing towards Jay's vacant seat.

Apparently, even in his absence, Jay had the power to rile Tag.

Fuck it, he thought. *I need a proper drink.*

And maybe a few more uncomplicated smiles from Will, the cute barman. After encountering both Austin and Seb in one cursed night, Jay thought he bloody well deserved a decent Scotch and, maybe, some meaningless sex.

Avoiding the awestruck crush around Seb, who was perched artfully on the edge of the low stage with Niccolò pressed up against him, Jay escaped once more to the bar. Thankfully, it was still relatively empty.

Finding a spot, he caught Will's eye and smiled. "Told you I'd be back," he said as Will strolled over.

"Did you win?"

"*Leeches* did—for the screenplay."

"Cool." Will set a glass on the bar. "One for the road, is it?"

Jay nodded, but when Will slid the glass towards him, he said, "Not really for the road, though, since I'm actually staying here tonight..."

"Yeah?" Will rested his elbows on the bar, leaning closer. "Nice room?"

Will had a pleasant face and attractive hazel eyes lit by a playful gleam when he smiled, which he was doing a lot.

Jay smiled too and said, "It's a suite."

"That *is* nice." Will grinned. "Are you maybe up for a little room service later?"

Jay laughed. "That depends on—"

Someone jabbed him hard on the shoulder. "Oi, what the bloody hell do you think you're doing?"

Startled, Jay turned to find Tag O'Rourke standing behind him, arms folded across his chest, glaring at him with those arresting honey-gold eyes of his.

"What the hell...?" Jay said indignantly.

Tag's glower deepened. "I asked what you think you're doing, skulking out here and leaving Mason..." He shot a look at Will. "—his *date*, by the way—alone all night."

Straightening to his full height, Jay fixed Tag with his most imperious glare. Unfortunately, the movement brought them rather too close together. So close, in fact, that Jay became aware of a subtle, spicy scent on Tag's skin that brought back visceral memories of their brief close encounter at the Hallowe'en party, months ago—when Tag had been dressed in nothing but body paint and those obscenely tight silver shorts...

Swiftly cutting off that distracting train of thought, Jay glanced over at Will, wary of being overheard. Thankfully, Will was already beating a tactful retreat, heading for the other end of the bar. Jay could hardly blame him.

Relieved and irritated in equal measure, he swung back to

Tag. "I should ask what *you* think *you're* doing," he hissed. "There are *press* here. How dare you make a scene—"

"How *dare* I?" Tag leaned in closer, so close that Jay's skin prickled. "Jesus Christ, you really do think you're a cut above, don't you?"

Scowling, Jay said, "You have no idea what I think."

"No?" Tag scoffed. "Well, I know you have a *date* tonight. Remember him? *Mason,* who you've fucking abandoned with Misty—"

"Oh come on, hardly *abandoned.*"

"—while you flirt with the bar staff. It's bloody rude, is what it is." Caustically, he added, "Besides, isn't mingling with the help against your rules?"

"For God's sake." Jay ran a hand through his hair, unreasonably flustered by Tag's sarcasm. "You know it's not a *real* date with Mason. All he's interested in is getting the pictures he needs for his socials."

"Are you sure? Because to me he looked—"

Out of nowhere, a wry—and slightly slurred—voice drawled, "I wondered where you two had got to."

Jay jumped, and so did Tag, both of them turning to find Mason standing not two feet away. He swayed slightly, regarding them with sardonic amusement.

"Mason," Jay said, taking in his inebriated state with guilty concern. "God, sorry, I—" Mortified by his own bad manners, Jay glanced at Tag, who, weirdly enough, looked as guilty as Jay felt, maybe because he'd been spending his time raging at Jay rather than paying any attention to Mason himself.

"We, uh, lost track of time, I guess," Tag said, a faint flush in his cheeks. "We were so busy arguing—"

"*Arguing.*" Mason snorted, staggering a little. He looked pale and definitely the worse for wear. "Right…"

"We were," Jay said. "I was having a quiet drink when Tag came over to tell me off for abandoning you with Misty." He grimaced. "He was right. I'm sorry. She's just really hard work, you know?"

"*Now* you admit I was right?" Tag exclaimed, outraged.

Jay shot him an irritated look. "I never said you weren't right. It was the way you said it, like I was being—"

"Jesus Christ!" Mason looked somewhere between amused and despairing. "What *is* it with you two?"

Jay had no answer for that; he had no idea why Tag got under his skin so easily, but he couldn't deny that he did.

"You know what?" Mason went on. "I don't even care. Whatever. Let's just... end this farce, okay? No more dates. With either of you."

"What?" Tag sounded genuinely dismayed. "No, Mason, I—"

"Come off it," Mason slurred, lurching when he held up a hand to silence Tag. "Who do you think you're kidding with this bullshit anyway? Why don't you just go fuck each other's brains out already, instead of pretending this weird competition has anything to do with me?"

Jay's gaze darted to Tag, who was staring at Mason in... horror? Jay couldn't quite label the expression flickering over Tag's irritatingly handsome face, but yeah, it was something close to horror. Probably something close to what Jay was feeling to be honest. Jay opened his mouth to assure Mason that there was nothing like *that* between himself and Tag, but Tag got in first, hissing, "See what you've done?"

As always, Tag's anger was like a flame to touchpaper. Immediately, Jay's resentment flared. "What *I've* done?"

"Yeah." Tag jabbed him in the chest. "You left him alone all night!"

"*You* could have talked to him." Jay jabbed him right back. "But here you are, haranguing me, instead!"

"Haranguing?" Tag exclaimed. "I was not *haranguing* you."

Vaguely, Jay was aware of new arrivals, another conversation starting up beside them, but he paid no mind because he and Tag were toe-to-toe now, Tag giving it to him with both barrels. Jay couldn't look away, his gaze intent on Tag's angry, handsome, *infuriating* face.

"This is so typical of your type," Tag spat. "If someone like me—a working-class man trying to break into the profession —just *dare*s to point out when you're behaving in a shitty way, you immediately dismiss them as aggressive and hysterical and—"

"My *type?*" Jay cut in, furious. "What the hell is that supposed to mean?"

"You know exactly what it means," Tag shot back. "People from your privileged little elite, with your expensive educations and family connections that give you a handy leg up while the rest of us—"

"I *beg* your pardon?" an angry voice interjected, and this one was too loud to ignore—not to mention it sounded horribly like Austin Coburn.

Fuck. Austin was the last person Jay wanted to witness his public spat with Tag. God knew how he'd use it in his despicable '*A Little Bird Tells Me*' column. Jaw clenched, Jay braced himself to find Austin's gimlet gaze fixed on him—but it wasn't. No, all of Austin's furious attention was focused on Lewis Hunter's brother, Owen, of all people.

Owen appeared to be entirely unmoved by Austin's spiteful glare, regarding him with a sort of amused indifference, while Mason looked between the two of them, the third point of their triangle, swaying a little on his feet.

"I saw you taking pictures on your phone," Owen told Austin mildly. "And I don't think anyone here wants that right now." He looked at the rest of them, as though to confirm his assumption, his calm gaze taking in Tag, Jay, and Mason. "Right?"

Photographs? Jay felt a rush of fury. He clenched his jaw and his fists, nails biting into his palms. What an utter fucking prick. Coburn called himself an 'arts critic', but Jay knew he could be as sleazy as the worst tabloid hack.

Tag's gaze moved from Austin to Jay, clearly picking up on the tension, and for an instant he looked surprised, as if he'd glimpsed Jay's anger—which was galling because Jay prided himself on his ability to act professionally in even the most trying of circumstances. Hastily, he donned his usual mask, languid and unconcerned. "Yes, that's right," he said, channelling Dame Cordelia's most contemptuous tone. "Do run along, Austin, old chap."

Austin shot him a venomous look, then turned on Owen to continue the argument. But Jay stopped listening because, right then, he glanced over at Tag, and found the other man staring at him with an odd expression—an odd expression that transformed into a crimson flush when Jay caught him looking.

Their gazes locked awkwardly, only breaking apart when Austin noisily stormed off, and Owen said, apologetically, "Sorry about that, but I saw him sneaking photos of you, and you all looked like you were, er, preoccupied... I hope I haven't put my foot in it or anything?"

"Not at all," Jay said quickly. "Quite the opposite in fact. Austin Coburn is a pompous prick who's hated me since prep school. I'm grateful you spotted what he was up to."

Tag snorted and muttered, "*Prep* school."

Irritated, Jay ignored Tag, offering Owen his most charming smile and adding, "Watching you put him in his place is the most fun I've had in what's been a very long and tedious evening."

"Thanks a bunch," Mason huffed, folding his arms over his chest, his expression genuinely hurt.

Jay could have kicked himself. "Oh, Mason, I didn't mean anything by it," he said, feeling awful.

"No," Tag interjected, "you never *mean* to be insulting, do you? But somehow, you always are."

Jay turned on Tag. "Insulting? Me?" That was bloody rich, coming from Tag. "You're the one who just accused me of being an elitist!"

But Tag's gaze had moved past Jay, and when Jay glanced over his shoulder, he saw the reason why. Owen was guiding a distinctly wobbly Mason away, in the direction of the bathroom.

Shit.

"Do you think he's okay?" Tag said uncertainly, glancing back at Jay with genuine concern. The expression softened him, tempering his prickly shell, making him look younger, and sweeter.

And just like that, all the fight went out of Jay, leaving behind only remorse and guilty self-loathing. "Probably feeling sick," he said. "He looked pretty green. Maybe I should…"

He trailed off, but didn't move. Owen had a protective hand on the small of Mason's back and was saying something to him, head bent close, a solicitous look about him as Mason leaned into him, trustingly.

"I think Owen's got it covered," Tag said, staring after them with a surprisingly wistful expression.

And yeah, he did, didn't he? Jay felt suddenly very inadequate.

For a few moments, they were both silent. Then Jay sighed and rubbed a weary hand over the back of his neck. Reluctantly, he admitted, "You were right. I *was* neglecting Mason. And now we've both lost our dates for the evening, so—sorry about that, I suppose?"

Tag turned back to look at him, and, for the first time that night, he smiled at Jay. It was a rueful smile, rather than the bright, dazzling one he wore so often, but it was just as disarmingly attractive, and it made Jay's belly clench with a disturbing, aching *want*.

"I haven't lost anything," Tag said with a shrug. "Owen

65

wasn't actually my date." He moved to stand beside Jay at the bar and waved at the barman.

"You and Owen just came as friends?" For reasons Jay didn't want to examine, the news buoyed him. He scrambled to hide the feeling before Tag noticed.

"Sort of. It was actually Aaron who invited me," Tag said. "Owen was coming for Lewis, and I was just making up the numbers at the table." He gave a self-mocking smile, which lacked something of his usual spirit. "It wasn't a complete waste of time, though. At least I stopped you from winning the dating contest."

Despite himself, Jay gave a soft chuckle. "You're very competitive, aren't you?"

Tag opened his mouth, but, luckily, the bartender arrived before he could retort. Not Will, Jay noted ruefully, but an older man. "What can I get you, gents?"

"Do you want another?" Tag said, indicating Jay's empty tumbler. He did, but he doubted Tag had pockets deep enough for an eighteen-year-old Highland Park.

"Why don't you let me get these?" he offered, and without waiting for Tag to object, told the barman to charge the drinks to his room. "I'll have another shot of the Highland Park," he said, "and whatever he wants, please."

The barman nodded, then turned his attention to Tag. "And for you, sir?"

Tag looked rather mulish, as if he was considering standing on his pride, but after a moment, he made a little gesture of surrender and muttered, "Um, the same, thanks."

Christ, Jay thought, *is it that hard for him to accept a drink from me?*

Once the barman had moved away, Tag said, "So, you're staying here tonight? At the hotel? I assumed you lived in London."

"I do. Well, just outside it. In Chalfont St. Giles?" Tag looked blank, and Jay shrugged. "It's just northwest of the

M25. I thought it would be easier to take a room here than go all that way and back tonight."

Tag raised his brows. "A room here must cost a fortune."

"Well," Jay said, uncomfortable now, "it's not just because of tonight. I've got a meeting in town tomorrow, so it'll give me an extra hour or two in bed. Which, as far as I'm concerned, is worth every penny of the extortionate room rate."

Tag gave him a wry look, but only said, "Yeah, I feel your pain. My shift starts at seven tomorrow."

He turned away then, intently watching the barman pour their drinks, and Jay was fascinated to see colour rising in his cheeks, very noticeable beneath his pale complexion.

When Tag didn't elaborate on that comment, Jay prompted, "Your shift?"

Tag flashed him a bright, breezy smile that Jay didn't buy for a second. "City Beans, remember? I'm a barista when I'm not filming *Bow Street*—which, in fairness, is most of the time. I'm also a waiter and a barman and a labourer on construction sites. Whatever work I can pick up, really." He gave a short, harsh laugh, and his whisky-coloured eyes glittered. "So, you see, your first impression of me was pretty accurate —I do fit in better with the crew than the cast."

"I never said—" Jay began, but then the barman was there again, sliding their drinks in front of them, and Tag blatantly seized the opportunity to divert the conversation.

"*Anyway*," he said, "I had some amazing news today. Things are looking up, and if it all works out, it could turn out to be my big break. *Finally*."

He looked so unaffectedly pleased and excited that Jay couldn't help smiling. "Well, in that case, congratulations. I'm delighted for you. Genuinely."

"Thanks." Reaching for his glass and lifting it up to the light, Tag added, "So, this is the good stuff, eh?"

"It is," Jay acknowledged. "Are you a whisky drinker?"

"Tried it once and hated it." Tag grinned, an appealingly boyish expression, and clinked his glass against Jay's. "Let's see if I like it more now."

Then he knocked back a huge mouthful, making Jay wince, and immediately slapped a hand over his mouth. His eyes went wide and watery, and he convulsed as if trying to contain a cough, then failed spectacularly and began sputtering and gasping, hanging onto the bar like a drowning man.

Jay couldn't hide his smile. "Hmm, still not for you?"

"Fuck off," Tag rasped between coughs. "I don't care how expensive this stuff is. It tastes like fucking *paint stripper*."

Jay laughed properly then. "You're *supposed* to sip it," he said, "but yes, it *is* an acquired taste."

"Yeah, well, I don't think I'll be acquiring it." Tag's voice still sounded rough—rather sexy, in fact—as he slid his glass towards Jay. "Here, you may as well have it."

"Let me get you something else," Jay offered and raised a hand to summon the barman.

But warm fingers closed around his wrist, and Tag gently pushed his arm back down. "Don't," he said huskily, meeting Jay's gaze very directly. "I don't want another drink."

On one level, the words were a rejection, but on another… was Tag saying he wanted something else? A jolt of excitement shot through Jay at the note of assurance in Tag's voice, at the feel of those strong fingers still holding his wrist as their eyes held uncomfortably, as though snagged on thorns and unable to disentangle. "Okay," Jay said eventually, but he didn't look away and Tag didn't lift his hand from Jay's wrist. Instead, he swallowed, his throat moving, eyes locked on Jay's as he moistened his lips with the tip of his tongue.

What the fuck was happening here?

Then, with the world's worst timing, someone cleared their throat nearby. Jay startled, pulling free of Tag's grip as he turned to find Owen Hunter standing next to them, holding Mason's blue velvet jacket. He was watching them with wry curiosity.

"Sorry to interrupt," Owen said, "but Mason's not feeling well, and I'm going to make sure he gets home all right." He glanced at Tag. "Will you be okay catching a ride back with Lewis and Aaron?"

"Of course," Tag said. "Is Mason okay?"

Owen grimaced. "Better now he's thrown up."

Shit. "This is my fault," Jay said, mortified once more by how neglectful he'd been. "I should have been looking out for him. Let me call a cab—"

"No." Owen cut him off hurriedly. Then, looking a little self-conscious, he added, "Um, there's already a cab on the way. Mason just asked me to let you know he's going. He's pretty embarrassed and just wants to head off without any fuss."

Ah. So, Mason didn't actually want to see Jay right now. Well, Jay couldn't really blame him for that. He swallowed a smile and said, politely, "I understand. Tell him I hope he's feeling better soon."

"Yeah," Owen said. "I'll tell him." And then he was striding out of the bar towards the stairs with Mason's jacket folded over one arm.

"Well," Tag said, breaking the silence. "I'm not sure how I'll compete with this date. You really set a high bar tonight." The words were mocking, but when Jay glanced at Tag, it was to see that rueful smile again. A smile that mocked them both.

"Luckily, you won't *have* to compete," Jay replied. "Since there won't be any more dates with Mason for either of us." He sighed heavily. "I behaved like a total arse tonight. I owe him an apology."

"Yeah, well, we were both arses." After a pause, Tag added, "I don't think fake dating is for me."

Jay raised an eyebrow at him. "No? You seemed pretty into it to me."

Tag grinned, the tip of his tongue peeking out one side of his mouth, caught between his teeth. It was a cheeky, silly expression he used a lot, and Jay reluctantly found it cute. "Too frustrating. I prefer the real thing."

"Frustrating, huh?" Jay said. He tried to pull on his game face, but he could feel his heart beginning to thud anxiously, and had someone just sucked all the air out of the room?

"Yeah, in fact, now I really need to… let off some steam. Don't you?" Tag's voice was low and promising, and when he licked his lips, Jay's cock pulsed with desire. With another grin, Tag added, "I seem to recall that Mason suggested a solution for that."

"Why don't you just go fuck each other's brains out already?"

Heat washed over Jay's face, and he turned back to the bar, to his drink, but even as he did so, he was painfully aware of the man beside him, and despite all his usual worries, his gaze more or less immediately drifted back to Tag, who was now leaning against the bar, his jacket falling open to reveal the taut lines of his body. No accident, that; the display was far too deliberate, staged to be provocative.

"What do you say?" Tag raised an eyebrow. "It's just you and me left, after all."

"Not really," Jay said stiffly, certain Tag was teasing. "There's a whole bar full of people here."

"Is there?" Tag's eyes were heavy-lidded, unmistakably inviting.

"Come off it," Jay said, suddenly rather airless. "I thought you hated 'my type'."

Tag shrugged, the gesture making his jacket fall a little further open, displaying the sexy lines of his trim waist and cocked hip. Jay recalled how beautiful the body beneath that shirt was all too well, and his mouth went dry at the memory.

"I'm not suggesting we become BFFs," Tag continued, his expression amused. "Just that we could… work off a little mutual tension. Besides, I feel like celebrating."

"Celebrating *what*?"

"My big break." Grinning, Tag said, "Come on, why not? I'm attracted to you, and I remember the way you were eye-fucking me at that Hallowe'en party."

Bloody hell, he was serious.

And Jay was suddenly *filled* with that aching want again.

Lifting his glass, Jay downed his whisky in one swallow, relishing the smoky burn, then immediately reached for Tag's abandoned drink and did the same, setting the glass down hard on the counter with a brisk exhale.

Fuck, he thought, as the alcohol made its fiery way to his belly, *am I actually going to do this?*

And then he looked at Tag again, and he knew that he was. Tag was still watching him, his molten gaze suddenly the only thing in the room that mattered. Helplessly, Jay swayed closer, his body thrumming with adrenaline, his skin tingling and heart pumping. His fight-or-flight reflex kicking in, maybe? Or perhaps his fight or…

"Fuck," he whispered, "this is a *bad* idea."

"Yeah," Tag agreed, smiling wolfishly. "The best ones always are."

CHAPTER FIVE

Tag

"Jesus Christ!" Tag laughed as he brushed past Jay and stepped into his huge hotel room. "This isn't a room. It's a fucking suite." He glanced at Jay over his shoulder. "This must cost a fortune."

Jay's face pinkened. "Yeah, well, a nice room helps me to relax, and Carly—she's my assistant—is pretty good at negotiating rates."

Tag snorted at that, but when he saw Jay wince, he felt an unfamiliar pang of regret. Still, it was pretty stupid to try to pretend he hadn't spent a fortune on this place. And all for an extra hour's kip in the morning.

Turning in a slow circle, Tag spent a few moments taking in the spacious living room area with its plush sofa and chairs, its huge TV, and, on the sideboard, a platter of sliced tropical fruit, a few mini champagne bottles on ice, an elaborate arrangement of yellow and pink roses—and, of all things, a box of After Eights, tied up with a ridiculously luxurious red satin ribbon. At first, he wondered if crap like this came as standard when you booked a bloody enormous suite, but then he realised…

"Oh my God." Tag laughed in disbelief as he stared at the sideboard. "Is that… is that the same stuff you have on your rider for *Leeches*?"

"Just the, um, the After Eights," Jay mumbled, looking embarrassed. "The rest would have been sorted out by Carly."

"Wow," Tag said, lifting his brows. "She really takes care of you, huh?"

Jay shrugged. "Yeah," he said. "She looks after me pretty well."

"Must be nice," Tag added, stepping closer. "You like that? Being taken care of?"

He was only teasing, didn't mean anything by it, but the way Jay's face immediately heated made him pause.

Their gazes locked, and Tag knew that he'd inadvertently stumbled onto something. There was an odd combination of fierce hunger and uncertainty in Jay's eyes, but he didn't answer Tag's question. He didn't say anything at all.

Christ, those eyes. Dark as storm clouds.

Moving slowly, Tag stepped closer, lifting a hand to tug one end of Jay's bow-tie loose, his heart skipping at the sound of Jay's soft, indrawn breath. The black satin unravelled, and Tag pulled it free of Jay's collar, tossing it aside. "Want me to take care of you, Jay?" he murmured.

Jay briefly closed his eyes, and a muscle in his jaw ticked. But it was just for a moment. When he opened his eyes again, his gaze wasn't uncertain anymore. It was warm and teasing, and his mouth curved into a slow, wicked smile. "What I want," he said in a low voice, "is to get your cock in my mouth."

As he spoke, his hands were already moving to Tag's fly, undoing the buttons and lowering the zip. Tag's gaze dropped, and he watched, dry-mouthed, as Jay deftly slipped his hand inside to tease Tag's iron-hard cock with a sure, expert touch that had Tag moaning and his teeth sinking into his lower lip. Fucking hell, was this real? Jay Warren standing here, offering to drop to his knees and blow Tag? Surely this was too good to be true?

When Tag dragged his gaze back up to meet Jay's, catching him in an unguarded moment, he realised with a jolt that it *was* too good to be true. Because Jay looked... relieved.

It was like a bucket of cold water had been thrown over Tag. *Was he not into this?*

Jay must have sensed his change of mood because he drew back, his gaze on Tag as he said carefully, "Something wrong?"

And right then, Tag realised something. Jay had been *acting*. He'd decided to use that practised seduction routine to —what? Distract Tag from what he'd said about taking care of Jay? Those words must have hooked into something intense. Something Jay craved—maybe a craving he wanted to hide from Tag.

A craving Tag found himself longing to fulfil.

"No, everything's good," Tag murmured, sliding a hand around the back of Jay's neck. "But how about I blow you first?"

Jay swallowed, his dark brows creasing into a faint frown. "I'm happy to blow you," he said quickly.

"Yeah? Sounds like we have more in common than we realised," Tag said, arching a brow. He laughed softly but then caught a flash of worry on Jay's face that made his chest ache weirdly. More gently, he added, "Look, can I maybe just *kiss* you before we do anything else?"

"Okay," Jay whispered, his gaze watchful as Tag leaned in to capture his lips. For an instant, Jay's lips felt stiff under his own, but when Tag muscled in closer, taking a firm hold of Jay's hips and pulling him tight, something in him gave way. His eyelids fell, and his lips parted, welcoming Tag's tongue.

And when Tag pressed forward, Jay let himself be pushed backwards, tumbling onto the big king-sized bed that dominated the room. Tag followed him down, and they kept frantically kissing, the heavy scruff on Jay's jaw rasping against Tag's face, both of them groaning with pleasure as they began shucking off clothes with unholy haste.

When they were finally naked, Tag somehow found the strength of will to break the kiss for a moment, lifting up on one elbow to stare down at Jay. God, he really was a beautiful guy, his skin smooth and glowing, his lean, muscled body perfectly proportioned.

"You going to let me blow you then?" Tag murmured softly, leaning down to press a kiss to one golden shoulder.

"Uh, I—" Jay looked embarrassed, seeming unsure what to say. Tag frowned and smiled at the same time, curiously charmed. He would never have expected this reaction from Jay, a man who, until now, Tag had thought of as annoyingly suave and overconfident.

"Come on," Tag prompted gently, studying Jay. "Let me take care of you."

And there it was again, that flare of *want* in Jay's eyes. For an instant, Tag saw Jay struggle with it. Then he said, his tone strangled, "I really think I should go first."

Tag didn't agree. That *'should'* said it all. He wanted this to be fun, not an obligation. "It doesn't need to be tit for tat," he said, smiling. He stroked a hand up Jay's flank, enjoying Jay's responsive shiver. "Just let me make you feel good, and we can… go from there, yeah?"

But Jay still looked unhappy.

"What is it?" Tag prompted, watching him carefully. "Have I done something wrong? I want you to feel good." He stroked Jay's warm side again, and Jay arched into the touch with a moan of pleasure that made Tag's cock harden and his balls ache. Jay seemed to want him, so what was the problem?

"Nothing's wrong." Jay said at last. "I just—" He flushed,

a crimson wash that was strangely appealing. "It's just that sometimes I… can take a while? To come, I mean."

And suddenly, it all made sense. Tag felt a rush of sympathy at the uncertainty in Jay's voice, the faint anxiety in his grey eyes, but he kept his voice light. "Hey, that's not a problem," he said. Then he stabbed his tongue lewdly in one cheek and added, "Believe me, I won't be complaining about spending more quality time with your cock."

Jay gave a startled chuckle at that, and Tag took the opportunity to move down the bed and settle himself between Jay's thighs. "Mmm," he said, "I won't be complaining *at all*."

Jay had a nice cock. Very nice indeed, a good length and a decent girth, with a plump, glossy head that was already flushed with want. Tag leaned down and licked the damp tip, relishing the briny flavour that burst on his tongue, and the hoarse gasp Jay gave at just that small contact.

So responsive. Fuck, Tag was going to enjoy this.

Urging Jay's thighs apart, he shimmied in between them, running the tip of his nose up the crease between Jay's thigh and groin, inhaling his delicious scent. Jay groaned and widened his thighs to accommodate Tag's shoulders.

"You smell amazing," Tag muttered, pressing more kisses along that same crease, making Jay groan again, and squirm a little. Turning his head, Tag licked a broad stripe all the way up Jay's shaft, before engulfing it in his mouth in one smooth, downward move. The spongy head prodded insistently at the back of his throat, making his eyes smart even as he began to slowly retreat, dragging his lips back up to the crown, his fingers curling around the base.

Pulling off, Tag lifted his head, his gaze skimming back up Jay's lean, golden body, taking in the neat bush and the dark trail of hair that arrowed up Jay's flat belly and continued between his ribs before dusting his firm pecs. He seemed to be naturally less hairy than Tag, who needed to manscape pretty ruthlessly. But Tag was pleased—and maybe a little surprised—to see that neither was he waxed perfectly smooth.

When his gaze finally reached Jay's face, it was to find Jay eying him strangely.

"Like what you see?" Jay asked, and Tag wasn't sure how to read his tone. Was that arrogance? Or had there been a note of insecurity in there?

In all their previous interactions, Jay had oozed privilege and self-confidence, but right now, his cheeks were pink, and his gaze was sliding away from Tag's.

"Yes," Tag said without hesitation. "I bloody love it."

Without waiting for a response, he leaned back down, trailing kisses down Jay's belly before engulfing that lovely cock in his mouth once again and beginning to slowly, patiently, work Jay's shaft with his mouth, relishing every gasp and moan, every desperate, straining thrust of Jay's lean hips against his firm hands.

Tag loved giving head, and his own cock grew painfully, achingly hard between his legs. It was all so good, the heft of Jay's dick in his mouth, the sight of him lying there, debauched and helpless, the sound of his moans and gasps. Knowing Tag was doing this to him.

Tag knew, without arrogance, that he gave excellent blowjobs. In fact, when he put his mind to it, he could usually get a guy to come obscenely quickly. In this case, he was very glad it was lasting a bit longer than usual, since his own dick was enjoying itself immensely. But as the time ticked by, his jaw inevitably began to ache, and eventually, he was forced to briefly pull off Jay's dick.

"Just need a second," he murmured, leaning back on his heels and moving his jaw from side to side.

Jay's eyes flew open at that, and he stared at Tag in mortification. "Shit," he said. "I'm taking ages, aren't I? Fuck, I'm sorry."

He began to sit up, but Tag stopped him, again with a

hand to his chest. "What are you doing?" he said, genuinely puzzled.

Jay gave a rueful huff. "It's way past your turn. Lie down. I'll do you."

I'll do you? Tag winced.

"Lie back down," he said softly.

"But—"

"Jay," he said firmly, "I told you I'd take care of you. Lie down."

Slowly, reluctantly, Jay lay back again, but his stormy eyes remained troubled. "This isn't fair on you," he said. "You're doing all the work, and I'm just—"

Tag leaned down, silencing him with a kiss. When he pulled back, he grabbed Jay's hand and pressed it to his own hard cock, enjoying the startled expression on Jay's face. "This isn't work for me," he whispered. "I can come just from this." He quirked a smile. "So, be a good boy and lie still while I suck you dry, yeah?"

Jay swallowed and nodded, and Tag shimmied back down the bed to take him in his mouth again. Only this time, he took hold of his own cock at the same time and began to stroke himself in tandem, determined to show Jay how much this turned him on. That it wasn't *work*.

Jay got into it faster this time, and soon he was moaning beneath Tag again, his hips shifting as Tag worked his dick mercilessly, deep-throating him and making obscene noises. It wasn't long at all until Tag felt Jay's shaft swelling that last tiny fraction more, and then Jay's hand was in his hair, clutching him as his hips punched up and he began to unload in Tag's willing mouth.

It was the taste of it—the salt-sweet flavour of Jay's spunk flooding his mouth—that tipped Tag over too. His hand stripped his cock once, twice more before he erupted over the bedcovers, then collapsed onto his side.

As he lay there, gasping, he felt insanely light-headed,

partly from Jay's dick being shoved so far down his throat he simply couldn't suck in air, and partly from his own inability to even remember to breathe when he was coming so hard.

For what felt like an indeterminate period of time, they just lay there, gradually coming back to themselves. At first, Tag felt amazing, his whole body drenched with the happy chemicals of good sex. But then, inevitably, reality poked its nose around the door and said, *Well now, what have you been up to?*

What indeed? Had he really just given Jay Warren, of all people, a blowjob? Turning his head, he glanced at Jay, who lay beside him, one arm thrown over his face.

Tag felt… well, he felt a lot of things. Fuck-drunk and wary and like he wanted to pull Jay into his arms, all at the same time.

He was thinking of how to break the silence when, from under his protective arm, Jay shakily said, "I can't believe I let you do that."

It was like a knife between Tag's ribs. "I need to clean up," he muttered, rolling away from Jay and off the bed, scooping his boxer shorts from the floor en route to the bathroom and locking the door behind him.

Once inside, he took a deep, unsteady breath and let it out again, rubbing his hand over the back of his neck. When he caught his own reflection in the mirror, he winced. He had that just-fucked look, lips swollen, pale skin flushed, dark hair wild from the way Jay had been pulling at it.

Fuck. He'd hooked up with Jay Warren. And it hadn't felt like a normal hook-up. Tag wasn't shy about sex—he enjoyed it, and he didn't hesitate to open himself up physically to his partner in every way. He was affectionate too, and friendly, but emotionally, he tended to keep a certain casual distance. He wasn't looking for anything serious, not with anyone. Certainly not now, when his focus had to be his career.

It hadn't been like that with Jay, though, had it? Strangely, the fact that Jay had been a bit inhibited physically had made it feel *more* intimate than usual. More emotional. Was that why Tag was feeling so weird right now? So spooked?

Was that why he felt so pissed off about Jay's dismissive words? Christ, was he feeling *hurt*?

He realised, suddenly, that he didn't know what he was going to do, or say, when he left the bathroom. What would he normally do with a hook-up? Probably make a cheeky joke. Put his clothes on, give the guy a quick kiss—sometimes his number, if he liked him a lot and thought he wouldn't be too clingy—and head on out. But something in Tag didn't like that idea. Not at all.

Oh God.

In the mirror, Tag's eyes widened, and he felt his heart start to pound in a panicky way. What was he even thinking? Jay clearly regretted what they'd done, and if Tag had half a brain, he'd feel the same. He *did* feel the same, didn't he? Tag kept himself footloose and fancy free for a reason, and right now, he had other priorities. Christ, the opportunity of a lifetime had just landed in his lap—he could *not* afford to be distracted.

The best thing he could do right now was make a swift exit with as little drama as possible. Even so, his stomach twisted when he cracked open the bathroom door and slipped back into the bedroom.

His vague hope that Jay might be the sort to come, roll over, and fall asleep was immediately dashed. Jay was perched on the edge of the bed watching the bathroom door intently. His expression was difficult to read. It had something of his usual aloofness, although his flushed cheeks and ruffled hair hinted at the vulnerability Tag had witnessed earlier. The knots in his stomach tightened.

Jay had donned his briefs and a t-shirt, and that left Tag feeling exposed, standing there in just his boxers.

"Well," Tag said brightly. "That was fun."

Jay blinked and after a moment said, "I, er, don't normally do this, but if—"

"You're kidding," Tag cut him off before he could say more, adopting a deliberately teasing tone. "Well, that was pretty good for your first time."

Jay looked unsettled. "Um. Obviously, I've had sex before…"

"Yeah, I know. I was just fucking with you." Giving a brittle laugh, Tag snatched up a knot of clothing that included his trousers, shirt, and socks and began untangling them hurriedly, adrenaline making his fingers clumsy.

After another pause, Jay said, "You're leaving."

Tag wasn't sure whether that was an observation or an order. Stomach churning, he gave Jay a stagey wink as he started dressing, saying, "Always leave them wanting more, right?"

After a pause, Jay said flatly, "Right."

The silence that followed was intensely awkward.

Tag didn't look at Jay as he dressed, but he could feel Jay's gaze on him as he slipped back into his rented tux. He stuffed the bow-tie into his trouser pocket and started pulling on his socks. He really wished Jay would stop looking at him. "Feel free to jump in the shower while I get dressed," he said breezily. "I can let myself out."

After another painful pause, Jay said in a chilly tone, "I assume we'll be keeping this between ourselves, then?"

Well, *that* sounded more like the man Tag knew, cool and condescending. It was a relief to Tag, even as it needled him. Maybe *because* it needled him. "Really?" he said, aping surprise. "I was going to put it on my Insta."

Jay visibly paled. "You wouldn't—"

It had been a joke, but Jay's obvious horror still stung.

"Calm your tits. I'm joking," Tag said. "What do you think I am? No, don't answer that." He was fully dressed now, except for his tux jacket, which he swung over one shoulder, holding it there with a finger crooked through the loop. "Look, I don't really do secrets," he said, "but I'm not about to go to the press, if that's what you're worried about."

"I'm more worried about work stuff," Jay said stiffly. "I'd rather this wasn't the subject of RPP gossip."

Even though Tag had been trying to make a quick escape not two minutes earlier, he felt his hackles rise at those words. "Oh? And why's that?" he said. "Don't want people to know you like a bit of rough?"

Jay's expression grew flinty. "For God's sake, don't be so childish."

The flare of irritation Tag felt at that was almost a comfort, and he embraced it, letting it wash away his more confusing feelings. *This* was the real Jay, after all. "Oh, I'm childish now, am I?"

Closing his eyes, Jay took a deep breath. "This was a mistake."

Tag felt like he'd been punched. "You're telling me," he shot back hotly. "I've never had to work so bloody hard at a blowjob in my life."

He regretted the jibe the moment it left his mouth. It was cruel and untrue, but the damage was already done. Jay stiffened, and just for an instant—no more—Tag saw that he was genuinely hurt, his eyes widening and his lips pressing together. And then, in the blink of an eye, he changed. His expression hardened, and all that hurt melted away. When he finally spoke, he sounded amused, in a biting sort of way. "Well, in that case," he said in crystal tones, "I hope you don't charge by the hour."

"*Charge...*?" Tag spluttered, unable to even attempt a witty retort. "Fuck off!"

Jay swept his arm towards the door. "Don't let me stop you..."

So Tag didn't, stalking out of the room without another

word, letting the heavy door slam behind him. And good riddance.

For a moment, he glared at the closed door. As he turned away, though, he realised someone was standing a few doors down, staring at him, one hand raised, about to insert the keycard he was holding into the lock.

It was that journalist. Austin Coburn.

Tag's first instinct was to panic—to hide—but that was swiftly replaced by a surge of annoyance. Why should he care, after all?

So instead he just flashed Coburn a careless smile and strode past him down the hotel corridor.

CHAPTER SIX

JAY

The next morning, Jay was woken by housekeeping tapping at the door of his hotel suite.

He opened his eyes, disorientated for an instant, but when he heard the door handle begin to turn, he jack-knifed up in bed. "Sorry," he called out, his voice croaky, "could you come back later?"

The door handle was released, and moments later, he heard the rumbling sound of a housekeeping trolley being trundled away.

Jay flopped back down, covering his face with his arm as his mind returned remorselessly to the events of the night before: the awards dinner, the embarrassing episode with Mason, the absurd confrontation with Austin Coburn... and allowing Tag O'Rourke to blow him. To *take care of him*, as Tag had called it.

A distressed moan escaped his throat, loud in the silent hotel room.

Jesus Christ. What had he been thinking?

Well, *thinking* wasn't the issue, was it? The issue was that he *hadn't* been thinking. At some point, he'd just stopped. Switched off his brain and let his dick take over. Or rather, let *Tag* take over. Which wasn't his usual strategy. Usually, Jay was careful to stay in control of his hook-ups. That way he could manage his—well, his tendency to get a bit uptight. Once he'd made a guy come, it was amazing how often his interest in Jay's orgasm dwindled. Not Tag, though. No, he'd seemed very interested indeed.

Christ, the heat in his voice when he'd pushed Jay back into the pillows.

"I told you I'd take care of you. Lie down."

Jay shivered, aroused at the memory of what he'd let Tag do to him, and mortified by the things he'd confessed. What had possessed him to give over control like that, to a man he barely knew? To confide his most embarrassing secret to him, a man who'd already amply demonstrated that he despised Jay? Tag could make him a laughing stock, if he chose. What a fucking idiot he'd been.

"I've never had to work so bloody hard at a blowjob in my life."

A pained grunt escaped Jay at the humiliating memory. He rolled over, pulling one of the pillows over his head.

Up until Tag had uttered those words, Jay had thought Tag had enjoyed their time together. That he'd been as into it as Jay. That the patience and understanding he'd shown had been genuine.

But apparently, Tag had just been going through the motions. Doing what he needed to do to get Jay to climax, so he could bust his own nut and leave.

Fuck.

Thank God Tag had interrupted him before he could stammer out the invitation to stay the night that he'd been working up to while Tag was in the bathroom. At least Jay had been spared the humiliation of Tag turning him down.

Yet, somehow, even though he hadn't said the words, that was still the worst part. Knowing that when he'd made the conscious decision to trust Tag, he'd got it so utterly wrong. Again.

Christ, he wanted to curl up and die. Why was he so bloody gullible?

Tag must be laughing his head off at how eagerly Jay had lapped up his bullshit. Would he tell Mason? Or maybe Aaron? Or maybe he'd drop a hint to Austin Coburn— everyone knew that bastard relied on industry sources for his '*Little Bird*' column. That last thought prompted a bolt of sheer panic that hit him right in the middle of his chest.

Fuck.

Beneath the pillow, Jay squeezed his eyes closed even tighter, trying in vain to block out the memories of the night before. Trying to un-see the image, burned into his brain, of Tag stalking out of the suite, the door slamming behind him.

His only consolation was that he'd managed to hide his feelings from Tag, masking his humiliation with icy disdain. Hurt was always easier to bear when nobody knew you were suffering.

Still, it had taken Jay hours after that to finally fall asleep. It was only as the grey light of dawn had begun to rinse away the darkness that he'd finally dropped off.

Jay lifted the corner of the pillow just enough to glance at the clock on the bedside table. He was due to meet Bea Lawson in just over two hours. As tempting as it was to go back to sleep, he needed to get washed, dressed, packed, and checked out before making his way to the restaurant.

Pull your bloody self together.

Gritting his teeth, he threw aside the pillow, shoved the bedcovers back, and got to his feet. As he headed for the bath-room, he pushed Tag O'Rourke to the very back of his mind, stuffing the awful mess of last night into a box and locking it up. *Do not open.*

He'd have plenty of time to obsess over that particular

mistake later. For now, it was time to get himself into the right frame of mind for his meeting.

Bea had invited Jay to lunch at a restaurant in Camden. It was only a couple of miles from the hotel so he could easily walk it, even with the annoyance of dragging his wheeled suitcase behind him.

The walk gave him plenty of time to think about how he would approach the meeting.

Once he'd expressed his regret that he wouldn't be able to take the role Bea had offered, he'd tell her that he would love to be involved in other ways. Perhaps he could come and see the show when it premiered in York? He could tip off the press that he'd be there in the hope that would get the play some attention, and of course he'd ask Carly to post about it on his socials.

There was just one problem with his plan: he'd honoured his promise to his mother and read *Let Us Go Back*.

And he'd loved it.

It wasn't even just that he'd loved the play, he thought, as he strode through the busy city streets, weaving through the throng of single-minded city types, lugging his case behind him. It was that he hadn't been able to stop thinking about it, or about the character of Sassoon with his comfortable, somewhat Bohemian upbringing. The man had been surrounded by easy wealth and artistic talent from a young age. And Jay knew that life. He knew what it was to grow up in such rich pastures. To learn, painfully, how different reality could be.

Jay had read about Sassoon and Owen years before, how they'd met at Craiglockhart Hospital during the First World War. How Owen, fresh and impressionable, had been entirely awed by the more experienced, upper-class Sassoon, and how Sassoon had condescended to read Owen's poetry and gift him with his insights. Back then, Sassoon had seemed lofty, even self-important, to Jay, but in Bea's play, a more vulnerable side to the man emerged. Sassoon was unsettled by Owen. Stunned by his talent. Maybe even envious of it.

It had been a long, long time since Jay had craved a role the way he craved this one. It wasn't only that he wanted to play Sassoon—it was that he didn't want anyone *else* to play him. He wanted the role all for himself with a selfish, hoarding greed he barely recognised.

Well, he told himself, as he approached the restaurant where he was meeting Bea, *you're just going to have to live with the fact that someone else* will *be playing him.*

Bea was already at the table, waiting for him, when he went aside. Spotting him, she half-rose out of her seat, lifting a hand and smiling broadly. With her slightly frizzy mane of red hair and tall, slender build, she was the spit of her father, Timon Lawson, one of Dame Cordelia's closest friends.

Jay raised a hand in answer and began to make his way over to the table.

"You're looking as amazing as always," Bea said, after the obligatory air kisses. "Oberon's dreamy, of course, but I've always said you're the best-looking Warren brother."

"Flattery will get you everywhere," he retorted with a grin, only to regret that statement an instant later when he remembered he was about to tell her he couldn't take the part.

Bea sparkled at him. "Ah, well in that case, I'll promote you to the best-looking Warren *child*. Portia's now officially second."

Jay chuckled. "She'll hate that. She's so competitive."

"You all are!" Bea said. "I remember those parties your mother used to throw, with all of you trying to outdo each other with your party pieces."

"Not *me*," Jay said, laughing. "I was always trying to get out of doing a party piece."

"Oh, you fibber!" Bea replied. "You obviously loved the limelight." Jay chuckled again, though the comment surprised him. That wasn't how he remembered it.

A waiter, in a denim apron with leather straps, arrived to explain the menu to them, which seemed to take an inordinate amount of time. Bea, perhaps sensing Jay's lack of interest, offered to order some plates for them to share, and Jay was happy to agree, paying scant attention as she made her choices.

For the next while, they chatted about inconsequential stuff. Bea was funny and vibrant and full of stories about people they both knew, so it was no hardship. A jug of water was brought and served with as much reverence as if it was liquid gold. The wine Bea had ordered came next, a lovely, crisp white. Then they were offered bread from a small, burlap sack and solemnly informed that the butter had been made in the restaurant kitchen and was infused with truffle. Jay smiled wanly. He didn't much like truffle.

Despite the butter, the rest of the food was very good, if a little on the small side. It was fine. Jay wasn't particularly hungry anyway. He picked at the shared plates, happy to let Bea have the lion's share.

"So," she said at last, when they'd finished eating. "This play of mine…"

She left the words hanging in the air, waiting expectantly, excitedly.

Awkwardly, Jay said, "Bea, it's—it's really wonderful. I mean that."

Her eyes sparkled with pleasure, and she leaned forward, elbows on the table. "You think so? I'm so glad, Jay. I mean, I'm more grateful than you can imagine that you agreed to take the role, but it makes it so much sweeter knowing you actually *like* the play."

Jay blinked. "Um, Bea, are we not"—he broke off, heat

climbing in his face—"I thought we were just meeting to discuss the *possibility* of me taking the role."

Bea looked shocked. "Oh," she said. Then, visibly, she wilted, like a pin-pricked balloon, "Oh, shit."

Jay stared at her, unsure what to say. She looked *devastated*. "I'm sorry," he blurted. "I think there's been some kind of misunderstanding. My mother said you wanted to offer me the part and asked me to meet you to discuss it. I didn't realise..." He trailed off.

"I see," Bea said, her voice very small now. "I, uh, I think there may have been some crossed wires then. I had the impression that you—well, that you'd said yes. I thought this, today, was kind of a formality." She grimaced. "Is this where you tell me you don't want the role?"

Jay felt terrible—and a little angry, suspecting his mother had a hand in this confusion. "Well," he began, determined to yank off the sticking plaster. But when he saw Bea swallow, the vulnerable bob of her pale throat, and the real fear in her eyes, somehow, he just... couldn't do it. Weakly, he finished, "I wasn't sure I could do justice to the role."

Bea's troubled expression cleared. "Is that all? Jesus, Jay, you're my dream casting. I love your work. You do restrained vulnerability—which is the core of this character—better than anyone. That period drama that went out last Christmas. God, you were good in that."

Jay couldn't help but smile. Rehearsing and filming *The Year of No Summer* had taken up every spare minute between shooting *Leeches* seasons. It had been a gruelling year, but he'd been incredibly proud of that piece.

"What do I need to do to persuade you?" Bea said urgently. "Please, Jay. I don't have anyone else in mind. My rehearsal space is booked. Henry's agreed to direct—"

"Henry Walker?"

"Yes!" Bea nodded enthusiastically, perhaps sensing a breakthrough.

Jay had studied under Henry at RADA and had never felt more understood as an actor. In fact, he'd always wanted to work with Henry professionally, and back then, before Seb, he'd blithely assumed that one day he would…

"We're so lucky." Bea went on. "Henry's doing it as a favour to my dad, bless him, and we've just cast the Owen role together. He's Henry's first choice—a fantastic young actor. You'll love him. He'll be here soon actually."

"Bea, I—"

"Look, I'm not asking you to tour the play around the country after the festival—I know you don't have time for that." She tried to deliver a cheeky smile. "And I've kind of promised that gig to your understudy anyway. All I'm asking from you is the festival run. It's just two weeks, and your mother told me you don't have any *Leeches* commitments over the summer, so the timing's perfect."

Fuck. Panic was building in Jay's chest, his heart pounding now. How could he get out of this? Should he just admit the truth? That the thought of getting up on stage terrified him out of his wits? That was a secret he'd been determined to take to his grave.

He opened his mouth to speak—to say what, he wasn't even sure—but was forestalled by Bea's gaze shifting away from his own as she spotted someone over his shoulder. "Oh, here he is!" She lifted an arm to wave, beckoning the person over.

Jay turned in his seat.

When he saw the man approaching their table, his stomach plunged.

It was Tag O'Rourke, looking as sexy as ever, his gait loose and confident, his gaze fixed on Bea. He was wearing that gorgeous, open smile of his, eyes bright with pleasure, dark hair a little tousled from the wind. And then he spotted Jay, and his smile froze. For an instant, he looked shocked.

Bea gave a strained laugh. "Hey Tag," she said. "I guess

now you know who that big name is." She turned to Jay. "This is Tag O'Rourke—we cast him as Wilfred Owen yesterday. Tag, this is Jay Warren. You've probably seen him on TV."

For a second, they just stared at one another. It was probably only a couple of moments, but it felt ages longer. Jay saw Tag's astonished disbelief turn to dismay, then something that looked almost like grief. He had an instant of savage satisfaction—*regretting last night's exit now, are we?*—but swiftly on the heels of that came realisation. This role was the *big break* Tag had been celebrating last night. And now he was sure he'd fucked up that chance.

Somehow, Jay found himself pushing back his chair and getting to his feet. Putting out his hand and saying smoothly, "Great to see you again, Tag." He let his lips quirk into a smile. "It's been too long."

Tag just stared at him, wide-eyed. Then, after a hesitation, he reached out and took Jay's proffered hand. They shook briefly. Tag's touch was cold from being outside, and Jay tried not to think about its heat last night.

"You know each other?" Bea put in, surprised.

"A little," Jay said. "We have some mutual friends."

Tag was catching up now, scrambling his game face back on as he turned to Bea. "Um, yeah. I'm good friends with Aaron Page—Lewis Hunter's partner."

"Ah, a *Leeches* connection," Bea said. "Well, it's a small world. Would you like a glass of wine, Tag?"

Tag shot Jay a quick, questioning look, and Jay gave a slight shrug.

"Sure," Tag said carefully. "That would be nice."

"Great." Bea stood up, grabbing her bag. "Take a seat. I'm going to the bathroom. I'll grab the waiter on the way and ask him to bring another glass and bottle. You two can catch up while I'm gone."

And with that she strode off, leaving the two of them

alone. Tag stared after her for a moment. He looked as though he wanted to call her back.

"You may as well sit down," Jay said gruffly.

"Yeah," Tag said. "Of course." Shouldering out of his jacket, he made a bit of a production out of arranging it on the back of his chair before finally sitting down.

Underneath the jacket he wore a black, flatteringly tight City Beans t-shirt, and Jay realised he must have come straight from work. Why that should make Jay uncomfortable, he couldn't say, except that *he'd* spent the morning in bed, wallowing in his regrets, and that pointed up starkly the difference in their circumstances.

After a moment, Tag puffed out a breath. "So," he said. "This is awkward."

Jay sipped his wine and set the glass down carefully. He kept his expression bland. "Yes. I take it you didn't know about my involvement?"

"I knew the Sassoon role was going to a 'big name'," Tag replied. "I had no idea it was you. If I had, I wouldn't have…" He trailed off.

"You wouldn't have what?" Jay asked, raising a brow. "Walked out last night? Blown me? Treated me like an enemy for the last few months?"

Tag winced. "Jay—"

But whatever he was about to say was swallowed as the waiter arrived, placing a fresh glass in front of Tag with a flourish before setting about uncorking the wine. They both watched in silence, Tag's expressive mouth set in a tense and increasingly unhappy line.

He managed a smile for the waiter, though, when he poured Tag a glass. "Cheers, mate," he said, flashing that heart-stopping grin.

And then they were alone again, or as alone as they could be in the middle of a slightly pretentious Camden restaurant at the tail end of the lunchtime rush. Tag sipped his wine without appearing to notice the taste—philistine—and Jay considered his options. The truth was, as humiliated as he felt by this situation, it could also work in his favour. Obviously, given the personal situation between them, they couldn't work together. Which meant Jay had a legitimate reason to bow out of the production, generously standing aside to allow Tag to take a role he so clearly coveted. Dame Cordelia could hardly blame him for that, for allowing an up-and-coming young actor an opportunity at his own expense—it was exactly the sort of noblesse oblige she expected of all her family. And of herself.

He opened his mouth to say as much, but Tag got in first.

"Look," he said leaning forward across the table and speaking in a low, urgent voice, "I know you can get Beatrice to recast the Owen role, and I suppose you're entitled, but that would be really bloody unfair. I've worked hard for this, I earned it, and I bloody well deserve it."

Tag's passion, the fire in those liquid gold eyes of his, tripped something in Jay's chest, setting his heart galloping. He hid the bizarre reaction behind the quizzical lift of one eyebrow. "I see that I'm still playing the villain in your personal drama."

Tag said nothing, lips pursed.

"You'll be pleased to learn," Jay went on, "that I haven't actually accepted the Sassoon role yet. And now—given the situation between us—I tend to think it would be best if I decline. Without wishing to sound conceited, the play is clearly more important for your career than mine, so I'm happy to stand aside." He lifted his glass in salute. "You're welcome."

Tag, however, looked neither grateful nor pleased. His expression only darkened. "You're kidding, right? You're going to storm off in a huff and ruin everything?"

"I—*what*?"

"For fuck's sake," Tag hissed, "you're the big name. Beatrice is counting on you. The success of this project is built around you. But I suppose you don't care about any of that."

"You have no idea what I care about," Jay shot back, startled by his own vehemence. "You don't know anything about me."

"I know you're willing to screw us all over out of pique!"

Through gritted teeth, Jay said, "Would you rather I asked Bea to recast Owen, then?"

"No!" That was rather loud and set a couple of heads turning their way. Tag hunched down, lowering his voice. "I'd *rather* you behaved like a professional and agreed to work with me."

Jay just stared at him. "You—you can't possibly imagine that we can work together."

"Why not?"

"You know why not!"

Tag shook his head, looking frustrated, and clenched a hand in his thick dark hair. With a startling flash of clarity, Jay remembered the silken strands running through his fingers while Tag had been—

"Shit," Tag sighed, slumping back in his seat. "It's such a great fucking play, as well."

After watching his crestfallen expression for a couple of moments, Jay conceded, "It is, yes."

"You've read it?"

Exasperated, he blurted, "Christ, don't look so surprised!" Immediately, he was annoyed at himself for the brief loss of his cool, but Tag's habit of always thinking the worst of him was beginning to grate on his nerves. Determinedly pushing his irritation aside, he took a deep breath and added more calmly, "It's a brilliant play, and I confess that Sassoon… speaks to me as a character."

"I can see that he would," Tag said, his expression turning thoughtful. "Yeah, you've got all that starchy upper-class reserve going on, but underneath…" He trailed off, a slight flush rising into his cheeks. "You'll be good as Sassoon."

"Not too wooden?" Jay said pointedly.

Tag's flush deepened, but he brazened it out with a grin. "I'm willing to be convinced I was wrong about that."

Cheeky bastard. And, despite everything, Jay found himself reluctantly charmed by Tag's chutzpah.

Still, he couldn't accept the role. After the near disaster with the Dracula thing, he'd sworn to never, ever put himself through the trauma of live theatre again. The very thought made his throat close in panic.

"Look," Tag said, leaning forward, his keen gaze on Jay. "How about this? We forget everything that's happened before today. It's water under the bridge. Gone. We start again from now. Just two actors embarking on an exciting new production together."

Jay drummed his fingers on the table. He wanted to say no, but Tag looked so eager sitting there in his City Beans shirt, watching Jay intently, as if he held Tag's life in his hands. Which he did, in a way, he supposed. And then he remembered the tearful bob of Bea's throat when she'd realised that Dame Cordelia had over-promised regarding Jay's involvement in the play. His bloody mother... Christ, he could practically hear her now.

Darling, always be generous with your talent and your time. We, at the summit, are obliged to extend a hand down to those still climbing the slopes.

And Tag *was* still climbing, living hand to mouth but fired with ambition. Bea was climbing too, although she'd started rather higher up the mountain than Tag. Jay, of course, had been born at the top.

That wasn't his fault, but his mother *was* right; it did burden him with responsibility, whether he liked it or not.

"The success of this production is built around you."

If Tag had meant that to prick Jay's conscience or

stroke his ego, he'd been way off the mark. Nothing could be more terrifying. Jay couldn't deny it was true, though. The problem was, Tag didn't know that Jay was hopelessly flawed, a cracked foundation, and that any production built around him was liable to collapse at the last moment.

He chewed his lip, considering. "What about—?" He cleared his throat, saw Tag watching him with his clenched fingers turning white on the table. "What about the romantic scenes? How would we deal with those?"

Tag just shrugged. "We *are* actors, Jay. Adults, too. Anyway, we're starting fresh, remember? Everything before today is forgotten."

Easy for him to say, but there was no way Jay could forget last night. Neither the intensity of the sex, nor what had come after. This morning he'd expected—hoped, rather—to never see Tag again, and here he was, facing the prospect of spending a couple of months working intensely with him. Christ, it was impossible.

"Sorry I was so long," Bea said, breezing back to the table and taking her seat.

Tag shifted awkwardly. "No problem," he said. "Jay and I were just, uh, discussing the play."

"Yes?" Her hopeful gaze travelled to Jay. "Tag did a *marvellous* audition for Owen. He's going to be wonderful. You both are." She pressed her hands to her chest, eying them. "Oh, you look amazing together. Henry said you would. Owen and Sassoon are sitting right here, right now. I'm getting goosebumps!"

Across the table, Tag met Jay's eyes. His brows lifted in a question. Or maybe a plea.

Heart thudding, Jay took a long swallow of wine. He felt rather like a man forced to walk the plank, balancing on the end with a pirate poking him in the back with a cutlass. Only it wasn't a pirate, it was his mother poking him with her expectations, it was Bea with her hope, and it was Tag with his bright, burning ambition.

All depending on him to make the right decision.

More than all that, though, it was the play itself, the character of Sassoon, calling to him from the deep with an elusive pull that he'd not felt in a long time. Whispering that maybe he could do it, that maybe this time, under Henry's steady hand, everything would be all right. That the risk was worth taking for a chance at regaining what he'd lost.

Jay set down his glass so that the others couldn't see the sudden tremor in his hand. "Well," he said graciously, "I am very fond of York."

ACT TWO

CHAPTER SEVEN

TAG

Three months later - May

With relief, Tag manoeuvred himself and his luggage onto the final escalator heading up from the tube, trying not to take out a tourist with his massive rucksack while he dragged his wheeled suitcase onto the step below him.

Gradually, the huge station concourse came into view, and his stomach squirmed excitedly. King's Cross and the 11:05 to York awaited.

This was *it*.

The station was busy as Tag made his way through crowds of travellers, some striding purposefully, headphones on, others milling about in groups staring up at the train information boards. Tag had left plenty of time, so he didn't need to rush. Briefly, he considered grabbing a coffee from one of the myriad eateries—the place looked more like an airport departure lounge than a train station—but he'd packed a sandwich and a drink and couldn't afford to splash out on anything if he was going to make it through the next eight weeks. So he did a leisurely loop of the concourse instead, too keyed up to take a seat.

Keeping an eye on the ever-changing information boards, he strolled past families, business people, a noisy school trip, and the constant queue of tourists waiting to have their photos taken with the luggage trolley half embedded in the wall beneath the *Platform 9 ¾* sign.

Tag checked the time on his phone. Walked on, checked again. It felt like forever, but eventually, when he looked up, he saw that his train had an assigned platform and he hurried to join the throng heading towards platform six.

It felt odd to be leaving London. This would be the longest he'd ever been away from the city. York looked interesting, though, and very quaint. He hoped the people were nice and didn't hate Londoners on principle. Not that he'd have time, or money, to be sampling the local nightlife. Work, work, and more work was all he was there for, and most likely the only people he'd spend time with would be the cast and crew... including Jay.

Christ, *Jay*.

They hadn't met since that bloody awful lunch, back in February, when he'd thought everything was going to screech to a halt before it had even begun. His heart had just about stopped when he'd realised that Jay Warren was the 'big name' Beatrice had been so excited about. The possibility had never even crossed his mind. As far as Tag knew, Jay never did theatre. And then Jay had turned around in his seat, his brief, betraying look of horror—definitely horror—swiftly hidden behind his practised polish. Almost as if they hadn't had scorching sex followed by a blazing row only hours earlier.

Tag still couldn't believe Jay had agreed to take the role.

In the restaurant, he'd been convinced that he'd blown his biggest and best ever professional chance, that Jay would refuse to work with him. He hadn't felt much better about it after he'd left, Jay's gaze cool and inscrutable as they'd said their goodbyes. Over the weeks that followed, he'd jumped every time his phone rang, dreading the call from Beatrice telling him that Jay had changed his mind and Tag was out of the production.

That call had never come, though, and now here he was, hauling his luggage onto the 11:05 to York.

This was really happening.

Stowing his suitcase and overstuffed rucksack in the luggage racks at the front of the carriage, he fished out his lunch and made his way to his pre-booked seat. Luckily, at this time on a Tuesday morning, the train was relatively quiet, and he had two seats to himself.

Settling down, he popped in his earbuds and pulled out a battered copy of *The Collected Poems of Wilfred Owen*, which he'd been reading obsessively over the last few weeks. At least, he'd been reading it obsessively when he hadn't been working. Knowing he'd have to scrape by on peanuts in York, Tag had taken as much work as possible over the last couple of months—shifts at City Beans, working on site with his dad, and as many corporate catering gigs as he could fit around everything else. He'd built up a little cushion of cash, but it wouldn't stretch far.

It would all be worth it, though, on opening night.

That's what he'd tried to explain to his mum and dad, neither of whom were happy that he'd quit City Beans—his only 'steady income'.

"Don't worry," he'd assured them as he calmly explained his plans. "I'll still be able to pay you my rent while I'm away."

They'd protested, of course, but Tag had ignored them. Yes, paying rent to them, plus paying for a room in York, would be difficult, but the fact was they couldn't meet their mortgage payments without his money. "Think of it as a retainer," he'd said cheerfully, "so you don't rent my room out to anyone else while I'm gone."

He'd watched them struggle with the idea, exchanging uncomfortable glances, and he'd seen the worry darkening his dad's face. They all knew the consequences of getting into financial trouble, knew how far into the future its shadow could fall, how it could knock you down and keep its boot on your back.

Yeah, Tag knew *exactly* what he was risking, chasing his dream. He'd always known. Which was why he could only keep chasing it while there was a realistic chance of success. If his big break never came, he'd have to get a real job so that he could afford to move into his own place and let his parents downsize and pay off their whacking great mortgage.

Despite squeezing in a couple more auditions over the last two months, though, Tag hadn't been cast in anything else. He'd got close once. The casting director had assured Tag he was her first choice. She'd waxed lyrical about his 'nuanced and subtle conveyance of complex interior states', but had eventually confessed that the money men wanted someone with more star power for the role. In other words, someone who'd put bums on seats. And that wasn't Tag. Yet.

He wasn't about to give up, though. Everything could change with *Let Us Go Back*.

Tag smiled, his excitement swelling as the train started to move. Slowly at first, it pulled out of the station but then quickly gathered speed, rocking from side to side as it accelerated, powering north through London towards York and Tag's future.

It was overcast when they pulled into York station two hours later and Tag dragged his luggage off the train. Following the signs to the exit, he lugged his case up the stairs of an iron bridge that crossed the tracks and then down the other side onto a small concourse with a couple of shops.

Standing to one side to let people pass, he dug out his phone and opened Google Maps. His digs were walkable from the station, and to the rehearsal space that Beatrice had organised too. They'd be meeting there tomorrow at ten, so he'd given himself half a day to settle into his room, unpack, and get the lay of the land.

Heading off, he marched out onto a busy street, past a bus stop, a rank of taxis—and what looked like a castle on a hill. Nice. Although it was May, the air in York was noticeably chillier than at home. Fresher, too. He liked it. Excited, full of that springtime feeling of hope and new beginnings, Tag headed along a grand street lined with tall, grey imposing old buildings.

According to Google Maps, it was a thirty-minute walk to his new house. Following the map, he crossed an elegant stone bridge over a wide river—the Ouse, apparently—and found himself walking past ancient city walls and into the centre of York, passing the looming and awe-inspiring Minster. He stopped there, staring up at its towering Gothic stonework, statuary, and stained glass windows, then snapped a selfie and sent it to his mum. *I'm here!*

York really was a gorgeous city. And almost as full of tourists as London. He had to dodge a couple of large tour groups as he navigated his way past the Minster and into the city's picturesque cobbled streets. Eventually, though, his map led him out of the city centre and the buildings gradually became less quaint and more ordinary. Well, that was to be expected.

The room he'd rented, a single in a shared house, was the cheapest he could find. It looked okay on the website, but far from luxurious—a 1930s mid-terrace, his room being the front parlour with shared use of the bathroom and kitchen. Really, he only needed a bed, didn't he? Somewhere to sleep and leave his stuff. It would be fine for eight weeks.

The house was a few streets back from the grandly named Broadway, which Tag took to be a good sign. Off Broadway— where else would an actor stay in old York, right? Modest houses lined the road, a mix of red brick terraces and a handful of semis. Most were in good nick, well maintained and lovingly gentrified. Others, less so.

One other, especially less so.

Tag's heart sank as he came to stand outside the address he'd been given, the place where he'd be spending the next few weeks of his life. A car up on blocks filled the neglected front garden, and next to it lay a fridge with its door agape. The battered front door of the house stood ajar and from inside came the sound of… hoovering? That was a good sign, he hoped. The curtains to the front, upstairs bedroom were closed, one hanging crooked, while a smear of grey net curtains slouched across the window of his own downstairs bedroom.

Steeling himself, Tag approached the door, dragging his case over the cracked crazy paving. He knocked and called out, "Hello?"

No answer.

He tried again, louder. "Hello?"

The hoover stopped, there were footsteps, and a middle-aged woman appeared wearing neon pink leggings and a Disney t-shirt proclaiming *It's a Princess Thing*. A cigarette dangled from the corner of her mouth. She looked Tag up and down and said, "Yes?"

Clearing the tightness from his throat, he said, "I'm Tag. I'm renting a room here?"

"Tag?"

"Tag O'Rourke. Uh, I've been emailing someone called Maggie?"

She nodded. "That's me. I didn't expect you to be so…"

She gave him another once-over, then shrugged. "All right, then. This way." She turned and headed back inside. Tag followed in trepidation. The place stank of cigarette smoke, with a strong undertone of weed, and he had to make an effort not to cough.

"I've hoovered," Maggie said, sounding rather defensive as she led him into his room.

Tag had to work hard to control his expression. The single bed which he'd seen on the website advert had been reduced to a rather dingy mattress sitting on a carpet that had probably been new in the sixties. The bedframe appeared to have disappeared entirely. An ancient and frankly lethal looking gas fire hung at a rakish angle on the chimney breast, with a dirty pink curtain covering each alcove.

Helpfully, Maggie shuffled over to pull one curtain aside and reveal a single pole spanning the alcove space. "Wardrobe," she announced, which Tag felt was pushing the definition.

"Right," was all he could manage.

"Kitchen's this way," Maggie went on, stepping over the Henry Hoover she'd abandoned in the hallway.

The kitchen contained a rickety table and chairs, a fridge, a microwave, a toaster, a kettle, and an ancient-looking electric cooker with a pan of something greasy and congealed festering on top. The sink was crammed with dirty plates, and an overflowing bin crouched beneath the counter.

"They never bloody empty it," Maggie muttered, kicking the bin as she passed it and dislodging a minor avalanche of rubbish. "Bathroom's through here."

And so it was. An avocado-green suite, the bathtub stained a disturbing brown and with a plastic shower hose wedged onto its taps. A mildewy curtain hung listlessly from its pole. Tag didn't dare look too closely at the loo.

Fuck, he thought, *I can't stay here.*

But where the hell else could he go? He'd already paid a month's rent in advance.

He felt a little breathless.

"You're not the usual type," Maggie said then, eying him curiously as she took a drag on her ciggy. "What is it you do?"

Faintly, although even now with a sense of pride, Tag said, "I'm an actor. I'm rehearsing a play here. In York."

Her plucked eyebrows rose. "Actor, eh? Been in anything I know?" Then she cackled. "I suppose not, if you're staying here." She laughed again, tickled by her own joke.

Tag smiled, wanly. "Well, I haven't been in anything you know—yet."

She grunted at that, unimpressed, and squeezed past him, heading back through the kitchen. Crouching, she unplugged the hoover and then stamped on the cable button. The cable whipped along the floor and back into the hoover with a noisy rattle.

"The others won't bother you much," she said when it was done, gesturing to the rooms upstairs. "They're only really awake at night, anyway. Mostly they're stoned or working."

"Great," Tag said faintly. "So, uh, you don't live here, then?"

"Me? God no." She looked offended by the idea as she picked up the hoover and headed for the front door. "Keys are in your room. Best to keep it locked when you're out." Over her shoulder she grinned, cigarette waggling between her lips. "*And* when you're in, if you know what I mean."

Then she was gone, leaving Tag alone and staring down at the stained mattress, the grotty floral carpet, and the grey light filtering in through dirty net curtains.

CHAPTER EIGHT

JAY

Jay rather liked the little riverside studio apartment Carly had found for him in York.

It was small, true. Just one big room really, with a bathroom off. Half of the space was given over to the bedroom, and the other half was split between the lounge and dining area and a tiny kitchen. As compact as it was, though, it was more than ample for his needs, and it was nice to be right on the river. This was his second morning here, and already he was enjoying his new routine of having breakfast in the little dining nook in front of the big picture windows. He could look out onto the peaceful, sleepy river as he sipped his coffee. There wasn't even a whisper of traffic noise or city bustle.

Jay gave a contented sigh and leaned back in his chair, cupping his coffee mug between his hands.

Carly had been pretty horrified when he'd picked this place from the shortlist she'd sent him. It had been the cheapest one, right at the bottom of the list.

"It's so threadbare!" she'd protested when he'd pointed to

it. Which was ridiculous. It was perfectly comfortable, with a king-size bed, nice furnishings, and, thankfully, a very decent coffee machine. Okay, it was a bit basic, but Carly tended to think that anything that wasn't a five-star hotel was a hovel.

He had asked her to find him a place that his salary for the play would more or less cover. In the end, she hadn't quite managed to meet that challenge, but since this place was only a couple of hundred a week more expensive, he didn't feel like he was being too much of a prima donna. And he *was* going to be living here for the next eight weeks.

Jay's gaze returned to the dog-eared script sitting on the table, beside the open jar of his favourite thick-cut Seville marmalade. Today was the first day of rehearsals, and already his stomach was a mass of rigid knots. He must have read the script a hundred times by now, and made countless notes. For the last couple of weeks he'd been slowly building his character, though not too completely, not yet. He knew how Henry Walker worked and wanted to stay open to the ideas that would inevitably arise at the read-through, curious to discover what the others would say. Would their ideas be aligned with his?

Would Tag's?

If he was honest, he was having a little difficulty imagining Tag playing Wilfred Owen. Tag was such a vital, vivid personality—brash even, inhabiting his own skin so fully that it was difficult to picture him playing someone like Owen, who had reputedly been an introspective, nervous young man.

What sort of an actor would Tag be, Jay wondered, as he sipped his coffee. He'd googled him, of course, but the only thing he'd found was a toothpaste advert, and that told him nothing. Well, nothing more than he'd already guessed—that Tag had a superb face for television. And very white teeth. What he'd be like on stage, though… Bea had raved about him, but Jay wasn't entirely sure about her judgment. As good as her writing was, Bea was young and inexperienced. However, she *had* said that Tag was Henry's first choice for Owen, and that definitely carried weight as far as Jay was concerned.

Henry was one of those people that everyone in the theatre world knew and admired. He'd done it all, acting, directing, writing—teaching too. The one-act play he'd directed Jay in as a drama student was, to this day, the best acting experience of Jay's life.

Which probably explained why, on top of his other anxieties, Jay was feeling pretty nervous about dusting off his rusty theatre skills in front of him—and, if he was honest, Tag too. Luckily, he probably wouldn't have to flex his acting muscles too much today. The first table read was usually a pretty relaxed affair. At drama school, he'd loved these early stages of rehearsal, the bright back-and-forth of ideas, the building out of the script as scenes were blocked and characters developed. Like building a house from blueprints, gradually turning the dialogue and instructions on the page into something real and tangible. Or maybe more like a tent, he thought, smiling to himself. Something that had to be assembled and disassembled every night.

Every night for two weeks.

As always, when his mind snagged on that thought—of actual performance—his breath began to feel short and his chest grew tight. Closing his eyes, Jay forced himself to take deep breaths. Gradually, the feeling passed.

When he opened his eyes again, he said aloud, his voice firm and determined, "Time to go." It was the voice of a man with a mission. A man with something to prove. A man who was determined to face his fears.

That was who Jay Warren was playing today.

∼

Jay had visited the rehearsal space briefly the previous afternoon, just to get his bearings and say a quick hello to Bea. The room she had secured was in a small conference centre, not far from the venue where they'd be performing. It was a decent size with four rectangular tables that could be configured however they wanted, and a stack of chairs. The walls were painted white, the floors covered in a utilitarian grey carpet, and several large whiteboards were fixed to the walls, probably for when the rooms were used for corporate events. It had struck him as a bit depressing.

This morning, though, when he walked into the room, he saw it rather differently. It had been overcast yesterday afternoon, and he hadn't really noticed the big, arched window at the far end. This morning, it was sunny, and the morning light streamed into the room, softening the starkness of the white-painted walls.

"Jay!" Bea said happily, rising from her chair to greet him. The tables had been pushed together to make one big table in the centre of the room. In the middle were vacuum jugs of coffee and tea, a big plate of pastries, a bowl of fruit, a few pads of paper, a selection of pens, and a couple of iPads.

Jay lifted his messenger bag off and set it down on a chair before moving forward to greet Bea with a quick hug. "Am I the first to arrive?" he asked when they broke apart. "Besides you?"

"Yes," she said. "I got here about half an hour ago. I'm so excited to get started. I can't believe I'm about to start rehearsals for my first full-length play!" She gave a self-conscious laugh. "God, I'm really not being at all cool about this, am I? I'm so nervous!"

Jay gave a short laugh. "That's understandable," he said. "If it helps, I'm also pretty nervous."

"You? Why would you be nervous? You've been in the business for years."

He shrugged one shoulder. "Well, it's been a while since I did any theatre."

"Don't you worry, Julius," someone said behind him. "It's just like riding a bike."

Jay whirled around, his smile already unfurling, because he knew that voice. And sure enough, there stood Henry Walker. He looked a bit older than the last time Jay had seen him, but just as disreputable in battered old jeans and a woolly jumper, topped off with his characteristic neckerchief and pork pie hat. He smiled wide and opened his arms, and Jay couldn't help but walk right into them, pulling the older man into a tight hug.

"Henry," he said, surprised to find his voice so hoarse. "It's good to see you."

When they broke apart, he cleared his throat, embarrassed by his own unexpected display of emotion. He tried to step back, but Henry kept hold of his upper arms, his kind gaze very penetrating.

"Julius," he said.

He said Jay's name like it was a complete sentence, with layers of nuance, and Jay couldn't help laughing a little, because it was so very Henry to do that. And, because Henry was the least stuffy person Jay had ever met, he laughed too.

"Ah, this is wonderful," Henry said, his pale blue eyes dancing. "I'm so glad you took this role, Julius." He paused then, tilting his head. "Or should I call you Jay? Do you prefer that now?"

"Um, yes please," Jay said. "If you don't mind. It's… easier."

"Mmm-hmm." Henry nodded, as though Jay had said something rather more profound. Then he clapped his hands on Jay's upper arms and released him.

"I didn't realise you two knew each other so well," Bea said. "But then the acting world *is* pretty small, isn't it? And I suppose it stands to reason since Daddy's such good friends with Henry and with your mother, Jay."

Jay didn't get a chance to point out that he'd met Henry for the first time at drama school because Henry was walking off, calling out, "Hello, Tag O'Rourke! Welcome, young man. Come in, come in."

Jay's heart jolted alarmingly.

Fuck.

He forced himself to turn slowly, not wanting to seem too eager.

Tag stood in the doorway, looking as annoyingly hot as ever in black jeans, jacket, and a fitted burgundy t-shirt, his hair a little tousled from the breeze outside. For an instant, his expression was oddly uncertain, his dark brows a little furrowed, but as Henry moved towards him, he broke out that killer smile and stepped inside, stretching out a hand to Henry, who took it in both of his own, keeping hold of it as he repeated his words of welcome.

For far too long, Jay stared at Tag, taking in the toned body, trim waist, and long, muscled legs. And then his self-awareness came back online, and he managed to tear his gaze away before Tag caught him eye-fucking him. Again.

As Henry drew Tag further into the room, someone else appeared in the doorway. A robust, middle-aged woman with a crown of unapologetically grey curls and sparkling dark eyes. She wore faded denim dungarees, flowery Doc Martens, and a biker jacket. In one hand she held an enormous black travel mug proclaiming its content as 'Witch's Brew', and in the other a huge canvas bag.

Jay laughed. "Freddie? I might have guessed Henry would rope you into this one, too."

Winifred Gould, universally known as Freddie, was one of Henry's closest friends, and a top-notch stage manager. Henry rarely worked with anyone else, but even so, Jay was surprised he'd persuaded her to get involved with this little production. She mostly worked at the National.

"Julius," Freddie scolded as she sailed into the room, depositing her cup and bag on the closest table, "you can't talk about being roped into anything when the bloody writer's standing right behind you. Bea, sweetie, hello, how are you? Nervous? Yes, of course you are." Bea didn't have a chance to respond before Freddie turned back to Jay. "And you! About bloody time *you* were back on stage, Julius Franklin Warren, instead of slumming it in *television*." She leaned in and kissed his cheek, a real kiss, not an air kiss. "Your mother sends her love, of course."

"And here she is!" Henry exclaimed, turning away from Tag to greet Freddie.

As they gushed, Jay found his attention drawn back to Tag. He stood slightly apart from the group, watching Henry and Freddie with a tense expression Jay couldn't quite parse. It reminded him of a boy with his face pressed to the toyshop window.

"So," Henry said then, turning to Bea. "It looks like we're just waiting for our understudy."

Bea looked briefly uncomfortable at this. "Rafe might, er, be a little late," she muttered. "He was…going out last night."

Jay's gaze returned to Tag, as though drawn by a magnet. This time, though, it was to find Tag was looking at him too. His pale skin flushed hard when their gazes tangled.

"All right," Henry said in a let's-get-down-to-business tone, and Jay hurriedly returned his attention to him. "Why don't we get ourselves sorted out with our coffee while we wait for Rafe to arrive?" He began shepherding them all towards the table. "These pastries look delicious, Bea. Did the venue supply them?"

"God, no," Bea said, making a face. "They just gave us some horrible, cheap custard creams. But I thought we should kick off with something a bit better for our first read-through."

"Wonderful idea," Henry said, pulling out a chair and nudging Tag into it. "Though I must admit I'm rather partial to a custard cream. They were my nan's favourite."

He kept up a stream of chatter along these lines for several minutes as everyone helped themselves to drinks, selected pastries—Tag devoured his on the spot—took their scripts out of their bags, and grabbed whatever else they needed. Jay remembered, now, how good Henry was at this part—making everyone feel comfortable and welcome and creating a safe space for the whole company, no matter how large or small.

"Okay," Henry said when they were all settled. "It's a pity Rafe's not here yet, but shall we dive in?"

Bea cleared her throat, setting both hands down on the table. "Before we do that, can I just say a few words?"

"Of course," Henry said, sitting back. "This is an open space. I want everyone to feel they can speak up at any time."

Bea nodded. "As the playwright, I just want to explain a few things up front about the play and the characters. I think it's important that we start off with a shared understanding of the key points."

This didn't sound to Jay much like the way Henry worked and, sure enough, when Jay glanced at him, he was frowning slightly. So was Tag.

"Okay," Henry said slowly. "Can we pause here for a second, Bea? I'm absolutely with you on getting your thoughts out there. In fact, I'm keen to get everything on the table, just not in a way that shuts down anyone else's thoughts, you know?"

Bea looked startled. "I'm not shutting down anything—I just think it'll be beneficial for the company to hear firsthand from the playwright what the intent and themes of the play are. If anything, it should save time. There's no point wandering down false paths when I'm right here to lead the way."

Henry sat back in his chair, seeming to consider her words. Then he said, quite gently, "Bea, I can guarantee you this: everyone around the table wants to honour the intent and themes of the play. What I'm saying is that, in my experience, it's a good idea, before the playwright states their view" —he paused, waving his hands in search of the right words— "*too decisively*, to listen to the actors' thoughts on the characters." He gestured at Jay, then at Tag. "These young men have studied their craft for *years*. They've learned how to build a character from scratch. And they've spent the last few weeks poring over your script—just look at how crumpled those pages are and all the notes on them." Bea's glance darted to the script in front of Tag which, sure enough, was as dog-eared as Jay's copy. Henry smiled encouragingly. "My advice is to listen to what their take is before you start setting down limits. You'll find the whole always exceeds the sum of its parts."

Bea's colour had been rising throughout Henry's kindly lecture. "Of course I'll listen to them. I never suggested I wouldn't. All I was saying was that it might be useful to—" She was interrupted by the door flying open.

"I'm *so* sorry," said the attractive young man hurrying into the rehearsal room. "Bloody alarm didn't go off."

Dark-haired, well spoken, and inoffensively handsome, he looked somewhat familiar to Jay. Maybe he'd met him at one of his mother's parties? Or maybe he just looked like half the people he'd studied with at RADA.

"Rafe!" Bea beamed and hurried over to greet him. "You made it."

Rafe gave her a careless one-armed hug. "Only just," he said, with a laugh. "Had a bit of a sesh last night. You should have come!"

Without even meaning to, Jay's gaze found Tag's, and an

unexpected flash of *Oh God* passed between them. Jay had to struggle to master a smile as he rose politely to his feet. From the corner of his eye, he saw Tag hesitate and then do the same.

"Everyone," Bea said, turning to face them. "This is Rafe Fitzroy. He'll be understudying for both Sassoon and Owen." She threw a look at Jay and gave a little, embarrassed laugh. "Just in case!"

Jay wasn't offended. In fact, he'd insisted that his contract include a requirement for the company to provide a suitable understudy for his role, even though Bea had already confirmed Rafe was on board. God knew they might need him. Standing, he offered his hand to shake. "Rafe. I'm Jay Warren. Good to meet you."

"You too. *Huge* fan," Rafe replied, shaking firmly. "I know your sister, actually. Portia? She shared a flat with my ex-girl-friend at uni."

"Ah," Jay said. "Well, the theatre's a small world."

"Tag O'Rourke," Tag said then, also holding out his hand. "It's nice to see you again, Rafe."

Rafe gave him a blank look as they shook, followed by an equally bland smile. "So sorry, have we met? I'm terrible with names and faces."

Colour rose in Tag's face, his shoulders stiffening as he bristled. "A couple of times, yeah." Then a sharp smile tugged at the corner of his mouth. "At the auditions."

As if Rafe would have forgotten that, Jay thought.

"Rafe and I were at boarding school together," Bea jumped in quickly. "*So* talented. He's just finished a year in New York, haven't you? Studying at Julliard."

"God, Bea." Rafe rolled his eyes but was transparently pleased. "Nobody wants to hear about *that*."

Jay exchanged another glance with Tag, who still looked irked by Rafe's rudeness. Jay couldn't blame Tag, but now at least he understood what was going on. Rafe had been up for the role of Owen, had lost out to Tag, and despite his polish couldn't quite mask his jealousy. Well, jealousy was par for the course in this business. Rafe would have to get over it, and Tag would have to deal with it.

On the other side of the table, Henry rose and gave Jay a quick smile. "Everyone, take a seat," he said. "Rafe, nice of you to join us at last."

Rafe's handsome face fell. "Sorry, Henry, late night yesterday." He gave a charming, rueful smile. "And I'm not really a morning person."

"Well, you are now," Henry said briskly. "Take a seat."

As Rafe did so, claiming the chair next to Bea's, Henry turned to the rest of them. "For those of you who don't know me, my name's Henry Walker. I'm the director…"

Henry talked briefly about his approach to rehearsals, explaining how he liked to run each stage of the process. Since the rest of them knew Henry to one degree or another, and knew how he worked, Jay suspected this was mostly for Tag's benefit, which was typical of Henry. Unlike Rafe, or Jay himself, Tag obviously hadn't grown up in the theatre, and from his eager interest in what Henry was saying, this was probably all relatively new to him.

Jay found himself oddly envious of Tag's innocence, of his excitement still unsullied by experience. As far as the theatre was concerned, Jay had been jaded by the age of five.

"…and we all need to give of our best for this production to succeed," Henry was concluding. "So I'm sure we'll see you bright-eyed and bushy-tailed tomorrow morning, Rafe. Yes?"

Henry sounded jovial enough, but there was steel behind his smile; he'd never had patience for dilettantes.

Rafe, obviously taken aback, glanced at Bea for support. "Of course," he said defensively. "Like I said, I had a late one."

"And I sincerely hope you made the most of it," Henry

said drily, "because for the next two months, we'll be doing nothing but eat, sleep, and breathe *Let Us Go Back*." He clapped his hands twice. "Now, we have six weeks until we open, ladies and gentlemen. Let's begin."

There was a general rustling of papers as everyone turned to the first page. Jay dug his glasses out and popped them on while Tag, who was sitting across the table from him, shrugged out of his jacket and rolled his shoulders. Jay looked away, disturbed by how distracting he found the sight of Tag's bare arms and the intricate curls of the tattoos winding across his skin. His palms tingled with sense-memory, Tag's smooth, muscled biceps warm beneath his hands, Tag's lips—

"I've never had to work so bloody hard at a blowjob in my life."

The remembered words slashed across his memory, and Jay sucked in a breath, looking down sharply at his script, face heating.

Fucking hell. He needed to get that night out of his head, or he was going to make a right hash of this.

"...and I'll read the direction," Henry was telling Bea when Jay managed to tune back into their conversation. "I'm sure you'll want to make notes. Table reads are such a vital tool for refining dialogue, aren't they?"

She nodded, looking as if she wasn't sure whether he was doing her a favour or stealing the limelight. Christ, she really was very young.

"And are we ready?" Henry asked, glancing around the table.

Jay murmured a yes and prayed that it was true. Tag just gave a brisk nod, fingers flexing, bottom lip caught between his teeth. Nervous, Jay realised with surprise. He'd never seen Tag nervous before.

Well, he wasn't the only one. Jay's own stomach was in knots.

He wondered what Henry would make of him today.

Would he think the promise Jay had shown at RADA had matured or atrophied? He was afraid it would be the latter. It had been a long time since Jay had done a table read with anyone but the familiar cast of *Leeches*, and he was out of practice. Longer still since he'd had to perform with someone he'd gone to bed with. In fact, after Seb, he'd vowed never to make that mistake again…

So much for good intentions.

Then there was no more time to worry about anything else because Henry cleared his throat and started to read. "Act One, Scene One. The stooped figure of an old man, bent double and hobbling with a stick, appears from the dark, making his way towards a blinding white light centre stage. From far away comes the wail of an ambulance siren. As he walks, the man begins to transform. The siren fades into the dull thud of distant guns, and the figure slowly unbends until he is no longer an old man but a soldier, his stick becoming his rifle, his stooped back his pack. He stands in the light and looks up. Now, he is somewhere else. A bar. There are tables and chairs, a piano in the corner, its cheerful music not quite masking the distant thud of the guns. Another soldier sits alone at one of the tables, writing in a notebook…"

Henry looked over at Jay, who took a breath and began. "Owen?" He made the accent clipped and precise. "I can't believe it. What are you doing here, old boy?"

"*I* never left." Tag looked at him across the table, but it wasn't Tag. Not exactly. The transformation was subtle, exciting. He sounded different, too, his natural London accent replaced by something soft and lilting. Slightly West Country, perhaps. "You're the one who got lost, remember?" He smiled, engagingly shy. "But I'm glad you're back, Sassoon. I've missed you. Here…" He reached out as if to pass Jay something. "What do you make of this?"

And so they went on, working through the scenes with Jay reassessing Tag almost moment by moment. He was a *good* actor; that was the first thing Jay recognised. Bea had been right about that. From what Jay could tell, Tag was generous, receptive, and instinctively responsive to Jay's performance. Impressively well prepared, too. Henry might consider him *over* prepared, but Jay knew to leave that kind of conversation to the director. By the end of the first couple of hours, though, Jay knew that he and Tag would be able to work together despite their...awkward personal history. It was a huge relief.

He glanced across the table while Henry and Bea discussed the next scene, watching the concentration on Tag's face as he studied his script. The scene was a big one for Owen, and Jay was curious to see how Tag played it.

"The dreaming spires!" Tag began when Henry cued him in, eyes full of awe and excitement. "Or maybe *I'm* the one dreaming. I can't tell you how often I've—"

A loud gurgling rumble cut him off, and Tag slapped his hand over his belly. "Oh God," he said, Tag once more. "I'm so sorry!"

Henry laughed. "I think perhaps it's lunchtime? We'll tackle this next scene once we're all refuelled."

"I'm fine to keep going," Tag protested, although his stomach gave another betraying grumble. He laughed, flashing that brilliant smile of his, and Jay felt a sharp stab of attraction.

Damn it.

"No, no." Henry was already pushing to his feet. "I could do with stretching my legs anyway. But good work this morning." He looked between Jay and Tag, nodding. "Very good work. If I didn't know better, I'd suspect you'd rehearsed together before. I'm sensing a real chemistry between you, right off the bat. It's marvellous."

Tag's slightly strained smile was no doubt a mirror of Jay's own.

"What did I tell you?" he said to Bea as he passed behind her chair.

"You were right," she said, smiling. "They *are* perfect together."

At her side, Rafe cleared his throat pointedly.

"Oh, and you will be too, Rafe." She squeezed his arm in apology. "I'm just so excited! I can't tell you how amazing it is to have you all reading my words." She pressed her hands to her chest. "Such an honour."

Jay smiled. "I'm glad you feel we're doing justice to the work."

"And thank *you* for the opportunity," Tag added. He smiled too, but he looked tired. Well, he'd been acting his socks off all morning, Jay supposed. If he kept up that level of intensity, he'd be exhausted before opening night.

"Can I tempt you, old girl?" Henry had produced a packet of his trademark cigarillos from a pocket and was wiggling them at Freddie.

"No, you bloody well can't," she said, brandishing a vape pen back at him as she too got to her feet. "But I'll keep you company outside and inhale some of your poisonous fumes…"

Bea, meanwhile, had her phone out and had turned to Rafe. "Selfie? I'm teasing the hell out of this all over my socials." Blushing, she added, "And you look fabulous today."

Rafe made a show of considering, then shrugged one shoulder. "Outside, then, the light's better."

Jay watched them leave, arm in arm, marvelling at how young they were. They couldn't really be that much younger than him—well, perhaps ten years—but somehow he felt a lifetime older.

When the door banged shut behind them, Tag let out a long breath, eyes closing and head falling back to reveal the long pale column of his throat. A throat that Jay had kissed. He still remembered the soft warmth of Tag's skin against his lips, the prickle of his late-evening stubble. Remembered too the way he'd felt being with Tag that night—appreciated, understood. *Looked after*. At one point he'd even imagined something profound was happening between them. Christ, what a bloody idiot.

Embarrassed, he looked away.

From outside came the sounds of the street: cars passing, people talking, a child laughing. In the distance, a siren wailed. But inside the rehearsal room, the silence swelled. Jay could feel it pressing on his chest, making it hard to draw breath, because now they were alone together.

Alone for the first time since that night.

As if animated by Jay's thought, Tag opened his eyes and lifted his head. In the sunlit room, his dark hair gleamed as his lips curved into an impish smile. "So," he said, "*Julius* is it?"

Jay shook his head. "Don't start."

"Or do you prefer Caesar?"

"Trust me. I've heard them all before."

Tag huffed a laugh. "Yeah. I bet that was fun at school."

"You have no idea."

"Are you kidding?" Tag flashed a grin, tapping his own chest. "Tag, remember? Gift Tag. Hash Tag. Name Tag… Endless fun."

"Fair point." Jay smiled, determined not to be charmed by that grin. But then their gazes tangled again, Tag's honey-coloured eyes looking paler in the sunshine but still as captivating as Jay remembered, and his heart began to skip and skitter, his skin prickling hot.

Fuck.

Hurriedly, he got to his feet, breaking their locked gaze. "I, er, passed a nice-looking deli on my way here," he said hurriedly. "Fancy grabbing a sandwich before the others get back?"

"A sandwich?" Tag sounded nonplussed.

Jay lifted an eyebrow, hiding behind the practised expression. "Two pieces of bread with some kind of savoury filling between them. They're quite common in Chalfont St. Giles."

"You should consider stand-up," Tag said drily.

"I'd rather deep-fry my own eyeballs."

Tag made a sound that wasn't quite a laugh, then sighed and tapped his script. "Thanks, but I'd better stay here and, er, read over the next scene."

That would have felt like a brushoff had Tag not sounded so rueful. Jay frowned. "You're extremely well prepared already, Tag. And aren't you hungry?"

Curiously, a flush touched Tag's cheeks. "Oh, I'll just finish off these," he said, waving airily at the last two pastries slumped limply on the plate between them. "That'll be fine."

Given how loudly Tag's stomach had been rumbling earlier, two small pastries hardly seemed like enough food. Perhaps Jay ought to bring him something back from the deli? Oddly, he found that thought deflating. "Come on," he coaxed, "you can afford a few minutes. You know what they say about all work and no play…"

"I do, yeah." Tag's gaze sharpened. "Unfortunately, *Julius*, some of us have to work twice as hard in life to get half as far as others."

Okay. Jay spread his hands in surrender. No way he was getting dragged into *that* conversation.

"Fine," he said shortly, grabbing his jacket from the back of his chair. "I'll see you later, then."

Striding towards the door, he decided that he wouldn't bring anything back for Tag. Sod him. If Tag wanted to play a smoking bloody martyr, then far be it from Jay to cramp his performance.

CHAPTER NINE

TAG

When Tag got back to his new—and thankfully temporary—home after the first day of rehearsal, he finally met his new housemates, ignoring each other in the kitchen. One of them was slouched at the kitchen table, fair head resting on the wooden surface. Asleep? The other, a skinny girl, dressed all in black with long, mousy hair and massive headphones, stood at the counter, pouring oat milk into a bowl of chocolate cereal.

"Hi," Tag said, giving the girl a wave and a friendly smile. "I'm Tag O'Rourke. I just moved in."

"Okay," she said, her gaze on her cereal. "I'd appreciate it if you don't use my milk." Without looking at him, she replaced the cap on the carton, put it in the fridge, grabbed her bowl, and walked out. Tag stared after her, taken aback.

"Don't mind her."

Tag turned at the voice. The fair-haired guy was now propping his head on one hand and offering a friendly if somewhat sleepy smile. "Clem isn't very social," he said. "I'm

Mikey. I'm pretty friendly but… fuck." He gave a long, slow blink. "I just had some really strong skunk. I, like, need a minute?" He set his head back down on the table.

Tag waited for a few moments, but the guy didn't move. Eventually, he said, tentatively, "I was going to make myself a cuppa. Do you want one?"

"Ohmigod," Mikey whispered, without lifting his head. "That'd be so fucking amazing. You got any snacks? I'm starving."

"I don't really have any groceries yet. Just some teabags." Tag paused. "If you've got food, I could maybe make us something?"

"Do your worst, man. Everything that isn't cereal or oat milk is mine."

"Sure, okay." Tag crossed the kitchen and opened the fridge. It wasn't exactly bursting at the seams, but there was a mould-free block of cheese and some butter, and he'd already spied a loaf of bread sitting next to the toaster.

Ten minutes later, he was setting two mugs of tea and a plate of cheese-on-toast on the table. "Here you go."

Mikey slowly raised his head. "That smells fucking *amazing,*" he said, reaching for a slice of melty, cheesy good-ness, then groaning in pleasure as he stuffed it in his mouth. "Did you fucking *make* this?"

Tag laughed, grabbing a slice for himself. "It's just cheese-on-toast."

Mikey waved that off. "You've got serious cooking skills," he mumbled. "This is the best cheese-on-toast I ever ate."

"Nothing to do with the skunk, right?" It wasn't particu-larly funny, but Mikey laughed, spraying crumbs, then laughed harder at the crumbs.

Tag couldn't help but grin at Mikey's silly good humour. Was it weird that this was the most at home he'd felt all day, sitting here with this easy-going stoner he'd only just met?

There was something about the guy's working-class accent that just… put him at ease. While the initial table read had gone well, and, yeah, everyone had been welcoming and friendly, they were all just so… bloody posh. They couldn't be more different from him.

"It probably *is* the skunk," Mikey admitted, drawing Tag's attention back to him. "But this still tastes fucking lovely. Any chance of more?" He sent Tag a hopeful look, big puppy dog eyes rimmed with eyeliner.

"I reckon you've got enough bread and cheese for a couple more slices," Tag said, levering himself up and heading for the counter. He began grating the last of the cheese. "Is that a Sheffield accent, by the way?"

"Good catch," Mikey said, sounding impressed. "Especially for a Southerner. Is your family from Sheffield?"

"Nah, but I've studied accents a bit—I'm an actor."

"No shit?" Mikey brightened. "You been on TV?"

"Just in one toothpaste advert," Tag said, with a wry grin. "But I'm in a new show coming up."

"Yeah?" Mikey chugged his tea. "What's it called?"

Tag sprinkled the grated cheese on the bread. "*Bow Street*. It's sort of a historical crime drama."

"Sounds awesome. I'll definitely watch out for it. So, what are you doing in York?"

Tag transferred the bread to the grill pan and slid it under the heat. "I'm in a play—it's part of the York Drama Festival. We're rehearsing for the next six weeks. Then it's a two-week run."

Mikey looked gratifyingly impressed. It wasn't a reaction Tag got often, and it had an involuntary smile tugging at the corners of his mouth. He turned to the grill, pretending to check the toast, to hide his pleasure.

"Amazing," Mikey said. "Though I'm guessing you're not getting paid much, if you're staying in this shithole."

The cheese was bubbling now. Tag slid the slices onto the waiting plate and took it over to the table, dropping into the seat opposite Mikey, who was now looking much more alert.

"You're right about that," he admitted, as Mikey crammed another slice of cheese-on-toast in his mouth. "I've got to pay for my own accommodation and expenses out of what I get, plus I've got financial commitments back home. And I had to give up my steady barista gig to take this part." He sighed heavily. "I'm going to be living on baked beans for the next couple of months."

Mikey looked thoughtful. "Well, if you've done bar work, I can probably sort you out with some shifts?"

"Could you?" Tag said hopefully. He'd been planning to see if he could pick up some casual work but knew it wouldn't be easy with him only being in town for such a short time. "That would be fantastic. And yeah, I've been a barman. And a waiter, kitchen porter, cleaner, labourer—I can turn my hand to a lot of things."

Mikey grinned. "In that case, I can definitely hook you up. The guy I work for owns a bunch of bars and a club in town, and he's always looking for staff, especially for late shifts and call-offs at weekends. He needs someone who can rock up and fill in wherever he needs them—like a floater? I used to do that, but now I'm a manager, so I'm permanently in one venue. Would that work for you? It sounds like you've got the experience."

"That would be perfect for me," Tag said fervently—having even a little bit more money would be a ton of help. He might even be able to afford the odd lunch sandwich, though maybe not the gourmet deli ones Jay apparently liked. Christ, the one Jay had brought back today... practically half a baguette stuffed with deli meat and cheese and salad and pickles. And the way Jay had been groaning as he ate it. That had been... hard to ignore. Thrusting that thought aside, Tag determinedly dragged his attention back to Mikey. "We have our rehearsal space from ten till four each day, and the director wants to use it to the full, so I think day shifts will be pretty much out for me, but I'm expecting to be available most evenings while we're rehearsing."

Mikey stuck the last piece of cheese-on-toast in his mouth, then pulled out his phone. "Perfect," he mumbled through the food. "I'll text Graham right now. He's gonna be stoked.

When Tag headed off to the Salter Street Centre the next morning, he was feeling considerably less nervous and more optimistic than the day before. He'd met the rest of the cast and crew and, with the possible exception of Rafe, liked them all. Plus he'd bonded with one of his housemates *and* found himself a job—Mike's boss, Graham, had cheerfully offered him as many casual hours as he could fit in from Wednesday till Sunday for the next few weeks. Things were definitely looking up.

It was a couple of miles to the Centre, and Tag found his mind returning to yesterday's table read as he walked the route. It had been an interesting start. Henry clearly had a way he liked to work. Bea seemed a little impatient with it, but while Tag had some sympathy with her—the play was her baby after all—he was instinctively attracted to Henry's actor-centred approach.

As the Centre came into sight, Tag saw Freddie walking up the path to the front door ahead of him, a stout, colourful figure in purple leggings and Doc Martens, weighed down with a backpack and a large shoulder bag.

He followed her inside, where Henry and Jay were already chatting, coffees in hand. Freddie was standing at the table, extracting a large binder from her backpack. This was her promptbook, a huge bible of documents containing her own marked-up copy of the script, another clean copy she had started marking up yesterday with blocking notes, a props list, a costume list, scene breakdowns, and God only knew what else besides. Tag, who had never worked with a professional stage manager before—only student ones at drama college—had been fascinated as he watched her work yesterday. Despite her slightly chaotic air, Freddie's prompt-book was meticulously maintained, bristling with sticky tabs and colour-coded annotations.

"Morning, Freddie," he said, walking towards her.

She looked up. Her eyes, which were a very light blue, were bright against her tanned skin, and the laughter lines around her eyes and mouth were deep grooves. "Good morning, beautiful boy," she said, beaming at him. "Ready for day two?"

"As I'll ever be," he said. "Can I get you a coffee?"

"Please, lovely," Freddie said. "A cappuccino with double chocolate sprinkles would be perfect, but I daresay a cup of that awful, tepid filter will do for now."

Tag laughed and reached for the vacuum jug, loosening the lid. "Ordinarily, a cappuccino wouldn't be a problem for me," he said as he poured out two mugs of rather wishy-washy brown liquid. "I've been working in a coffee shop for the last few years, and I'm pretty good with a steamer wand if I do say so myself. But there's not much magic I can work with this, I'm afraid."

She laughed, accepting the mug from him, then doctoring it with a slug of semi-skimmed. "And I see we're reduced to the custard creams today," she said, wrinkling her nose. "They look like the same ones they gave us yesterday." She prodded one of them experimentally, and, ominously, it gave a little beneath her finger.

Tag grimaced. He'd skipped breakfast since he still hadn't

bought any groceries yet, and his stomach felt like it was trying to eat itself.

"So," he said, trying to distract himself from his hunger. "I gather you work with Henry a lot?"

"All the time, darling, for my sins."

"Then you probably know how long we're going to be spending on this stage of the rehearsal process?"

Freddie sent him an amused glance. "Do you know, practically *every* actor who works with Henry for the first time asks me that?" She shrugged. "Honestly, it depends, but it's certainly the case that he likes to spend a *lot* more time than any other director I've worked with. He calls it the 'getting to know the play' phase." She grinned, her expression conspiratorial. "I think poor Bea's finding it rather irritating, don't you?"

Tag couldn't stop the huff of laughter that escaped him at her mischievous look. "Perhaps," he demurred, not wanting to jump into company gossip on day two.

"Well, it's hardly surprising," Freddie said blithely. "She's very like her father. They're both incredibly bossy and single-minded. I mean, Henry adores Timon—he really is a *marvellous* actor, you know—but he gets very cross with him too, because Timon simply *cannot* take direction. Honestly, the rows they've had over the years!"

Tag tried not to look like he was hanging on Freddie's every word, but he couldn't help but lap up this sort of backstage gossip. The truth was he felt starved for it, and his nerdy little theatre brain was happily filing away every story-nugget to revisit later.

"If Bea spent more time listening to Henry," Freddie continued, warming to her subject, "she'd benefit enormously from this experience. I mean, what other young playwright gets the chance to have *the* Henry Walker directing their debut play? You can't buy that sort of opportunity."

Tag's good humour dimmed at that reminder. The truth

was, pretty much *no* other young playwright could swing such a coup. Bea had been given it on a silver platter because Henry and Bea's father, Timon Lawson, the foremost Shakespearean actor of his generation, were good friends.

It *wasn't* fair, but the fact was, for the first time in his life, Tag was a beneficiary of that unfairness, if an indirect one, and he wasn't sure what to make of that. There was much made of lucky breaks in the theatre world, and maybe that was how he should think about it. He'd struggled to land paid work since he'd left drama school and was not in a position, when he finally got an opportunity, to look a gift horse in the mouth.

"Good morning," a new voice said, interrupting Tag's reverie.

Jay.

Tag turned to see Jay standing beside him, reaching for the coffee jug to refill his mug. He wore jeans today, a faded blue sweatshirt with the sleeves rolled up, and those horn-rimmed glasses Tag had seen for the first time yesterday and that made him look like a sexy professor. Jay was clean-shaven too —Skye Jäger's trademark facial hair was out, and Siegfried Sassoon's smooth jaw was in. He'd need a haircut before opening night, though, Tag mused. It was too long for an officer, the thick, dark fringe falling into his eyes.

Jay set down the coffee jug and turned to face Tag and Freddie, mug in hand. He gave a slightly lopsided smile, and Tag's stomach twisted. Why did he have to be so fucking *handsome*? So perfect, with his golden skin and that shiny, dark hair. Tag could still remember the feel of it between his fingers, slippery like silk. And his skin, so smooth and warm...

Tag swallowed back a groan at the memory and tried to make his features expressionless. To look like a normal person. It must be working because Jay didn't give him a second glance, just lifted his mug to take a slurp of coffee, only to quickly grimace.

"Christ, that's even worse than yesterday's brew," he said. "Thank God I've already had a decent coffee today."

"Did you buy one on the way?" Freddie asked. "You *rotter*. You should have got me one while you were at it. I'd *kill* for a cappuccino right now."

Jay laughed. "Calm down. I had my coffee at home, sitting at my little breakfast table, looking out over the river. Thankfully, my apartment has a good coffee machine. Just as well as I'd never be able to get going in the mornings otherwise."

"Lucky you," Freddie said enviously. "What kind? Is it one of those pod machines?"

"No, it's actually a really fancy Gaggia one. It has one of those proper espresso drip things and the pipe for steaming milk."

"Ooooh!" Freddie said, impressed. She elbowed Tag. "Do you hear that? We should go round to Jay's, and you can make us all a proper cappuccino." She glanced at Jay and added, "Tag's a professional barista."

Tag's face heated. Suddenly, he wished he hadn't confided that to Freddie. The contrast was too painful: Jay was staying in a fancy riverside apartment complete with a top-of-the-range Gaggia machine. The nearest Tag got to one of those was when he was working a shift at City Beans.

And didn't that just fucking say it all about the yawning gulf between him and Jay?

"Uh, yes, I know," Jay said, offering an awkward smile. "Maybe you could give me some tips? I don't think I'm heating the milk right."

Tag's smile felt tight and unfriendly. "Sorry," he said. "I can't be giving away my trade secrets to helpless rich dudes. Not when I'll be needing my old job back when this is over."

"Oh," Jay said. He gave a weak, unhappy laugh. "Yeah,

um, right." He dropped his gaze to his coffee, staring into the black depths as though he might find some answer in there.

Tag looked quickly away, only to catch Freddie eyeing him with blatant interest, her head tilted to one side. It was unnerving, and he was glad when Henry clapped his hands and moved towards the table, saying loudly, "All right, people, let's get started."

CHAPTER TEN

JAY

As much as he hated to admit that Dame Cordelia was right, after two and a half weeks in the rehearsal room, Jay had to concede that he was enjoying himself. Henry's deep-dive into character discovery was a luxury you didn't often get in television work, at least not in the projects Jay shoehorned in between *Leeches* seasons. And of course he'd been playing Skye for years and knew him inside out, so no need for this level of exploration there.

This process was a change, and he was relishing the intellectual challenge of getting to grips with Sassoon's spiky, contradictory character, discovering him in tandem with Tag's discovery of Owen.

Tag…

Jay glanced surreptitiously across the rehearsal space to where Tag sat on the floor, leaning against the wall, head tipped back and eyes closed while they all took a break. As usual, Jay's stomach gave a mortifying little flutter at the sight of his handsome, boyish face and tousled black hair. Christ, and that beautifully sculpted body, poorly hidden beneath faded jeans and an old t-shirt...

If only he could forget the night they'd shared, but every moment of it was burned into his memory—Tag's touch, his taste, his unexpected tenderness. The only part starting to fade was the sting of Tag's angry words before he'd left Jay's room. In truth, neither of them had covered themselves in glory during that unpleasant scene—Jay cringed when he remembered suggesting Tag charged by the hour.

Christ, what an arse.

Anyway, the Tag he'd got to know over the last couple of weeks was different from the mercurial, prickly himbo who'd stormed out of his hotel room back in February. This Tag was bright, funny, and kind-hearted. Sure, he carried a chip the size of East London on his shoulder, but deep down, he was a very likeable guy. And Jay did like him. A lot. So much so that it was becoming a problem. Try as he might, Jay couldn't seem to master the intense attraction to Tag he'd felt from the very first moment they met.

If anything, it was getting worse.

Tag didn't seem to have any such problem with regard to Jay, however. His whole attention was on the play, and he was throwing himself into the rehearsal process with infectious abandon. Unapologetically himself, Tag laid himself wide open, day after day, in ways Jay found both impressive and terrifying. It was certainly part of why Jay was enjoying himself so much; working with a focused, collaborative, and energetic actor like Tag was a joy. Even when Jay found himself plagued by a ridiculous crush that was becoming increasingly hard to hide.

"Looks like someone's sleepy," Rafe said, glancing at Tag as he strolled towards Jay. In a louder voice, he added, "Too many late nights, Tag?"

"We've been working hard today," Jay said mildly, glancing at Tag, who was blinking his eyes open. They'd been concentrating on a tricky scene that Tag was finding especially difficult. Henry was keen for Tag to find his own way into it, and Tag was certainly trying—he was a hard worker—but today, he'd seemed to lack his usual focus. In truth, he *had* seemed rather tired.

"Talking of late nights," Rafe went on, "Bea and I are going to hit the Black Bear on Saturday night. Fancy tagging along?"

Absolutely not. Forcing himself to be polite, Jay said, "What's at the Black Bear?"

Rafe pantomimed shock. "Only, like, the best gay bar in York. You don't know it?"

"Why would I know it?" Rafe looked nonplussed, and into his silence Jay said, "Anyway, why are you going to a gay bar?"

"Research."

"Er, for what?"

Rafe rolled his eyes. "I'm a straight actor understudying *two* gay characters? Obviously, I need to get the full gay experience to inhabit them completely." He tossed his floppy hair. "It's something we did a *lot* at Julliard."

From across the room, Tag said, "You'll certainly get the full gay experience at the Black Bear on a Saturday night. Wear your tightest jeans."

Jay glanced over and caught the mischievous sparkle in Tag's eyes when they briefly met his own. "You know the place?" Jay couldn't keep the surprise out of his voice. Maybe Rafe was right. Maybe Tag really had been out partying during the week.

But Tag just shrugged, then stifled a yawn. "I know a lot of places," he said.

Jay wasn't sure what to make of that.

Rafe, meanwhile, looked rather uncertain. And young. With all of his insufferable Julliard crap, and his frankly high-handed manner, it was easy to overlook Rafe's youth and basic lack of experience. Both in acting and, Jay suspected, in life.

"Listen," he said, putting a reassuring hand on Rafe's shoulder. "You're doing fine. You don't need to hang out in a gay bar to understand Sassoon. It's all there in the script. Just trust Henry. Trust the process. You're an actor, remember? You're portraying Sassoon, not impersonating him."

It didn't have the reassuring effect Jay had intended. Instead, Rafe bristled. "I suppose we all have our preferred techniques," he said stiffly and walked away.

Jay sighed and from the corner of his eye spotted Tag climbing to his feet. Turning, he was surprised to see a small, puzzled smile on Tag's face as he walked over to him.

"That was kind of you," Tag said quietly. He looked over to where Rafe was talking—flirting—with Bea. "He needs to listen more."

"He's young," Jay pointed out.

Tag huffed a laugh. "He's the same age as me."

Startled, Jay looked over and found Tag watching him wryly. Just then, a sudden flood of sunlight filled the room, catching Tag's raven hair, highlighting hidden strands of copper. Jay's heart gave a hopeless twang. Clearing his throat, he said, "Then I'd say you've made much better use of your time."

Tag's smile broadened. "Yeah?"

"Yeah." In a lower voice, he added, "You're more talented than the Rafes of this world. As I think you know."

Tag didn't deny it, although his smile dimmed and he scrubbed a hand over his eyes. The sunlight dimmed too, as suddenly as it had arrived, and in the greying light Tag looked tired again, faint shadows gathering beneath his eyes. "It's not just about talent or hard work, though, is it?"

"True, there's always an element of luck."

This time, Tag's laugh sounded more brittle. "Yeah, and some people are born with more luck than others."

Jay had no answer to that, because of course Tag was right. Bea was a prime example, as was Jay himself. And Rafe. In fact, now he thought about it, Tag was the only person in the room without the advantage of connections. He'd have thought that would make Tag feel even more proud of his achievement, but he only looked weary.

"Right, people," Henry called, re-entering the room with a faint waft of cigarillo smoke on his heels. "Let's get cracking. Tag, Jay—I'd like to go from, 'Ah, now we come to it'."

They returned to the table and two chairs that had been set in the centre of the room. An empty water bottle was standing in for the wine. Tag sat; Jay remained standing. They'd rehearsed this scene enough that they were both more or less off-book, although Tag's script still sat on the table.

He performed that little roll of the shoulders he always did before they started, something Jay was determined not to find in any way endearing. For himself, he just closed his eyes for a moment, gratefully blocking out the sight of Rafe doing some kind of centring exercise in the far corner that apparently involved standing on one leg.

"When you're ready," Henry said quietly.

Jay opened his eyes, met Tag's, and they were off.

"Ah, now we come to it," Tag said in that lilting voice he'd chosen for Owen. "Were you jealous of my death, Sassoon?" He made a rueful sound. "You needn't be, you know. It wasn't much of a lark."

"I never envied your mortality." He allowed his gaze to linger on Tag, feeling truth well into his voice. "It was your *immortality* I coveted." Tag laughed, meeting Jay's eyes, and it was thrilling to feel the connection being forged through their performance.

His heart sped up as Tag said harshly, "So you begrudge me the only thing I ever had that you didn't."

"What did *I* have that you didn't?"

Tag's brows rose as he lifted the 'wine' to top up their glasses. "Wealth, connections, education…"

"But you had everything that mattered. For God's sake, Owen, *you* had the greater talent. You had potential."

Tag pushed to his feet, knocking his chair over. "Have you forgotten that I died a boy?"

"You died a *poet*."

"But *you* lived!"

They were staring at each other across the table. Tag's gaze was blazing, and Jay let the moment stretch, and stretch some more before he turned away and said, "Of late, I've begun to wonder whether that was quite appropriate."

Into the charged silence that followed, Bea gave a heavy sigh. "The thing is, Tag," she said, "I still think you have Owen being too aggressive here. This isn't meant to be an argument. It's a discussion. A revelation of Sassoon's truth."

Jay clenched his jaw, let his eyes close briefly. His heart was still racing from the intensity of their exchange, and he knew Tag would be feeling the same. More so, probably, since he was struggling with this scene—struggling to play it as Bea wanted.

"We're still very much in the exploration stage, Bea," Henry chided. "Let's not shut anyone down. Every interpretation is valid. Tag," he went on before Bea could say more, "I'm interested in this feisty Owen. Where's that coming from for you?"

Tag, picking up the fallen chair, said, "I suppose… I mean, Sassoon had all this privilege, right? He lived his whole life as a poet, which Owen would have loved, but *Sassoon's* the one who's jealous. Owen died in a ditch, for God's sake. He was twenty-five—that's my age. Why wouldn't he push back when Sassoon starts whining about how hard he's had it?"

Jay laughed a little at that, drawing Tag's attention. "In defence of Sassoon," he said, "it's Owen's fame he envies. His immortality."

Tag was scowling. "I get that, but in the end fame is *all* Owen had. And it wouldn't be much comfort for a bloke who never got to live his life. Christ, he was twenty-one when he went to war—his whole adult life was war, and then he died. Boom. I just—" He glanced at Bea, moderating his tone. "I feel like he'd push back on Sassoon's pity-party."

"Let me ask you both this," Henry said, rising and walking towards them. "If, as a young man, Sassoon could have chosen between the immortality Owen achieved—every schoolchild in England is taught *Dulce Et Decorum Est*—or the long, but ultimately disappointing, life he led, which do you think he'd have gone for?"

"Life," Tag said immediately, then frowned.

Jay said, "Immortality. Sassoon believed he was born for greatness—his mother had convinced him he was destined to be a famous poet. Anything less would have been a disappointment, and men like Sassoon can't bear to be a disappointment."

"Interesting," Henry said.

"But that's how Sassoon felt at the *end* of his life," Tag countered. "I don't believe he'd have chosen death when he was young. He and Owen are talking to each other across a lifetime—Owen's saying what Sassoon's younger self would have said. That's why I think he'd challenge him. Push back."

Nodding thoughtfully, Henry said, "And I think there's a good place to leave it for today. Thank you both, we're really getting somewhere. Now—" Smiling, he turned to address the whole room. "Freddie prodded me on this at lunchtime, and I realised, to my horror, that we're halfway through week three of rehearsals and haven't had a company night out yet. So I suggest we repair to the nearest hostelry and get ourselves some dinner. What do you say?"

"Fabulous idea!" Rafe gushed. "There's an amazing Lebanese Tapas bar on High Petergate? We can *probably* get in without a reservation, since it's early."

Bea nodded, clearly torn between lingering irritation at Henry's rebuke and desperation to agree with Rafe. Her crush on him was becoming even more obvious than Jay's crush on Tag. At least he bloody well hoped it was.

"I was going to suggest going out too, actually," she said, smiling at them all and then beaming at Rafe. "Lebanese *does* sound amazing, but do they have many vegan options?"

That led to further discussions and both of them pulling out their phones.

Meanwhile, Freddie got to her feet and started closing her huge folder. "Personally, I'd prefer a pub," she said. "I could murder some gammon and chips right now. How about you, Tag?"

Which was when Jay realised that Tag looked decidedly uncomfortable. "Um," he said, running a hand through his hair, "I actually kind of have a thing tonight."

A moment of silence followed, which might have been funny had Henry not looked genuinely disgruntled. "You do?" he said. "Remember, your focus needs to be one hundred percent on this production, Tag."

"It is!" Tag assured him hurriedly, colour rising in his cheeks. "It's just, uh, a thing my flatmate organised. A getting-to-know-you thing."

Henry nodded, though his gaze remained sharp and fixed on Tag. "Another night, then?"

"Definitely," Tag said. "How about, er, Sunday?"

That was three nights away. Did Tag have plans every night until then?

"My, you do have an active social life," Rafe said, cattily echoing Jay's own unworthy thoughts.

Tag looked like he didn't know how to respond, but before things could get too awkward, Freddie chimed in with, "Sunday suits me better, to be honest. I'm knackered tonight, Hal. It's been a long week, and it's only Wednesday."

"Me too," Jay added quickly, picking up his cue. "To be

honest, I was planning on a hot bath and an early night. Plus, Sunday will give us time to book a table somewhere nice."

"Oh!" Bea piped up. "And you know what would be awesome? I could invite Giles Cox." To Jay, she added, "He's the artistic director of the York Drama Festival. He's been so supportive." Her eyes twinkled. "And he's dying to meet *you*."

Jay felt his heart sink. Clearly, she was expecting him to butter this guy up.

"All right." Henry had ceased his scrutiny of Tag and clapped his hands, decision made. "Sunday it is, then. Bea, why don't you find somewhere suitable and ping round the details?" To Tag he said, "Enjoy your evening. Bright-eyed and bushy-tailed in the morning, yes?"

"Absolutely," Tag said, nodding. He looked embarrassed, though, and Jay felt a flash of resentment on his behalf; no need for Henry to treat Tag like a naughty schoolboy in front of everyone. He'd never once been late for rehearsal, and always gave his all.

As they were getting ready to leave, Jay strolled casually over to where Tag was shrugging into his jacket and murmured, "Hey, don't worry about Henry. He's pretty old school, you know? Company first, cast is family and all that. My mother's the same."

Tag looked up at him from under an unruly fall of dark hair, which he quickly pushed back from his face. "Is she?"

"Oh, you can't imagine." He smiled. "As long as you keep bringing it at rehearsals, Henry will be fine." Jay attempted a laugh, although it sounded somewhat strained, and added, "Just don't have *too* much fun, or we'll all be jealous."

Tag gave him a rather flat look. "I think I can guarantee that I won't." Then he nodded, gaze lingering for just a beat too long before he swung his backpack over one shoulder, and said, "Have a good night, Jay. See you tomorrow."

When the door closed behind him, Jay realised that he'd

been staring and quickly looked away, only to find Freddie eying him with the look of a woman who'd seen it all before.

"That's a young man who's got a lot on his plate," she observed to nobody in particular.

∾

There was no rehearsal on Sunday, and Jay spent an enjoyable morning sleeping in, followed by a leisurely afternoon exploring the beautiful city of York with its winding cobbled streets, ancient city walls, and, of course, its glorious Minster.

He was spotted a few times and took a couple of selfies with people, but mostly he tried to keep a low profile behind his dark glasses and baseball cap. The weather so far had bucked the stereotype for Yorkshire and the sun had shone most days, warming the May air into something that felt like summer.

As he ambled home along the river, he found himself wondering what Tag had been up to all day. Resting, hopefully. He'd obviously been exhausted again at yesterday's rehearsal, forgetting lines and losing focus. Henry clearly wasn't happy about it, and that worried Jay. If Tag carried on like this, Henry might do something drastic—he wouldn't be the first undisciplined actor Henry had cut during rehearsals.

Not that Jay thought Tag *was* undisciplined. But he couldn't help remembering the first time they'd met, at the RPP Hallowe'en party, Tag gorgeous and flirtatious in those obscene silver shorts, joking about blowing Jay in the loos and then spending the rest of the night trying to get into Mason Nash's pants.

A starfucker, Jay had assumed. A beautiful young actor looking for a good time—and maybe a career boost.

And then, at the awards dinner, Tag had been the one to drag Jay into bed. Not that he'd needed much dragging, but still...

Was *that* the real Tag? A fun-loving party boy who'd already found the best gay bar in town?

Maybe. Yet somehow it didn't add up, not when he thought about how *good* Tag was, how seriously he took his work. Surely he wouldn't blow this chance for the sake of a couple of Jägerbombs and a quick shag at the Black Bear?

No, it didn't make sense. Jay felt like he was missing something important.

By the time he'd returned to his cosy little apartment, it was time to shower, change, and head out for the evening. The restaurant Bea had chosen turned out to be a charming brasserie nestled on the banks of the Ouse in a lovely old brick building that, according to the plaque out front, had once housed the pump engine for the waterworks.

Jay was shown to their table by a wide-eyed waitress who blushed furiously when she recognised him. Jay took care to thank her, offering a smile that only deepened her embarrassment. He'd found that some fans felt quite overwhelmed around him, and the kindest thing to do was let them deal with it themselves without appearing to notice.

Henry, Bea, and Rafe had already arrived. They were sitting at a round table surrounded on three sides by floor-to-ceiling windows that looked out over the river on one side, and a small park on the other.

"This is great," Jay said as he took a seat next to Henry. "Good choice, Bea."

She beamed. "It is, isn't it? Giles suggested it. He's coming, by the way."

Yes, Jay hadn't forgotten. Something they didn't prepare you for at drama school was the fact that, as 'the talent', you'd be expected to schmooze with executives and money people. Jay had always known, though. After all, he'd been trained in the art at his mother's knee; Dame Cordelia could charm the stars from the sky when she wanted to get one of her projects off the ground. Jay wasn't nearly so persuasive, but he thought he could manage the director of a regional drama festival without too much trouble.

Freddie showed up next, accompanied by a man Jay didn't recognise but assumed must be Giles Cox. He and Freddie clearly knew each other, and they came in chatting.

"… and so I said, no, you can't have a cue line, it's the bloody dress rehearsal!" Freddie laughed, her voice booming through the restaurant. "And that was the last time I ever worked with *him*. Ah, here we are!" She beamed as they reached the table. "Hello, hello everyone. Look who I found outside."

"Giles!" Bea jumped up and went to greet him. "*So* glad you could make it." They bussed cheeks. "Everyone, this is Giles Cox, director of the York Drama Festival. He's who we've got to thank for our amazing venue."

Giles was younger than Jay had expected, mid-thirties he guessed, and attractive in a well-heeled way. His sandy hair was styled in a slicked-back pompadour, and he wore chinos and a casual pink linen shirt. "No thanks needed," Giles said, smiling. "It's an honour to have you at the festival." His gaze flickered to Jay, then came to rest on Henry. "I'm a huge admirer of your work, Mr. Walker."

"Henry, please," Henry said, rising and shaking Giles's hand across the table. "And thank you. I'm excited to be part of your festival. Let me introduce you to Jay Warren, one of our lead actors."

Giles's eyes sparkled as Jay stood to shake hands, his grip lingering suggestively. "Here's where I confess to being a little star-struck," Giles said with a disarming smile. "I'm something of a *Leeches* fan."

"Is that so?" Jay said, turning on the charm. "Well, don't tell anyone, but so am I."

He laughed. Giles laughed. They all laughed.

Which was when Tag appeared at the table sounding a little breathless and with the air of a man trying not to look like he'd been rushing. Jay felt a little breathless himself because, even in dark jeans and a plain, long-sleeved t-shirt, Tag was stunning. The healthy colour in his cheeks, probably from running, only added to his rumpled just-got-out-of-bed charms.

"Sorry I'm late," Tag said as his gaze flicked to Henry. "I, uh, got a bit lost."

"It *is* rather hidden away, isn't it?" Henry said easily. Then he turned to Giles. "Let me introduce you to our other lead, Tag O'Rourke."

Giles smiled and leaned past Freddie to shake Tag's hand. "Nice to meet you, Tag. I've heard great things about you."

"Yeah?" Tag looked surprised, the expression lighting up his face. "Cool. I mean, thanks."

Giles chuckled, and Freddie patted Tag's shoulder. "You'll need to get used to that, Sunshine. You've got a bright future ahead of you."

Jay smiled at the embarrassed pleasure on Tag's face as they all took their seats, Giles claiming the chair next to Jay and Freddie the one next to Giles, which left Tag the remaining seat next to Rafe. On cue, Rafe gave a pointed cough. Bea, like a puppet whose strings were being tugged, sat upright and said, "Oh, Giles, let me introduce Rafe Fitzroy. He's understudying both roles in the play. We're *so* lucky to have him on board."

Across the table, Giles said, "Hi Rafe, it's good to meet you. It must be exciting to be working with Henry Walker and Jay Warren—what an opportunity."

Rafe raised his eyebrows and said, "Oh, I've known Henry for yonks. And I studied with *lots* of incredible people when I was at Julliard." He smiled. "Besides, Grandy knows all the A-listers—I never get star-struck."

Grandy? Jay repressed the urge to roll his eyes and met Tag's laughing gaze across the table.

Giles, proving he had decent manners—and that he'd

probably met a lot of actors—simply laughed and said, "Well, of course." His gaze moved back to Jay and, in a warmer voice, he said, "Would it be terribly boring if I asked you about *Leeches*? I promise not to go on about it all evening."

"Ask away," Jay said, "but I can't tell you anything about the new season, I'm afraid. I haven't seen the first scripts yet, and even if I had, Lewis Hunter would have my balls if I leaked any spoilers."

"That's a shame," Giles said with a lingering smile, "because one of the things I wanted to ask about was the rumour that there's going to be a kiss between Skye and Faolàn…"

Jay mimed zipping his lips shut, and Giles laughed.

"All right, all right," he said, resting his hand on Jay's forearm. "Perhaps it's safer to talk about *Let Us Go Back*. How are rehearsals going?"

"Oh, amazingly," Bea cut in and launched into an excited retelling of the past few weeks.

As she talked, Jay glanced back at Tag, only to find him looking quickly down at his menu, as if he'd been caught staring. Jay felt an inappropriate flutter of excitement, then quashed it, reminding himself that Tag was more likely to have been staring at Giles than at him.

Whoever he'd been looking at before, though, Tag was frowning as he studied his menu, brows drawn together. Jay glanced at his own menu—he thought it all looked very good, with interesting choices and a couple of decent-looking veggie options. Reasonably priced as well, with the main courses coming in at about thirty pounds.

He glanced back at Tag, saw him worrying at his lower lip, and a thought struck him that probably—definitely—should have struck him sooner. Considering it for a moment, he said, "Seen anything you fancy, Tag?"

"Oh, umm…" A tell-tale flush rose into Tag's cheeks.

"Actually, I'm not all that hungry. I might just have a starter or something."

Jay nodded. "They do look good," he said, but he was thinking about Tag having given up his job as a barista, about Tag skipping lunch in favour of slightly stale custard creams, and about the modest sums they were both earning.

Suddenly, he felt like a bloody idiot. He looked around the table at the rest of the company, all of them complacent well-to-do theatre types, just like him. No wonder Tag had a bloody chip on his shoulder. It wasn't even a chip. It was a genuine grievance.

He looked back at Tag, who was still chewing on his lower lip, and made a decision. "You know what?" he said, cutting across Bea's monologue to address the table. "I think tonight calls for champagne, don't you?"

A general murmur of approval followed, although unsurprisingly not from Tag, whose frown deepened.

Jay turned, summoning the waitress with a smile. "Could we have two bottles of your best champagne, please?" he said, pulling out a credit card and handing it to her. "And put everything on this, if you would, food included." To the table, he said, "Tonight's my treat. Order whatever you want and let's celebrate *Let Us Go Back*!"

"That's very generous of you," Henry said, beaming his approval. Of course, it was exactly the sort of thing Dame Cordelia would do, so naturally, Henry approved.

Rafe said, "Well, in that case, I'm having a cocktail…"

"Ooh, good idea," cooed Bea, practically climbing into his lap to look at the drinks menu. "What looks good?"

Tag said nothing but when Jay casually glanced his way, he saw immediately that Tag had relaxed, that his frown had disappeared, and that he was smiling slightly as he browsed the menu.

Bingo.

And when Tag ordered, it was pan-roasted scallops with

peppered swede, followed by a 10oz chargrilled, Yorkshire-raised steak, with treacle tart and whipped creme fraiche for dessert. He ate every bite.

Jay was glad to see it, but at the same, he was mortified it had taken him so long to realise Tag was struggling financially. And it got him wondering how else Tag might be struggling for the sake of this production.

CHAPTER ELEVEN

The day after the cast dinner, Tag was the first to arrive at rehearsal. He scarfed down three custard creams, poured himself a cup of the horrible coffee, and settled down to wait for the others.

It was a beautiful morning. The sun streamed through the window, making the utilitarian space look bright and promising. Or maybe Tag was seeing it differently because he felt properly rested for the first time all week. As much as he'd agonised over turning down a shift to go to dinner last night, it had been worth it. Not just for the chance to spend some downtime with the rest of the company, and to enjoy a slap-up meal at no cost, thanks to Jay's generosity, but also to hit the sack before midnight for the first time in ages. As thankful as he was for his temporary bar gig, the hours were proving to be punishing. Last night's uninterrupted eight-hour kip had been glorious.

The only damper on the evening had been having to watch Giles Cox flirt with Jay all night. That had been weirdly irritating. Tag didn't give a shit who flirted with Jay, or whether Jay flirted back, but yeah, watching the two of them making eyes at one another had left Tag grinding his teeth. Maybe it was because their whole conversation had been a roll call of all the famous people they both knew, or were related to, or who happened to be their fucking godparents. Christ, how many godparents could one person have? Whatever. One thing was undeniable—Jay had a lot more in common with Giles than he did with Tag.

Tag scowled into his coffee. Giles had spent most of the evening gazing into Jay's eyes and asking him endless questions about *Leeches*, monopolising his attention ruthlessly.

Selfish twat, Tag decided. Not that he cared for himself, of course, but it *had* been a company night out. Hadn't it occurred to Giles that Jay might want to talk to anyone else? But then, maybe Jay had been quite happy being monopolised. He hadn't seemed like he needed rescuing at any point. Tag remembered how the two men had looked with their heads bent together, one fair, one dark, laughing about their mutual friends—*"Oh my God, you shared a flat with Annabelle Ryan? We were in the same year at RADA!"*

Tag had found himself wanting to reach over and mess up Giles's stupid pompadour hairstyle. Or 'accidentally' spill some red wine on his artfully creased linen shirt. Annoyingly, on the odd occasion when Giles had actually spoken to Tag, he'd been nice, all smiles and easy grace.

"It's wonderful to have brilliant young actors like yourself coming to York, bringing your talent to the provincial stage. That's exactly why I took this festival directorship on."

Twat, Tag had thought when he'd said that, even as the more reasonable inner-Tag quietly pointed out that Tag wouldn't be thinking that if Giles had been flirting with him, or at least, if he hadn't been all over Jay.

The rest of the company started arriving in ones and twos, first Henry, then Bea and Rafe, then Jay. Jay looked as relaxed and well-rested as Tag felt, and Tag found himself wondering whether Jay had left the restaurant with Giles last night. Whether anything had happened between them.

His stomach soured at the thought.

"What's up?" Freddie asked, plonking herself down beside him. "You're glaring."

"Nothing," Tag said. "Everything's great." He flashed her a quick smile.

Perhaps he protested too much—she sent him an odd look but didn't press further.

Henry decided to start the rehearsal with Jay's opening soliloquy in the second act, meaning that Tag, thankfully, didn't have to do much of anything right away, other than pay attention.

Jay walked into the centre of the room. He was wearing those horn-rimmed glasses that Tag liked so much. They enhanced the clean, elegant lines of his handsome face, particularly now that his customary facial hair was gone. Jay suited a beard, but that clean-shaven jaw accentuated his movie-star good looks. His hair was getting longer too, and Tag found himself imagining it longer still, brushing his shoulders. Maybe tied back in a messy ponytail. He'd suit it like that, Tag mused, but then Jay would suit pretty much anything.

Tag watched Jay move through the blocking for the scene with Henry. Henry wanted to try something a bit different, and Jay dutifully paced through the new suggestion. Then Bea was chipping in, and Freddie was flipping through her prompt book, making hurried notes. Tag was only half listening to what was being said, his attention taken up with how Jay was moving, his fluid grace, his expressive face.

Within himself, Tag recognised something shifting, a sudden switch in perspective that left him remembering, in bemused embarrassment, those months after they first met, when he'd looked at Jay and seen nothing but an over-privileged, condescending adversary…

"Tag, come here, will you? I want to try something."

That was Henry, beckoning him over. *Shit*. Tag felt a stab of panic even as he lurched up from his seat and hurried over. He should have been listening properly instead of navel gazing.

"Yeah?"

"You remember what we were planning when Jay gets to the end of this monologue, when it's your line?"

"Yeah, I'm going to be sitting in the dark, stage left, waiting for the spotlight to come to me." The instant the spotlight hit Tag, Jay's side would go dark, taking the audience from Sassoon in the present to Owen in the past.

Henry nodded, but he was frowning. "It's too static," he said. "It needs more movement. It needs to be more *dynamic*."

"I think you're right," Freddie said, tapping her pen against her chin. "That lighting break—it's a bit clichéd, isn't it?"

Beside her, Bea bristled, probably because the lighting direction was in the script. "I think it could be very effective," she said defensively.

"Oh, it's *effective*," Freddie said agreeably. "Clichés are popular for a reason. The question is, is it the effect you want? You're basically splitting the scene by switching the spotlight from Sassoon to Owen, but it's *one* scene, isn't it? That's how I read it."

Bea's brow pleated in a frown, but she didn't disagree.

Henry was nodding. "The scene needs to drive forward when Jay's monologue ends, not stop and start again. We want continuity from Jay's last line into Tag's first one." He looked at Bea, his gaze searching, as though willing her to understand.

"I see what you mean," she said at last, turning to Tag and Jay. "What do you think?"

Tag, aware that he'd missed some of what had been said earlier, was relieved when Jay spoke up first.

"I agree. Those last couple of lines are so *angry*. Sassoon's

154

not just remembering the past. He's feeling it in the moment. He's saying it *to* Owen."

"Yes," Henry said, pointing at Jay. "Yes. So, perhaps we begin to illuminate Tag's side of the stage while you've still got a few lines to go? Maybe starting from the line about the ward at night? *Silence falls. But soon after…*" Shouldering out of his threadbare, oversized cardigan, he handed it to Tag. "Try this. You're taking off your dressing gown, about to go to bed, pottering around a little. Bedtime routine stuff. And then"—he stilled, thinking—"then when Jay starts the line, *Real or not, the dead haunt me to madness,* you show the audience something. A moment of vulnerability."

Tag glanced at Jay. He was listening intently to Henry, but as though he felt Tag's attention, his gaze flickered to him, and their eyes met briefly. Tag felt a rare, brewing excitement, deep in his belly.

Dragging his gaze back to Henry, he said hoarsely, "What then? Does Jay stay on his side of the stage, looking over at me? Does he come to my side of the stage?"

Henry cocked his head to one side. "What do *you* think?"

That was a typical Henry move, Tag was discovering. He shared a lot of ideas but he also asked a lot of questions, seeming endlessly fascinated by everyone else's views. Honestly, it was kind of thrilling for a young actor. Tag would never have guessed that someone of Henry's reputation and experience would be so open to his ideas.

Buzzing now, he thought about it. At last he said, "I think he should cross the stage," he said. "Yank back the curtain on the past and walk right into it. Say the last line to Owen directly. I think it could be really powerful."

"Yes," Jay said urgently, pushing his glasses up to the top of his head. "Yes, I like that idea. That last line is *for* Owen, after all. Sassoon's angry. Furious. It's almost an accusation."

Bea nodded. She still wasn't smiling, but she looked less unhappy. "All right, let's try it."

Tag moved to the left side of the rehearsal space, trying to sideline the happy energy bubbling in his gut at the intoxicating exchange of ideas and to get into his Owen headspace. It was hard, though. This was why he wanted to act, why he had chosen this insane career. He was hit by a rush of deep affection for the people standing around him, eccentric Henry and forthright Freddie and clever, difficult Bea.

And Jay. Who had proven to be a surprisingly sensitive actor. Sensitive in a lot of ways, Tag mused, which you wouldn't guess when you looked at the red carpet photos. Jay Warren, star of *Leeches*, was impossibly gorgeous, and always —like his alter ego, Skye Jäger—exuded unassailable masculine confidence.

Tag had seen another side of him, though, that night in Jay's hotel room, and the more Tag saw of him now, the less surprised he was that Jay had been so sensitive in bed. So... vulnerable.

And the more he regretted the way the evening had ended.

Jay pulled those sexy, horn-rimmed glasses back down onto his nose and ran his gaze quickly over the script one last time before tossing it aside and crossing the room to stand a good ten feet to the right of Tag.

Behind Tag, there was a thud, and when he looked round, it was to see that Freddie had just set a chair down behind him, a prop for later. She raised a brow at him and pointed at the baggy cardigan Henry had passed him—his dressing gown in this scene—which he was still holding. Hurriedly he pulled it on, imagining the minimal settings of a bedroom around him. A bed, a chair, a small mirror above a cracked sink in the corner of the room.

And then Jay began to deliver the monologue. Tag stared at him, rapt. He was doing it differently than the last time they'd read this scene, his tone more driven, less dreamy, giving the familiar words new tone, new nuance.

Christ, he was good. And that was another thing Tag hadn't expected before their rehearsals had begun. Jay was contained and effective, with a still magnetism that drew the audience in so well he barely needed to raise his voice. He'd have them all straining to hear his every word, just with the sheer force of his personality.

Tag felt a wild, almost pleasurably masochistic stab of envy at how easy Jay made it look, to just stand up and perform these lines in a new way, right on the spot. To have the confidence to try to find his way to the character, to the scene, right in front of everyone.

From the corner of his eye, Tag saw a waft of movement, and his gaze flickered to Freddie, waving at him. Oh yes, he was now in this scene too, wasn't he? He sent her a small nod.

Jay was saying, "… and the dead are more real than the living. In my dreams, I find them every night: in the trenches, on the field, in the hospital wards…"

Tag's cue was coming, and he readied himself for it, moving to the imaginary mirror and beginning to play out the motions of slowly shaving, thinking himself into the mind of Wilfred Owen as he lived his quiet routine at the Edinburgh hospital, away from the front.

Jay's voice was an anchor, pulling at him with every word.

Tag wiped his face and moved away from the mirror, slowly removing the cardigan and carefully laying it over the back of the chair. He found himself thinking, *Owen is just a memory. I am just a memory.* The thought struck him as terribly sad, unbearable even, and he fought the urge to hide away, allowing the full force of his sudden grief to show on his face, even though it made him feel very naked, very exposed. But there was something exhilarating too about being this honest, this real. In giving this unfiltered, unpractised performance.

"Real or not," Jay carried on, "the dead haunt me to madness."

Acting by instinct now, Tag moved towards Jay, coming to

a stop halfway across the distance between them, as though at an invisible barrier. *See me*, he thought, letting his face plead his case.

Jay walked toward him, coming to a halt less than an arm's length away. Their gazes met, and Tag felt a stab of satisfaction at the pain he saw in Jay's eyes. *He sees me*.

In a painful, bitter tone, Jay spoke his next line, and then he stepped forward, reaching for Tag, taking hold of his biceps and pulling him roughly forward, till their chests collided. The thrill of the contact made Tag's heart slug hard, his breath feeling locked up and tight in his throat. He stared at Jay's face, mesmerised.

"Why can't I exorcise you?" Jay said harshly. "Why won't you *leave me alone?*"

Tag twisted in his grasp. "Why won't you let me go?"

Jay stared at him, stunned, as though it was the first time he had heard the words.

It felt like the first time Tag had heard them too. This wasn't two soliloquies. It was a dialogue. Jay lifted one hand from Tag's arm as if to caress his face, but then, quite abruptly, he dropped it to his side and stepped back, glancing over at Henry. Tag felt his chest ache, not quite certain whether it was Owen's or his own disappointment he felt.

"What do you think?" Jay asked Henry. "Should I step into Tag's scene at this point? Or stay here, on the border?"

Henry glanced at Tag. "What are your thoughts?"

"Maybe I sort of pull you across?" Tag said, taking Jay's hand. "Invite you into the memory?"

"Do we need to be prescriptive?" Bea glanced at Henry. "Maybe we're fluid here, and don't have a border per se? Freddie's probably right that it's a cliché to divide the scene."

"I could just wander through Jay's scene?" Tag suggested. "I mean, that's how memories work, right? They're unpredictable, intruding where they're not wanted, popping up when you don't expect—"

"No," Jay said sharply. "Absolutely not."

Tag blinked, totally thrown by Jay's angry tone and uncompromising words. He hadn't reacted like this to any other suggestion anyone had made over the last few weeks.

"No?" Tag said. "Just *no*? I thought this was a collaborative exercise?"

"It is, but that's a stupid idea."

"A *stupid*—"

"There are no stupid ideas here," Henry chided gently. "Now, Jay, I know—"

"He can't just drift about the stage, for God's sake!" Agitated, Jay pushed a hand through his hair, dislodging his glasses and only just catching them. "He has to stick to the blocking—that's just basic stagecraft."

Tag's cheeks heated. "I *know* that. I wasn't suggesting I drift—"

Just then, the door banged open, and Rafe announced, "Here we are, Giles, the rehearsal room!"

Nobody moved for a couple of seconds, but as Tag watched, Jay's eyes squeezed shut and his agitated expression smoothed out almost instantly. As though he'd put on a mask.

"Giles," Henry said, more clipped than usual. "How nice to see you."

"I hope I'm not interrupting," Giles said from behind them. "Rafe showed me the way in."

Jay let out a slow breath, opened his eyes, and for a moment, his gaze fixed on Tag. He looked rueful and slightly embarrassed. Tag didn't know how to react. He didn't know what the fuck was going on, or why Jay had blown up like that.

One minute they'd been flying, connecting eye to eye and mind to mind as they'd played the scene together. Acting could be like that when it was good, when it was flowing— like you were in an altered reality. That was when you knew it was working. And it *had* been working. Really fucking well. And then—

"That's a stupid idea."

It was so unlike Jay. At least, it was unlike the man Tag had come to know over the past few weeks— generous, collaborative, and creative. But it *was* more like the Jay he'd thought he knew before they'd come to York. Maybe *this* was the real Jay?

Behind them, the others were talking loudly. Bea laughed, saying, "I'm so glad you came, Giles! We're just working on a new idea, actually…"

"We *were*," Henry said drily. And then, to Tag and Jay, "Excellent work, you two. I want to explore this further." He made a face. "But I suggest we take a short break before we carry on."

"Good idea," Jay said tightly, although he was all smiles as he turned and strolled past Tag to greet Giles. "And hello to you! I didn't expect to see you again so soon."

"Did you think I'd wait when I had a personal invitation to drop in and see how things are going?" Giles was all but batting his bloody lashes. "Please, carry on as if I'm not here…"

Tag had to make an effort not to snort. *Not likely*, he thought sourly. He wasn't about to carry on baring his soul while Giles stood in the corner drooling over Jay.

Rolling his shoulders, trying to relax, Tag watched Jay, casual and handsome with his glasses pushed up into his dark hair again, one hand in his pocket. Laughing easily, as if schmoozing with Giles Cox was exactly what he wanted to be doing today. And perhaps, it was. Clearly, Jay had invited him here last night. Or this morning, Tag thought with a sour squirm in his belly.

Maybe Jay had left Giles's bed this morning, inviting him to drop in later.

There was no reason that thought should feel so uncomfortable, so much like…what? Betrayal? That was fucking ridiculous.

"Great work," Henry said, walking over to where Tag still lingered next to the chair in the middle of the rehearsal space. Henry glanced over his shoulder and then said in a low voice, "Listen, don't worry about Jay. I'm sure he didn't mean to sound so…"

Henry waved a hand, searching for the right word, and Tag supplied, "High-handed and entitled?"

"Right." Henry gave a rueful smile. "It's tough, I know, dealing with people of Jay's…pedigree, shall we say? There's always a sense that the rules are different for them."

Tag snorted softly. "It's more than a sense."

"I know how you feel, believe me. But in this case it really isn't what it seems." Again, Henry glanced back to where Jay was chatting with Giles before adding even more quietly, "Jay has a particular sensitivity around blocking. I wouldn't normally tell you this, but given that Jay probably won't… I understand from Ronnie, Jay's brother, that there was an incident during the opening night of Jay's West End debut. You may have heard about it?" When Tag shook his head, Henry carried on. "It turns out that another actor deviated from the blocking they'd rehearsed. It threw Jay so badly that he couldn't recover. He blanked, suffered a panic attack on stage, the poor sod, and couldn't go back on for the rest of the run."

"Jesus," Tag said softly.

"Yes. So, you see, Jay's very particular about blocking and people sticking with what's been rehearsed."

"I wasn't suggesting that I didn't—"

Henry put a hand on his arm. "I know you weren't. I'm just giving you the context—I'd hate to see this little upset damage the incredible chemistry I saw between you two today."

Tag felt a swell of emotion at Henry's praise, professional pride and… something else. Personal satisfaction?

"That information isn't widely known, by the way," Henry went on. "So please keep it to yourself."

"Of course I will." After a moment's thought, Tag added, "What did you mean when you said you know how I feel?"

Henry shrugged. "Only that my background is closer to yours than to Jay's, or Rafe's for that matter. My dad was a postie for forty years. My mum worked in the local sorting office. Of course, back when I was fighting my way into the business, there were more opportunities for people like us, kids with nothing but talent, ambition, and a shovel-load of grit." He grimaced. "These days, it's all kids like Rafe with pushy parents and fancy educations."

Tag laughed softly. "Tell me about it." Then he said, "But I didn't realise that about you. I mean, you talk like you're…"

"One of them?" Henry laughed. "Must be all that Shakespeare, darling. And sometimes it pays to fit in." He clapped Tag on the shoulder. "The truth is there's ten Rafes to every one of you, Tag, and that's a bloody shame. But don't let it stop you—this industry is crying out for your talent and perspective."

Pleased, embarrassed, Tag said, "Thanks. And I'll keep in mind what you said about Jay."

"Good. And now," Henry said grimly, "I need to give Rafe a little reminder about respecting the sanctity of the rehearsal room and not barging in wearing hobnail boots…"

Tag huffed a laugh as he watched Henry stride over and collar Rafe, escorting him towards the door, but his thoughts were on Jay and what Henry had told him. He'd heard something, he now remembered, about Jay leaving a production. He'd thought the story was that Jay had stormed out in a strop, but he couldn't really remember the details, only that Jay had supposedly been difficult and divaish. If Henry had got his information from Jay's brother, though, it was more likely to be true, wasn't it? It definitely chimed better with what Tag now knew of Jay…

He glanced over to where Jay was still talking to Giles, only to see Giles resting his hand on Jay's forearm as he chuckled at whatever anecdote Jay was telling. Giles had done that last night, too, lots of unnecessary touching. Not that Jay seemed to mind. And not that it was any of Tag's business, so why was he staring like a—?

Fuck.

Jay must have felt his gaze because, right then, he glanced over, and their eyes met for a puzzled moment before Tag awkwardly looked away. Shit, that made it worse. Now he looked like he was jealous. Which he wasn't, obviously. Why would he be jealous? He was just pissed off that Giles had interrupted their rehearsal, that was all, and he wished the bastard would bugger off.

As if on cue, Jay said, "Well, we should get back to work but, yeah, tonight would be great. Looking forward to it."

Tag's stomach gave an irritable lurch. A date, then. Whatever.

"*Fantastic,*" Giles gushed. "I'll pick you up at your place and we can walk from there. Text me the address?"

Tag tried not to pay attention to the faffing about with phones, or the extended goodbyes after Henry reappeared with a chastened Rafe in tow. It wasn't like Tag *cared* that Jay was going on a date with Giles, although he couldn't help noticing that nobody gave Jay any grief for going out on a work night.

But then, as Henry had said, the rules were always different for people like Jay, weren't they?

CHAPTER TWELVE

Tag

Tag had been half joking when he'd put the frighteners on Rafe about the Black Bear on a Saturday night. Partly, he'd wanted to dissuade him from showing up and making an arse of himself, but mostly, Tag had wanted to avoid Rafe finding out that he pulled the occasional shift at the Bear and grassing to Henry.

Saturday nights *could* be rowdy, although nothing like the riotous London scene. Like everything else in York, the Bear was a bit more genteel, and on Mondays, it was much like any other pub, albeit catering to a more diverse clientele. It was actually a pretty nice place, and Tag had been more than happy to oblige when Graham called to ask if he could cover a last-minute sickness absence this evening. Mondays were a breeze, and although he wouldn't make half as much in tips as he would at the weekend, he'd probably get away by eleven. The extra money was very welcome after missing out on Sunday's shift.

The Bear offered good-quality pub food, a decent selection of fancy craft beers, and a relaxed ambience, with scrubbed wooden floors, twinkling fairy lights, and a light dusting of rainbow flags. Tonight, Tag was working with a young crew, mostly students from the two local universities. They seemed like a nice bunch, although he didn't know them well—lots of earnest opinions, big smiles, and excitement at working in a real-life gay bar. They were kind of cute, in a puppyish way.

Tag's shift would cover both the bar and food service tonight, supporting the pink-haired young bar manager who went by the name of Zab—short for Elizabeth, apparently. She was in her second year at Uni, studying Maths and Philosophy, and was stressing about her upcoming exams.

"I mean, eight a.m.?" Zab complained as she polished glasses behind the bar. "It's such a discriminatory time of day to start an exam, right? There are studies that literally prove people under twenty have different circadian rhythms to older adults. Basically, there shouldn't be any exams until the afternoon."

Amused, Tag said, "Well, I empathise with being sleep-deprived." He eyed the door as a group of young women crowded in, laughing as they looked for a table, and called over, "Hi there, sit anywhere you like! Order food at the bar."

As they settled at a large round table in the corner, there was a call from the kitchen, and Tag went back to pick up a huge sharing plate of nachos for table fifteen—a couple of guys in casual office wear, who might have just been work colleagues if you missed the way they were shyly holding hands across the table. They were sweet, in a quiet, suburban way.

"Here we go, guys," he said as he set the plate down between them, forcing them to release each other's hands. "Nachos Grande with extra sour cream, cheese, and guac. You okay for drinks?"

The older of the two said, "I'll take another Pumphouse Pale. Jamie?"

Jamie ordered the same, and Tag was heading back to the

bar to fetch their beers when the pub door opened again, and a blond man entered, holding the door for his companion—a gorgeous, dark-haired man who looked startlingly like Jay Warr—

—who *was* Jay Warren.

Tag stopped so fast he almost fell over his own feet. For a panicked moment, he considered diving behind the bar and hiding. No time, though, because with the slow unfolding of a nightmare, Jay stepped through the door and looked directly at Tag.

For an instant, he seemed surprised but…pleased? Then he must have noticed Tag's Black Bear t-shirt and the short apron tied around his hips because Jay's expression changed. Surprise turned to shock, and then to embarrassment, before he got himself back under control and pasted on a smile.

"Shall we sit by the window?" said Giles, who hadn't noticed Tag at all. Generally, people overlooked bar staff unless they were trying to order. "Or would you like to sit outside? It's a bit cool out, but—"

"Just a moment," Jay said smoothly. Then, to Tag, "I didn't know you worked here."

Tag suppressed a ridiculous impulse to beg, *Please don't tell Henry!* Nothing he could do about the heat in his face, though, and that pissed him off because why should *he* be embarrassed? There was nothing embarrassing about earning a living for fuck's sake. "Yeah," he said bullishly, "I pick up a couple of shifts here and there." *So what?* He met Jay's eyes with a challenge and held them until Jay looked away, obviously uncomfortable.

With a sudden pang, Tag remembered their rehearsal that morning when they'd been so closely connected, working as one, their past antagonism subsumed in the performance. They'd eventually recovered their groove after Jay's weird blow-up, but now this. *Fuck.*

Giles turned towards them, looking alarmed when he

recognised Tag but then smiling when he understood the situation. "Oh, hi," he said, a quick once-over taking in Tag's uniform. "Good to see you again."

"You too!" Tag beamed, putting on a bravura performance as the host with the most. "None of the tables are reserved, so sit where you like and order at the bar. Have a great evening, guys!"

With that, he turned and escaped back to the bar, busying himself by collecting the beers for table fifteen. He couldn't help sneaking a peek, though, as Giles ushered Jay over to a table for two by the window. Jay moved with his usual, easy grace, but there was a subtle self-consciousness about him that Tag hadn't noticed before. Whether it was because Tag was there, or because Jay was out in public, Tag wasn't sure.

A short flurry of customers arrived after that, and Tag got busy making and serving drinks. Then, two of the women who'd come in just before Jay and Giles arrived, wanted to order food for their table.

"Mine!" Zab hissed, muscling ahead of Tag to sparkle at the women as she took their order. No doubt angling for a larger tip.

Which meant Tag was the only staff member free when Jay prowled towards the bar, menu in hand, presumably to order food for himself and Giles. Or possibly, judging by his expression, to murder Tag.

Shit.

Well, there was no avoiding it. He'd have to have this conversation with Jay at some point, so he might as well get it over with here and now. Rolling his shoulders, Tag braced himself. "Hey," he said, smiling as he moved over to where Jay stood tapping his menu on the bar. "What can I get you?"

Jay raised his brows. "How about a straight answer?"

Tag bristled. "What does that mean?"

"You've got a job? On top of rehearsals?"

"Shock!" Tag gasped. "Actor has side gig! Come on, Jay... Even you must know how it works."

In a low voice, Jay said, "Actors working with *Henry Walker* don't have side gigs."

"Yeah, well, they do if they want to eat. Or pay rent, or keep their digs at home." Honestly, he didn't know whether to laugh or cry. "Is this really a shock to you? They're paying me peanuts, Jay. It's probably less than you spend on your deli lunches, so I—"

"You should have said something." Jay frowned, all patronising concern. "I could help."

Tag felt his hackles rise but bit back his instinctive response—*I don't need your bloody help!* Tomorrow morning, he'd be acting with Jay again, trying to find his way back into that space of mutual connection they'd discovered. He couldn't risk fucking things up between them, not when they'd made so much progress.

"Look," he said calmly, "I appreciate the offer, but I don't need anyone's help. I'm fine." He gestured to the menu. "Now, you want to give me your order or what?"

For a moment, Jay held his gaze, those grey eyes of his searching. Then he looked down at the menu with a sigh and said, "Fine, I'll have the beef and ale pie and a bottle of Pinot Noir, with two glasses. Giles wants the vegan cheeseburger with salad and no bun. And no cheese."

Tag gave an unprofessional snort and was surprised when Jay laughed softly. "Yeah," he sighed. "I know."

"Date not going well?"

Jay raised an eyebrow, giving Tag another of those searching looks. "It's not a date."

"It looks like a date. Pretty sure Giles thinks it's a date."

"I'm schmoozing, that's all. For the sake of the production. It's expected."

Feeling weirdly buoyant all of a sudden, Tag turned to fetch the wine and glasses. "Wow," he said, when he set them on the bar, "and you think me working *here* is inappropriate. At least I'm not selling my—"

"Oh shut up," Jay said, but he was smiling when he pushed away from the bar. More seriously, he added, "We're not finished with this conversation, by the way."

"You can't tell Henry."

"I won't, but…"

"But what?"

Jay shook his head. "We'll talk about it later." He grabbed the wine with one hand and the glasses with the other. "And we *will* talk about it, Tag."

What the hell did he mean by that? Frowning, Tag watched Jay make his way back to his table, as graceful and elegant as a dancer. If Jay insisted Tag quit his bar work, things would be impossible financially, but if Jay gave him no choice—if he threatened to tell Henry—what would Tag do? What *could* he do? A payday loan to tide him over? Accept Jay's 'help', whatever that might be? Tag's pride revolted at the idea, but one thing was certain—he wasn't giving up this role.

"Oh my God," Zab hissed in his ear. "Do you know who that is?"

He blinked, rattled out of his thoughts. "What?"

"That guy!" She nodded towards where Jay was rejoining Giles. "It's Jay Warren, from *Leeches*. The actor who plays Skye."

"Oh yeah," Tag said, grinning. "I'm actually—" He caught himself in time. Jay's involvement in the production was under wraps—at Jay's insistence, according to Bea—and they were under orders not to let the cat out of the bag. "I'm… actually a big fan."

"He is *so* lovely," Zab sighed. "He makes my little bisexual heart go all wobbly."

Tag laughed and glanced back at Jay, who was pouring a glass of wine for Giles. "Yeah, he's pretty nice-looking."

Zab looked at him like he was an idiot. "*Nice-looking*? He's bloody gorgeous." She leaned closer, lowering her voice to a whisper. "Is that guy his date, do you think? He *is* gay, you know."

"I'd heard that, yeah."

Which was more delicate than saying, *Yeah, I guessed as much when I had his cock in my mouth.*

It felt strange now, remembering what he and Jay had done together that night. How it had felt to be with him, to share that slow, careful, ultimately mind-blowing journey. There'd been a connection between them that night, before Jay's buyer's remorse had kicked in, and Tag had ruined everything with his big mouth.

"I've never had to work so bloody hard at a blowjob in my life."

Wincing at the memory, he wondered what had it cost Jay to trust him again, to trust him enough to be so vulnerable with him in rehearsal…

Tag's heart gave a confused, pained jolt.

"Definitely a date," Zab said as Giles reached over and put his hand on Jay's forearm. She patted Tag's shoulder in faux-sympathy as she headed towards a customer at the other end of the bar, "Sorry, Tag, you're out of luck there."

With a disconcerting lurch of disappointment, he realised Zab was right. He'd messed up his chance with Jay. Not that anything could ever have come of their hook-up, but still… That ship had very much sailed, and the thought made Tag feel inexplicably sad.

The bar got busier after that, and Tag didn't have time to keep tabs on Jay and Giles, which was probably for the best. When their food was ready, he let Zab take it over and watched, amused, as she set the plates down in front of them, blushing furiously, then said something that made Jay laugh. A moment later, he was standing up to take a selfie with her, both of them hamming it up as he pretended to bite her neck vampire-style. Meanwhile, Giles looked on with a rictus of a smile that screamed impatience.

Unfortunately for Giles, Jay's antics with Zab drew enough attention that others in the bar began to recognise him. A couple more customers crept over, hesitatingly, to say hello and ask for a selfie, and Tag was reminded of Wilfred Owen timidly knocking on Sassoon's door clutching a copy of *The Old Huntsman* for him to sign.

Jay was being more generous than Sassoon had been, by all accounts, warm and patient with everyone. Giles was not, but luckily none of Jay's fans seemed to notice; they only had eyes for Jay, and who could blame them? Smiling and joking with his admirers, Jay was in his element, and he was *dazzling*.

Later still, when Tag was passing their table to start clearing the empty one behind, he couldn't help overhear Giles say, "...but it's just intrusive, isn't it? People are so entitled these days. I don't know how you put up with it, to be honest."

Quietly, Jay replied, "It's not always like that, and anyway, I don't mind. It's part of the job. And most people are very nice. You get a few oddballs, of course, and some people are a bit over-familiar, but..." He paused and then added, "I'm sorry if it's bothered you this evening, though."

"Oh, it hasn't bothered *me*," Giles said, which was clearly a lie. "I'm thinking about you."

Ha, Tag thought wryly, *I bet you are*.

In a silkier voice, Giles added, "But perhaps we could go somewhere more private now?"

Ugh. Tag didn't need to see Giles's face to picture his flirty smile. He'd been flashing it at Jay all last night.

Building pressure in his chest made Tag realise he was holding his breath, waiting for Jay's answer... and that made him realise he was being a creepy weirdo. Quickly, he gathered the coffee cups and dessert plates from the vacant table and carried them back to the kitchen without waiting to hear Jay's reply.

It was none of his business, after all, just like Tag's side gig was no business of Jay's.

When he got to the kitchen, the orders were just coming up for a table of eight in his section. He carried the meals out, then had to quickly nip behind the bar to help with a sudden rush. The next time he glanced Jay's way, it was to see him pulling on his jacket and heading out. He was hit with the oddest pang of disappointment at the sight. Jesus Christ, what was wrong with him?

Just as Jay reached the door, he turned his head, and their gazes met. For an instant Jay looked embarrassed—maybe Tag did too; they'd both been caught looking after all. Then he raised his hand in a quick farewell and followed Giles outside.

The door closed decisively behind them.

Tag felt suddenly, weirdly low. But he didn't have time to dwell on it. Already, another punter had stepped forward with a long, complicated order, and it was back to work.

The rest of his shift was busy, despite it being a Monday, and honestly, he was glad. He knew he'd probably only brood otherwise. Even with him providing sick cover, they were a bit short-staffed tonight, so in the end, he didn't even manage a proper break to eat dinner, plus the clear-up at closing took longer than he'd expected. It was almost eleven-thirty by the time he finished up, and when he got outside, it was to discover the rain had come on. Turning up the collar on his thin jacket, he hunched his shoulders and began trudging back to the house.

By the time he arrived, he was feeling thoroughly out of sorts, cold, wet, hungry, and exhausted. And, more than that, he felt down. Just—sad really. *Christ*, he thought as he shoved his key in the lock and shouldered the door open. Was he still moping over Jay going out with Giles? And if so, *why*? What the fuck did it matter to him?

Inside, the house was dark and quiet. Despite his hunger, he decided to go straight to bed, too tired to cook. A rim of flickering light showed round the door of Clem's room at the top of the stairs. No noise. She'd be gaming, headset on, probably eating bloody cereal and oat milk as usual. There'd been no light on in Mikey's room upstairs, so it looked like he was out. Probably working.

Yawning, Tag opened his own bedroom door, snapped on the light… and froze in the doorway.

"Oh fuck," he breathed and closed his eyes.

It had already been a long night, and it wasn't over yet.

CHAPTER THIRTEEN

J AY

The next day, Tag was late to rehearsal. Properly late. Thirty-six minutes.

Henry was seriously pissed off by the time he slunk in, muttering an apology about sleeping through his alarm. Taking hold of Tag's shoulder, Henry walked him straight back outside, and when they returned, ten minutes later, Henry was thin-lipped while Tag just looked crushed.

After that, everyone was on edge and nothing went right. It was obvious to Jay that Tag was struggling to get into character. He kept glancing at Henry worriedly, which was only making things worse. As hard as Jay tried to continue as though everything was normal, it was no good. The tension was palpable.

Eventually, Freddie intervened. "Henry, I think everyone needs a break," she said bluntly. "Long lunch today." Without waiting for his agreement, she hefted her backpack over her shoulder and headed for the door. "See you all at two."

Henry glared after her for a few moments. Then his scowl melted away, and he sighed heavily. "She's right. Let's all take a couple of hours to get our heads back in the game. Clean slate when we come back at two, yeah?" As he walked past Tag on his way out, he patted him on the shoulder. It was a gesture of apology, but Jay wasn't sure whether Tag realised that. He still looked upset.

Bea and Rafe began chatting about where to go for lunch, debating the respective merits of an Italian bistro and the Dog and Duck.

"Do you two want to come?" Bea asked, after they'd decided on the Italian place. "The seafood linguine is amazing, and the pizzas are pretty good too."

Rafe glanced at Tag and added silkily, "Maybe a couple of glasses of vino would relax you for this afternoon, Tag?"

Jay felt an uncharacteristic urge to punch Rafe's stupid face for that crack, but Tag didn't even react, just shook his head tiredly and said, "I think I'm going to head back to my place for a bit. I've, um, got some stuff to do."

Shit, he looked so *defeated*. Where was his usual fire? That annoying chippiness that drove Jay up the wall, but that he also reluctantly… *liked*.

"How about you, Jay?" Bea said, interrupting his thoughts.

Ugh, no. The thought of spending two hours watching Bea flirt with Rafe, while he droned on about everything he'd learned at Julliard, was not Jay's idea of fun. Especially not after spending the whole of the previous evening fending off Giles Cox—both his attempts to persuade Jay to let the festival put out a 'quick press release' about his involvement in the play and his repeated invites to join Giles for a 'nightcap' at his place after they left the Bear. Giles hadn't taken Jay's polite rejections—on either count—with particular grace.

"I think I'll pass," he told Bea with what he hoped was a regretful smile. "I'm not really hungry. Besides, I could do with getting out and burning off some energy instead. Might go for a run."

Bea, looking positively delighted to have Rafe to herself, grabbed his arm and began steering him towards the door. "Come on, Rafe, I'm *starving*. I haven't had a thing since breakfast."

Once they were gone, Jay turned around to see Tag zipping up his bomber jacket and still looking beaten down.

"Listen," Jay said gently. "Don't take this morning to heart. Some rehearsals are just cursed. You start off on the wrong foot, and it's like nothing can go right after."

Tag sighed. "Yeah, I know. I just—" He broke off, rubbing a hand tiredly over the back of his neck.

"What?" Jay prompted softly.

"Well, it's my fault, isn't it? I'm the one who arrived late. And I know that's really unprofessional—no wonder Henry's pissed off."

Jay studied his unhappy face, noting the dark shadows under his eyes, and the weariness etched there. He stepped closer. "Are you all right?" he asked carefully. "You look pretty exhausted."

Tag gave a huff of unamused laughter. "I didn't get much sleep last night."

Jay felt suddenly stupid. "Oh, was your shift last night a long one? I didn't realise the Bear stayed open late."

"It doesn't," Tag said. "I was done before midnight but—" He broke off. He seemed to be considering saying more, but in the end only shook his head. "I think I'm going to try and grab a quick power nap while we've got some time. I feel ready to drop." He pulled out his phone and swiped the screen, checking the time. "If I go now, I can probably grab an hour and get back for two." Seeing Jay's frown, he added with a small smile, "Don't worry. I'll put an alarm on. See you later, okay?"

"Okay," Jay echoed, but as he watched Tag leave, he felt unhappy, unsettled even.

It was only as he was lifting his messenger bag over his head that he remembered Tag saying, when he'd arrived this morning, that the reason he'd been late was that he'd slept through his alarm. Was it possible he'd do that again? If he did, Henry would be furious—and Tag would take that badly. Jay bit his lip, uncertain what to do. Maybe he should give Tag a call at one-thirty, just to make sure he did wake up? The company had its own WhatsApp group, so he had Tag's number. But what if the reason Tag had slept through his alarm was because his phone was on mute? Henry insisted they muted their phones during rehearsals, and it was easy to forget.

Jay glanced at the closed door, unsure what to do.

"For fuck's sake," he muttered at last, yanking the door open and jogging out, hoping he wasn't too late to catch up with Tag.

When he burst out the front door of the centre, Tag was nowhere in sight, but Jay had noticed he always headed left when they finished at the end of the day, so he went that way, hoping for the best. A couple of minutes later, he caught sight of Tag disappearing round a corner. Relieved, he followed, and when he turned the corner himself, Tag was about fifty yards ahead of him, walking quickly, purposefully. If he kept jogging, Jay would soon catch up with him, or he could just call his name. But he didn't do either of those things. Instead, he found himself slowing his pace to match Tag's and hanging back. Hesitating.

Tag's phone rang then, and he yanked it out of his pocket, seeming eager to take the call. By the time he put it away again, they'd been walking for a quarter hour, and it was too late for Jay to just casually call out to Tag. It would be obvious that Jay had been following him, and how would he explain that? He was struggling to explain it to himself beyond his weirdly intense need to make sure Tag made it back to rehearsal on time.

Glancing around, Jay began to notice that the houses were looking rather less salubrious. After a few more minutes, the area had become distinctly down at heel, and it only got worse as they continued. When Tag finally came to a halt, it was in front of a house that frankly summoned up the word *slum* in Jay's mind.

Surely Tag hadn't been living *here* for the past three weeks.

Maybe Jay was being a judgmental, privileged prick, but it *was* objectively awful, wasn't it? The door Tag was currently opening—which seemed to involve a lot of key jiggling and shoulder-barging—was a battered-looking thing with peeling paint, surrounded by blank-faced, grimy windows, and there was an actual car up on blocks in the neighbouring garden. Jay blinked at the sight. So that really *was* a thing people did and not just a useful poverty cliché they used in television dramas.

How hard-up would Tag have to be to live here? He was getting paid the same as Jay—and okay, that wasn't enough to fully cover Jay's accommodation, never mind any other expenses—but this place surely had to cost a lot less than Jay's apartment. And Tag *was* supplementing his acting salary with bar work. Jay wondered how much Tag would be making from his shifts at the Bear and realised, with some shame, that he hadn't the faintest idea how much people were paid for that kind of job.

As Tag disappeared inside the house, and the door closed behind him, Jay suddenly felt very much out of place and very aware of his expensive clothes. This was nothing like the well-heeled area where his riverside apartment was situated, with its hipster coffee shops and micro-bars. It didn't even look like there was anywhere he could grab a bite to eat; he hadn't seen so much as a corner shop, never mind a deli.

What was he supposed to do now? He couldn't just hang

around outside Tag's house to make sure he got up on time. Hell, he'd probably get mugged. Maybe he should walk back into town, grab a sandwich at his favourite lunch place down the road from the Salter Street Centre, and then head back this way later? With luck, he'd run into Tag on his way back to the rehearsal room, and everything would be fine.

Relieved to have landed on a solid plan, he was just about to get going, when a car pulled up, and an angry-looking woman in a pink velour track-suit got out of the driver's side, slamming the door behind her. As she stormed up the short path to Tag's front door, Jay noticed the word 'juicy' was plastered over the bum of her leggings in sparkly silver sequins. She knocked aggressively on the door.

What the fuck?

Half a minute later, the door opened, and Tag stood there, looking pissed off but entirely unsurprised to see her.

She pointed a hard, angry finger at him. "Any damage to that room is coming out of your deposit!"

"Fuck that!" Tag replied angrily. "*You* owe *me*. It happened while I was at work! Either get me another room or pay me my rent back."

"It was fine till you moved in," she snapped. "Let me see it."

Pressing his lips together, Tag stood aside, waving her into the house with sarcastic politeness. She barged past him, and he followed her inside.

Jay stood, uncertain, on the other side of the road. He stared at the grim little house, his stomach churning with a weird sort of dread. Which was both stupid and pointless—nothing was going to happen to Tag—but still, Jay felt oddly protective of him and couldn't bring himself to leave while Tag looked like he might need help.

Barely five minutes later, the door opened again, and the angry woman stalked back out.

She turned to glare at Tag, who was standing in the doorway. "You know what?" she said in a nasty tone. "Go for it. Sue me. Seriously, I don't actually give a fuck. It'll take you months and cost you thousands. Your choice." Then, yanking a bunch of keys out of her pocket, she stalked back over to her car, got inside, and peeled away.

Tag just stared after her, his expression angry and bleak. Then his gaze shifted—and he saw Jay.

As Tag's eyes went wide, a jolt of alarm shot through Jay. He began walking forward, crossing the road and heading up the weed-strewn path. "Tag, listen," he said, his tone calm but driven. "I'm sorry. I—I followed you. I know I shouldn't have, but I was worried you might sleep through your alarm again and—" He came to halt, realising that he was now less than an arm's length from Tag, who was staring at him in disbelief.

The silence between them was suddenly deafening, the small space that separated them unbridgeable. But Jay *had* to bridge it. And so he reached out, gripping Tag's shoulders with both hands and saying, "Are you okay?"

Tag stared at him, and his eyes, which were usually so bright and determined, brimmed with such misery Jay couldn't stand it. "*Tag*," he said, and it was a plea. *Let me in.*

"I should never have fucking come to York," Tag rasped, his voice cracking. "I gave up a regular job for this, and now I'm broke, Henry thinks I'm useless, I don't even have a fucking bed to sleep in and—" He made an inarticulate sound that was something between a scoff of laughter and a sob and swiped at his eyes with the back of one hand.

Jay's heart pinched hard. "Henry *doesn't* think you're useless," he said firmly, squeezing Tag's shoulders. "And what's this about not having a bed?"

Tag shook his head, then said, "Come in. I'll show you." He began to turn, dislodging Jay's hands from his shoulders, leaving Jay feeling curiously bereft even as he followed Tag into the house and down a narrow corridor. Tag opened up one of the doors and leaned back to invite Jay to look inside.

"*Shit,*" Jay breathed. The room looked like an actual bomb had hit it. Plasterboard, dust, and bits of wood lay everywhere. He glanced up at the ripped-open ceiling—almost the whole thing had come down. If Tag had been sleeping there when it happened… Jay's scalp prickled, and he realised he was furious. "Was that bloody woman trying to blame this on *you*?"

"Yeah." Tag sagged against the door frame and rubbed a weary hand over his face. "I feel like an idiot," he croaked. "The room was incredibly cheap, but I had to pay the rent and deposit up front to secure it—I only realised how bad it was when I got here, and then it was too late. There's nothing I can do in the short term to get my rent back. Even if I take her to court—which I can't afford to do, obviously—I'll be back in London before the case gets anywhere." He shook his head disgustedly. "I'm stuck here."

Jay's gaze took in the horror of Tag's room. While efforts had clearly been made to clear up, it was still covered in filth —and damp filth at that. The whole atmosphere felt unhealthy. Jesus, what kind of spores would Tag be breathing in at night?

"You can't sleep in here," he said, before he could think better of it.

Tag laughed, without humour. "Yeah. Not right now anyway. Last night, I tried to sleep on the couch in the living room, but it's only five feet long and lumpy as hell. I barely got an hour's kip."

"You need to go somewhere else," Jay said, turning to him. "You're not going to get through the next five weeks without a decent night's sleep."

Tag's expression was agonised, and worse, ashamed. "I know, but I can't *afford* anything else. Didn't you hear what I said? I paid for this place up front. I'm fucked."

Jay stared at him. "It can't be that bad," he whispered, but even as he said the words, he knew that was just wishful thinking.

Tag's amber eyes sparked with irritation. "It *is* that bad," he snapped. "I know you can't understand what it's like to have no money, but when I say I haven't got a spare penny, I mean that literally!"

"But what about the money Bea's paying you? And your bar work?"

Tag gave a frustrated snort. "I have other commitments—I pay rent to my parents every month, and they rely on it to meet their mortgage. I can't just stop paying while I'm pissing about up here. Jesus, you really don't get it, do you? Do you think I'd live in this shithole if I didn't have to?"

"I'm sorry." Jay swallowed. "No wonder you think I'm a prick."

Tag sighed heavily. "I don't think you're a *prick*," he said. "But you're fucking naïve about life sometimes."

Jay nodded. That was fair. He'd been clapping himself on the back for buying dinner for everyone at the company night out, thinking he was so insightful about Tag's financial issues, but the truth was, he'd been just as blind as everyone else. He'd had no real idea how tough things were for Tag, and he hadn't bothered to ask.

"So, is your landlady at least going to get this cleaned up?" Jay asked, gesturing at the wrecked room.

Tag shook his head. "She says it's my problem, so I reckon I'm going to be sleeping on the couch till I clean it up." He shrugged. "At least I don't have a shift tonight, so I can make a start after rehearsal."

Jay stared at him, horrified. "*Fuck that,*" he heard himself saying, his voice hoarse with outrage. "You're not cleaning this shit up for that...that *woman*. Pack your stuff. You're coming with me."

Tag's eyes widened. And honestly, Jay wondered if maybe his did too. He hadn't planned to say that—it just came out.

"Coming with you where?" Tag said faintly.

Where?

The obvious solution was a hotel until Tag could find somewhere else to stay. Of course, Tag couldn't afford a hotel, or somewhere else to stay, and knowing Tag, he'd probably rather sleep under a bridge than let Jay pay. So what, then?

Jay pictured his riverside apartment. Okay, it was just a studio apartment, but it was roomy, and the couch converted into a good-quality sofa-bed. Tag couldn't object to crashing on a friend's couch, could he?

"You're moving into my place," Jay said firmly.

"What? No!" Tag protested. "You don't need me under your feet."

"What I *need*," Jay snapped, knowing instinctively that the best approach was to fire up Tag's drive and ambition, "is a co-star who can fucking do his job and get up for rehearsal in the morning. And who'll be there on opening night because he's not come down with some lung infection from breathing in deadly bloody spores!"

"Spores?" Tag blinked at him, seeming taken aback. "I didn't—" he began and broke off.

"Come on, Tag," Jay said, more gently. "This is your big break. You have to give it your best shot, right? And if you insist on staying here, you won't be doing that. You know it, and I know it. So for once, will you put your pride aside and just let me help you out?"

Tag swallowed, his throat bobbing hard. "Okay," he whispered.

CHAPTER FOURTEEN

JAY

Five days later

On the first Sunday morning after Tag moved in, Jay found himself lying in bed and staring up at the ceiling as the glorious bells of York Minster rang the hour at ten o'clock.

From the other side of the room came the steady sound of Tag's sleeping breaths, and Jay knew, if he looked over, that he'd see him stretched out on his stomach, one arm curled up over his head, face turned and half smooshed into the pillow. The t-shirt he slept in would probably have ridden up to expose the small of his back, possibly the waistband of his underwear. And his black hair would be tousled against the white pillow, his lips parted—warm, and soft, and infinitely kissable.

Jay knew all this without looking because that's what he saw every morning now. Not that he made a point of *looking* at Tag as he padded past the sofa-bed. It was just that he tended to wake up first, and it was a small apartment. He couldn't avoid seeing Tag when he went to the bathroom to grab a shower. And if his gaze had occasionally lingered over the lean curve of Tag's back and the swell of his arse beneath the covers, well… He was only human.

Human and horny, apparently.

That was just too bad, though, because pursuing anything with Tag was out of the question. Even if Tag hadn't made his feelings crystal clear after their night together months ago, Jay had a strict rule about relationships with co-stars. The rule being absolutely never, not under any circumstances. He'd been badly burned by Seb and would never put himself in that position again.

At best, he and Tag could be friends.

Funny to think how impossible any friendship with Tag had seemed at the start of rehearsals. But things had shifted between them, especially in the week since Tag had moved into the apartment. Tag's prickles had softened, and the time they were now spending together outside rehearsals was surprisingly fun. Tag was an entertaining and easy companion, and they had a lot in common. Not just their profession but their tastes—in theatre, films, television. Even the stuff they disagreed on was fun to talk about with Tag. He was sarcastic and mischievous, his amber eyes glinting with good humour as they debated the respective merits of Miles Davis and Britney Spears.

There was certainly no shortage of stuff to talk and laugh about over their snatched breakfasts of toast and coffee, or during the walk to and from the Salter Street Centre, or on the two occasions they'd cooked dinner together in the apartment's tiny kitchen. Tag had been working on the other nights, though he'd promised to take fewer shifts, now that he was living with Jay and some of the financial pressure on him had eased.

Jay languidly stretched and thought about the day ahead. For almost the first time since they'd come to York, they had a whole day to themselves, with no rehearsal. And thank God, because the week had been a slog. It would have been hard even without Tag's housing situation knocking him off balance for a couple of days. They'd been working through the last of the knots in the script, and tensions had been high, with everyone increasingly aware of opening night speeding towards them like a freight train.

Thankfully, yesterday, Henry had pronounced himself satisfied with the exploratory stage of the process, and tomorrow, they were moving the rehearsals to the venue where they'd be opening in just a few weeks.

The prospect of appearing before a live audience had Jay's gut pitching nauseatingly, and he shoved the thought aside to be dealt with later. For now, he had a whole day ahead of him with no plans.

No plans... and Tag asleep on his sofa-bed. Would Tag want to spend today with him, Jay wondered? He felt both excited and anxious about the possibility. But maybe Tag would prefer some time to himself? That thought was oddly deflating, not to mention ridiculous, given Jay's own rules.

Nevertheless... He turned his head towards Tag—and was startled to find Tag's whisky-gold eyes open and watching him. They both looked quickly away.

There was a rustling of bed covers from Tag's side of the room, and then he said, "Sorry, I couldn't tell if you were awake. I didn't want to disturb you."

"I'm awake," Jay said, "just enjoying not having to get up." That was true, but he'd also not wanted to wake Tag, who'd been working last night and must have got in late because it had been almost one when Jay went to bed, and he hadn't heard Tag come home.

Tag huffed a laugh. "Yeah," he said, "it's been a long week." After a silence, he added, "Look, you probably want some time to yourself this weekend, so I can make myself scarce if—"

Jay threw a pillow at him, smiling at Tag's surprised yelp. "Will you stop it?" he said. They'd had this discussion at least once a day all week. "I like having you here. I'm enjoying the company to be honest." Sitting up, he scratched a hand through his hair and looked over at Tag again. "But, I mean, if you'd rather look for somewhere else…?"

Tag was sitting up now as well, the bed covers pooled in his lap. He looked soft and appealingly sleep-rumpled in a way Jay thought the chippy side of Tag might not appreciate. And he was regarding Jay with an expression it was difficult to parse. "No," he said eventually, his gaze flickering down and away, "it's nice here. But you have to let me pay my way."

This was another conversation they'd had a few times now. "I told you," Jay said, getting out of bed, "we can settle up when you get your rent money back from that woman."

Tag sighed. "Yeah, well, that'll be sometime never."

"I'm pretty sure Geoff will sort her out," Jay said. He'd called his lawyer, Geoff Hall, the day after Tag had moved in and asked him to send a scary letter to Mrs 'Juicy'. When he'd told Tag what he'd done, he'd added a little white lie, namely, that it wasn't costing Jay anything. Luckily, Tag seemed to believe him, which was good because Geoff's bill would undoubtedly be more than the money Tag got back. And Jay *was* hopeful he'd get it back—Geoff was nothing if not effective. Look at the way he'd taken down Charlie Alexander last year.

"We'll see," Tag said and sighed. He sounded like he'd given up the money already.

Briskly, Jay clapped his hands and said, "Let's both just focus on the play for now. It's just over three weeks until opening night, God help us. And if we're not off-book tomorrow, Henry will string us up."

Tag cocked his head, frowning. He sat cross-legged on the sofa-bed, looking up at Jay through dishevelled hair. "You're already off-book," he said. After a pause, he asked, "Are you worried about it?"

"No," Jay said quickly. Too quickly, probably—*The lady doth protest too much.* "No, I'm usually okay with my lines."

Tag's frown deepened. "What then? You're worried about something. Is it opening night?"

Shit. He couldn't talk about this, and certainly not with Tag. If Tag suspected that Jay was...unreliable, it would be a disaster for both of them. Affecting a nonchalant shrug, he said, "Well, everyone's nervous about opening night, aren't they?"

"True," Tag agreed, although he didn't look like he'd bought Jay's misdirection. "It's exciting too, though?"

"Yeah," Jay said, forcing a smile. "Yeah, it is."

Much like being pushed out of a plane with no parachute.

Fuck, he couldn't think about it anymore; his stomach was churning, and he felt slightly sick. "Do you know what?" he said brightly. "I fancy a run. Want to come? There's a nice route along the river I could show you."

Tag looked surprised, but then nodded. "Yeah, all right. Sounds good."

Jay smiled, pleased, and a moment later, Tag smiled too, their eyes meeting and holding a fraction too long for comfort before Tag gave an odd little laugh and started to get up. Which prompted Jay to flee to the bathroom so he didn't accidentally ogle Tag in those snug black boxer briefs.

It took a few minutes for them both to get ready, mostly because Tag got distracted by his phone. He was sitting on the sofa in his running gear, frowning as he typed a message, when Jay came out of the bathroom.

"Trouble?" Jay asked as he went to the door to find his trainers.

"Hmm?" Tag glanced up, distractedly. "Oh, no. It's just my mum. She's having a family get-together when *Bow Street* drops on Thursday and she's desperate for me to be there, but of course, I'm up here so..."

"That's a shame," Jay said.

"Yeah, it's kind of a big deal to her. And to me, but…" He shrugged. "Just bad timing."

Doubtfully, Jay said, "I suppose you could ask Henry if you could take Friday off—?"

"No way," Tag said, shaking his head. "The play comes first." He put his phone away and stood. "Anyway, like I told Mum, there'll be other things to celebrate. This is just the beginning."

Nevertheless, he looked a little crestfallen.

"It's your first TV role?"

Tag nodded, then added with forced brightness, "But not the last, right?"

"I'm sure of that," Jay said earnestly. Still, it was a pity Tag couldn't mark this milestone with his family and friends.

Shoving his feet into his running shoes, Tag crouched to lace them. "I usually run for about half an hour," he said, "but if you want to go longer…?"

Jay took the hint and dropped the subject. "No, that sounds good to me," he said, pocketing the apartment keys and grabbing his sunglasses and baseball cap.

Tag gestured to them as they trotted downstairs to the front of the apartments. "Do you get recognised often? It was a bit mad in the Bear the other night."

"Sometimes," Jay said, slipping on his sunglasses as they stepped outside, even though the morning was drab and overcast. "Depends on context, really. At a posh London restaurant, I'll usually be spotted—which is why I avoid them. At McDonald's, probably not so much."

Tag laughed. "You do *not* go to McDonald's."

"Well, maybe not often," Jay conceded.

"Not ever, more likely."

"You know, you have a very strange view of my life."

"All right," Tag said, following as Jay led him around their apartment block and down to the river. "When we've finished our run, we're going to McDonald's for breakfast. My treat."

"And undo all the benefits of exercising?"

Tag gave him a slow and unashamedly flirtatious once-over, eyebrows twitching suggestively. "Come on, you can afford a McMuffin. You're in fantastic shape—for your age."

Flustered by that look, Jay felt his cheeks heat, but hid it under a burst of mock outrage. "My age?" He shoulder-checked Tag. "Why, you young whippersnapper, you!"

Tag laughed. "Was that—? Was that meant to be an American accent?"

"Oh shut up."

"Because if it was, I know a great dialect coach. And it's not true what they say about old dogs and new tricks…"

Jay snorted and began to run. "Come on, keep up!"

From behind him he heard Tag's laugh, and then a few seconds later, Tag was jogging along at his side, and then overtaking. Which led to several silly minutes as each of them tried to outpace the other, at the end of which they were both sprinting at full tilt and then staggering around laughing, gasping for breath, and both claiming victory.

After that, they settled into a steady run, heading along the pretty footpath next to the river and into the city. They passed a few other joggers and dog walkers, and a couple of people did do a subtle double-take, but nobody stopped them, which was a relief. Eventually, though, the path widened out and became more crowded, making it difficult to run. They'd almost reached the bridge by then anyway, so Jay slowed to a walk.

"That was great," Tag said, catching his breath as their pace dropped.

Glancing over, Jay felt a twist of desire at the sight of Tag's flushed cheeks and bright eyes, his hair pushed back and his sweat-damp t-shirt clinging to his chest. Christ, he looked hot. In every sense of the word.

"It *was* great," Jay agreed, walking over to grab the railing next to the river as he started to stretch, aware of Tag's eyes on him. When he looked over, Tag's gaze flicked sideways, and then his eyes widened, and he laughed. "Oh my God, look," he said, pointing to a white sign attached to the railing. "This is called Dame Judi Dench Walk."

And so it was. Amused, Jay said, "Thank God my mother isn't here."

"Yeah?" Tag pulled one foot up behind him, holding it there, hip pushed forward to stretch out his thigh muscle. "Would she be jealous?"

"Jealous? No." Resisting temptation, Jay kept his eyes firmly on Tag's face and no lower. "But we'd have to listen to about three hours of anecdotes about 'dear Judi'."

"That's so cool," Tag said, and for once, there was no edge to it. He actually sounded wistful. "Your mum's a legend. I love her."

"Everyone does," Jay agreed. "Including me. I'll introduce you some time, if you like."

Tag's eyes went comically wide. "Seriously? Oh my God."

"I think she'll like you," Jay said, pushing back on one heel to stretch out his calf. "She admires anyone who's serious about 'the work', and you are."

"So are you."

Jay changed to stretch his other calf. "Well, in her view, television work isn't real acting, so..."

"What?" Tag sounded offended, which made Jay feel stupidly warm. "That's bollocks."

"But *darling*," Jay gushed, in his best imitation of Dame Cordelia, "to be the best actor you can be, you simply *must* spend some of your time on stage. Television pays well, but artistically, it's not as nourishing."

Tag laughed along, but his expression grew serious when he said, "Did she really say that to you?"

Suddenly, Jay was afraid he'd revealed too much. Although he felt like he could trust Tag, how much did he really know him? Backpedalling, he said, "She means it kindly."

"Yeah, parents usually do." Tag moved to lean against the railing and look out over the river. It was a dark brown on this overcast day and moving slowly. "Every few weeks, my dad'll say something about me 'keeping my options open'. By which he means maybe I should get a proper job. He means it kindly, too. He loves me, and he's worried that I'm not getting my foot on the ladder, you know? That I'm going to regret wasting my time chasing a dream. I get it, but it still feels undermining when you know you're not living up to their expectations, doesn't it?"

Jay didn't know what to say at first, because somehow Tag had arrowed straight to the heart of a pain Jay had never articulated to anyone. Not even his siblings. He swallowed, joining Tag at the railing. "Yeah," he said softly, "that's exactly how it feels."

As Jay leaned his arms on the metal rail, Tag's elbow bumped his and a jolt, bright and electric, shot through him. Tag glanced over, as if he'd felt it too, his honeyed eyes warm and full of understanding—and something else. Jay's heart leapt into action, racing like he was sprinting again.

"Well, I think you're a brilliant actor," Tag said seriously.

"Do you?" Jay couldn't resist teasing. "Not too wooden?"

Tag grimaced. "Do me a favour and forget everything I said that night? I always say stupid shit when I get angry. In fact, forget everything I said before we came to York."

Jay offered a rueful smile. "I'm sure we both said things we regret. I know I did."

"Yeah?" Tag smiled, and Christ, he had a fantastic smile. It lit up the whole day. "Then maybe we could—?"

"Oh my God, it *is* him!"

The loud stage-whisper and accompanying giggles came from a few feet away. Tag looked over—rookie mistake—and so Jay had no choice but to slap on his professional smile and do the same. A group of three teens, two girls and a boy, stood clustered together watching him with wide eyes and flushed faces. One, the gangly boy, wore a *Leeches* hoodie and an expression of confused adolescent adoration. Jay wanted to give the kid a big paternal hug.

"Hey there," he said, raising a hand and lifting his sunglasses. "Having a good day?"

"We are now," the boldest of the girls said, and they all burst into more giggles.

"We love *Leeches*," said the other one. "We're, like, huge fans."

"Yeah? Cool." He glanced at Tag, who was grinning at him. "Want a picture?" Jay asked the kids.

"Ohmygod, yes!" said the bold girl, pulling out her phone.

"Come on then." He beckoned them over, and they grouped together in front of him so they could take a selfie—several selfies.

And then Tag said, "Hey, give me your phone, and I'll take a couple."

Which resulted in a little impromptu photo shoot, with each of the kids getting a separate picture with him.

"Nice hoodie," Jay said when it was the boy's turn, and the kid laughed and blushed, and then grinned when Jay gave him a fist-bump just as Tag snapped the picture.

They were nice kids and thanked him profusely as he and Tag extricated themselves and headed up to the bridge. Jay knew, if they weren't careful, a crowd might gather, so he didn't want to hang around.

"That was fun," Tag said as they ran up the steps. "I bet you made their year."

Jay laughed, but it was a nice thought. It made him appreciate the importance of what he did in *Leeches*—the joy it brought to people, the small difference he made to their lives. There was a value to that beyond what his mother considered the significance of 'the work', and Jay honestly loved that part of the job.

"But you know those pictures are already all over Snapchat and TikTok?" Tag carried on. "Their mates are probably on their way already."

"Yup, probably."

After a pause, Tag said, "I'm still getting you that McMuffin, but maybe we should head back to the flat and get it delivered? No point in causing a scene in McDonald's."

Jay laughed. "You read my mind."

"And we could run some lines after, if you like?" Tag added, almost diffidently. "Make sure we're both okay for tomorrow."

And that, Jay knew, was a kindness; Tag thought Jay was worried about being off-book and was offering to help. Touched, he said, "That would be great. Thanks."

Tag didn't reply, but his smile broadened, and somehow Jay felt its warmth deep in his chest.

Later that afternoon, sprawled on the sofa, Jay listened as Tag spoke the last line of the play. A quote from one of Sassoon's later poems.

"All right then, Sassoon," he said from the floor where he lay, his legs up against the wall—some kind of yoga pose, apparently. "*Since you and I are one, Let us go back. Let us undo what's done.*"

And that was it.

"Word perfect," Tag said, smiling.

"Thank God." Jay dropped his script to the floor in a rustle of papers and checked his watch. Half past six. He looked over at Tag, feet in the air, arms spread out crucifix-style, eyes closed. "Are you working tonight?" he asked.

Twisting his head to look at him, Tag hesitated. "I've got

the night off." He paused then, pulling his legs down and rolling onto his knees. "I was thinking… They're showing *The Burying Party* tonight at this independent cinema in town. Have you seen it? It's about Owen's final year."

Stupidly, Jay's heart began to slug in his chest. "I haven't seen it, no." His voice felt tight and too small.

Tag cleared his throat. "I was thinking of going, if you fancy it? Might be helpful for background."

This wasn't a date, obviously. Even so, Jay's heart was racing, though he tried to play it cool. "You're not afraid it might influence your performance?"

"I don't think so?" Tag considered. "No, I know *my* Owen. I'm interested to see other takes on him, though. I totally get it if you don't want to. Sassoon features too, and you might—"

"No, I'm in," Jay said and tried not to worry about his eagerness to spend even more time with Tag. Christ, he was overthinking this. "When does it start?"

Tag looked pleased. "Eight-thirty. It's not that long."

"I'll make us some dinner, then." Jay stood up, hoping Tag hadn't noticed his stupid overreaction. "Pasta okay?"

"You know," Tag said, "you don't have to keep feeding me…"

"Fine, I'll make pasta for me, and you can sit in the corner with your bread and water."

"Ugh." Tag pushed easily to his feet. He was very limber; Jay had noticed that in rehearsals too. Must be the yoga. "I *am* paying you back for all this."

"I know you are," Jay said, seriously. "In the meantime, I have a packet of penne and some tomato-and-basil sauce in a jar. If you're interested in this gourmet meal?"

"How the other half lives," Tag said, sounding amused.

"It's not all champagne and caviar, you know."

"I hope it's posh sauce in a jar… Like, Harrods or something."

Jay turned to the kitchen. "I don't know where it's from. I asked Carly to get some food in…"

"Oh my God, that's worse!" Tag exclaimed, prodding him in the ribs. "You got your PA to do your shopping?"

Jay laughed, squirming away from Tag's fingers. "Okay, okay, that *is* worse. You're right."

They carried on like that, bickering amiably while Jay got the pasta cooking and Tag tipped a bag of salad into two bowls. After they'd eaten at the little glass table by the window, they headed out. The overcast day had turned into a gloomy evening, the air warm with the promise of approaching rain, and Jay was glad the cinema was only a short twenty-minute walk away.

Slipping in after the house lights had gone down, with a warm box of salty popcorn Tag had insisted on buying, they found their seats while the adverts were playing. It wasn't full—perhaps a dozen other people were scattered across the small auditorium—and nobody paid them any undue attention. Jay settled in happily as the feature began, conscious of Tag in the seat next to him, their elbows almost touching.

The story was as familiar as it was tragic. So much senseless death, so much wasted potential. As he watched the camera linger on Owen's body, prone on the wooded riverbank, he thought of the Sassoon he'd come to know through Bea's script—thought of the grief, the envy, and the love Sassoon had felt for Owen as his own life had continued onward while Owen's was cut desperately short.

When Owen's mother received the news of her son's death just as the victory bells were peeling out on Armistice Day, Jay heard a sniffle from his right and glanced at Tag. Full of life and passion and talent, Tag wasn't dissimilar to Owen, and in that instant, Jay understood something of what it must have been like for Sassoon to continue on without him. To fade and age, to slowly, bit by bit, lose the youth and vitality that Owen, in death, had retained.

Tag turned his head, his eyes bright in the light from the screen. "I always cry at films," he confided in a whisper.

"Me too," Jay whispered back, pressing his shoulder against Tag's in solidarity and feeling Tag press back. Neither of them pulled away until the credits started to roll.

They were quiet on the way home, both lost in their own thoughts. Eventually, as they headed down to walk back along the river, Tag said, "Do you think they were lovers?"

"Sassoon and Owen?" Jay looked at him; Tag's expression was thoughtful, distant. "I don't know. Probably not. What do you think?"

"I think Owen was properly in love with Sassoon. I'm sure of that, even if it was half hero-worship. Owen loved him."

Jay thought about it some more. "If they weren't lovers, I think Sassoon must have regretted it later. When he looked back, I think he recognised in Owen something he'd spend the rest of his life chasing."

"A kindred spirit, you mean?"

"Or a soulmate, perhaps, if that's not too sentimental." They'd stopped by the river's edge, standing side by side, the lights from the other bank gleaming in the dark water. "In our play, Sassoon thinks that he envies Owen's fame and his talent, but I wonder…" He glanced at Tag, at his handsome profile, his crop of black hair stirring in the night breeze, and felt a sudden clarity. "Maybe it isn't really envy he's feeling?"

"What then?"

Jay thought. "Maybe… regret."

Tag considered that; then he nodded thoughtfully. "He regrets what they could have had."

"More than that, I think. He regrets that, together, they could have achieved more than either of them managed alone. Sassoon could have nurtured Owen's career. And Owen's talent—his love, maybe—could have inspired Sassoon to greatness again."

Tag made a soft sound of surprise. "You think Owen was

Sassoon's lost opportunity, his path-not-taken." He turned to Jay, eyes bright in the half-light. "How was it he described Owen's death again?"

"*A chasm in my private existence,*" Jay supplied, surprised to find his voice rasping with empathy for these long-dead men. "*An unhealed wound.*"

After a silence, Tag reached out and took Jay's hand. "That's so sad."

"Yeah." Exhaling softly, Jay threaded his fingers between Tag's. "It is."

Standing there, looking out across the light-bejewelled river, Jay had a stark vision of himself as a regretful old man like Sassoon.

What risks might he wish he'd taken? What paths might he wish he'd walked?

What rules might he wish he'd broken?

Then Tag gently squeezed his hand and let him go. As his hand fell back to his side, Jay's heart tripped and skipped in answer to his silent questions.

This one. This one. This one.

CHAPTER FIFTEEN

TAG

For the next few days, Tag's mind was entirely taken up with three things: the progress they were making on the play, his mounting excitement and anxiety about *Bow Street* airing on Thursday... and how things were developing between himself and Jay.

Given that the first two of these three things had the potential to transform his life professionally, it was insane that the third thing was taking up any of his headspace at all, but the truth was, it was taking up just as much of his attention.

Maybe more, if he was honest.

When he'd first come to York, Tag had known that his history with Jay meant there would be bear traps ahead. After all, they hadn't ever officially made peace over their past bickering—all those months of sniping at one another and using poor Mason's social media likes as proxy trophies in their feud. And then there was the unfading memory of the awards dinner, when Tag had both acknowledged and given into his attraction to Jay. That too remained unaddressed and unresolved.

Yet somehow, he and Jay had slowly bonded, despite their prickly start. Jay, without really trying, just by being himself, had won Tag over. In the rehearsal room, his professional generosity and humility had surprised Tag, and not only in terms of how he interacted with Tag himself. He'd been incredibly patient and kind with Rafe too, going out of his way to give him helpful advice and making sure he got plenty of opportunities to rehearse alongside Jay and Tag. One by one, Tag's prejudices about Jay had been punctured by his humour, his modesty, his thoughtfulness. Tag had come to York determined they would find a way to work together, but he hadn't expected it to be so easy. Hadn't expected to *like* Jay as much as he did.

One thing he had expected, though, was to still be attracted to Jay—and that expectation had certainly been met. The attraction wasn't just there, it was even more intense, amplified now by their constant proximity. Tag felt like he spent most of his time in the riverside apartment trying to ignore or hide an erection.

So yes, Jay was proving to be a major distraction from the other things playing on Tag's mind.

That said, by the time Thursday actually rolled around, it *was* the airing of *Bow Street* that was dominating his thoughts. He was useless in rehearsals all that day, preoccupied and inattentive, his mind constantly wandering. It occurred to him, eventually, that Jay must have told the others about *Bow Street*, because Henry was being more forbearing than usual, and Freddie just kept grinning at him. By early afternoon, Henry had evidently given up on Tag contributing anything useful. For the rest of the day, he concentrated on a few of Jay's solo scenes, while Tag sat off to the side, ostensibly observing.

By the time they got back to the apartment, Tag was jittery with nerves. "I think I'll go for a run. Want to come?"

Jay dropped onto his bed, yawning. "I'm pretty tired. I'll give it a miss today."

"Oh, right. Okay," Tag said, surprised by how disappointed he felt. They went running together most days now. But fine, Tag was perfectly capable of going on his own. It was what he did at home, after all.

Flipping open his large case—which he hadn't got round to unpacking since he'd moved into the apartment—he rummaged around, pulling out his running stuff, and heading for the bathroom to get changed. Even as he did it, a small part of him wondered why he didn't just get changed in front of Jay. He'd never been shy about his body, and in all honesty, it felt a bit prissy to scuttle off like this. But this was what Jay did, and Tag felt like he should follow his lead. And yes, fine, it was probably best to keep a few boundaries in place. Tag still remembered, all too well, that unexpected, and wonderful, and terrible night in Jay's hotel room. He didn't think he'd ever forget what Jay had looked like, lying under him, those stormy eyes glittering with lust, and his mouth swollen from their kisses. His bare, golden skin and the noises he made as Tag stroked and kissed him.

He'd certainly never forget the devastated look in Jay's eyes when Tag had angrily said, *"I've never had to work so bloody hard at a blowjob in my life."*

Now, standing in front of the bathroom mirror, remembering that moment, Tag grimaced, a hot tide of shame threatening to overcome him. God, he wished he could go back and unsay those words.

Weird to think that had all happened months ago. Right now, it felt like yesterday, the memory still so vivid and bright. Other times, it felt like years ago, a distant time before, when Tag had been a different man entirely. Jay too. A very different man from the one Tag had spent these last weeks getting to know.

Christ, what a fuck-up that night had been. What a fuck-up *he* had been.

Exiting the bathroom, he dumped his clothes next to his open case and sat on the edge of the sofa-bed to pull on his trainers.

"Do you want me to get anything for dinner on the way back?" he asked as he knotted his laces.

"Nah," Jay said, without opening his eyes. "There's plenty of stuff in the fridge. See you later."

Grabbing his phone and strapping it to his arm, Tag shoved in his earbuds and headed for the door. "Yeah. Later."

After running one of his favourite routes twice over, Tag was exhausted and sweaty, but the antsy feeling that had been under his skin all day had finally eased. He spent a good few minutes stretching, then used the short walk back to the apartment to cool down his muscles and plan the evening ahead. A shower would be the first order of business, he decided, then dinner, then *Bow Street*. Jay had seemed tired earlier, so maybe he'd let Tag cook for them tonight?

He'd just turned the corner into the development when his phone buzzed with a text. It was from Graham.

Any chance you could pick up a shift at The Bear tonight?

Tag's steps slowed to a halt as he stared down at his screen. He'd wanted to stay in and watch *Bow Street*, but he could do with a few extra hours, and it wouldn't be a late one. These casual shifts would be coming to a complete end soon —once the play opened, his evenings would be spoken for. That thought might not fill him with quite as much panic as it would have just a week ago, thanks to Jay's generosity in taking him in, but the realisation that he'd be missing out on this extra cash still made his stomach hurt. Besides, did he really have to see *Bow Street* the second it came out? He could watch it on catch up any time he liked—it wasn't as if he was going to be with his family for this airing anyway. Hell, he hadn't even asked Jay if he wanted to watch it tonight. Maybe Jay would rather do something else? It was his apartment after all, his TV. Not that he thought Jay would be a dick about it. Tag knew if he asked to watch *Bow Street*, Jay would agree. He was a nice guy, and he'd seemed excited for Tag when Tag had mentioned it. Plus, he'd understand, better than any member of Tag's family ever could, just how much blood, sweat and tears had gone into his relatively brief time on screen.

But would Jay really *want* to watch it?

Suddenly, Tag felt depressed. Shoving his phone back in his pocket, he trudged towards the main door of the apartment building and pressed the bell.

"It's me," he said when the intercom came alive with a burst of static.

"Hey," Jay said, sounding a bit breathless. A second later, the door buzzed.

In the course of the short walk from the atrium to Jay's apartment, Tag made his decision. There was no reason not to take the shift. He pulled his phone back out of his pocket, ready to start typing a quick reply to Graham, but when he stepped inside the apartment, he came to an astonished halt.

The little table was set for two, and squeezed onto its small surface—alongside placemats, glasses, cutlery, a bread-basket, and an ice bucket with a bottle of champagne in it— was one of those ridiculous balloon arrangements, with a weighted base and a riot of helium-filled balloons bopping around on their shiny silver ribbons.

The balloons—and hell, there had to be at least ten of them —were a variety of colours, shapes and sizes, but they all had the same words emblazoned on them: '*Congratulations Tag!*'

Tag's eyes stung, a lump swelling in his throat.

He turned towards the kitchen area, where Jay stood, smiling at him, a wooden spoon in hand. A delicious savoury smell filled the air.

"Surprise," Jay said softly, setting down the spoon.

"It definitely is," Tag said hoarsely, embarrassed to hear the emotional note in his voice. "What's all this for?"

Jay shrugged. "It's not every day your debut show airs on TV. I thought a small celebration was in order."

"Yeah?" God, was Tag going to cry like a baby over this? He felt like he might.

"Yup," Jay said cheerfully. "I'm making dinner—nothing too fancy, just lasagne, but it's my mum's recipe, and it's delicious. Plus I've got some fizz for us to toast your success and some fancy gourmet popcorn for when we're watching the show."

"That's—" Tag broke off to clear his throat. "That's really kind. Thank you."

Jay looked gently amused. "Why don't you grab a shower while I assemble the lasagne and bung it in the oven?"

"Okay." Tag said hoarsely. As Jay turned back to the hob to resume his efforts, Tag crossed the room to his suitcase to yank out clean clothes, then typed out a quick message to Graham—*Sorry mate, can't do tonight*—before putting his phone on to charge and heading to the bathroom for a long, hot shower.

Twenty minutes later, clean and warm and loose-limbed in his favourite ancient joggers and a Planet of the Apes t-shirt, Tag watched as Jay untwisted the metal cage on the champagne bottle and popped the cork with practised ease.

"Nicely done," he said admiringly.

Jay grinned and poured the champagne, handing one glass to Tag before sitting on the sofa beside him. "To you," he said, "and to *Bow Street*. I hope it brings you all the success in the world, Tag, I really do." He touched the rim of his glass to Tag's.

"Thanks," Tag said, and he felt choked up all over again, which was bloody ridiculous. Jesus, was he going to blub? Why Jay's thoughtfulness was making him feel so emotional, he wasn't sure, but it was. Maybe because he'd been feeling low about not being with his family, and because of all the stress of the last few weeks.

"*You and your leaky head*," his mum would say, with her twinkly grin, and the thought made him smile. Tipping back his glass, he took a long swallow of the cold, dry wine, enjoying the bubbles fizzing on his tongue.

"I could get used to this," he said when he lowered the glass. He quirked a smile at Jay and said cheekily, "I suppose you already are."

Jay chuckled. "I won't deny I like a nice glass of champagne." His thigh was grazing Tag's now, partly because the sofa was small and partly because, being a sofa-bed, it sagged a little in the middle, causing both occupants to roll towards the centre. "But my life's not all champagne and oysters, you know."

Tag shifted subtly away. "I know. You also like a McMuffin." Did his voice sound strangled? "And After Eights," he added.

Jay laughed. "True. I fucking love After Eights. Seriously, I can eat a whole box on my own—and I mean the big one."

Tag made a face. "Ugh. All that super-sweet mint fondant. How can you?"

Jay just laughed again and performed a chef's kiss. It was meant to be funny, but Tag's gaze went straight to his mouth, to those beautifully carved lips, and he felt suddenly airless, remembering them pressed to his own.

Tearing his gaze away, he said, "I should give my parents a quick call. Tonight's a big deal for them too."

"Good idea," Jay said easily, rising to his feet. "I'll get dinner sorted while you chat to them."

He ambled over to the kitchen area, moving with that easy grace that Tag had become so used to over these last weeks of rehearsing together, and for a few moments, Tag just enjoyed the simple pleasure of watching him. He was an incredibly hot guy, no question, and that was certainly part of his pleasure, but it wasn't just that. Now every line of Jay's body, every facial expression, every movement he made was imbued with his... *Jay-ness*. With the person Tag had come to know and—

Fuck. What was he thinking? Dragging his gaze away, he yanked his phone out of his pocket and, with shaking hands, called his mum.

She answered immediately. "Tag, is that you?" Her voice was bright with anticipation, her ever-present Irish accent warmly familiar.

"Hi, Mum," he said. "Thought I'd give you a quick ring before the show."

She was a talker, so he settled down to listen to her chat for a while, peppering her monologue with "*hmms*" and "*ahs*" and "*she never dids?*" Once his mum was done talking, he spoke to his dad for a few minutes, and then his sister, and then his mum came back on for a bit to interrogate him about his eating habits and check yet again that he'd sorted out tickets for them to come to the play when they came up to York.

"You know we don't mind buying them, like everyone else," she said for the fortieth time.

"Don't worry about it, Mum," Tag said, torn between amusement and exasperation. "It's all sorted."

After another few minutes of goodbyes—his dad and sister were put back on again for half a minute for that purpose—his mum said her final farewells. "Bye-bye, darlin'. You take care of yourself and make sure you're eating plenty of fruit and veg, all right? I can't wait to watch the show." With a bubbly, "Love you, love you!" she hung up.

The screen informed him that the call had taken forty-nine minutes, and he looked over at Jay guiltily. "Sorry that was so long," he said. "My mum can talk for Ireland—and that's saying something. Have I messed up dinner?"

Jay shook his head. "Not at all. It's perfect timing. The lasagne's had time to rest, which will save us from burning off the roofs of our mouths." He pointed a spatula at the table. "Go and sit down and I'll bring it over."

Tag was topping up their glasses with more fizz when Jay set down their plates. The lasagne looked and smelled amazing, and it tasted amazing too, as did the crusty bread and the green salad and the dry, bubbly wine. It was, all of it, just... lovely. And Jay was lovely too, making Tag laugh and making his heart feel warm and full. Making this very ordinary day into a special occasion that Tag knew he would always remember.

As he swallowed the last bit of champagne in his glass, that thought—that this would one day be a distant memory— sent a stab of sadness through him. Which was stupid. Of course this would be a distant memory one day. Everything would, *one* day. And that was especially the case for actors, who often formed intense, short-term bonds with their colleagues that did not—could not—last. Tag was going to have to build up a thicker skin for dealing with this kind of thing if he was going to make a success of his career.

Thrusting the melancholy thought aside, he smiled at Jay. "Thank you for dinner. It was delicious. I'll clear up, though."

"You will *not*," Jay said severely, steering a protesting Tag over to the sofa and pushing him down. He quickly cleared the table and stacked the dirty dishes next to the sink.

"I'll sort them tomorrow," he said with a wave of his hand. "I can't be arsed tonight."

"I'll do them," Tag insisted.

"Nope," Jay said, pointing at him. "This is your special night, and you will not touch those dishes either tonight or tomorrow. No arguments!"

Laughing, Tag subsided, lifting his hands in a gesture of surrender. "Okay, okay."

"What do you want to drink now?" Jay asked. "I've got red or white."

"*More* wine?" Tag asked, raising a brow. "Henry would not approve." Henry had views on drinking the night before rehearsals.

Jay said drily, "*Bow Street* starts in ten minutes, and if you're anything like me, you're going to need a drink when you watch yourself on screen."

"Good point," Tag said feelingly. "Red then."

Jay set the wine down on the little coffee table in front of the sofa, along with a bowl of popcorn, which Tag was way too full to eat. Before he sat down, Jay switched off the main light, leaving only one small light on, next to his bed. A small glowing point in the now-dark apartment.

It felt like they were at the cinema, and as Jay sank onto the sofa beside him, Tag felt the oddest surge of excited antici-pation. Alarmed, he shifted back, leaning into his own corner of the sofa, trying to move his centre of gravity away from Jay. Which was ridiculous, given that Jay seemed entirely oblivious, his attention focused on switching on the TV and finding *Bow Street*.

"I've been looking forward to watching this," he said, without moving his eyes from the screen. "And not just because of you. It's a great premise, and of course Derek Brookes is brilliant in everything."

Derek, a well-known television actor, played Arthur Thorne, one of the main characters in *Bow Street*. Tag's own key scene near the end of the pilot was opposite Derek and had been the single most exciting moment in Tag's career so far—well, until he'd been cast in *Let Us Go Back*. It didn't get much better than playing opposite Skye bloody Jäger in a fourteen-night stage run. Not that Tag had felt that way when he'd first learned that his co-star would be Jay... Tag gave a strangled laugh as he remembered his dismayed reaction, and Jay turned towards him, his face faintly lit by the ghostly blue light reflected from the TV. He raised an eyebrow in query, but Tag just shook his head and took a gulp of his wine.

The show was starting now, and Tag's stomach was a tangle of nerves. Which struck him as absurd—it wasn't like he was about to go on stage, but still, his heart was thudding as the pre-titles prologue scene began. This first scene was set twenty years earlier from the point of view of Mary, who viewers would later learn was Bishop's—Tag's character's— mother. The scene began in a vibrant, busy tavern, the camera roving over various groups of men. Mary wove her way around the pub, chatting and flirting in a brassy way. After a while, she slipped out into the dark, grimy night, hurrying through a web of alleys, before arriving at the docks. A man in a long coat stood waiting, leaning against a post, his hat pulled down low over his face.

"Where is he?" the man said, his voice deep and gravelly. His face remained in shadow.

"In the White Hare, sitting near the bar wiv two other coves. He's got a fancy green-and-yellow striped waistcoat on."

"Good girl," the man said. He levered himself away from the post and stepped right up to her. For a long moment, their faces were very close, the man's still obscured as they stared at one another. Then he pressed a glittering coin into her hand. "Best get yourself home now, Mary."

As he walked unhurriedly away, Mary watched him go, something angry, and longing, in her expression. The last image of her slowly faded, the screen darkening as the title, *Bow Street*, shimmered to the surface in stark letters, and the ominous, rolling music began.

CHAPTER SIXTEEN

Jay paused the screen on the final credits, white words on black.

Jude 'Bishop' Morton—Tag O'Rourke.

Tag still sat as he had throughout his fantastic final scene, knees up to his chest, arms wrapped around them. In the glow of the television, his eyes were wide and luminous, his face cast in shadow and light.

"Bravo," Jay said into the soft silence. "As my mother would say, you were wonderful, darling."

That broke the spell. Tag gave a relieved laugh and began to uncoil, tension seeping out of him as he moved. "Yeah?" The look he gave Jay was familiar: pleased, uncertain, hopeful. Which was exactly how Jay always felt after watching his own performances.

"Absolutely," Jay said. "You were nuanced and subtle. Fantastic characterisation. And that final confrontation...? There was so much emotional truth in your last few lines. I'm afraid you rather stole the scene." At Tag's look of dismay, he added, "In a good way! You were compelling. I couldn't take my eyes off you."

Afraid that might have betrayed more than he'd intended, Jay quickly asked, "So come on, tell me what the deal is. Bishop's got some ulterior motive, hasn't he, for betraying his gang? It's not just the money. I could see it in your eyes."

Tag looked pleased by that, though he seemed to be trying to suppress his smile, biting at the corner of his mouth. "Actually, I don't know his motivation for certain," he said. "I mean, in my head he's got a reason—I made up this little backstory about his father—but I don't think the writers intended it to be more than just the money. Pete Graves, the director, picked up on what I was doing, though, and liked it, so..." He trailed off, seeming not to know what the consequence of Pete liking it might be. Or maybe just afraid to say it aloud. To jinx it.

"I bet he did," Jay said. "I know Pete, and I bet he *loved* it."

"Yeah." Tag grinned, boyishly proud of himself, and Jay's belly seized with a sudden spike of longing. God, he shouldn't have had so much bloody wine tonight; look what had happened last time they got drunk together…

Oblivious to Jay's consternation, Tag carried on talking, his tone almost shy as he confided, "Pete did say he might look into expanding Bishop's role if *Bow Street* gets picked up for a full season."

"I don't think there's any doubt it'll be picked up," Jay said, which was a half-truth. *He* thought the show was excellent, but the viewing public—not to mention studio executives—were fickle beasts, and there were never any guarantees.

"Touch wood," Tag said, tapping the coffee table in front of them.

"Touch wood," Jay echoed, though he tapped his own temple, making Tag laugh and shake his head.

"Funnily enough," Tag went on, settling back into his

corner of the sofa, "it was that scene that got me the audition for *Let Us Go Back*. Pete's the one who put me in touch with Bea."

"Is that so?" Jay smiled. "Then we both owe him a thank you." More seriously, he added, "I honestly can't imagine anyone else playing Owen."

Tag's face softened, his expressive eyes gleaming in the light of the TV. "Yeah? Well, I can't imagine anyone else playing Sassoon."

Jay's smile froze. Although rehearsals had been going well, now that they were getting closer to opening night, he kept second-guessing himself, questioning his connection with the character. Panicking at the thought of the audience, of the reviews. He kept that to himself, though, lifting his glass again in a brief toast. "Then I hope I'll do you justice."

"Of course you will," Tag said, as Jay threw back the last of his wine. "You've already helped me so much." His voice dropped, growing husky. "With everything."

Touched, Jay turned his head back towards Tag, intending to respond with a *Thank you*, or maybe *You've helped me too*. Afterwards, he couldn't remember precisely, because at the very moment he turned, Tag leaned forward to deliver a kiss, one that was plainly intended for Jay's cheek, but that instead landed clumsily on his mouth.

They both froze, eyes open and staring at one another. And in the stunned, timeless moments that followed, Jay became insanely aware of Tag's body leaning against his own: its tense strength, the bunched muscles in the arm he'd braced against the back of the sofa, the kindling look in his eyes. The softness of his lips. "Sorry," Tag murmured at last. But he didn't move back.

And he didn't sound sorry.

Jay's heart thundered, his mind a riot of conflicting feelings: panic, hope, pleasure, fear.

Desire.

"It's okay," he whispered, which wasn't much of an answer, but it seemed to answer something for Tag, because his lips tugged into a small smile.

"Yeah?"

Then, slowly, deliberately, he brushed his mouth against Jay's again, eyes open, searching Jay's gaze. Jay took in a shaky breath, but he didn't pull away, and when Tag did it again, his lips a little firmer this time, Jay returned the faint pressure, closing his eyes on a sigh.

Oh God, this was a Bad Idea.

That didn't stop him parting his lips, though, and allowing Tag to deepen the kiss. It didn't stop him kissing Tag back. Hell, nothing could stop him now, because he *wanted* this. He'd wanted it for weeks. Wanted *Tag*.

Jay shifted, letting Tag muscle closer, his taut, gorgeous body bearing Jay back into the soft cushions of the sofa.

Sliding his hands beneath Tag's t-shirt, Jay caressed his smooth, warm skin. His hands moved upwards, pushing Tag's t-shirt up, baring his chest to Jay's hungry gaze. Leaning up on one hand, Tag reached behind his shoulder, grasping the back of his t-shirt and hauled it off over his head. He tossed it aside, then lowered himself back down, grinning at Jay, his dark hair sexily ruffled. And then they were kissing again, and Jay couldn't get enough of him, couldn't kiss him deep enough, couldn't hold him tight enough. Could hardly breathe for wanting him.

They arched and ground against one another as they kissed, wrestling and tussling on a sofa that was too small for two grown men. Jay heard the coffee table scrape across the floor, the empty wine bottle hit the rug and start to roll, but he didn't care. As messy and ungainly as this was, it felt fucking fantastic. "Fuck," Tag gasped against his mouth eventually, sounding as shaky and breathless as Jay felt. "Why did you have to be so bloody gorgeous?"

Jay laughed unsteadily. "I could say the same to you."

Tag pulled back enough that they could see each other properly. His hair was wild, eyes dark with desire. "I don't want to fuck things up," he said desperately. "Will this fuck things up?"

He meant the play.

Yes, Jay should say. *Yes, it'll be a bloody disaster.* Who knew better than him that fucking your co-star was an incredibly awful idea?

But right now, he couldn't think rationally. He wanted Tag so much his body physically ached for him. And it wasn't just his body; something deeper and far more terrifying clamoured for this connection.

And yet he felt compelled to honesty.

"It's a risk," he admitted through numb lips. "But... it doesn't have to be serious. I mean, it could just be some fun, right?"

"Right." Tag didn't sound too sure. After studying him for hours in rehearsal, his face was very familiar to Jay, and the expression he wore now, brows pinched in unhappy concern, made Jay's chest ache, and his confidence sink.

"I know last time wasn't exactly fun..." Jay trailed off, his heart shrinking from the memory of that night. A memory fresh enough to still be viscerally painful. He swallowed against the lump that had appeared in his throat. "Actually," he said, trying to sit up without pushing Tag away, "maybe we should—"

"Jay, wait." Tag placed a firm but gentle hand on his chest to keep him in place. "About last time. I've been wanting to apologise for ages..." He gave an embarrassed laugh. "It's not exactly come up in conversation, but... What I said that night? About, you know, having to work hard or whatever?"

"It's fine," Jay said, face burning. "I know I'm not—"

"Jay, don't. *Please.*" Tag looked agonised. "It would've been a shitty thing to say even if it was true, but it *wasn't* true. It was the opposite of true, and I'm sorry. I had a fucking *fantastic* time with you. I was just—" He blew out a breath, pressing his lips together in that expression he wore when he was dissatisfied with his own performance. "I don't even know. I didn't know you then, and I thought I sort of hated you—which was really fucking immature." His sheepish gaze met Jay's. "It was just, well, at the start of the evening, you were my archenemy."

Jay couldn't help but smile at that. "Your archenemy?"

Tag gave a lopsided grin. "My over-privileged nemesis."

"Ah."

More seriously, more softly, Tag said, "I know you better now. I like you better." He wet his lips, eyes darkening as he reached out and stroked Jay's arm, making him shiver. "And yeah, I do want to... have fun with you. As much fun as possible if I'm honest. After all, we're only going to be in York for three more weeks."

Jay's mouth dried, his skin prickling beneath Tag's slow caress. And then, amazingly, his cock stirred too, just when he'd thought the mood was well and truly gone. Breathlessly, he said, "Right. It doesn't have to be a big deal. We can just... fool around."

Tag's gaze was careful. "And no one has to know, do they?"

Jay blinked, uncomfortably reminded of Seb's insistence on secrecy. "You'd want to keep this quiet?"

Tag made a face. "Do you mind? You know how people are. I don't want anyone saying I earned the Owen role on my back. I'd never be taken seriously again."

Jay nodded, relaxing. "Yeah," he breathed. "I get it." And he did, because Tag was right—that's exactly what people would say. Hadn't Jay thought something similar, back when he'd first met Tag? Besides, Henry had strong views about romantic entanglements between cast members. So, really, it was good that Tag had raised it, good that they were on the same page. It made sense to set the ground rules. A quick fling. Nothing serious. And kept private, just between the two of them.

Tag lowered himself back down, covering Jay's body with his own. "So, if we're in agreement," he murmured, "shall we get back to where we left off?"

Oh fuck. "Tag…"

"I want to make you feel good," Tag murmured, leaning down and brushing his lips over Jay's mouth again. "Do you trust me?"

And that was the question, wasn't it? Jay's heart began an anxious thump in counterpoint to his racing desire. *Did* he trust Tag?

With some surprise, Jay realised that, yes, he did—at least, he trusted him in rehearsal. He trusted Tag's performance, his talent. Trusted him as a generous and creative performance partner who wanted their play to succeed as much as Jay did.

But did he trust him with this, too? Last time he got involved with a co-star…

No, *fuck* that! Tag wasn't Sebastian Talbot. He couldn't be more different from Seb.

Smothering his misgivings, Jay plastered on a smile that was neither wholly genuine nor wholly fake, his heart hammering now with nervy excitement. "Okay, but this time, it's your turn."

Tag's eyebrows shot up. "For what?"

Reaching forward, Jay tugged on the drawstring of Tag's joggers with shaking fingers. The soft fabric was doing a nice job of outlining his sizeable erection. "Come here and find out," he suggested hoarsely.

That sounded like a line Skye Jäger might have used. It probably was; he had a tendency to fall back on learned lines with his hook-ups. It was all part of the performance, the familiar, comfortable mask. It was part of how he took control, how he managed his nerves.

Maybe that was why it felt so wrong now. So *off.* Because

he didn't *want* to wear a mask with Tag, but he wasn't sure how to do this any other way.

"Hey," Tag said softly, drawing Jay's attention back to the moment, to him. His expression was curious, and Jay wondered how transparent he was. "Did I lose you there for a sec?"

"Sorry," Jay muttered, mortified. *Focus, for God's sake.*

"It's okay," Tag said gently. "And for what it's worth, the way I see it, sex isn't about taking turns or returning favours." He grinned. "I'm not keeping score." Then he leaned down and pressed his lips to Jay's.

It was a deep, slow kiss that knocked all thought out of Jay's head for several long, blissful moments and brought his distracted cock back to pulsing, achingly hard life.

When Tag pulled back, his smile was satisfied. He levered himself up and clambered off the couch, almost tripping over the discarded wine bottle. Laughing, he caught his balance. He made quite a sight with his gorgeous bare torso, lewdly bulging joggers, and with his hair all sexily ruffled. Utterly fuckable. Helplessly, Jay's hand went to his own aching prick, still trapped in his jeans, and then, embarrassed, he pulled it away.

Tag's smile only deepened. He held out his hand. "Come on," he said. "Let's go to bed before we break this fucking sofa."

Laughing, Jay took his hand and allowed himself to be pulled to his feet and towed to the bed. When they got there, Tag gripped the waistband of his joggers and, in one flamboyant move, shoved them down and kicked them off, along with his briefs. And then he simply stood there in all his naked, uninhibited glory, arms outstretched and smiling his phenomenal smile. "Ta-da!"

Playing the audience for laughs, and still sexy as hell.

Jay was suddenly certain he'd never wanted anyone, or

anything, in his life more than he wanted Tag in that moment. The raw force of his desire left him breathless.

Maybe Tag saw that—Jay knew, now, how intuitive he was—because his amused grin gentled into something more serious, and he stepped forward, reaching for Jay. Kissing him sweetly on the mouth as he began to undress him, his nimble fingers working Jay's jeans open, then closing around his painfully hard prick, startling a needy sound from Jay's throat. Christ, had he ever been this turned on before?

"Mmm," Tag murmured, nuzzling Jay's neck, "you're so hard. Is that all for me?"

"Fuck, yes," Jay gasped thrusting with embarrassing eagerness into Tag's hand. "All for you."

Tag gave a little breathless sound of pleasure, which only made Jay's cock stiffer still. "Let's get these off," Tag said, tugging at Jay's jeans. "I want to see you."

After a few moments of ungainly struggle—fuck, why was he even wearing socks?—Jay had kicked away his tangled clothes. Tag's appreciative gaze felt warm as it roved across his body, like sunlight against his skin, something to bask in, something to relish.

A roguish smile tilted the corner of Tag's mouth. "Yeah," he said, prowling closer, "look at you. Fucking breathtaking."

Tag's hand landed warm on Jay's hip, sliding up over his ribs to his back, then running down his spine and stroking his backside, little golden shocks rippling across Jay's skin in the wake of his touch. Then Tag leaned in, pressing against Jay, chest to chest, thigh to thigh, prick to eager prick.

Sliding his arms around Tag, navigating the beautiful contours of his body, Jay couldn't help but thrust his hips forward with embarrassing neediness as their lips met again.

"Jesus," Tag gasped after a while, pulling back and grinning, "I'm going to make you come so fucking hard tonight." He tumbled them both onto the bed, still kissing, and they began rutting together in a happy frenzy, led only by what felt good, what felt right. It felt fucking incredible to just let go like that, to simply act on instinct. Jay had rarely—make that never—felt so abandoned, so liberated.

He began to kiss his way down Tag's gorgeous body—all ivory skin and black hair, neatly groomed around his straining prick and tight balls. His cock was a nice size, in proportion with his trim, muscular body.

Jay kissed the warm softness of Tag's belly, his jutting hipbone, and listened with a racing pulse to the soft sounds of frustrated pleasure Tag made as his hips thrust restlessly forward. Jay's cock throbbed, and his mouth watered, and yet he felt strangely… uncertain.

He glanced up the lean landscape of Tag's body and found Tag's gaze fixed on him in return. One arm was bent, cushioning his head, and his free hand lifted to brush Jay's hair.

Tag gave another of those quizzical smiles. "You don't have to do that, Jay. Like I said, I'm not keeping score."

"It's not that," Jay whispered. "I want to."

"Okay. What is it?" Tag stroked through his hair again, and Jay wanted to lean into his warm hand.

What *was* it? Jay wasn't sure he could say himself. The truth was, the confident mask that had served him well for years of casual hook-ups didn't *fit* anymore. At least not with Tag. Tag had seen through it right away, that very first night. He knew Jay wasn't the sexually assured guy he pretended to be.

Tag was going to see right through *him*.

"I don't want to disappoint you," he said thickly.

Tag cupped his jaw with one hand, his expression unusually grave. "Someone's done a real number on you, haven't they?"

Jay blinked at him. "What?"

Tag shook his head and smiled, kind and teasing at once, his eyes warm as he gazed at Jay. "You could never disappoint me. Besides, I'm so turned on right now you could probably make me come with one of your trademark smouldering glares."

Jay frowned, confused, and Tag grinned. "Yeah, that's the one." He flopped back on the bed, arms spread wide. "So come on, Julius, you sexy beast, let me have it!"

Jay couldn't help the laugh that bubbled up from his chest, helpless and irresistible. God, but it really was impossible to worry too much when Tag was just... so much *fun*. So in the moment, so open to the experience.

Still smiling, Jay settled in between Tag's spread thighs and nuzzled into his groin, loving the soft, musky scent and the weight of Tag's hand coming to rest lightly on his head, neither guiding nor demanding, just present. He settled his attention on Tag's prick, taking in its flushed head and silken length, curling his hand loosely around the shaft, feeling its heft, delighting in Tag's groan of pleasure.

He kissed Tag there, then took the head of his prick into his mouth. *Tag's* prick. That was a turn-on in itself, the thought that this was *Tag*, that he was giving Tag this pleasure.

"Fuck yeah," Tag breathed, his fingers flexing in Jay's hair. "That's it, that's good. You're so good, Jay..."

He kept that up, a constant stream of approval as Jay sucked him deep, backed off to nuzzle his shaft and balls, then took him into his throat again. It was wet, and messy, and disorganised—nowhere near as polished as his usual performance, but it felt so much better. Incredible. Exciting. So exciting that his own prick was demanding attention, and he found himself thrusting helplessly against Tag's leg, desperate to ease his own tension as Tag squirmed and gasped and babbled praise.

Time stopped. Or perhaps the world stopped beyond the little bubble of space between them. Jay wanted to stay there forever, suspended on the cusp with Tag's hand clenched in his hair as he kissed and worshipped Tag's body.

Eventually, though, Tag's hand tightened, tugging. "Come up here," he rasped, "or I'm going to come, and I don't want to yet."

Jay looked up at him, his lips feeling swollen and spit-slick.

"Fuck," Tag said in a low growl of a voice, "I want to kiss you. Come here."

And so Jay went—slowly, taking his time to work his way back up Tag's body, making him laughingly protest until Jay was lying on top of him, elbows braced on either side, and he could lean down and take Tag's glorious mouth.

Their kiss was deep and debauched, tongues tangling, hands in each other's hair, bodies grinding together in joyful abandon. Tag lifted his legs, wrapping them around Jay's waist, bringing their pricks closer together as they writhed and gasped their way towards the edge.

Oh, God, he was close. So close.

But not close enough.

Shit. Jay felt the familiar flush of panic, the fear that it wouldn't happen, that his climax would slide away, out of reach. That he'd fail to perform. Then came the realisation that he'd lost his concentration and, with that, the easy rhythm between them. Now Tag was slowing his movements too.

Fuck. *Fuck!*

"Hey," Tag said, hands running up and down Jay's back. "Shall we try something different?"

When Jay pulled back enough to see him, Tag wasn't frowning or looking frustrated. His honey-gold eyes were as warm as ever, darkened by huge black pupils, his pale face flushed pink, his lips the colour of crushed raspberry. Christ, he was gorgeous. Absolutely bloody gorgeous.

"Do you have lube?" Tag asked.

Jay blinked, his panic returning with a jolt. Did Tag want to fuck? Shit, of course he did. He probably didn't think it was proper sex without penetration. Okay, well, Jay could do that—he was pretty worked up; he'd probably be fine with only a little more prep. Or he could go into the bathroom and prep himself—

"I've got some in my washbag," Tag went on, "but if you've got any closer to hand?"

As it happened, he did, in a drawer in his nightstand. For solo use, usually. He reached for it, considering condoms. He didn't have any, hadn't considered hooking up while he was here, but probably Tag—

"Ooh, this looks nice," Tag said, taking the lube from him. "Aloe vera."

"Do you have a condom?" Jay blurted. "Because I don't, actually."

Tag looked at him oddly. "Do you want to fuck?"

Jay's mind went blank; he couldn't fumble a response. He knew he should say yes—that he should *want* to say yes—but somehow he couldn't find the words.

And then, before he could say anything at all, Tag added, "Because I was thinking of something different. Come here."

He pulled Jay closer, organising them both so that they were spooning—Tag behind, his prick nestled against Jay's arse, and one arm draped over his hip, stroking Jay's slightly deflated cock with lube-slick fingers. It was…nice. Sort of relaxing, which wasn't something Jay usually associated with sex.

Tag's breath was warm against the back of Jay's neck as he said, "You have a great arse, you know? And a fucking lovely dick."

Jay couldn't help smiling. "You do say the sweetest things."

After a moment, Tag laughed, a warm rush of breath against Jay's ear. "You're also very charming," he said, kissing Jay's shoulder. "Irritatingly charismatic. Thoughtful. Generous…"

He punctuated each word with a kiss, pushing up on one arm to nibble at Jay's ear, which made his breaths shorten alarmingly. Who the hell knew there was a direct link from his ear to his prick? But suddenly, he was as stiff as stone in Tag's confident grip.

"Mmm," Tag mused, nuzzling his ear again, "you like that."

"Fuck," Jay murmured, striving to squirm away but held in place by Tag's strong arm around his waist, the swirling lines of his tattoos vivid in the room's half-light.

Tag was relentless, nibbling and nuzzling while his hand stroked Jay's prick in a steady rhythm that meant business. At the same time, his hips were thrusting forward, driving his prick against Jay's backside, the lube thick and slick between them. And then he changed angle, and Tag's prick slipped between Jay's thighs, nudging the back of his balls with each stroke. Jay gave a startled, strangled sound, but got the idea immediately, tightening his thighs as Tag pushed between them, his heavy cock sliding across sensitive skin with each urgent thrust.

Everything started gathering speed and momentum, and Jay could do nothing but let it happen. Tag was in control; Tag was taking care of everything.

Another feeling began to rise alongside Jay's building physical pleasure, some undiscovered need opening as if to the first rays of the sun. He could feel it in his chest, in his throat. In his stinging eyes.

"Tag…" Jay half choked his name as his body tensed, a white heat gathering in his thighs, his belly, running the length of his spine. Close, so close now.

Tag's hand on his prick sped up, his voice thick as he rasped, "That's it, let go. Let me see you come."

On command, everything detonated.

With a shout, Jay arched and shuddered in Tag's arms, his climax roaring through him with blinding brilliance, and with it a bursting joy so absolute it was impossible to contain. It was everywhere, drenching him as he felt Tag stiffen and thrust one last time, his own cry hoarse as warm, sticky heat erupted between Jay's thighs, against his balls, and Tag sagged against his back, his hand still cradling Jay's prick, his chest heaving.

"Jesus," Tag gasped after a long, breathless moment, and then he started to laugh softly. "Fucking hell."

He kissed Jay's ear again, sending aftershocks of pleasure shivering through him, then rolled away onto his back. Jay followed suit, and they lay there, side by side, sprawled diagonally across the bed, catching their breath.

Jay was a sticky mess, breathing hard, his heart thundering, but that joy… It hadn't left him. Far from it, he felt it saturating every part of him. He wanted to laugh. He thought he might cry. Maybe he was losing his mind.

"I think you may have literally fucked my brains out," he told Tag. His words sounded wobbly, and he didn't even care.

"Ditto," Tag agreed, and he didn't sound all that steady either. In fact, he gave a little shell-shocked laugh. "Fucking *hell*, Jay, that was…"

"Yeah…"

Neither of them said anything more. After a while, Jay went to clean up in the bathroom and brush his teeth. Tag went after him, and while he was in there, Jay turned off the TV and straightened up the bedcovers.

He couldn't forget what had happened last time they'd done this, and he was braced for anything when Tag reemerged from the bathroom in a clean pair of boxers. Neither spoke as their eyes met. Tag glanced towards the sofa, not yet converted into his bed, and then back to Jay.

And somehow, despite his terror, Jay managed to smile and lift the bedcovers in invitation. To his enormous relief, Tag's brilliant grin broke out right away, and he padded across the room and back into Jay's arms.

Thank God.

They kissed lightly as they settled down together in the big bed, hands exploring each other's bodies with less urgency now. It felt good to hold Tag like this, warm and sated and comfortable.

"That was amazing," Tag said after a while, snuggling closer so that his head rested on Jay's shoulder.

"It was." Jay kissed his head. "It really was."

"*You* were amazing," Tag went on, stroking Jay's stomach. "You're so…responsive. I love it."

Nobody had ever called him *that* before, and Jay didn't quite know what to make of the compliment. He was smiling, even so, trailing his fingers over Tag's shoulder, tracing the whorls of one of his tattoos. "What do they mean?" he asked, keen to divert the conversation away from the awkward subject of his performance. "Or are they just decorative?"

He felt Tag smile against his shoulder. "They mean different things," he said. "That one?" Lifting his head, he peered at the black lines—letters?—that Jay was tracing. "That's my first. It's meant to say 'Be Yourself' but it was a crappy tattooist. I got it done when I was a kid, after I landed my very first professional role." He gave a wry laugh, laying back down against Jay's chest. "Mum did her nut."

"Your first role," Jay said, smiling. "What was that?"

"Young Ebenezer Scrooge. It was at our local theatre. They were putting on a Christmas production. Quite a big thing, you know? Professional, but they always cast the kids' roles locally. Anyway, my drama teacher told me to go along to the auditions, so Mum took me. And all the other kids…" He broke off, looking up at Jay with a rueful expression. "They were all from drama schools, all really posh. They all knew each other, too. I was the only one there from a normal school, definitely the only one with a proper London accent, and I could hear them… sniggering. I was meant to hear, of course. I almost left, to be honest, but Mum wouldn't let me. *Be yourself,* she said. *Show them what's what.* And so I did. And I went and got the bloody part, and all." He grinned, although Jay could see more behind that smile—could see the lingering humiliation and anger at how those kids had treated him. "Anyway, being a dumb fourteen-year-old, I decided to ink my mum's profound advice on my arm at a dodgy tattoo parlour that didn't check IDs. I got the next one to try and make the first one look better, and then I just kind of got hooked."

Jay ran a hand over Tag's arm, tracing the badly formed words, almost hidden now by the elegant swirling pattern that surrounded them. The thing that struck him about that story was what Tag had said about his accent. Because Tag was brilliant with accents—the subtle Shropshire burr he gave Owen was perfect—and if he'd chosen to, he could probably have sounded exactly like those snobby kids who'd tried to knock him down. Exactly like their adult counterparts who almost certainly still did the same. Jay had wondered before why Tag didn't make his life easier by softening his natural Estuary twang—and now he knew.

"Theatre kids can be total shits," he said eventually, his voice rough with feeling, "but I'm glad the casting director saw your talent. And I'm glad you're still following your mum's advice. I like who you are, and I know you're going to get all the success you deserve."

Sounding sleepy, Tag said, "Yeah? Well, I hope so. If it doesn't come soon, I'm going to have to go with plan B— getting a real job. At least it'll make my dad happy. "

It would also mean Tag giving up on his dreams.

The idea of Tag being forced to do that when he had so much talent and potential made Jay feel an unfamiliar hot fury. Deep in his gut, maybe for the first time, he felt how very wrong it was that Tag's success should be determined more by his family's ability to support him than by his own talent, drive, and hard work.

"It'll come," Jay said determinedly, although he wasn't sure who he was trying to convince. "You're a very talented actor, Tag, and—and I'll do everything I can to help people see that."

"You're already helping." Tag lifted his head, meeting Jay's eyes. "Agreeing to work with me despite our history. Putting so much of yourself into *Let Us Go Back*." With a sleepy smile, he added, "The way I see it, appearing on stage with you is my big break. It's up to me to make the most of it. Loads of actors never get a chance like this."

Jay's heart lurched uneasily. "You know, *Bow Street* is probably the bigger opportunity…"

"Are you joking? No way. *Let Us Go Back* is a way bigger deal. Bea says they've got some big-name theatre critics coming up from London. "

"Really?" Jay hoped he didn't sound as panicked as he felt. London critics? Please, God, not Austin Coburn.

"Yeah, thanks to Henry directing," Tag said. "And when it comes out that you're in it? Bea reckons there's going to be a media frenzy."

That was what Giles Cox thought too. It was why he'd spent most of their evening in the Bear trying to persuade Jay to agree to a press release about his involvement before opening night. And it was why Jay was desperate that nobody should find out until he'd walked out on stage that first night and proven that he could actually get through a performance.

Tag settled his head back down, heavy and relaxed on Jay's shoulder. "I just hope I don't fuck it up."

"You won't fuck it up," Jay said faintly. "You're going to be incredible."

As for himself… Christ, it was bad enough that he'd let his mother railroad him into this role, but it hadn't occurred to him until now that, if he screwed up again, he'd be risking more than his own embarrassment. He'd be risking Tag's future.

The prospect of letting Tag down so badly made it difficult to breathe all of a sudden.

Why the *hell* had he agreed to do this stupid bloody play? He should have lived with his mother's disappointment and let the part go to another actor, a *better* actor. Someone who didn't have a panic attack at the thought of a live fucking audience.

It was too late for that now, though. Opening night was barrelling down the tracks, and Jay, like a cartoon heroine, was tied firmly to the bloody sleepers.

There was no escape.

Which meant that, one way or another, Jay had to find a way to tame his crippling stage fright before he ruined Tag's chance of achieving the success he needed so badly.

CHAPTER SEVENTEEN

Tag

The morning after *Bow Street* aired, Tag woke feeling warm and content. Then he rolled over and saw Jay's dark, rumpled head on the neighbouring pillow, and the events of the night before came flooding back to him in a headlong rush. He braced himself for awkwardness, but when, moments later, Jay stirred and turned over... he smiled. And that made Tag smile back. He had no idea quite *how* goofy his smile was, but he knew it must be goofy, because it was so wide his cheeks actually hurt. But he couldn't put the smile away, or even make it smaller. And maybe that was a good thing, because Jay kept smiling too, in fact, his smile widened, and when Tag moved towards him, he let Tag kiss him.

Kissing Jay in the morning light, completely sober, was just as amazing as kissing him the night before had been. Maybe even more amazing because it felt so *easy*. Jay's body relaxed beneath Tag's, and he wrapped his arms around him, returning the kiss. And when, a few minutes later, Tag took both of their cocks in hand and began to lazily stroke, Jay arched up into Tag's grip, moaning with pleasure, till Tag brought them to a satisfyingly mutual orgasm.

And that was how it went for the next whole week, at least when they were alone in the apartment. At night they slept in Jay's bed, and in the morning, they woke up together. And those nights and mornings were fucking perfect, even when Tag was easing under the covers in the early hours after working a late shift.

They'd agreed to keep what was happening between them secret. Tag didn't want to get a reputation as someone who slept his way to success, but that wasn't the only reason to stay quiet. Henry discouraged romantic entanglements between cast members because they could throw off delicate company dynamics. That wasn't a risk worth taking when they were so close to opening. So, at rehearsal, in front of the others, they acted like nothing more than friends.

It made things a bit weird between them sometimes, though. They didn't just flip back to intimacy as soon as they got back to the apartment after rehearsal. Tag felt like he had to coax Jay back to him each evening.

It helped that Tag was a tactile guy, not only with his romantic partners, but with everyone. He would hug his friends, kiss their cheeks, squeeze their shoulders. Now he lavished all that easy, warm affection on Jay, and Jay responded, like a thirsty plant that had finally been watered. It wouldn't happen right away, but once they'd been home a while, he would slowly *unfurl*, relaxing into Tag's touch, letting Tag tangle their limbs together and shower him with affection. It was weirdly gratifying. Like winning over a standoffish cat.

And then there was the sex. The sex was... fucking amazing actually, though not in an easy-breezy way. Tag had realised by now that Jay had some issues with sex. They hadn't discussed what those issues were, not yet, but it was pretty obvious to Tag that someone in his past had hurt him.

Damaged his confidence. Jay seemed to think he wasn't very good in bed, which Tag found incomprehensible. But Jay clearly believed it. There were a lot of little self-deprecating remarks to that effect, and sometimes—not always but sometimes—he'd get visibly anxious, pulse racing, breath coming quick and shallow, erection wilting. Strangely, it often happened just when he appeared to be most turned on, as though some trap in his mind had been sprung.

At first, Jay was mortified every time it happened. He seemed to assume Tag would find it pathetic, or maybe funny, but when Tag kept reacting with the same calm, easy-going patience, he gradually began to relax. He was still wary and embarrassed when it happened, but Tag thought he was beginning to trust him, to believe the soothing words Tag would say to reassure him. And once the panic passed, it wasn't difficult to build his arousal back up. Not to mention that the climax, when it came, was always intense, almost as though the enforced wait made the final payoff that much sweeter.

Afterwards, Jay would get this look in his eyes, like Tag had done something extraordinary or heroic. And honestly? It made Tag feel about ten feet tall. No one had ever made him feel so fucking accomplished before in his life.

So far, they had stuck to blowjobs, handjobs, and frotting. It was good every time—hell, it was *fantastic*. Tag didn't need anything else. But yeah, it was maybe a little weird that they didn't even discuss other options. Ordinarily, Tag would have raised it with a partner by now, but he wanted to be patient with Jay. He had a sinking suspicion that if he raised the possibility of having penetrative sex, Jay might not be honest about how he really felt about it. And the very last thing he wanted was for Jay to agree to something he didn't actually want to do.

So instead, he stayed quiet and just tried to give Jay all the space he needed to tell Tag silently—with his body, and his

expressive stormy gaze, and his incredible responsiveness—
what he wanted. And right now, it seemed to Tag that Jay
already had everything he wanted. He didn't seem to need
anything more. Which was good because there were other
pressing matters to think about, not least the fact that the
festival was starting next week. Opening night was just five
days away.

Bea and Henry seemed happy with how the production
was shaping up, though there were still a few scenes Henry
wanted to perfect. Jay was working a lot with Rafe, insisting
he get to rehearse every scene. Meanwhile, Freddie was
running around like a blue-arsed fly most days, finalising the
set, lighting, and costumes and updating her promptbook.
Although it was a fairly minimal production, there were a lot
of moving parts and, with little technical help on offer from
the venue, Freddie had her work cut out.

As for Tag himself, he wasn't sure there were words for
how he felt about the play. He'd always loved acting, but this
was the first time in his life he'd experienced a sense of real
community with a company—and in Jay, a genuine, deep
connection with another actor. He had the sense that what he
and Jay were creating together was more than their indi-
vidual performances, and that was exciting. A little scary too.
In a strange way, it was scarier than doing a one-man production. Something about it being just the two of them, how fully
they had to rely on one another, made it feel more perilous
somehow. Letting himself down would be one thing, but
letting Jay down would be a thousand million times worse.

On top of all that, the reactions to *Bow Street* had started
coming through. And they were good. Really good, both from
the critics and in terms of viewing figures. The cherry on the
cake, though, was hearing that Tag's own performance had
been singled out for praise by a couple of big-name critics. A
fact that he only knew because his mum was sending him
links to each and every complimentary review that

mentioned his character. Which was nice because he'd been following Jay's rather stern advice not to read the reviews until the play's run was over, in case a bad one damaged his performance. So it was good to see some of the glowing praise, pre-vetted by his mum.

He *did* understand where Jay was coming from, though. Especially with the play opening so soon.

"You don't want anything to undermine your self belief," Jay had warned one evening over dinner. "Focus on your process, on your performance, and don't think about what the critics are saying. They're only trying to make themselves sound clever, anyway."

Tag didn't think his ego was so fragile that a bad review or two would knock his confidence; God knew he'd dealt with bigger obstacles than that over the years. It clearly concerned Jay, though, and he did have more experience than Tag. So, if Jay reckoned there was a risk that a bad review of *Bow Street* might impact Tag's performance in the play, it wasn't a risk worth taking. Tag wouldn't do anything to jeopardise the dynamic he and Jay were creating together in *Let Us Go Back*.

On Friday morning, a full week after they first got together, they were walking to rehearsal when Jay said, out of the blue, "My mother called me yesterday."

Tag, who had been thinking about how much he wanted to tangle his fingers with Jay's as they walked, glanced at him. "Yeah?" Jay hadn't mentioned this yesterday, but it wasn't an unusual event. Dame Cordelia called at least once a week, though unlike Tag's mum, she was never on for long.

"She's coming to York—she'll be here now, actually. She's staying with my godparents." Jay gave a little grimace and added, "Apparently, my godmother is *insisting* on throwing a pre-opening party for us tomorrow night." He rolled his eyes.

"That's nice," Tag said carefully. It was pretty obvious Jay didn't think so, but Tag wouldn't be human if he wasn't a little bit pleased at the thought of meeting *the* Dame Cordelia

Warren at a party being thrown in honour of the play he was starring in.

Jay sighed. "She says it's going to be very small, but it won't be. It never bloody is. And it's obviously not Mandy's idea. This has my mother written all over it."

Tag felt a pang of sympathy that was tangled up with other things—fond amusement at Jay's frustrated expression, schoolboyish excitement of his own. Brushing the back of his hand against Jay's, he said, "Hey. It'll be fun. I'll *make* it fun for you, I promise."

Jay glanced at him, mouth quirking. "Yeah?"

"I'm *very* good value at parties," Tag said immodestly. "You know that; you've seen me in action."

"I have," Jay agreed. "And you are, it's true—especially in those silver shorts." He sent Tag a heated look. Tag laughed and waggled his eyebrows.

"I know I sound like an ungrateful sod," Jay added. "I do realise she *means* well."

"I get it," Tag said.

He would have said more, but a voice behind them called out, "Hey, you two!" and they turned to find Bea jogging towards them. She persuaded them to take a diversion to her favourite coffee shop where she sprung for coffees and pastries for everyone. When they reached the venue, this offering prompted much *oohing* and *aahing*, not to mention a good-natured tussle between Henry and Freddie over the only chocolate twist. Once the pastries had been divided up and they were all eating, Jay told the others about his mother's plan.

Tag had half-expected Henry to disapprove, but he seemed delighted.

"We're in great shape for opening night," he said. "I was already planning to tell you all to take the weekend off and completely relax before the final push on Monday." He grinned. "I think a party is just what the doctor ordered—and your mother's parties are always wonderful, Jay."

No doubt on Henry's part, then, as to who the real hostess of this bash was.

Everyone else seemed equally excited. Freddie was delighted that she'd have an opportunity to wear her new dungarees, while Bea was already texting her father to find out if he would be coming. Only Jay seemed indifferent as he sat quietly, shredding his uneaten Danish into a pile of crumbs.

When breakfast was over, Henry announced that he wanted to run through the first scene of the second act again. They all groaned, mostly good-naturedly. They had tried this scene two different ways at the last few rehearsals and Henry couldn't seem to decide which he preferred.

"Today, we decide," he said firmly.

Bea announced, somewhat irritably, that since she had already given her view on the matter the day before, she'd go and 'deal with her inbox' for the next couple of hours.

They were running the scene for the second time when someone slipped through the door at the back of the auditorium and sat himself down a few rows back from Henry and Freddie.

It was Giles Cox, Tag noted with irritation. Now that they were at the main festival venue every day, Giles had taken to popping in from time to time, usually hanging all over Jay like a bad smell. Even though Jay had told Tag that nothing had happened between him and Giles, Tag still felt an irrational bolt of jealousy whenever Jay so much as smiled at him. He tried not to show it, but it bothered him that Jay seemed to feel it was his responsibility to keep Giles happy. Particularly since Tag knew Giles kept badgering Jay to 'let the cat out of the bag' about his involvement, when it was obvious Jay didn't want that.

"Tag!" Henry said sharply, and Tag realised he'd got lost in his own head.

"Sorry," he mumbled. "I got distracted by—" He waved in Giles's direction, and Henry frowned, turning to see who he was gesturing at.

"Don't mind me," Giles said, unabashed. "Just observing for a bit."

Henry turned back to face the stage, his expression tight. But all he said was, "Take it from *'What is this place?'"* and they resumed.

They'd barely been going five minutes, though, before they were interrupted again. This time, the door was flung open, and the new arrival swept inside with unapologetic regality.

"*Mother,*" Jay said, and there was a note of resigned exasperation in his voice that was not echoed by the other cries that followed an instant later.

Henry, delighted: "Cordy, darling!"

Giles, awestruck: "*Dame* Cordelia Warren!"

Freddie, affectionate: "Cee, you old tart!"

They all left their seats and went to her, moths to a flame.

Dame Cordelia in the flesh was a little shorter than Tag had expected—a good head shorter, if not more, than her son —but she certainly packed a punch. Her high-necked dress, which hugged her ample curves, was a deep emerald green. She'd paired it with bold, jet jewellery and clunky black boots, and her short hair was styled into irreverent spikes. But it was her expressive face that really captured you.

As she greeted Henry and Freddie, she was all sparkling delight, eyes merry as she laughed. Then, as Giles introduced himself, she was graciousness personified, her gaze warm and interested as he spoke, modestly pleased when he showered her with obsequious compliments.

"Now where is this son of mine?" she demanded, though she had clearly already spotted Jay, standing on the low stage beside Tag. She eyed him, her eyes twinkling with mock reproach. "Come here and give your mother a hug, you heathen! I haven't seen you in forever!"

Jay rolled his eyes at her theatrics, but there was a smile tugging at his mouth as he left the stage to go to her, and when he reached her, he pulled her into a tight, affectionate hug. Tag knew that Jay's mother wasn't the easiest parent— from the things Jay had said, Tag had the feeling that everyone in Dame Cordelia's life, including her children, came second to her greatest passion in life—but they were clearly very fond of one another, and seeing them like this made Tag's chest ache a bit. He missed his own family.

When they broke apart, Jay turned and beckoned Tag over. "Come and meet my mother, Tag." A bolt of pleasure went through Tag at that invitation, and he wasn't sure whether it was at the thought of finally meeting one of his acting idols, or at the intimate note in Jay's voice that made the invite feel oddly special. Just for him.

In truth, it was probably both.

He hopped down from the stage and jogged over to them, smiling shyly at Dame Cordelia, who beamed at him and grabbed hold of his hands, squeezing them lightly as Jay said, "Mother, this is Tag O'Rourke. Tag, my mother, Cordelia Warren."

"It's just *marvellous* to finally meet you, Tag," she gushed, looking right into his eyes. "Henry speaks very highly of you, and he's *very* difficult to please!" She grinned at Henry, who just shook his head wryly.

"You're very kind," Tag said. "I'm absolutely star-struck right now, as you can probably imagine."

"Oh, *pshaw!*" Dame Cordelia scoffed, but she liked what he'd said; he could tell. She clearly adored being the centre of attention.

Dame Cordelia looked around then, frowning faintly.

"Where's Bea?" she said at last. "I wanted to talk to you all together."

"She'll be back soon," Henry said. "What did you want to talk about?"

"Well, I'm not sure if Jay has mentioned," she said, turning slightly to address everyone. "But my dear, *dear* friend Mandy, who *lives* in this gorgeous city, wants to throw a little shindig for your production tomorrow evening." As soon as she began to speak, Dame Cordelia somehow assumed the lead role in the room. It was as though the spotlight had found her, and she was instantly centre stage. Everyone else naturally gravitated around her, her own personal audience.

"It's just a *little* party," she went on, "since we're having to throw it together at the last minute." Here, she rolled her eyes at Freddie, adding more quietly, as though only the two of them could hear her words, "Mandy's *such* a Last-Minute-Lucy!" Then she turned her attention back to the wider group and said, "*Please* say you'll come?" She clasped her hands in front of her chest and looked around hopefully, as though anyone would even think of refusing.

It was beautifully done, and Tag felt sure no one had ever declined an invite from her in her life. She had a sense of expectation about her that you just felt you had to meet. And that you *wanted* to meet. It occurred to Tag suddenly how different she and Jay were. Jay could don his confident star persona with ease in social situations but, as Tag had come to realise, it was basically just an act—a facsimile of this.

"Of course we'll come!" Henry exclaimed.

"No chance of us missing out on all that lovely booze," Freddie added, grinning.

Dame Cordelia gave a tiny clap of her hands, then turned to Giles and said, "And you must come too, Giles."

Giles beamed. "You're very kind. I'd love that, thank you."

Stifling a groan, Tag sent a sidelong glance at Jay, whose jaw tightened betrayingly.

Giles cleared his throat. "I actually have a friend coming up for the weekend. Would it be all right if I brought him along?"

"Of course," Dame Cordelia carolled. "The more the merrier!"

Tag relaxed a little at that news. With any luck, Giles's friend would keep him busy and well away from Jay.

The next few minutes were taken up with Dame Cordelia getting Giles's number—which she insisted in writing in a little green leather notepad while refusing to let anyone show her how to add the number directly to her phone—*then* finding Mandy's address in the same notepad and reading it out painstakingly slowly, *then* telling everyone at least five times to come along any time after seven and absolutely *not* to bring a single thing, on pain of death.

"Mandy's ordered simply *crates* of booze and it's all on sale or return," she said blithely, as though that meant it was free. "And she has some caterer friend who's going to rustle up some delicious nibbles—though when we last spoke, she hadn't even *called* him yet!" She gave a peal of laughter and added, "Better have some pasta before you come, darlings, or we'll all be pissed as farts by nine."

"Oh God," Jay groaned.

Dame Cordelia laughed again and set a hand on Giles's forearm. "Poor Julius. He lives in fear of what I'll get up to at parties." Turning to Jay, she added, "Don't worry, darling. I can't go swimming in the nude this time. Mandy doesn't have a pool."

Jay palmed his face and groaned again, and everyone laughed.

"Right-o!" Dame Cordelia said, clapping her hands together. "I daresay I'd best get back and help Mandy with the arrangements. *Lovely* to see you, darling. Especially lovely to see you *here*, where you belong." She waved a hand towards the stage and then tugged Jay into another quick hug. After that, she went round bussing everyone else's cheeks with formidable efficiency, and telling them to make sure Bea and Rafe came too, and that, if anyone else wanted to bring a friend, just to let Jay know so he could text her.

"It'll be absolutely fine," she told them all. "It's just that Mandy needs to know, for security and all that boring nonsense." She rolled her eyes, then sent them all a final wave and sailed out the door.

It was as though half the occupants of the room had left, rather than only one. Suddenly, the space felt empty and echoey.

"Your mother," Henry said to Jay fondly, clapping his shoulder. "What a woman."

CHAPTER EIGHTEEN

JAY

That evening after rehearsal, Jay was shoving his water bottle into the backpack he'd left in the front row of the stalls, when a teasing voice said, "You do have a dressing room, you know. No need to camp out in the auditorium."

It was Giles Cox.

Jay suppressed a sigh. Zipping up his backpack, he plastered on a smile and turned to face him. "I do," he agreed. "But I prefer to keep that for performances only."

Giles chuckled. "Actors and their superstitions, eh?"

Jay smiled stiffly. "Something like that."

"And do you have any superstitions about getting a Friday night drink with the festival director?"

Jay's smile froze. Going out with Giles was the last thing he wanted to do; Tag wasn't working tonight, and Jay had been looking forward to spending the evening with him. Alone. He began scrambling for an excuse, but his brain felt weirdly sluggish. "Um…"

And then, into the silence, a voice said brightly, "Hey, Jay! Are you ready to go?" Jay looked over at the stage to see Tag hopping down and walking towards them. He already had his jacket on, messenger bag slung across his body, and there was a glint in his eyes that Jay recognised from their earlier, more hostile acquaintance. This time, though, the challenging glitter wasn't directed his way. "All right, Giles?" Tag said, flashing an insincere smile. "Didn't realise you were still here."

Giles's smile was equally artificial. "Oh, hello. Jay and I were just talking about going for a drink."

"Yeah? Sounds good, but I'm afraid we can't." Tag ran a hand up Jay's arm and squeezed his bicep—it wasn't exactly intimate, but it was certainly proprietorial—and despite wanting to keep their intimacy secret, there was a part of Jay that loved that possessive touch. Smiling broadly, Tag added, "Early nights all weekend. Right, Jay?"

Torn between alarm and amusement, Jay struggled to keep a straight face as he gave Giles an apologetic look. "I'm afraid he's right. Henry's orders."

Giles's gaze shifted to Tag, dipping to his hand still resting on Jay's arm. "What about your mother's party?"

"Ah, well, nobody can say no to my mother," Jay admitted with a laugh. "Not even Henry. But Tag and I will be taking it easy and heading home early. We've got a demanding couple of weeks ahead of us, and the production has to come first."

"I see." Giles's obvious displeasure suggested that he *did* see, that he saw more than Jay would have liked.

Smiling, Jay added, "I'll catch you at the party, yeah? We can get a drink there. I'd love to hear about everything you've got going on at the festival."

"Of course," Giles agreed coolly. "I'll look forward to it."

"Me too," Jay said, which was a barefaced lie. Or, as his mother would describe it, a 'necessary social performance'.

Either way, he was relieved, if unsettled, when Giles said his goodbyes and left.

"God, he's a wanker," Tag muttered as they watched Giles stroll up the aisle and out of the auditorium.

Jay stifled a laugh. "Why do you say that?"

Tag made a face. "He acts like he has some kind of claim on you. Like you're a—a perk of the job or something." He shook his head, as though to dislodge the thought, then offered Jay a rueful smile. "Sorry, I'm not being very subtle here, am I? Do you think he guessed that we're, you know…" He waved a vague hand, making Jay smile despite his unease.

"Yeah, maybe," Jay admitted.

Tag made a face. "Sorry."

"It's okay," Jay said. "But, you know, he *is* the festival director, and his family's one of the biggest donors as well. It's kind of expected that we'll make a *bit* of an effort with him."

Tag eyed him for a moment. Then he said, "Yeah, but that doesn't mean you have to agree to go out with him. You're allowed to have boundaries, Jay. You know that, right?"

Tag was looking at Jay like he was unsure whether Jay did understand that, and Jay realised he wasn't sure how to respond. The truth was, he'd learned at his mother's knee that part of an actor's job was to keep the money guys happy, and at this point, the lesson had become so ingrained he was programmed to be agreeable to people like Giles.

But actually, Tag was right, wasn't he?

Taking a breath, Jay tried to shake off his disquiet. "Come on, let's get out of here."

The walk home should have been pleasant. Blue skies and warm spring air hinted at the arrival of summer, and the streets were busy with locals and tourists enjoying the weather, but Jay found himself preoccupied.

His thoughts kept circling back to Giles and the suspicion he'd seen in his eyes when Tag had acted so possessive. It was silly that it bothered him so much. So what if Giles Cox had guessed that he and Tag were... together? Was that even the right word? Involved? Given what they'd agreed, 'hooking up' was probably more accurate.

It didn't feel like hooking up to Jay, though. They might have only been together for a week, but if he was honest, Jay was already emotionally invested. And okay, maybe that was partly down to how Jay was built, but it was also because of Tag, because of the man Tag was. He made Jay want to throw caution to the wind. He made Jay want *more*, emotionally and physically. But, Jay didn't know how to ask for more. Or whether it would be a mistake to even try.

Jay glanced over at Tag as they walked, and his heart lifted at the sight of his familiar face, caught in profile in the low evening light. He would have liked to take Tag's hand, but that would be risky for any number of reasons—not least of which was the possibility of them being photographed and ending up on some sleazy gossip site. He didn't care that much for himself, but Tag had been clear that he didn't want to be publicly linked with Jay, and Jay respected that.

No doubt picking up on his introspective mood, Tag sent him a questioning smile. Jay smiled back, bewitched by the openness in Tag's expression, by his curiosity and his concern. Everything about him was real and honest. Yes, sometimes that honesty meant you got his prickles, but more often, it meant you got his warmth and interest, just like Jay was getting now.

He'd just opened his mouth to say as much when something hard and immobile slammed into the side of his face and body, sending him reeling back a step.

He'd been attacked...

By a lamp post.

Tag stood staring at him, both hands over his mouth, eyes wide. And then he let out a burst of appalled laughter. "Oh my God, are you okay?"

"Ow!" Jay said, touching his cheekbone, half laughing and

half glaring in embarrassment at the bloody lamp post he'd walked into. "Who the hell put that there?"

"I thought people only did that in movies," Tag said, still laughing as he came closer. "Let me see." He pulled Jay's hand from his cheek. "Have you got a bruise? Henry will do his nut if you do."

"I'm fine." More than fine, in fact, with Tag gently probing his face.

"You need to look where you're going."

"You need to stop distracting me."

Tag chuckled softly. "How was I distracting you?"

"By being so…" Jay met Tag's smiling eyes and grinned helplessly. "God, you have no idea how much you distract me."

"Yeah?" The humour in Tag's expression shifted into something more intimate. "Good. I like distracting you."

"And you're very good at it," Jay murmured.

"I am, and I plan to distract the hell out of you later on." Tag waggled his eyebrows outrageously. "But first, let's get you home and put some ice on that cheek."

Jay really didn't think he needed ice, but once they were back in the flat, Tag insisted on getting half a bag of frozen peas, wrapping it in a towel, and pressing it to Jay's cheekbone.

"To stop any bruising," he explained, kneeling on the sofa next to Jay. His other hand rested lightly on Jay's thigh. It probably wasn't intended as a sexual thing, just a casual intimacy, but nonetheless, Jay was suddenly tensely aware of his touch and his closeness.

The tension was frustrating. He and Tag were often physically close in rehearsals, touching and holding each other as the play dictated, and Jay was fine with all of it. But once they got home, it took him ages to relax back into being intimate again. If only he could be more like Tag, who was always so at ease with himself, so present in the moment.

"I think that'll do for now," Tag decided eventually, setting the bag of peas on the coffee table and leaning forward to kiss Jay's cheekbone. His lips felt warm against Jay's chilled skin. "No permanent damage."

"Thank you," Jay said, finding himself a little choked up by Tag's ministrations. He wished he could articulate why, but he couldn't find the words, so he just covered Tag's hand where it still lay on his leg and squeezed.

Turning his own hand over, Tag threaded their fingers together. "Are you worried that Giles might have guessed about us? I know we're trying to be discreet, but when I saw him pressuring you like that..." He gave a self-conscious shrug. "I'm sorry. I didn't mean to go all caveman."

Jay laughed, and it released some of his tension. "You *were* a little possessive. But I quite liked it, to be honest."

Tag gave him a teasing look. "*Did* you?"

In answer, Jay leaned forward and brushed his lips against Tag's in a gentle kiss that swiftly deepened as Tag's hand came to rest on the back of Jay's neck, holding him in place. Instinctively, Jay's body resisted slightly, but when Tag responded by gentling his hold, Jay felt himself start to relax, the stresses of the day easing from his muscles as he lost himself in the feel of Tag's mouth moving against his own, Tag's fingers flexing in his hair.

"Better?" Tag murmured after a while.

Jay's eyes flickered open to find Tag watching him with an affectionate, tender expression that made his chest ache. "Yes, much."

Tag kissed him again, gentle and warm. "You've been stressed today."

"I know." He sighed, disappointed that he'd let it show. "I'm sorry."

"Don't apologise." After a pause, Tag asked, "What's up, though? I mean, other than Giles. And your mum's party.

And the fact that we're opening next week." He mimicked a gasp of horror. "OhmyGod!"

Next *week*. Jesus.

Jay's answering smile felt as watery as his guts. He couldn't think about opening night. He knew that he should, that he *had* to, sooner or later, but right now, he couldn't.

Instead he said, "I was thinking that I like how easy you find all this."

"All this what?"

"This." Jay squeezed Tag's hand. "Us. It doesn't freak you out or anything, does it?"

"Only when I remember I'm sleeping with Dame Cordelia Warren's son." He grinned, then, more seriously, added, "Does it freak *you* out?"

Jay considered. "I suppose it does, in a way…" He looked down at their threaded fingers, then back up to Tag's face. "I wasn't spinning you a line when I said I have a rule about not getting involved with co-stars. I do, and it's there for a reason."

"Yeah, I figured. What was his name?"

"Oh God," Jay groaned, slumping back on the sofa. "Is it that obvious?"

Tag grinned. "Tell me his name and I'll punch his lights out."

That made Jay laugh. "Yeah? Maybe not."

"You don't think I could take him?"

"I'm sure you could take him," Jay said, smiling ruefully. "But it might not be a great career move."

Tag's eyes rounded. "Really? Oh my God, who is it?"

Over the years, Jay had become so used to keeping the secret that he hesitated, even though he'd long ago realised that his loyalty had been misplaced. But it actually felt strangely empowering when he looked over at Tag and said, "Sebastian Talbot."

Tag's jaw dropped. "Shit. You're kidding me."

Jay shook his head. "We were in *The Birthday Party* together. I was straight out of RADA..." He made a face. "The whole thing was a fucking disaster."

"But he's like..." Tag was obviously doing the maths. "Isn't he in his fifties?"

"He is now, but this was over ten years ago."

"So, what? He was in his forties, and you were... Twenty-two?"

"Twenty-one."

Tag winced. "Yikes."

"Yeah. And of course Seb wasn't out back then, so it all had to be this big bloody secret." He shook his head. "It was a huge mistake."

"*His* mistake."

For the most part, Jay had come to accept that was true. "I could have said no."

"*Could* you?" Tag held his gaze, lips pursed. They both knew the score; the power dynamics in the industry could be toxic, and plenty of young actors fell victim to coercion.

It hadn't been that, though. Even after a decade, Jay felt embarrassed to admit the truth. "Yeah, I could have, but he was...charismatic and commanding. I idolised him. I *trusted* him." He grimaced. "I thought I was in love. I thought he was too."

"Oh Jay," Tag said softly, leaning in to hug him. "What happened?"

Jay didn't want to go into all the gory details, and it was a pretty dull story anyway when you stripped it down to its core. He blew out a breath. "In a nutshell? Seb liked the idea of me, but the reality? Not so much. I frustrated him. And let's say my, uh, performance disappointed him—both on stage and off. The play was a disaster. Well, *I* was a disaster in it, and Seb dropped me like a hot coal. That's pretty much it."

"Jesus," Tag said, looking appalled. "What a fucking arsehole."

"Yeah, well, lesson learned." Jay smiled at Tag, happy suddenly to be there with him, older and wiser. Reaching up, he ran his thumb over Tag's cheek, earning a smile in return. "So that's why I decided never to do this again…"

"Except that you are doing it."

"I am." Jay's smile felt crooked. "But it's different this time."

"Yeah?"

Jay nodded. "This time, we both know exactly where we stand. This time, nobody's going to get hurt."

Tag studied him for a moment. Then, lowering his lashes, he caught Jay's hand in his, brought it to his lips, and kissed his palm. "I'm glad."

"Me too."

Leaning forward, Tag kissed him, then sat back and held his gaze. "You can trust me, Jay. I promise. I'm on your side."

That simple promise affected him far more than it should have. Jay found he could only nod. And Tag, who somehow seemed to know him inside out, simply smiled and kissed him again, lingering longer this time, biting lightly at Jay's lips until their tongues touched and tangled, and Jay felt his heart leap helplessly towards Tag's.

Eventually, Tag pulled back, breathless and flushed. "So," he said, alive with the humour that was never far beneath his skin, "how about a little distraction…?"

CHAPTER NINETEEN

TAG

Evening sunlight suffused the room, turning the world warm and golden as they tumbled together onto the bed. For long minutes, Tag simply lost himself in Jay, kissing him, caressing him, tasting him—and revelling in the encouraging jut of Jay's prick nudging against his own.

He'd learned that Jay didn't like to be rushed, and that was more than fine with Tag. He was all for prolonging the pleasure. So he didn't hurry, concentrating instead on Jay and his responses, cataloguing them, noting every shiver and arch of his expressive body, every sound that escaped his throat.

"What do you want?" Jay gasped eventually. "We can do anything you want. Anything."

"Yeah?" That was new. *Anything.* Tag propped himself up on one elbow, studying Jay's earnest grey eyes. Carefully, he said, "What I'd really love is to know what *you* want."

Colour bloomed in Jay's cheeks. Jesus, the way this guy blushed.

"Me?" Jay looked away, unable to meet Tag's gaze. "Anything. Honestly."

"There must be something you'd prefer...?"

Jay didn't answer, his gaze still averted. Embarrassed, Tag realised with an ache in his chest. He stroked a soothing hand over Jay's chest and down towards his prick. "How about we sixty-nine?"

"Sure," Jay said quickly, lifting his eyes to Tag's again. "That's good."

Maybe so, but that wasn't *it*.

"Or maybe you'd like to fuck me?"

Jay's eyes widened, chest heaving as he sucked in a deep breath.

Warmer, Tag thought, feeling a tremor ripple through Jay's body. *Much warmer*.

More softly, he said, "Or *I* could fuck *you*?"

Jay stared at him with mute appeal in his stormy eyes.

"Is that what you'd like?" Tag's pulse quickened, but he kept his voice easy. The last thing he wanted was for Jay to feel pressured. "Do you want me to fuck you tonight?"

Face ablaze, Jay swallowed but he didn't look away. And, eventually, in a rough whisper, he confessed, "Yes. I want that. I'd *love* that. But... I'm pretty useless at all this." He gave a painfully awkward laugh. "I take bloody ages to get ready, you see, so it wouldn't be much fun for you—"

"Are you joking?" Tag smiled, but he had to work hard to mask his anger. Had fucking Sebastian Talbot told him that? "Getting ready is half the fun. In fact, why don't I start getting you ready right now?" He licked his lips invitingly, chuckling softly when Jay's nostrils flared. "Like the sound of that, do you?"

"Yeah," Jay breathed. "But only if you want..."

"I *do* want." Smiling, Tag shimmied down the bed, settling between Jay's thighs, before leaning back briefly to admire the view. There was no doubt that Jay was a beautiful man. Golden skin, burnished by the evening light, dark hair gleaming, eyes like storm clouds... and yes, a very nice cock too.

Wrapping his fingers around its satiny length, he gave it a few slow, teasing strokes.

Glancing up again, he caught Jay's lust-dazzled expression, his fingers clenched in the sheets, and felt a bolt of joy go through him. Joy, but with something else in it too. Something that chewed almost painfully at the edges of his heart. That was too much to think about right now, though, so he lowered his head and went to town, kissing, licking, and nuzzling Jay's prick, slowly but surely leading him towards the edge. No rush, no pressure, just building pleasure. And it *was* pleasure, for Tag too, his cock pulsing with unmet need, every nerve tingling in anticipation.

"You're gonna have to—" Jay gasped at last, his voice wrecked and desperate. "—*stop*, or—something. Because I'm gonna come before you even get inside me at this rate, and there's no way I'll be able to take you after that. Sorry."

Jesus Christ. The need in Jay's voice. What that did to Tag's prick. He slowly drew off Jay's cock and sat back on his heels, meeting Jay's wild gaze. "Don't worry," he said, his tone low and deliberate. "I'm going to get you so ready for me that by the time I sink inside you, you'll come in about two seconds." He smiled slowly, wickedly. "And then I'll fuck you till you come all over again."

"*God,*" Jay gasped. "I want that, I do, but, sorry, I need—well, *more* before I can take you." He swallowed visibly, his throat bobbing. "Could you grab the lube?"

Rather than reaching for Jay's lube on the nightstand, Tag got up and crossed the room to his own case. Opening up his wash bag, he unzipped the top section, pulling out not only lube but condoms too. Then he unhurriedly strolled back to the bed, tossing the condoms on the nightstand and lying down next to Jay, lube in hand.

Jay had that familiar tense look on his face now. He reached for the lube, not meeting Tag's gaze. "If you give it to me, I'll go into the bathroom and get myself ready really quick." He sent Tag a glance, arching one elegant brow. It was pure Skye Jäger. Pure artifice. "And then you can fuck me properly."

"I don't get to watch?"

"You wouldn't want to watch that. It's just prep."

Jay took hold of the lube, his fingers brushing Tag's, but Tag didn't let it go, his gaze moving over Jay's flushed face. Softly, he said, "Why don't you let me do this for you? I promise you'll like it."

Jay made a scoffing noise, and again, two patches of scarlet painted his cheeks. How endearing was that? Tag's heart was a fucking puddle right now because this was a side to Jay that nobody else ever saw, uncertain and embarrassed and a bit at sea, and Tag loved that Jay trusted *him* to see it.

"The thing is," Jay said, "I'm more, um—tight than average. It takes me a while to fully relax. It'll drive you nuts trying to get me ready—trust me, I know how this goes down —and anyway, I can get there myself way quicker."

"Quicker?" Tag echoed. "Why would you want this to be *quick?*"

Jay looked nonplussed, as if he'd never even considered the question before.

Tag was tempted to explore that further, but this wasn't the time—the conversation clearly wasn't helping Jay relax. His expression had tensed, his grey gaze faintly panicked. Tag needed to relax him, tease him. Turn him on.

He leaned in close, his lips just grazing Jay's as he murmured, "What if I *want* to do this? What if I *love* the thought of opening you up—slowly—for my cock?"

Jay's eyes went wide, and his throat convulsed.

Bingo.

"What if I tell you that, if *anyone's* putting their fingers inside you," Tag went on, "it's going to be me?"

Jay let out a thin laugh. His throat and upper chest were flushed now too, his eyes glittering with lust. "I'll take ages," he breathed. "You'll get bored."

"Er, no," Tag said, laughing. "What kind of loser gets *bored*?"

A self-conscious wince crossed Jay's face, and Tag understood exactly what kind of loser had been bored and impatient with Jay: Sebastian bloody Talbot.

He didn't pursue that, either. Instead he said, "I love getting a guy ready for my cock." Tag kissed him again, deep enough to demonstrate exactly how much he meant it. "I love it when I get him so turned on he's a whisper away from coming, just from having my fingers inside him, and he can't even think straight anymore."

Jay kept staring at him, his chest moving up and down as he breathed unevenly. "You don't have to—"

"I know I don't," Tag said, shimmying closer and skimming a proprietary hand over Jay's hip. "But I want to. And I honestly think that when you relax—and, believe it or not, you *will* relax—you're going to love it. So..." He grinned slowly. "Will you let me take care of you now?"

Jay's moan was helpless and obviously unintended. His face blazed with heat, and he turned his gaze away, as though he couldn't bear to be seen by Tag. But he didn't move his body away, not even when Tag slid one hand down to first stroke, then tug at his left inner thigh, making him shift and open up for him.

Conversationally, Tag said, "I'm going to play with you till you're *begging* me to fuck you."

Jay moaned again, his eyes tightly shut, skin all pink and self-conscious, while Tag opened the lube and drizzled some over his hand.

"I get that you're embarrassed," he said. "But you're still going to let me do this, aren't you? You'll do it for me because

I want it." Jay made another choked noise that Tag decided sounded enough like agreement, even as Jay threw his arm over his eyes. It was tempting to tug that arm aside and force him to watch, but Tag decided to let it go. For now. Another time, maybe, if he sensed Jay would like it.

Reaching between Jay's legs, he stroked his fingers up the sensitive crease, loving Jay's instant reaction, the way his body stiffened and arched, and the noises he made.

At first, Tag just stroked idly up and down Jay's crease, his fingers occasionally glancing over Jay's hole, but gradually, he began to home in, getting closer and closer to Jay's centre, till eventually, the pad of his index finger was teasing a light circle around his hole, and Jay was whimpering and shifting. Only then, finally, did Tag press a single fingertip inside him.

And Christ, yeah, he really *was* tight, the ring of muscle rigid on Tag's finger, the hard grip both demanding and resistant. "Sorry," Jay whispered. "I told you—"

"It's okay, shh," Tag murmured. Grabbing the lube again, he leaned up on his elbow and drizzled it straight onto Jay's body, letting it drench his fingers and drip down.

And then he began to move his hand, slowly but inexorably, using his strong fingers to gradually persuade the muscle to soften, the tight channel to ease. Jay was silent, eyes closed, expression pained, body held so tight. Tag leaned down and pressed a kiss to his mouth, and Jay moaned, parting his lips, letting Tag deepen the kiss, one hand curling round the back of Tag's neck while Tag slowly, patiently, worked his slippery fingers inside him.

Time seemed to slow as they kissed on and on, and all the while Tag kept patiently opening Jay up. He felt almost drunk on Jay. Occasionally, he'd break away to get more lube, to admire Jay's gorgeous chest, to suck and nibble a small, tight nipple. And then it was back to the task at hand, fingers pressing, reaching, scissoring, until eventually, he was thrusting his fingers firmly, rhythmically, and Jay was moaning and writhing under him.

Eventually, Jay wrenched his mouth free of Tag's and gasped, "*Jesus*. I've never—" He broke off with a strange, wild laugh. "I can't believe I'm saying this, but you were right. I *need* you to fuck me."

He really did look disbelieving too, face flushed with arousal, lips swollen, grey eyes glittering with lust.

"Your wish is my command," Tag said, the smoothness of the words at odds with his hoarse, desperate voice. He leaned away to swipe a condom from the nightstand. Seconds later, he was smoothing the latex down his shaft and grabbing the lube again.

"*More* lube?" Jay said, disbelievingly.

Tag smiled and waggled the tube. "Lube is good. Lube is our friend."

Jay gave a shaky laugh. "No argument from me on that front."

Tag paused, his gaze travelling over Jay's face. He looked a bit… emotional, and Tag wasn't sure why. "Are you okay?" he asked carefully, still searching Jay's face. "Do you want to keep going?"

Jay turned his head to the side, saying shakily, "Yes. *Please*."

Tag didn't know what it was that made his throat close—the tone of Jay's voice, maybe, or his carefully averted face. The bob of his throat as he swallowed. Whatever it was, it was unexpected, catching him by surprise. For just a moment, he didn't know what to do with himself. And then he realised he was still holding the fucking lube, so he snicked the cap and drizzled it over his sheathed cock.

When he leaned forward, between Jay's spread thighs, Jay breathed out, a long, shuddering surrender of a sigh. Tag notched his cock at the brink of Jay's entrance and carefully pressed forward, but there was no resistance now. Oh, there

was still tightness, but the move forward was slow and inex-
orable. Jay turned his head back, his eyes open now, and...
fuck. He was all need, all fire. That stormy gaze was wild, and
desperate, and when he grabbed the back of Tag's neck and
pulled him into a savage kiss, it was like being pulled under-
water. Like being submerged.

Tag's head was swimming. He was as far inside Jay's body
as he could go, and Jay's tongue was sliding against his own,
and Tag was moving, pushing in, pulling back, the rhythm
building, building, with every roll of Tag's hips.

Jay surrendered to the onslaught. The very last traces of
his body's resistance faded, till he was arching up, meeting
Tag's thrusts, and fuck, this felt so *good*. All that time Tag had
spent patiently opening Jay up was paying off now because
he got to have *this*, this strong, capable, complicated guy
giving in, surrendering to him, even though it was hard for
him. Even though it made him vulnerable. *Jesus*.

Jay was moaning, urging him on. "Yeah. Fuck me harder.
Please."

Tag grasped Jay's thigh and hitched it up, thrusting a fraction deeper, his head swimming with so much pleasure, it felt
like his brain might just explode.

"Oh God," Jay gasped in his ear. "Yeah, right there.
Fucking hell, Tag."

And there was something about that, the combination of
Jay's wrecked, gasping voice, and the sexy arch of his hips,
the sheer visual beauty of him as he revelled in Tag's cock
fucking him...

The orgasm ripped through Tag like a tornado, as sudden
as it was savage, tearing out of him, just as Jay cried out too,
his cock spurting between them, splashing warm and sticky.

As the final ripples of his orgasm faded, Tag blinked, his
shorted-out brain coming back online just in time to reach
down and keep the condom in place as he carefully pulled
out, registering Jay's soft hiss.

That disposed of, he rolled back onto the bed to catch his breath and bask in the hormone rush that was making him giddy. "Bloody hell," he breathed, grinning as he turned his head towards Jay—only to find Jay laying silent, one arm draped over his eyes, trembling very slightly.

Tag's belly swooped in concern. "Jay?" Pushing up onto one elbow, he tugged cautiously at Jay's arm. "Hey, you all right?"

Jay nodded, throat bobbing as he swallowed, but after a moment, he pulled his arm away. He was smiling, but it looked like an uncertain smile, and his eyes were very bright, lashes damp, cheeks hectic with colour and naked emotion.

Tag had never seen him so exposed before, and his heart swelled painfully at the sight. "Hey," he said softly, reaching over to stroke the damp hair back from Jay's face. "Okay?"

"Yes." Jay sounded husky, the word no more than a whisper. "It's just—I've never… You know, at the same time as someone else. It was…" He swallowed again. "It felt special, that's all."

Tag had to breathe through a sudden rush of feeling. "It *was* special. Jay, it was amazing. *You* were amazing."

Jay shook his head, looking embarrassed by the praise, but pleased too. And that gave Tag such a surge of satisfaction that he couldn't help adding in a low, teasing tone, "I told you you'd like it."

"You did. You were right." Smiling, Jay lifted one hand, curling his fingers behind Tag's neck again, gently running his thumb over the short hair at his nape. "I bloody loved it."

In the charged silence that followed, they simply watched each other, both of them smiling as they hovered on the brink of feelings too new, too tender to voice.

In the end, Tag looked away first, a little shaken by the intensity of the moment. "Let's recover for a bit," he suggested, settling down with his head on Jay's shoulder and letting the flood of emotions and endorphins wash through him. "We can make dinner or something later…"

Jay slid an arm under Tag's shoulders, pulling him even closer. And into his hair, he murmured, "I'm all for 'something later'…"

ACT THREE

CHAPTER TWENTY

JAY

Jay and Tag arrived at the cast party shortly after eight. A discreet security man met them at the end of Mandy's drive and another one waved them inside when they reached the mansion property's front door.

"Your godparents must be minted," Tag said, wide-eyed, as he took in the huge hallway with its marble-tiled floor. From somewhere in the house came the distant strains of music and voices.

"Sounds like the party's at the back," Jay said, pointing to an archway straight ahead. He glanced at Tag. "Shall we—"

"Darling, *finally!*" a voice interrupted, and Jay looked up to find his mother standing in the archway. She was wearing one of her favourite party outfits, a white tux, designed especially for an Oscars ceremony she'd attended in the nineties. Back in the day, she used to wear it *sans* shirt, the scoop-necked waist-coat displaying her famous cleavage to great effect. She had always been inordinately proud of her breasts, which, to Jay's utter mortification as a teenager, she insisted on referring to as 'the twins'. These days, though, she couldn't fit into the waist-coat—it no longer buttoned all the way the way up—and it looked like the trousers might soon have to be retired too, though they were still just about managing to contain her ample bottom. Being Dame Cordelia, though, she pulled the outfit off with an emerald green, semi-sheer blouse, matching green high heels, and her usual irrepressible chutzpah.

"I *know* I told you to come at seven," she told Jay severely, sweeping towards him and pulling his head down to kiss both of his cheeks. Her lips were tacky with lipstick, and she was wearing Shalimar, her favourite perfume, and probably his earliest scent-memory. "Why are you so late?"

He extricated himself gently from her hold and straightened. "We're only a little late." He offered an apologetically boyish pout that he knew would appeal to her and added, hopefully, "Fashionably late."

She melted on cue, shaking her head in remonstrance but indulgently now, patting his cheek fondly before turning to Tag.

"And how are *you*?" she said, taking his hands into her own and looking intently into his eyes, as though she'd known him for years, rather than only having met him briefly. Before Tag could formulate an answer, she added, "Oh my darling, your *eyes*! So beautiful! I said as much to Oberon, my eldest, the other day. We were watching that new television show of yours—you were marvellous in it, darling, just *mesmerising*—and we both commented on your darling peepers. Oh, Oberon's dying to meet you. He's coming tonight especially."

"Ronnie's here?" Jay said faintly. Christ, he hoped his brother was in England on his own business, and their mother hadn't forced him to come over just to see Jay's play. He was mortified by the very thought.

Ignoring his interruption, she squeezed Tag's hands again

and added, "Everyone's *so* excited to see Julius return to the stage."

"*Everyone*?" Jay said sharply, alarmed, and when she turned towards him, elegant brows raised in surprise, he added, "Who's '*everyone*'? We're not advertising that I'm in the play, Mother. You know that."

Dame Cordelia sighed. "Oh, darling, do wind your neck in. I just mean *us*. Your brother and me, and Mandy and Phil, of course. You know: the people who love you?"

She glanced back at Tag with a look that said, silently but very distinctly, *'You see what I have to put up with?'* Tag offered a slightly panicky grimace in return, but she was already moving away from them both, heels clacking on the tiled floor. "We're all in the orangery. Do come along."

Tag mouthed, "*Orangery?*" at Jay, and Jay bit his lip against a laugh that felt rather hysterical as they fell into step behind her.

Over her shoulder, his mother said, "Other than Oberon, you two are the last to arrive. We've got a nice little crowd— don't worry, Julius, nothing too big. Mandy just invited a few neighbours and some of the festival trustees. You know how she is with her community thing. Oh, and that nice festival director. Miles, is it?"

"Giles," Jay corrected automatically, even as he frowned. The trustees were one thing—at least they were part of the festival—but *neighbours*?

They were approaching a set of double doors now, which were ajar—the music and voices were clearly coming from there.

"Yes, yes, Giles. Oh, and you'll never guess who *he's* brought along!" Dame Cordelia turned on her heel, eyes sparkling with amusement. "That dreadful boy you went to school with. Do you remember? The one whose mother did that dreary family sitcom for decades. Talk about flogging a dead horse. He writes that wretched '*Little Bird*' column in one of the papers now."

Jay's blood ran cold. "Not Austin Coburn?" he said, even as he thought, *God, please, not him.*

He felt Tag's curious gaze shift to him, but didn't meet it.

"Yes, that's the one," his mother said cheerfully. She turned to Tag then, eyes twinkling. "Austin was *the* big cheese in the school drama club before Julius arrived. He wasn't best pleased to be ousted, was he, darling?" She pressed her lips together, trying not to laugh. "I mean, the poor boy had absolutely no talent—and I should know; I had to sit through his mangled Algernon Moncrieff in their sixth form production—but because his mother was on television, he'd inveigled his way into getting all the best parts. Until Julius joined the school. Obviously, they couldn't ignore *his* talent." She gave a stagey wink. "Or mine." With a tinkling laugh, she clapped her hands, then added to Tag with a wag of her finger, "Do *not* mention that if you end up talking to Austin."

Without waiting for an answer, she pushed the doors wide open and stepped inside, carolling, "Here they are! *Finally!*"

Oh God, *why* did she always do this? How many times did he have to ask her not to show him off like he was ten years old? Pressing his lips together, Jay followed her into the large, airy room, his gaze raking over the twenty or so people gathered there, all of whom had turned to look at his mother, himself, and Tag. And fucking hell, yes, there was Austin, glass of champagne in hand, standing with Giles, Bea, and Timon, Bea's father.

Jay looked quickly away, his heart thudding unpleasantly.

"Let's get you boys a drink," Dame Cordelia said cheerfully. "Champagne all right? Mandy ordered *vats* of it—oh, look there she is." She waved at Mandy, a tall, glamorous woman in a dark red cocktail dress, who was walking in their direction. "Yoohoo! Mandy, sweetie, could you grab a couple of glasses of fizz for the boys?"

Mandy waved and smiled, before seamlessly diverting to a table bristling with glasses of champagne, lifting two flutes.

Tag leaned in and hissed in Jay's ear, "Oh my God, your godmother is *Amanda Ffyfe*?"

Jay glanced back at him. "Didn't I mention?"

"No, you bloody didn't!" Tag whispered. Then, with a raise of his brow, he added, "Just like you never mentioned you and that journalist were playground rivals—that *is* the guy who was taking sneaky photos of us at the TV Best Awards, right?"

Jay sighed. "Yeah. He's not exactly my biggest fan."

"He sounds like a twat," Tag said, wrinkling his nose. "But I'm more interested in Amanda Ffyfe—do you think she'd let me get a selfie with her? My dad's had a massive crush on her since he was a teenager."

Jay huffed a laugh, absurdly grateful for the change of subject. "Your dad and every other straight boy in the early eighties." Mandy was best known for her very kitsch role as a model-turned-private-detective in a long-running American TV show called *Foxy PI*.

"She's an icon," Tag said, crossing his heart reverently.

"Jools, sweetie!" Mandy carolled as she approached them. "It's been forever!" She handed the two glasses of champagne she'd collected on the way to Dame Cordelia, then reached for Jay, pulling him into a tight hug. His mother immediately handed one of the glasses to Tag and sank half of the other one.

"I want a proper chat with you later," Mandy said in Jay's ear. "It's been far too long!"

He hugged her back affectionately. Mandy had no children of her own and had always taken her role as his godmother seriously. When she finally released him, she turned to Tag and said brightly, "And who's this handsome young man?"

"This is Tag O'Rourke," Dame Cordelia said, sliding a

proprietary arm around Tag's waist. "He's in the play with—" She broke off, then tipped her head in Jay's direction and added, "Well, you know."

Christ.

"Oh, wonderful," Mandy gushed, clapping her hands together. Her gaze moved between Jay and Tag, and she added, "Don't you two look cosy together? Are you…?" She trailed off meaningfully.

Jay didn't so much as glance at Tag, not entirely sure what Mandy might detect in his expression but rather afraid she might end up seeing more than he wanted her to. Laughing, he said, "Stop trying to pair me off. You're as bad as Mother. I can find my own dates, thank you very much."

Even without looking, he was aware of Tag stiffening beside him. Poor Tag. This sort of speculation was exactly why he'd wanted to keep their involvement private.

"She's right, though," his mother said, with a wistful sigh. "You would be a scrumptious couple."

God, they were excruciating.

Ignoring her, Jay turned to Mandy. "Um, Tag's a bit of a Foxy fan." It was an admittedly desperate attempt to change the subject, but he ploughed on regardless. "He was hoping to get a selfie with you, weren't you, Tag?"

Mandy smiled kindly at Tag and said, "Of course, darling, but can we do that later? I can't do photos under these lights, not at my age. I've got a nice little shadowy corner where we can take some lovely pictures."

"That would be awesome," Tag said earnestly. "My Dad and I love watching *Foxy PI* together—it's kind of our thing." He gifted her one of his killer smiles, sexy and modest at the same time. "He'll be *so* jealous that I'm meeting you."

Mandy preened at that, even as she demurred. As for Tag, perhaps he sensed Dame Cordelia's peevishness at ceding the limelight to Mandy, because he turned to her then, adding in a slightly breathless tone, "And I expect Jay's already told you what a *huge* fan of yours I am. When I was at drama school, I saved up for weeks for front-row tickets to see you in Beckett's *Happy Days*. You were… God, you were incredible. So much pathos, but humour too. I couldn't stop thinking about that performance for days after. Years, if I'm honest."

Dame Cordelia immediately thawed. Gripping Tag's forearm, she whispered, "Bless you, darling," her eyes glinting with emotion. Whether Tag knew it or not—and Jay suspected he did know it—he'd just said exactly the right thing, mixing fanboyish eagerness with professional admiration. The nicest part, though, was that he obviously wasn't putting it on—he meant every word, and now he was waxing lyrical about that long-ago performance, recounting details that only a true devotee would recall, and of course, his mother was lapping it all up.

Jay's heart melted a little at the sight of them getting on so well. Until he thought, *'What the fuck am I thinking?'* He was acting like someone who'd just introduced his boyfriend to his mother! Christ, Tag would be *horrified* if he knew that Jay had been feeling all squidgy and warm just because they'd been smiling at each other. *Jesus, get a grip.*

Luckily, Mandy distracted him, tucking her hand into his elbow and tugging him away from Tag and his mother's love-in. "Come and say hello to Philip," she said. "He'll be so pleased to see you." Phil was Mandy's husband and Jay's godfather. He was also one of Jay's favourite people, a quiet, intelligent man who was that rare thing amongst his mother's friends: a good listener.

"Where is Phil?" Jay replied, as he let Mandy lead him away. "Hiding out behind some vegetation?" Like Mandy, Phil had worked in the entertainment industry until his retirement, albeit on the business side rather than as a creative. Unlike Mandy, though, he was no extrovert, usually finding a quiet spot to hide out at parties.

"Pretty much," Mandy admitted with a grin. "He's parked

himself in his favourite chair looking out onto the garden… which just so happens to be hidden behind a lemon tree, where no one can see him."

Jay chuckled. That sounded like Phil, and it certainly wasn't difficult to find somewhere to hide here. The orangery was built on the back of the house and stretched across the full width of the building, creating a large, elegant space the size of several rooms that Mandy often used to entertain. The walls were exposed brick but most of the roof was glass, as were the huge doors that led out onto the garden. There were lots of chairs and sofas dotted around the place where guests could make themselves comfortable, and there was also plenty of room for people to stand around and mingle if they preferred to do that.

As Mandy led Jay towards the garden doors, a woman rose from a sofa they were about to walk past.

"Amanda," she said warmly, leaning in for a *mwah-mwah*. She was wearing a dress that resembled a shapeless, orange sack, but that Jay suspected was probably very expensive. "Quentin and I didn't see you when we arrived—I wanted to thank you for inviting us to your little get-together."

Mandy smiled genially. "Oh, you're very welcome, Lisette. I'm glad you could make it." Turning to Jay, she said politely, "Jay, this is my neighbour, Lisette Carter-Dunn—Lisette, Jay Warren." She gestured then at a man in an oddly naval outfit, still sitting on the sofa Lisette had bounced up from. "And this is Lisette's husband, Quentin." Quentin gave an amiable wave but made no move to rise, and Jay nodded back.

Turning back to the woman, Jay shook her hand briefly. "Nice to meet you, Lisette."

"Lisette's one of the trustees on the festival board," Mandy explained.

"I'm afraid so—for my sins!" Lisette gave a little laugh, then added more earnestly, "I jest, but it's truly rewarding being able to use my business acumen to support the arts. I've always been passionate about the theatre, and now that I'm retired, I have more time to give."

Jay smiled politely. "You ran your own business?"

"My own fashion label," Lisette said, gesturing at the sack dress as if to say, '*Obviously.*'

"How wonderful," Jay said. "A creative person with business experience—I'm sure you're a great asset to the board."

"Well, I like to think so," Lisette said modestly, clasping her hands at her chest. "Of course, this is a big year for us— our first season being an annual event. Until now, it's been every second year. We feel this will be a wonderful boon for local businesses." When Jay nodded agreement, she added, "And we're bigger too. We're putting on more productions *and* we have more big names." She beamed at him. "Such as your good self."

Jay's smile froze. "You… know about that?"

She tapped her nose. "Only those of us on the board," she said, then laughed and added, "Well, and Quentin, of course. As though I could keep anything secret from him!"

Quentin piped up then. "She knows I like your vampire show," he brayed from the sofa. "Very droll. Normally, I detest the theatre but I might come and see your play."

"Quentin! *Sshhh!*" Lisette hissed. "I told you on the QT!"

"Oh, sorry," he said without the slightest hint of remorse.

Jay felt a stirring of panic. Smiling tightly, he turned to Lisette and said, "Um, you *are* aware that we've deliberately not gone public about my involvement? We're keeping it under wraps till opening night."

"Oh, yes, yes," Lisette said airily, waving her hand as though to bat away some objection. "Don't worry. We're all friends here, tonight."

"Yes, well," Jay said slowly. "There are quite a few people here *I* don't know and who I don't think are on the board, so if you could be a little more circumspect, I'd be grateful."

Lisette frowned, plainly irritated now. In a less friendly

tone, she said, "I've lived in York all my life, Jay, and I can assure you that everyone here tonight is perfectly trustworthy. They're all the *right* sort of people."

Really? Jay thought angrily. *Like bloody Austin Coburn?*

"Besides," she went on blithely, waving a heavily beringed hand, "from a *business* point of view, I must say I question the value of keeping your involvement secret any longer. The board is dying to share the news. There'll be a ticket frenzy when it gets out, of course, but if we leave it too late, there's a risk we'll lose customers who can't travel at short notice. Or they'll only come for your play and not stay for the whole festival."

Jay's stomach gave an unpleasant lurch. That was exactly what Giles had argued the other night, and Bea had been dropping hints about making an announcement—or at least starting a rumour—for a while. They were clearly hoping Jay might soften, but he had been up-front about his feelings on this issue from the start and he had no intention of giving way. He simply couldn't.

That said, he had to face up to reality, and it seemed there were quite a few people here tonight who knew about him. Giles had apparently taken it upon himself to tell all the trustees. And bloody Lisette had told her other half!

That was already far too many people for Jay's comfort.

But worse than that was the possibility that Austin knew too. Hell, if he and Giles were friends, Giles had probably already told him. And even if Austin didn't know yet, there was a good chance that someone would blab it out in front of him tonight. Or Austin might just put two and two together for himself. There weren't exactly a ton of alternative explanations as to why Jay was here—with Dame Cordelia, too—especially when everyone knew there was a mystery about who was playing Sassoon.

Fuck.

Panic rising, Jay's gaze flickered over to Bea, who was still chatting to Austin and Giles. Right then, as though he sensed Jay's attention, Austin turned his head in Jay's direction and their gazes met. Austin's eyes narrowed. Then he lifted his glass in a small toast, offering a thin-lipped smile. There was nothing friendly about that smile and Jay quickly tore his gaze away, his heart slugging unpleasantly, palms damp.

He realised that Lisette was still talking, and that he hadn't heard anything she'd said for the last minute or more. Panic surged inside him.

Shit. He needed a minute alone to pull himself together.

"I'm sorry," he said. "Would you excuse me? I've just remembered something rather important that I need to make a quick call about."

Lisette stopped talking and frowned. Offended, probably, but Jay couldn't bring himself to care. Glancing at Mandy, he added apologetically, "I'll just be a few minutes."

"Take your time," Mandy replied easily. "Philip will still be sitting behind the lemon tree when you get back. Use his office for your call if you like."

Somehow he managed a smile and a few polite words for the now-frosty Lisette before he walked away, working to keep his pace unhurried and his expression neutral. His panic at bay.

Tag, who was still deep in conversation with Dame Cordelia, clocked him on his way out of the orangery. He frowned questioningly at Jay, and Jay shot him a quick, reassuring smile, though he didn't pause to speak.

Once inside Phil's office, he leaned back against the door and closed his eyes as the wave of panic he'd been holding back rose up, submerging him. His legs gave way and he slid to the floor, landing in a heap and burying his head in his hands.

"*Fuck,*" he whispered. "*Fucking hell.*"

The reality he'd been trying to ignore since he'd arrived in York hit him all at once.

People were relying on his celebrity to carry the play, but he just wasn't up to the job.

With sudden, ruthless clarity, he saw that, whether he liked it or not, the news of his role in *Let Us Go Back* was probably going to get out before opening night, maybe as soon as tonight.

It was exactly the sort of story that Austin Coburn would love to break. Jay Warren, back on stage, screwing up another play. Well, fuck Austin! And fuck Giles Cox, too, the treacherous bastard. He'd wanted to publicise Jay's involvement all along; all he cared about was ticket sales. And what better way to do it than by giving Austin Coburn the bloody scoop? Giles didn't even have to tell Austin himself, just bring him along and wait for the inevitable leak. After all, the champagne was flowing, and there were so many people here tonight who already knew. Hell, fucking *Quentin* knew. This was already the worst-kept secret in the history of badly kept secrets.

Well, sod them. They could have Rafe. All Jay had asked was for his involvement to be kept secret, but they couldn't keep their mouths shut, could they? So fuck them, he was out. He didn't owe them a thing.

Except… What about Tag?

The thought of letting Tag down like that made his throat hurt. Tag would hate him, despise him… Would finally know the cowardly truth about him. And that was intolerable.

Jay heard himself moan aloud, and it was an awful, broken sound. Animal-like and shocking. Christ. He had to pull himself together. None of this was objectively surprising. His plan to keep his involvement under wraps until opening night had always been a pipe dream, hadn't it? So why was he reacting like this?

Whatever the reason, suddenly all he could think about was standing on that stage. Act One, Scene One. All those people out there, waiting for him to speak. And Tag watching him fall apart, incredulous. Jay imagined looking out at the audience and seeing Austin Coburn sitting in the front row with that thin-lipped, malevolent smile on his face. Waiting for Jay to fail.

He didn't have to work hard to imagine standing there, with the words drying up on his tongue, his mind going blank. He'd lived it, and he remembered it in every excruciating detail.

Oh God.

He wasn't sure how long he sat on the floor of Phil's office, silently freaking out. But eventually, he became aware of light knocking on the door and someone with a mid-Atlantic accent saying his name.

"Jools? Jools, are you in there?"

Ronnie?

A wave of relief slammed into him. Miraculously, his big brother had arrived, just when he needed him.

"Hang on," he said hoarsely, clambering to his feet. He took a moment to smooth a hand over his rumpled hair and tug down his shirt before opening the door.

Ronnie stood on the other side, his pale grey gaze intense, dark brows creased with concern. "Are you okay? Mandy sent me to find you."

"Ronnie, I'm—I'm—" He couldn't seem to get words out, and Ronnie's frown deepened.

"Hey," he said gently, stepping into the room and closing the door behind him. "What's wrong?"

Jay moved back, letting him inside. "I've fucked up," he said. "I can't do it."

"Can't do what?"

"The play." Jay shook his head in disbelief. "We open on Tuesday. *Fuck.*"

Ronnie searched his face. At last he said, "Is it because you don't feel ready? That's not uncommon. It's amazing how often actors find that it's only just before opening night that things finally click for them and—"

"It's not that," Jay interrupted.

"Okay," Ronnie said calmly. "What then?"

"I think—" Jay broke off, swallowing hard. Was he really going to say this—admit this—aloud? "I think I've lost my nerve." He squeezed his eyes closed. "I should never have agreed to this."

When he opened his eyes again, it was to find Ronnie watching him tensely. "Come sit," he said, taking Jay's elbow and steering him towards a small sofa in the corner of the room. "Take a deep breath with me. That's it, in and then out… Now another…"

Jay did as he was told, trying to concentrate on his brother's reassuring voice and the feel of the breath in his chest, trying to ignore his racing pulse and shaking hands, the sweat trickling down his spine. The strangled scream trapped in his throat.

After a while, when Jay was starting to feel calmer, Ronnie said, "Is this about what happened with *The Birthday Party*? Are you still hung up on that?"

Ronnie was nothing if not direct. Tactless, some might say, but at least you always knew where you were with him. When *The Birthday Party* disaster had happened, Ronnie was the only person in Jay's life who actually asked him outright what had gone wrong. Everyone else tiptoed around him, pretending it hadn't been as bad as he imagined.

"Hung up?" Jay repeated dully. "Yeah, I guess you could say that. I walked in tonight and practically the first person I saw was Austin Coburn, and I just—I started having a panic attack." He shook his head, disgusted by his own weakness.

"Austin Coburn?" Ronnie was frowning. "Who's that?"

A laugh scraped out of Jay. "That critic. You know, the bastard who tore me apart in *The Birthday Party*. He's… not a fan. Always making snide comments about me in his stupid '*A Little Bird Tells Me*' column. Basically, he hates me."

"*Hates* you? That's kinda weird. Do you guys have history or something?"

Jay sighed. Ronnie, his oldest sibling, was a decade older than Jay, so he didn't know much about Jay's schooldays. "Yeah, we were at school together. I won't bore you with it—honestly, it's just bloody *stupid*—but the bottom line is, any chance he gets to run me down, he takes. When I saw him tonight, I just pictured him sitting in the audience for this play, and then all I could think about was how it felt that night, in *The Birthday Party*. Standing under the lights, sweating, my mind completely blank. And Seb just glaring at me, waiting for me to..." His throat closed on the final words, panic rising again, and he had to take in a deep, shuddering breath before he could add, "I'm just so fucking scared of it happening again. Oh *God*, I don't think I can do it. I *can't* do it." Dropping his head into his hands, he screwed his eyes shut. "But if I don't, I'll be letting Tag—everyone, down. And if I do, and I fuck up, it'll be even worse." He snatched another, panicked breath and scrubbed his hands over his face. When he finally looked up again, it was to find his brother watching him with a troubled, considering expression. "Help me, Ronnie," he whispered. "I don't know what to do."

Ronnie said carefully, "I guess the question is, what do you *want* to do?" When Jay just stared, unable to formulate an answer, his brother added, "Do you want to do the play, or not?"

Yes. To Jay's surprise, that was the answer that leapt to mind. He did want to do the play, he wanted to be there for Tag, and he wanted to bring all their hard work to fruition. "Yes, but I just don't think I can," he admitted.

"Sure you can," Ronnie said. "What's more, you will, if it's really what you want." He cocked his head, considering. "Doesn't your medication help with the stage fright?"

Jay frowned. "What do you mean, my medication?"

"Weren't you prescribed some anti-anxiety meds after *The Birthday Party?*" He shrugged. "I'm not judging. I know several actors who use medication to control their stage fright. I don't think it's the best tool myself, but it's not uncommon—I mean, Harmony uses meds." That was a surprise. Harmony, Ronnie's most recent ex, was an intense theatre actor, devoted to her craft. "It wouldn't normally be the first thing I'd suggest to an actor struggling with stage fright, but given how close you are to opening, and how short the run is, it might be worth a shot."

"I tried it once before," Jay admitted. "Just for a walk-on thing. It was a fucking disaster."

Ronnie looked curious. "How so?"

"I was like a zombie. Totally out of it. People thought I was drunk."

Ronnie winced. "How much did you take? Harmony only takes half a pill before a performance. She says it's just enough to take the edge off."

Jay considered that. It made a sort of sense. Two of the pills he'd been given had knocked him sideways, but maybe a fractional dose would be enough to get him through a performance. Just dial down the panic enough that he could function.

Jay looked at his brother. "Do you know what she takes?"

Ronnie frowned. "Not off the top of my head, though I can message and ask her. But, Jools—" He paused, then added, "I wouldn't recommend this as a permanent solution."

Jay flushed. "Yeah. I hear you."

"So maybe," Ronnie went on, "after this play is over, you could go see this woman I know in California? She runs courses—CBT, visualisation, mental strength, that sort of thing. She might be able to help you find a way to deal with this that doesn't involve popping pills. Okay, kiddo?"

Jay managed a watery laugh. "Okay," he said. "After the play."

Christ, after the play? Might as well say on the other side of the ocean, the distance between now and then felt so vast and unnavigable. Ronnie was offering a lifeline, though, and Jay knew he had to grab it with both hands or sink.

Ronnie had pulled out his phone and was shooting off a quick message. Before he'd even shoved it back in his pocket, it pinged with a response.

"I'm sending you the name of the meds," he said, his thumbs flying over his phone keyboard. Before he sent it, he looked up and met Jay's eyes. "Temporary measure only, yeah?"

"Yes," Jay said. "Promise."

"Okay then." Once the message had swished off to Jay, Ronnie said, "So, are you ready to get back to the party?"

Not really, but what choice did he have? The show must go on. "Ready as I'll ever be," he said. "And thanks, Ronnie."

His brother rose too, clapping him on the shoulder. "No problem. Now, I want you to introduce me to your co-star. Mother's charmed, and we both thought he was awesome in *Bow Street*."

"Give me five minutes," Jay said, "and I'll happily introduce you." He waggled his phone. "I just need to make one quick call."

Ronnie nodded and rose. "Fine, you have five minutes. If you're not back by then, I'm hauling you out of here by your ears, kid."

Jay laughed, but he was already busy searching his contacts and, as the door closed behind Ronnie, Jay's call was picked up. "Dr. Maynard speaking."

"Hello, Doctor. Sorry to call you out of hours. It's Jay Warren. I was hoping you could spare me a few minutes…"

CHAPTER TWENTY-ONE

TAG

Tag scarcely noticed Jay leaving with Amanda Ffyfe. When pinned by Dame Cordelia Warren's bright blue gaze, it was impossible to notice anything else.

He'd been raving—possibly too enthusiastically—about seeing her in *Happy Days* when Jay and Amanda had exited stage left. Now, Dame Cordelia was turning the conversation back to him.

"I can feel you have a love of the work. Not all actors do, you know. Not these days. Too many just want to be in the movies. But not you, I think." She pressed a hand to her chest. "You feel it *here*."

Tag laughed. "Well, I *would* like to be in a movie, but… No, you're right. I do love the process of acting. These last few weeks rehearsing with Jay have been…" He suddenly found himself lost for words, abruptly and acutely conscious that, not only was he talking to one of the country's greatest actors, but that she was *Jay's mother*. And that he wanted her to like him. *Shit.* "It's been a wonderful experience," he finished lamely.

"Yes?" Dame Cordelia's expression sharpened with interest—a mother's interest, human and honest. It helped Tag to see past the glamour of her talent and fame to the woman beneath, a woman interested in and—perhaps?—a little anxious for her son.

Tag nodded. "Jay's so talented. I, um, was afraid he might be a bit standoffish when we started. You know, with him being so much more experienced and well-known than me, but he's been great. Patient and encouraging, and so generous and responsive in rehearsal. He always listens."

"Oh yes," Dame Cordelia said earnestly. "Julius is *very* giving. He's such a sensitive performer."

"He is, yeah." Sensitive and responsive in lots of ways, Tag couldn't help thinking with an inappropriate rush of heat. "We've developed a great relationship... *Working* relationship," he amended quickly, since, earlier, Jay had been so keen to deny anything more. "And it's been fun working on a play that's never been performed before, exploring it together and developing our characters almost from scratch with Bea and Henry."

"Oh, how wonderful!" Dame Cordelia clutched both hands to her ample chest in delight. "Henry's a master at exploration. I envy you." After a slight pause, she asked, "And Jay's been...all right in rehearsals?"

Tag wasn't sure what she meant. "He's been great," he said. "He's pulled me through a couple of tough days, that's for sure." He considered mentioning their living arrangement, and how kind Jay had been about helping him out on that front, but decided against it; he wasn't sure what Jay had told his mother and didn't want to put his foot in it. Instead, Tag decided to lighten things, saying with a laugh, "The only real issue we've had is that Jay's been a little, er, *militant* about his involvement in the play being kept secret until opening night."

He expected Dame Cordelia to laugh in response—but she

didn't. "Hmm," she said, frowning slightly. "Yes, Henry mentioned that."

Just then, Tag's skin started prickling with the uneasy sensation of being watched. Glancing across the room, his gaze landed immediately on the man talking to Bea. It was the journalist from the TV Best Awards, the one who'd been sneaking pictures of Jay and Mason. The one who'd seen Tag leaving Jay's suite that night.

Austin Coburn.

Austin raised his glass at Tag, head cocked in invitation.

"Ah," said Dame Cordelia, clearly following Tag's distracted gaze. "That's Austin. The boy I was talking about who went to school with Julius. He's a critic and journalist now. Has a column in one of the big newspapers. I don't read it, of course, but I'm told it's very popular. You should probably talk to him."

Doubtfully, Tag said, "I'm not sure Jay likes him very much. He doesn't sound like a nice bloke."

Dame Cordelia made a scoffing sound. "Darling, you don't have to *like* him. He's useful to you, so make him *believe* you like him. Think of it as a performance—a social performance." She took his hand, drawing his attention back to her bright eyes. "I'm afraid, as I'm sure you already know, success in this business is as much about connections as it is about talent and hard work. Julius might be able to ignore that, but *you* can't."

That was true, and Tag was surprised by Dame Cordelia's frankness. Looking into her shrewd gaze, though, he realised that there was probably very little that got past her. For all her theatricality, Dame Cordelia was far more hard-headed than her son.

And talking of Jay, Tag spotted him at last, walking determinedly towards the door. He looked tense, his mouth pressed into a taut line, shoulders tight. He must have felt

Tag's eyes on him because he glanced over and gave a quick, tight smile as he passed.

Tag's instinct was to go after him, but Dame Cordelia still had his hand clasped in both of hers and was saying, "...so, come along, I'm going to introduce you to Austin and you're going to *sparkle*. Like him or not, darling, he could help launch your career with his review of this play."

It was beyond Tag's power to refuse Dame Cordelia Warren, especially when he knew she was right. This was his big break, and he had to seize every opportunity to make it a success, even if it meant schmoozing with Austin Coburn.

Still holding his hand, Dame Cordelia towed him through the crowd, throwing greetings like confetti. It made him think of a royal procession—everyone giving way, smiling and nodding, if not quite bowing, thrilled to have a moment of her attention.

"Now, look who I've found," she announced, blithely interrupting the conversation Bea was having with Giles, Austin, and her father. None of them seemed to mind, though, turning to Dame Cordelia with eager smiles, though Giles's smile dimmed at the sight of Tag. Tag ignored him. "Austin, have you met Tag O'Rourke? He's the marvellous young actor playing Wilfred Owen in Bea's play."

Austin fixed him with a beady look through the fashionably heavy frames of his glasses. "Not formally," he said, switching his champagne glass to his left hand and holding out his right to Tag. "A pleasure. I saw you in *Bow Street* a couple of weeks back. You were really quite good."

Austin's wry smile suggested this was a heady compliment, coming from him, and it was impossible not to take pleasure in it. Tag found himself 'sparkling' more easily than he'd thought he would, despite feeling uncomfortably disloyal to Jay. "Nice to meet you," he said, shaking hands. Austin's hand was clammy and cool, maybe from holding the sweating glass of champagne. "Will you be coming to see the play?"

"Well, that *is* why Giles dragged me all the way up here," Austin said with a supercilious smile. Glancing around the others, he said, "Do you mind if I borrow Mr. O'Rourke for a few minutes?" As an aside to Tag, he added, "I'll be reviewing the play, of course, and I'd love to get your insights into your character, if you have a moment?"

It was clear from the offhand way he said it that there was no question in his mind that Tag would have as many moments as Austin wanted, and Tag supposed that was true. At this point in his career, Austin had all the power, and it would be ridiculous for Tag to give him the cold shoulder just because Austin and Jay had been rivals in the school drama club. Besides, Bea was beaming at Tag, delighted that Austin was showing such interest.

Dame Cordelia smiled graciously at Austin. "Of course you may. I've been monopolising him for far too long." Then, to Tag's surprise, she leaned forward and kissed his cheek. "Now, don't you leave without saying goodbye."

She gave him an encouraging little shove in Austin's direction, then turned to Bea and Giles, launching into conversation. Austin was already strolling away, and Tag hurriedly followed him to a quiet corner of the room—sorry, 'orangery'—where a couple of deep armchairs sat together, a low table placed cosily between them.

A discreet waitress appeared with a tray of champagne just as they sat, and Tag helped himself to another glass. "Thanks," he said, giving her a smile.

She looked surprised—Tag knew from experience that most people didn't acknowledge the staff at parties like this—but she smiled back and murmured, "You're welcome."

Austin, predictably, ignored her as he dumped his half-empty glass on her tray and took a fresh one, saying to Tag, "Don't you just hate warm champagne?"

Tag gave a non-committal *hmm*, sending the waitress a discreetly apologetic glance as she glided away.

"So," Austin said, settling into his chair, legs crossed, champagne flute dangling from one languid hand, "this is an exciting opportunity for you, Tag. Can I call you Tag?"

"Why not?" Tag said, trying to exude his usual playful warmth, even as his skin crawled with dislike. "It's my name."

Austin gave a wintry smile. "Tell me, how did you come to be cast in the play?"

"The usual way, by auditioning."

Austin's eyebrows rose. "Oh," he said. "I rather thought…" He trailed off.

"What?" Tag said, keeping his expression neutral, his voice pleasant.

"Well," Austin said, drawing out the word, as though considering what to say next. "I don't *think* I'm wrong in saying that you and Jay Warren are friends, am I?"

Tag felt his own smile harden and grow wary. "What does Jay have to do with this?"

Austin laughed. "Oh, come on," he said. "Everyone here knows that Jay's playing Sassoon. I must have been told *in complete confidence* at least three times now."

Shit. Jay was going to freak out when he discovered the news was out. Perhaps he already had? He was certainly looking tense when Tag had last seen him.

"So," Austin prompted with an arch look. "You two are…?"

"Friends," Tag agreed, disliking the insinuation behind Austin's question. "But we didn't really know each other before we started working together. Like I said, I auditioned for the role."

Austin lifted a single sceptical eyebrow, a studied move. Tag wondered how long it had taken him to learn the trick. "You didn't know Jay before your audition?"

His incredulous tone and knowing expression suggested he remembered Tag leaving Jay's hotel room that evening. Widening his smile, Tag brazened it out. "Not really, no," he said. "We'd met a couple of times, but we certainly weren't friends, just acquaintances."

"I see." Austin took a sip of champagne, then said, "I'd assumed it was because you were friends that you decided to take the risk."

"The risk?" For a moment, Tag didn't understand. Then he got it. "Oh, you mean because it's a new play by a debut playwright? To be honest, I don't consider it a risk. I loved the play as soon as I read it. I think the audience will, too."

"Bea's very talented," Austin agreed smoothly. "But, actually, I meant the risk of performing on stage with Jay. Given his…history."

Tag stared. "His history?"

Now both eyebrows went up. "You must have heard of *The Birthday Party* debacle? It's infamous." Tag didn't know how to respond, and Austin didn't wait for him to gather his thoughts. "I was there that night, and let me tell you, it was a car crash. Jay completely froze, forgot his lines, forgot his blocking. They had to bring the curtain down and put the understudy on. Poor Seb—Seb Talbot? He was playing opposite him—was mortified."

Poor *Seb*? And then Tag realised: Austin was talking about the play Seb Talbot had dropped Jay from when they were together.

"Sounds like a nightmare," Tag said lightly, although from Jay's sparse description, he hadn't realised it was anything like that bad. "It *was* over ten years ago, though, and Jay wasn't very experienced."

"Oh, sure," Austin agreed. Then, curiously, he added, "But you *do* know he hasn't been on stage since, right?"

Tag had *not* known that. "What, never?"

"Well, there was that *Dracula* fiasco a year or two ago.

Thankfully it was only one night—a quick Hallowe'en cameo for his *Leeches* character—but I understand he needed some, er, artificial help to get through it." Austin shook his head sadly. "A little bird told me he was completely stoned that night. Tragic, really. Can't say I was surprised, though—we were at the same school. Terribly unreliable. Managed to avoid expulsion, thanks to Mummy's interventions, of course." He rolled his eyes, thin lips quirked in a cruel little smile.

Tag's gut was squirming now with a noxious mixture of anger at Austin for gossiping, at himself for listening, and a sick fear that there might be some truth to the story. Fear of what that could mean for their play. For himself.

Not that he wanted Austin bloody Coburn to know any of that.

Tipping back his champagne glass, he finished his drink in one big, insouciant gulp, then neatly set the glass back down on the table. Offering Austin a bright smile, he said, "You don't need to worry about Jay. He's absolutely fine. I mean, he's a fantastic actor, and he's brilliant in this role. He's going to be amazing when we open. My only worry is whether anyone will notice me next to him." With that, he rose, leaving his glass on the table between them. "You just wait. Jay's going to blow you away."

Austin's gaze, never warm, grew chillier. "Wouldn't miss it for the world," he said, teeth bared in an unfriendly smile as he patted the breast pocket of his jacket. "I've got front-row tickets."

"We'll see you on opening night, then," Tag said, keeping his smile in place as he walked away. He was starting to wonder whether success was worth having to suck up to twats like Austin Coburn. But then he remembered his precarious bank balance, and the constant shadowy threat of Plan B, and realised he was kidding himself. Of course he'd make that devil's bargain, just like every other actor in the business—including, apparently, Dame Cordelia Warren. He had no other choice.

Ruminating on that, he glanced around in search of familiar faces and spotted Henry holding forth to a gaggle of wide-eyed acolytes. Tag was heading in his direction when he saw Jay from the corner of his eye, talking to a tall, striking man with dark hair, impressive eyebrows, and an intensity that Tag could feel right across the room.

At the sight of Jay, Tag's heart gave one of those helpless leaps of joy that were new and exciting, and bordering on embarrassingly puppyish. He hoped he didn't have cartoon hearts in his eyes. Jay clocked him too, then, a flash of relief washing over his face that was swiftly shuttered. He turned, said something to the man he was with, and they both headed towards Tag.

Tag met them halfway.

"Hey," he said to Jay, taking in his tense expression with concern. "Everything okay?"

"Oh, you know, Mother's parties," Jay said, unconvincingly. Then he turned to his companion and added, "Tag, let me introduce you to my brother, Oberon Warren. Ronnie's the Creative Director of the Durham Theatre in New York. Ronnie, my co-star, Tag O'Rourke."

Of course the man was Jay's brother, Tag realised with something that felt mortifyingly like relief. Though he looked older than Jay, the likeness was obvious. "Great to meet you," he said, holding out his hand.

Oberon took it in a firm grip, meeting Tag's gaze with blue-grey eyes as intense as his brother's. "And you. Loved you in *Bow Street*. A real stand-out performance." His accent had a slight American twang, especially in his intonation. "Can't wait to see you in *Let Us Go Back*." He glanced at Jay before adding, "From what Jools tells me, you're a support-ive, collaborative actor." He glanced at Jay as though for confirmation.

Jay coloured faintly. "Uh, yeah," he agreed. "Tag's really great to work with."

Oberon smiled. "Yes, I can see you two have a bond. And I'm sure Tag'll be there for you on stage, right Tag?"

It struck Tag as a strange question, and he glanced at Jay, noticing with concern the stiffness in his jaw and the slight puffiness around his eyes. "Of course," he said. "We'll be there for each other, won't we?"

Jay nodded, but he wasn't meeting Tag's gaze. Into the silence Oberon said, "When you come down to it, it's all about trust and vulnerability. Trust is key. Trust in each other, and trust in yourself. Trust each other with your vulnerabilities. Then just let the magic happen."

"Very American," Jay said wryly. "You're going native, Ronnie."

"Hey, Dad was from California. I'm just getting in touch with my roots." Oberon smiled, revealing a set of very straight white Hollywood teeth. "But seriously, it's what I tell all my actors on opening night, and now I'm giving you two the benefit of my wisdom."

Jay huffed a laugh and met his brother's gaze in a silent exchange. "Thanks, Ronnie," he said eventually.

Oberon squeezed his shoulder and said, "You know where I am." To Tag, he said, "Good to meet you, and break a leg for Tuesday. But now, if you'll excuse me, I'd better go and say hello to Freddie before I get into hot water for ignoring her."

With that, and with a significant parting look for Jay that Tag couldn't interpret, Oberon strolled off, leaving Tag alone with Jay.

"Are you okay?" Tag asked immediately.

"I'm fine, why?"

Frowning, Tag studied his face. "I don't know. You seem stressed."

"No, just... Like I said, my mother's parties. I'm all schmoozed out, and it's not even been an hour."

Tag smiled, relaxing. "Yeah, I get that." He considered mentioning his conversation with Austin, but decided it wasn't the time or the place, not with Jay already so on edge. They'd talk about it later, at home. "We could always duck out early?"

"I wish. But if we leave now, she's liable to come after us and drag me back by my ears." He sighed. "I need to make a decent show of talking to Mandy's guests, and there's a couple of family friends here I really can't ignore—but I would like to get out of here soon. Maybe in another hour?"

"An hour's good with me. We *are* meant to be resting this weekend, after all."

Jay lifted his brows, his grey eyes darkening delightfully. "*God*, I need an early night tonight."

"Yeah?" Tag batted his lashes outrageously. "I think that can be arranged, though sleep might have to wait a bit."

Jay grinned, the tension dissolving from his face as their eyes met and held. Quietly, fervently, Jay said, "Thank God for you." And Tag's heart did another of those telling, playful somersaults.

They spent the next hour moving from group to group, chatting and laughing on demand, managing to get round most of the room while somehow never ending up in a group with Austin Coburn. Tag wondered once or twice whether Jay was deliberately avoiding Austin, but didn't have much time to muse over that, too busy meeting new people and trying to remember names. It was tiring being 'on' all the time, sparkling and attentive. Everyone was being tactful about the play, not mentioning Jay's involvement, though Tag suspected they all knew. The very fact that no one asked who was playing Sassoon made that much plain. All Tag could do was settle into his own role, 'Tag O'Rourke, star of the show', which he played with dutiful enthusiasm, giving everyone the performance they expected on that front, while Jay caught up with the people he knew, and charmed the ones he didn't.

A social performance, Dame Cordelia had called it, and Tag understood now what she meant. It occurred to him, watching Jay, that Jay had been giving this particular performance for almost his whole life. For so long, in fact, that it might be difficult for even Jay to tell where the performance ended and his real self began. What, Tag wondered, had that done to his personal boundaries?

Finally, Jay led Tag over to Dame Cordelia to say their goodbyes. She protested, but acquiesced when Henry stepped in to remind her that he needed his cast well-rested for the demanding week ahead.

"In fact," Henry added, looking across the orangery to where Rafe was standing with Austin Coburn, "I think I'd better have a word with our understudy about just that."

"I suppose you're right," Dame Cordelia said. She grabbed Jay, bussing him on both cheeks. "In which case I'll see you on Tuesday, darling, after the show. Break a leg! You too, Tag."

Jay just nodded, lips pursed, saying nothing, and Tag couldn't help recalling Austin's warning. Was it possible that Jay's tension was about more than the social strain of his mother's party?

They grabbed an Uber back to the flat and rode in silence most of the way. Jay seemed preoccupied, or perhaps he was just tired. Probably he was aware of the driver sitting right there. Tag hadn't quite fully absorbed yet that, for someone as famous as Jay, any conversation in front of a stranger could be a tweet thirty seconds later. But he was learning that silence was often safest.

So it wasn't until they were back in the privacy of Jay's cosy studio flat that Tag finally said, "God, that felt like a long evening."

Jay dropped onto the bed, arms out crucifix-style. "They always do." His eyes were closed, face drawn. "Mother means well, but sometimes…" He sighed. "I wasn't really in the mood tonight, I'm afraid."

"No, I sensed that," Tag said, kicking off his shoes and sitting on the bed next to Jay. Looking down at him—dark hair stark against the fluffy white duvet, shirt collar open to reveal the hollow at the base of his throat, skin golden against the navy fabric—Tag felt a complex rush of feelings: attraction, affection, concern, uneasiness. Pulling up one knee, he turned to sit sideways and set his hand on Jay's thigh. "Listen," he said carefully, "I spoke to Austin Coburn earlier…"

Jay's eyes flew open. "What? *Why*?"

Tag's brows drew together. "For publicity, why else? It was your mother's idea."

"Ugh." Jay made a face.

"Anyway, Austin said—"

"I don't want to hear what he said," Jay snapped, then softened his words by setting his hand on Tag's where it rested on his leg. "Sorry. I just—I don't want to think about him, or any of it, tonight. I just want…" Jay's gaze was painfully vulnerable, even as he moved Tag's hand up his leg towards his groin. "I just want you to…"

Tag's heart pinched at the longing in Jay's eyes; he was impossible to resist. "Yeah?" he said, squeezing lightly at Jay's stiffening prick through the soft material of his trousers. "You want me to take care of you, is that it?"

Jay nodded. "I do, yeah. I… I want you to fuck me until I can't think anymore."

Jesus. Tag's own cock was filling fast, desire overtaking reason and thought. He *did* want to talk to Jay about what Austin had said, but not now. Not when Jay so clearly needed something else. Something to take him out of his head and give him release.

Moving to straddle him, Tag leaned forward, braced on his arms, their cocks straining together through the fabric of their clothes, teasing and delicious. "I can do that. You know I love taking care of you," he said, smiling into Jay's storm cloud eyes. Lowering himself, he took Jay's mouth in a hungry kiss, delighting at the feel of Jay's arms closing around him, tugging him down, as warm and eager as his lips.

And then they were kissing, and wrestling, and pulling off clothes, and all talk, all concerns, were forgotten, as they got lost in the depths of each other.

CHAPTER TWENTY-TWO

JAY

On Sunday morning, Jay woke early, groggy after a restless night.

Given how relaxed he'd felt in the aftermath of last night's sex, it was disheartening to find himself awake before seven, his stomach already knotted with anxiety, his mind full of jumbled, circular thoughts.

He turned his head to look at Tag, who was lying on his side, facing him, hair bed-tousled, lips gently parted, the dark crescents of his eyelashes kissing his cheekbones. He looked content and untroubled and everything that Jay was not.

Jay gazed at him in silence, heart squeezing almost painfully. He was probably the hottest—and kindest—man Jay had ever been with. The most self-possessed too. He had an innate confidence that Jay suspected came from all the stuff he did that *wasn't* acting. All those different jobs, in retail and hospitality and construction. All that real-world stuff that Jay had never done. Tag might be five years younger, and have only a fraction of Jay's professional acting experience, but he was sure of himself in ways Jay suspected he would never be. Calm and laid back and easy-going in ways Jay envied.

Lying there, Jay thought back to his behaviour of the night before. Falling apart at the party, snapping at Tag when he'd tried to talk about his conversation with Austin, then all but begging Tag to fuck him so he could forget about it all. *Christ*. He gave a low groan at the memory. Seb had been right: Jay was too fucking needy. How long would it be before Tag grew tired of him?

Just then, Tag let out a soft snore and shifted in his sleep. He looked so peaceful, lying there, his hair dark against the white cotton pillow. Last night, after they'd both come, he'd suggested they have a lazy Sunday morning. A long lie-in, more sex, a late breakfast. It had sounded nice, *really* nice, but Jay was so fucking uptight he couldn't even relax enough to enjoy the simple pleasure of not having to get up. Here he was, before seven in the morning, his brain working over-time, his limbs itchy. There was no way he could just lie here until Tag woke up. If he tried, he'd only disturb Tag's rest.

A run, then. He'd leave Tag sleeping peacefully while he ran off his anxiety and hopefully come back in a better mood —or at least better able to pretend to be in a better mood.

Plan made, Jay carefully slid out of bed and quietly collected his running things, taking them into the bathroom to get changed. Tag was still dead to the world when he emerged and let himself quietly out of the flat.

It was an unremarkable, overcast morning, a little humid. After a few warm-up stretches, Jay set off on one of his more challenging routes.

When he finished, he was exhausted but feeling better— still squirmy in his gut, but less caught up in his own thoughts. On the way back to the flat, he stopped off at their favourite deli to buy breakfast sandwiches and coffee, and by the time he arrived back at the flat, he was doing a pretty good impression of 'normal'.

"Rise and shine," he said as he entered the apartment, chuckling when Tag groaned.

"I thought we were having a lie-in," Tag said in muffled tones.

"We are," Jay replied. "As soon as I've had a quick shower, I'm coming back to bed. In the meantime"—he set down the brown paper bag and cardboard drinks tray on the nightstand—"there's a double cappuccino here for you and an egg, spinach, and mushroom brioche roll with extra roasted tomato."

"My favourite," Tag murmured. "You're awesome."

"I know. Mine's the all-day breakfast roll, and I won't even complain if you nick some of my bacon."

Tag levered himself up on one elbow, grinning now, his dark gaze on Jay. "I think I love you," he said.

Jay's heart stuttered.

He froze where he stood, beside the bed. His shock was probably obvious. After a moment, he attempted a normal smile, but his face felt weird and stiff, and anyway it was too late—Tag wasn't looking at him anymore. He'd averted his gaze, reaching for the bag and rummaging for his sandwich inside, his cheeks blazing with embarrassment, his regret clear. *Shit*, it had obviously just been a throwaway, playful comment, but with his stupid, over-the-top reaction, Jay had made it awkward. Tag was probably mortified by that slip. Worried that Jay had taken him seriously.

Maybe because, for a fraction of a second, Jay had…

It was a thought that made Jay feel both intensely sad and incredibly foolish as he turned away and headed for the bathroom to shower.

～

They spent the rest of the day in amiable companionship, lounging in bed for a couple of hours, then heading out to a local cinema to watch an artsy Spanish film Tag was keen to see. Several times throughout the day, Tag tried to initiate conversation about the play, and once, he tried again to tell Jay about his conversation with Austin Coburn at the party, but each time, Jay closed him down quickly.

"Let's have one day where we forget about the play," he said, smiling to take the sting out of his words. "It'll do us both good."

Tag acquiesced with an easy smile, but Jay suspected he realised how uptight Jay was, his glances growing more concerned as the day wore on. When they went to bed that night and Jay—by then, desperate for oblivion—begged Tag to fuck him again, Tag gently refused. Instead, he gave Jay the longest and most insanely pleasurable blowjob of his whole life, waving him off when Jay tried to weakly insist on reciprocating.

"Go to sleep," he said with quiet firmness, settling his head on Jay's shoulder and wrapping an arm around his waist. "You're exhausted." And, finally, Jay did.

Again, however, the relaxing effect of orgasm was only temporary, and when he woke early the next morning, his first exhausted, anxious thought was, *Dress rehearsal day.*

Then, *Just one more day till opening night.*

Later, while Tag was showering, Jay sat at the breakfast table, ignoring his toast and reading the email he'd received from Dr. Maynard with details of the pharmacy where he could collect his prescription and dosage instructions.

He found himself thinking back to the *Dracula* fiasco. He'd had a massive panic attack at home that day and had pulled his meds out from the back of the bathroom cabinet in desperation. He'd taken the full dose, and, in fairness, the meds *had* killed the panic stone dead—but they'd also left him lumbering around the stage in a stoned stupor, tripping over his own feet and slurring his words.

"Shower's free," Tag said, interrupting his thoughts. Hurriedly, guiltily, Jay closed the email and shoved his phone into his pocket but when he glanced at Tag, Tag wasn't even looking at him, too busy pulling a tight, green t-shirt over his dark head and yanking it down over his muscular torso.

"I'll be quick," Jay said.

"Take your time," Tag replied cheerfully. "We've got ages. Plenty of time to grab coffee on the way."

Jay showered and dressed, and soon they were heading out. The pharmacy was on the way to the theatre. Jay waited till they'd been walking for a few minutes before pretending he needed some headache pills, and then it was easy enough to persuade Tag that he should go to the deli to grab their coffee while Jay popped to the pharmacy.

"I'll see you at the theatre," Jay said as he crossed the road, and Tag lifted a hand in acknowledgement before walking on.

Luckily, Jay didn't have to wait long for his prescription, and nobody recognised him. He tucked it inside his rucksack, making sure to push it down into the middle of the main section, before heading off.

He caught up with Tag just outside the theatre, relieving him of one of the cardboard cups he was carrying. There was already a buzz about the place when they got inside. Henry and Bea were talking animatedly while Freddie adjusted the placement of Sassoon's armchair and the other items on the stage. Jay and Tag got busy with make-up and putting on their first act costumes. And after that, it was time to get started.

As was often the case with dress rehearsals, they seemed to be bedevilled with endless issues, small but annoying things that Freddie took detailed notes on while Henry barked out orders. Everyone was getting a bit testy, even Tag, who was usually the most cheerful of them all.

When they finished the last scene in Act One, Jay stepped to the front of the stage and said, addressing Henry, "Before we break, should we run that scene again with Rafe? There were a couple of tricky moments with the blocking when Tag and I had that little scuffle—it feels different when you're in costume. I wouldn't want Rafe to be unprepared."

Rafe began to rise from his seat in the front row, only to sink back again when Henry waved him down irritably. "Not now. I want to run through from beginning to end with you and Tag and no interruptions. We can come back to this later —Fred, take a note will you?" Freddie, who was sitting at the end of the front row, with her massive promptbook on the seat beside her and an A4 notebook on her knee, waved a hand in the air in acknowledgement of the instruction even as she kept scribbling. Henry added firmly to Jay, "All I want you to do right now is concentrate on your performance, okay?"

Jay gave a tight nod. "Okay."

"Good. Let's start on Act Two then."

"Actually, can we take a quick break?" Bea said, standing up and rolling her shoulders. "I need to nip to the loo, and I wouldn't mind grabbing a coffee while I'm at it."

Henry gave a huff of annoyance, but Bea was already walking towards the door, a grateful-looking Rafe falling in behind her. Even Freddie was closing her notebook.

"Fine," Henry said with a sigh. "Back in ten, yeah?" The sound of the door closing behind Bea was his only reply.

"Come on, Henry," Freddie said, beckoning him. "You need a cig."

He made a face, but got up and shuffled after her.

When everyone else was gone, Jay turned to Tag. He was sitting on the floor of the stage, his uniform-clad legs stretched out in front of him, head leaning back, eyes closed. His officer's cap lay on the floor beside him.

"You okay?" Jay asked.

Tag lifted his head and opened his eyes. "Yeah, fine," he said, though he sounded a bit fed up. "You?" His gaze was direct. Searching.

Jay shrugged and paced to the other end of the stage, then back again, legs restless with unhappy energy.

After a moment, Tag said, "What was with the Rafe thing?"

"What Rafe thing?"

An impatient huff. "You wanting him to run the scene we just did."

"I don't know, I just—it felt different when we played it that time. It threw me a bit. It seemed sensible to make the point, you know?"

Tag shook his head, his dark gaze a little challenging. "Not really. We're doing a dress rehearsal. We're meant to be treating this like opening night, not taking time-outs to check in with the understudy and have a fucking coffee break."

Jay glared. "It's not my fault Bea decided she wanted a latte."

"Yeah, well, maybe she wouldn't have done that if you hadn't already interrupted the flow."

"Jesus, I made one bloody comment. Excuse me!"

Tag surged gracefully to his feet, gaze intent on Jay. "It's not just one comment, though," he said. "I've never known another actor to be so bothered about the understudy. Most of us spend our time hoping and praying we'll never need to call on them."

"Oh, in your vast experience, you mean?" Jay snapped. He pressed his lips together at Tag's wounded look and turned away, rubbing at the back of his neck.

"All I'm saying is that you seem pretty hung up about Rafe," Tag said quietly. When Jay didn't respond, Tag sighed and said, "Look, Jay, I know that you—" But he never got any further because, just then, the door flew open and Bea came charging through.

"Oh my God, you guys! Look at this!" She waved her phone at them and did a little skipping dance as she headed their way. "Austin Coburn wrote about the play—the link's on Twitter! National media coverage and we've not even opened yet!"

She held out her phone and, heart thudding, Jay took it from her.

"It's on Twitter?" Tag said as he jumped down from the stage and started rummaging in his bag for his own phone.

Jay looked down at Bea's phone screen. Austin had posted a tweet, with a link to an article. The picture in the link was of Jay at the TV Best Awards, standing beside Mason, Tag in the background talking to Lewis Hunter.

The tweet read, *"Bow Street's Tag O'Rourke confirms Jay Warren will be treading the boards with him at the York Drama Festival this week."*

"Click the link," Bea demanded excitedly, and when Jay did, he was taken to Austin's *'Little Bird'* column. It covered a few different stories, the last of which carried the usual sub-heading *"A Little Bird Tells Me…"* Underneath, it read:

"…Jay Warren, youngest son of Dame Cordelia Warren and star of TV angst-fest *Leeches*, has apparently stunned friends and family with his decision to perform on stage for the first time in years. He'll be starring in a brand-new play about the Great War poets, Siegfried Sassoon and Wilfred Owen. *Let Us Go Back* is written by Bea Lawson, daughter of renowned Shakespearian actor Timon Lawson, a good friend of Dame Cordelia.

"If you're a *Leeches* fan, don't hold your breath in hopes of scoring a ticket, though. The festival organisers predict a very quick sell-out, not least because opening night is Tuesday—

yes, *this* Tuesday—and the play will only run for the two-week duration of the festival.

"You may be wondering why this is the first we've heard of Jay Warren's involvement in the project. A *little bird* tells me that he's keeping his involvement lowkey so as not to overshadow the stage debut of close friend Tag O'Rourke, an up-and-coming young talent who recently stole the show as Bishop in Peter Crowley's new historical drama, *Bow Street*. Some believe it was O'Rourke who persuaded Warren to put aside his reservations about performing live—understandable given Warren's own <u>eventful debut stage appearance</u>. Whoever is responsible, there's no doubt that the York Drama Festival, a relatively new and modest event on the arts scene, will benefit hugely from securing such a big name. The only question now is whether Jay Warren can live up to the hype."

"Isn't it great?" Bea enthused as she retrieved her phone from Jay. "This is going to be so good for getting reviews! I bet we'll sell out in the next day or two." Jay tried to smile, but knew it was a poor effort at best. Not that Bea seemed to notice. Henry and Freddie had just walked back in, and she was already bouncing over to share the news with them.

Jay glanced at Tag, who was still staring at his phone screen, his thumb occasionally scrolling up. What was he reading? Had he clicked the link about Jay's <u>eventful debut stage appearance</u>? That would no doubt take him to Austin's years-old review of Jay's performance in *The Birthday Party*, with its brutal headline: *"When opportunity knocks… you flat on your back."*

The opening paragraph was still seared into Jay's memory, word for word.

"You'd have to be heartless to take any pleasure in watching an actor fall apart on stage, but when the Mill Cross Theatre brought down the curtain, mid-scene, on a frozen Jay Warren on Friday evening, it felt like a mercy kill. Warren was entirely out of his depth, a fact that was painfully obvious from the masterful perfor-

mance delivered by understudy Clement Harris after Warren's catastrophic collapse. One has to wonder why Harris, a veteran of the stage, was understudying someone straight out of drama school, but then, Warren is the youngest son of Dame Cordelia ..."

By now, Jay's heart was pounding in his chest, as hard as if he were sprinting. His breath felt trapped and tight inside him, anxiety swirling, and suddenly all he could think about was the little white box of pills he'd collected that morning.

Before he could think it through, he was turning on his heel and heading backstage, where he'd left his bag.

"Jay?" Henry called out. "Where are you going?"

"I'll be back in a minute," he answered, ignoring the question.

Once he was backstage, out of the others' sight and hearing, he let go of his iron control on himself. His breath began coming out in swift, panicky pants as he sank down to his knees beside his bag and tore the zip open, rifling through it till he found the box. Fumbling it open, he yanked out the blister pack of pills. The instruction leaflet fell out at the same time, drifting to the ground, ignored.

"Jay?"

The unexpected voice—Tag's voice—made him start guiltily.

"What have you got there?" Tag asked, lowering himself down to his haunches beside Jay. Jay didn't speak, or hand over the pill pack, but it didn't matter because Tag was lifting the leaflet, and when he opened it up and read the name, he clearly recognised it.

"I didn't know you were taking these," he said slowly.

"I'm not. I wasn't—" Jay paused. "That is, I haven't had any yet." When Tag didn't reply, he added, driven by honesty, "They're for stage fright." When Tag still didn't say anything, just stared at him accusingly, he snapped, "Oh don't look like that. Loads of actors use them to take the edge off."

"Take the *edge* off?" Tag said slowly, disbelievingly. "I'd have thought you'd want your edge intact when you're about to open a brand-new play. Jesus, Jay!"

Jay laughed, although he wasn't in the least amused. "Is that a view you've formulated from your vast experience of stage-acting? Or perhaps your medical expertise?"

Tag pulled back, clearly offended. "Well, excuse me for worrying about you! I just want to make sure you're okay."

"Yeah, it really sounded like *I* was your priority," Jay scoffed. "As I've said, I'm fine." Getting to his feet, he shoved the pills back in his bag. "You don't need to worry."

Tag rose too, his chest heaving, nostrils flaring. "Oh, *really*?" he said with savage sarcasm. "Because from where I'm standing, I've got a *lot* to worry about. Our dress rehearsal's a fucking shit show, all you seem to care about is making sure your understudy's ready, and now I find you popping pills that'll turn you into a bloody zombie." He threw his hands up in frustration. "Jay, this is my big break! If it's a fuck-up—"

"In case you hadn't noticed, this play isn't *all* about you."

"Yeah, I know!" Tag retorted furiously. "It's also Bea's first full-length work. It's a production that Henry and Freddie have put their hearts and souls into. *And* it's the fucking flagship event of this entire festival. It's important to lots of people!"

"You think I don't fucking *know* that?" Jay yelled. "Why do you think I'm so bothered about Rafe? Why do you think I got these pills? I want this play to be a success!"

"Then get your head in the game," Tag said in a low, driven tone. "Instead of looking for the easy way out, be fucking *present*. You don't need Rafe, and you don't need those pills. You've already got everything you need right here."

"You haven't got a clue what I n—"

"What the hell's going on back here?"

They both spun round to find Henry glaring at them.

"Henry—" Tag said, startled. "We were just—"

"—having a stupid argument," Jay interrupted, stepping forward. "You know how it is when we get to this stage. Tensions are running high." He turned back to Tag. "I'm sorry —my fault entirely. Shall we get back to rehearsal?"

Tag frowned and opened his mouth to argue, but Henry was already turning away.

"Come on, then," Henry snapped. "Let's make a start on Act Two."

CHAPTER TWENTY-THREE

Tag

Somehow, they managed to limp to the end of the disastrous dress rehearsal, though Jay remained stiff and distracted throughout, and Tag knew he hadn't been much better. Bea, watching from the middle of the stalls, had chewed her lip anxiously while Henry just looked grim.

As soon as possible after the final scene ended, Tag escaped backstage to the dressing room.

He sat slumped in front of the mirror, thoughts circling back to the sight of Jay holding those fucking pills and Austin's words of last night—"*Well, there was that* Dracula *fiasco a year or two ago. …I understand he needed some, er, artificial help to get through it. …he was completely stoned that night. Tragic, really.*"

Tag didn't know how much of that to believe, but there was no denying that he'd caught Jay with some pretty serious prescription medication. It was suddenly, shockingly clear that Austin had been right about one thing: Jay was suffering from stage fright so crippling that he needed meds to get through it. And not for the first time.

The enormity of it hit Tag all at once. Performing on stage with Jay was a huge risk, one that Tag hadn't even known he was taking. If Jay seriously fucked up, Tag's stage debut could turn out to be a disaster.

Why the *fuck* hadn't Jay told him?

Their personal relationship aside, they'd been working together for six weeks. He'd thought they were a team, that they had each other's backs, but not once had Jay said anything. Tag still wouldn't know if Austin hadn't warned him.

The truth was, he felt deceived. *Betrayed.* He'd given up his job to take this role, shouldering a financial burden he couldn't really afford. Would he have done it if he'd known Jay was maybe, *possibly* unreliable? Difficult to say, but he should at least have had the fucking choice.

He wondered, then, whether Henry and Bea knew. Bleakly, he concluded that they must, especially Henry, who'd known Jay for years. Yeah, they'd probably known and decided to accept the risk, which, *fine*, because at least they'd known there *was* a risk. Tag hadn't, despite having the most to lose. Bea and Henry—and Jay, of course—all had the wealth and connections to protect them if the play went tits up. Tag had nothing. He'd been operating without a safety net his whole career, and none of them apparently gave a shit about that. Or maybe they just hadn't thought about it. He wasn't sure if that was better or worse.

Tag stared at himself in the mirror, his hair slicked and parted à la 1918, make-up smudged around his eyes. He looked angry; he felt angry too. No, be honest. He felt *afraid*, terrified that his big break was going to end in disaster. Terrified that all his hard work and dreams would die here.

Maybe he should tell Henry about the pills? There might be something he could do to support Jay, or talk him down from his panic. If nothing else, as the director, Henry probably had a right to know.

Even so, going behind Jay's back like that…?

Still undecided, Tag scrubbed off his make-up, hung up his costume, ready for tomorrow, and dressed quickly before heading back to the stage. Jay was already down in the auditorium, back in his civvies and with his jacket on, talking to Henry, who had a firm hand on Jay's shoulder.

Okay, that was good. Tag felt a slight unwinding of tension at the sight of their earnest conversation. As he watched, Jay nodded, though his gaze remained fixed on the floor. A moment later, Henry gave him a firm pat on his arm and stood back.

"All right, everyone," Henry said, addressing them all. "That was a pig's ear of a rehearsal, I admit, but you know what they say: 'Bad Dress, Great Opening'. So go home, relax, and I'll see you back here tomorrow."

Jay was moving before Henry had stopped speaking, making it very clear that he wasn't waiting for Tag. Fine, whatever. A little time to cool down was probably a good idea. Crossing the stage, Tag made his way slowly down the steps to the stalls just as the doors closed behind Jay.

Henry and Freddie had their heads together by then, discussing something in Freddie's copious notes, and Bea was chatting with Rafe. Tag hesitated. Part of him wanted to tell Henry about the pills, wanted to do something to mitigate the risk, but despite his churned-up feelings, a bigger part of him recoiled from the thought of betraying Jay's confidence. He should at least talk to Jay first and make sure he fully understood what was going on. After that, if he was still worried, he could always phone Henry. With luck, though, he and Jay could talk it out without needing to involve anyone else.

Calling goodbye to the others, Tag left the theatre and started walking home. There was a light drizzle in the air, so he hurried, hoping he might catch up with Jay since he wasn't far behind. There was no sign of him, though, and Tag suspected he'd taken a cab instead of walking. That was confirmed when he got home to find the apartment empty and Jay's clothes scattered across the bed, his running shoes gone from their place by the door.

Well, that was probably for the best. Running always helped Jay work off his stress, and hopefully he'd be feeling calmer when he got back. Hopefully they both would.

Kicking off his own shoes, Tag eyed Jay's bag, dumped by the front door. Dithering only for a moment, he crouched down and opened it, ferreting around until he found the box of pills. Opening it, he was relieved to see that Jay hadn't taken any yet. Tag turned the packet over in his hand, then went to sit on the sofa to google the pills.

He'd been right about what they were: the same stuff his dad had taken during those first terrible weeks after the business collapsed, dragging his mental health down with it. Tag might be relatively new to theatre, but he remembered how the pills had affected his dad, and the idea that any actor took them before a performance had to be bollocks. The list of common side effects was as long as his arm, and right at the top were drowsiness, slurred speech, memory problems, and poor coordination.

Fan-fucking-tastic.

He couldn't believe Jay even had this stuff. What the hell was he thinking? The answer to that was obvious; he *wasn't* thinking. At least, he wasn't thinking about anyone except himself. He certainly wasn't thinking about Tag. None of them were. Not one of them had thought to tell him about Jay's stage fright. It hurt, but, honestly, why was he even surprised? He'd been dealing with people like this since he'd started acting as a kid. Did he really need reminding how different they were from him? Growing up with privilege made you careless, not cruel but blind to others' disadvantage. Jay had charmed him, and Tag had allowed himself to be charmed, but he'd been an idiot to let his guard down. He shouldn't have forgotten, even for a moment, that in this business, when it came down to it, you were always on your own.

Well, he'd remembered now, and he wasn't going to let Jay fuck this up for him.

Flinging the box of pills onto the kitchen counter, Tag went into the bathroom to wash off the remains of his make-up and shower. After that, he dressed in his comfiest joggers and a t-shirt in a futile attempt to relax while he waited for Jay to come home.

He had a long wait. It was almost an hour before the flat door opened and Jay came in, sweaty and breathing hard from his run. Tag, who'd been perched tensely on the sofa scrolling on his phone, stood up. For a moment, they just looked at each other. Then Jay turned away, bending to unlace his shoes.

"Sorry I didn't wait. I needed to…" He trailed into silence as he straightened, his gaze caught by something. "Have you been going through my stuff?"

Tag glanced down at Jay's open bag with a flash of embarrassment that he quickly quashed. "I'm not letting you take those fucking pills, Jay."

"You're not *letting* me?" Jay stared at Tag in haughty outrage. "Who the hell do you think you are?"

Tag's hackles rose. "Your fucking co-star, that's who I think I am. The one who'll look like an idiot if you're too out of it to give a decent performance. So, no, I'm not *letting* you screw this up for everyone just because you're looking for an easy fix instead of doing the fucking work."

"Jesus Christ," Jay growled, "the *work*? You sound like my bloody mother."

"Good! She knows what she's talking about."

Jay's expression twisted. "Oh yes, Dame Cordelia knows everything—she's a fucking national treasure, isn't she? Well, newsflash: she doesn't know *me*. And apparently, neither do you."

"Clearly," Tag snapped. "I definitely didn't know you were this bloody selfish."

Jay laughed, bitterly unamused. "*Selfish*? That's just... wow. Do you even—?" He broke off, shaking his head in disbelief. "You do realise I only agreed to do the sodding play for your sake? I'd have turned it down flat if you hadn't been so desperate."

"Come off it," Tag shot back, his anger rising now. "You barely knew me back then, and you definitely didn't like me. Why the fuck would you have agreed to do the play for *me*?"

"Because you were—" Again, Jay broke off, and this time he broke eye contact too, shrugging. "Because you made such a big bloody deal about how important it was. And I thought 'Why not? I'll do the man a favour.'" His scowl deepened. "Big mistake."

"Yeah, well, lying usually is."

Jay's gaze snapped back to Tag's. "Oh, I'm a liar too, am I? A selfish liar. Good to know you have such a high opinion of me."

Something like pain flashed across Jay's face as he spoke, but Tag ignored it, just as he ignored the stab of guilt that pierced him. Why should he care about Jay's hurt feelings when Jay had been lying to him for the last *six weeks*? "Why the hell didn't you *tell* me about your stage fright?" he demanded. "Why hide something this big?"

"Because I hoped I'd be okay." Jay prowled over to the window, staring out at the drizzly river. Bitterly, he added, "Maybe I would have been if you hadn't blabbed to Austin bloody Coburn."

Tag glared at his back. "Blabbed? Blabbed *what*?"

Jay's voice was flat now. "You told him I was in the play. You knew how I felt about keeping it under wraps."

"*I* didn't tell him!" Tag cried. "Everyone at that bloody party knew. That's why they were there, for God's sake. To meet the big TV star."

Jay turned back around, his expression grim. "But you confirmed it, didn't you? You even did it *on the record*. You gave him a bloody *interview*, Tag. You gave an interview to a journalist who I'd already told you fucking hates my guts."

"A journalist of a mainstream newspaper who will be reviewing our play! Was I supposed to tell him to take a hike? And anyway, why shouldn't I speak to him, or anyone else about *Let Us Go Back*? This is my play too, Jay. You might not want any media coverage, but I *do*. I need this to be a success. I'm risking a lot on it."

"So am I!"

Tag snorted. "What? A bad review? I'm risking my whole future."

"Christ, you have no idea..."

"Because you didn't tell me! I had to hear it from Austin."

Jay's lip curled. "And of course you believed what he told you. What was that, out of interest?"

"Nothing that today didn't confirm. He told me you hadn't been on stage since *The Birthday Party*, except for a walk-on in *Dracula* when you were totally wasted. And then I found you popping pills, so..." Tag trailed off, eyeing Jay unhappily. "What am I supposed to think, Jay?"

"You could try having a little faith in me."

"Faith in what? That you wouldn't take the pills *I saw you taking*?"

Jay flung up his arms in exasperation. "I didn't take any! And I wouldn't even have *needed* the sodding things if you hadn't outed me."

"*Outed* you?"

"It was that fucking article that set me off today! The one thing—the *only* thing—I asked for when I agreed to do this stupid bloody play was that my involvement be kept secret until we opened. That was it. But none of you could keep your bloody mouths shut, could you? Not you, not Giles, not Bea." Acidly, he said, "And *you* were happy to sell your soul

—or, rather, mine—for a mention in Coburn's shitty column."

"Oh, screw you," Tag snarled. As if Jay had ever had to worry about making a name for himself. "What does keeping it secret matter, anyway? It's not like people won't recognise you when you walk on stage."

"That's not the point."

"Then explain the fucking point!"

"It's—" Jay cut himself off, both fists clenching in his hair. Stiffly, as if the words were being dragged out, he said, "If no one knows I'm in the play, there's always a—a way out."

Tag stared for a long moment, floored. "A way out?" Then, as the truth finally dawned, "Oh my God, you were never planning to go on, were you?"

Jay rubbed tiredly at his temples. "Of course I was. But keeping my involvement secret was a sensible precaution— like the pills, and making sure Rafe was ready."

"All that fuss over Rafe! Fuck, I thought you were being *generous*, giving him plenty of chances to rehearse, but that wasn't it, was it?" A flush rose in Jay's cheeks, and with it, Tag's anger. "You knew all along that you wouldn't be able to go on, or that you'd be too fucking high. You knew Rafe would have to step in at the last moment, but instead of letting another actor—another name—take the role, you strung us all along. You let me think that all that work we did together was going to make it onto the stage, when the truth was, you always planned to leave me to get by with Rafe."

"I didn't," Jay said, his grey gaze bleak. "I was just trying to ensure that if—"

But Tag was on a roll now, his temper up, and he spoke right over Jay. "Jesus, don't you see how much this damages the production? How much it fucks up my chance of getting a break in this industry? Or maybe you just don't give a shit."

After a silence, Jay said quietly, "I can't say I'm surprised that's your opinion; you always did enjoy thinking the worst of me."

"Yeah," Tag shot back, "and it looks like I was right."

Jay's nostrils flared as he sucked in a deep breath, but his expression sank into the cool, haughty mask Tag had hated back when they'd first known each other. He recognised it now as one of Jay's 'social performances', the one he hid behind when he was feeling defensive. One that concealed every trace of the sensitive, vulnerable man Tag had come to know. "Well, in that case," Jay said, stalking over to the bed, "I might as well live down to your expectations."

Crouching, he yanked his suitcase out from under the bed and tossed it onto the mattress. Flinging it open, he began to empty the dresser, throwing his clothes haphazardly inside.

Tag felt a flash of panic. "What are you doing?"

"What does it look like? I'm leaving."

"You can't *leave*. We open tomorrow night!"

Jay didn't even look at him. "Why can't I? You're right. I'm a selfish fraud and a shitty stage actor. Seb was right; I'm not cut out for theatre. The production—*you*—will be better off without me."

"Better off with Rafe?"

"Rafe's fine. He knows the part inside out."

"Yes, Rafe's *fine*. But he's not *you*. He's not the Sassoon I want to play opposite. I want to perform the play *we* rehearsed, *our* characters."

Jay glanced up, a squally look in his eyes. "Think of it like this: Rafe will be fine, and you'll *shine*. And that's all you want, isn't it? To be the star of the show, to get all the good notices, to launch your bloody career." He slammed shut his suitcase, heaving it off the bed and heading for the door. "Well, now's your chance, Tag. The stage is all yours."

"For fuck's sake, that's *not* what I want, Jay!" To Tag's horror, his voice broke on the final words, and just for a second, Jay's step faltered. He turned, and his expression was regretful.

"You probably won't agree right now, but honestly, this is for the best. At least this way, I'm not leaving halfway through Act One." With that, he grabbed his keys and phone from the ledge by the door, shoving them into his bag before swinging it over his shoulder. "Use the flat for as long as you need," he said as he pushed open the door. "I'm sorry, Tag. I really am."

Hardly believing what was happening, and too furious to consider his words, Tag yelled after him, "Fine! Flounce off like a fucking drama queen. I always knew you were a selfish dick!"

But Jay didn't turn around, and when the front door swung shut behind him, Tag was left alone in the ringing silence of the flat.

Fuck.

CHAPTER TWENTY-FOUR

J<small>AY</small>

After leaving the apartment, Jay set off towards the train station at a swift pace, dragging his suitcase behind him, making it jump and rock as he yanked it angrily across the uneven paving. Still caught up in his argument with Tag, he barely noticed his surroundings as he stalked along. All he could think of was Tag's fury, the contempt on his face, the vicious things he'd said. His final words still rang in Jay's ears.

"I always knew you were a selfish dick!"

Fine. If that was what Tag thought of him after everything they'd shared over these last weeks, then fuck him. Why should Jay care? But as the adrenaline from their argument gradually leached away, his punishing pace slackened, and a quiet, inner voice murmured, *Why wouldn't he think you're selfish? You just walked out on the play. You just walked out on* him.

Jay slowed to a halt then, his suitcase bumping up against his heels as the full enormity of what he'd just done hit him. *Shit.*

He forced himself to take a deep breath, then another.

Then he glanced around, glad of the dark and grateful to see there was no one about to witness his odd behaviour. As preoccupied as he'd been, he'd walked further than he'd intended, over-shooting the train station by some way. Turning to head back, he checked his watch, grimacing when he discovered it was almost half past ten. Not exactly the ideal time to try to catch a train back to London.

Just then, the glowing sign of an approaching taxi caught his eye, and before he could think better of it, he was stepping towards the kerb and waving it down. Even as the driver swooped out of the traffic to pull up beside him, Jay had no clear idea of where he was going. For a moment, he considered doing something deliberately diva-ish, like asking the driver to take him all the way to Chalfont St. Giles, but by the time he'd shoved his luggage into the boot and got in the back, he'd decided to be sensible and gave the driver Mandy and Phil's address instead.

Once they pulled away, Jay turned to look out the window, staring at the neon blur of street lamps and signage streaking through the night. Thankfully, the driver didn't try to talk to him, leaving him to his jumbled, unhappy thoughts. Vaguely, it occurred to him that he should call ahead to let Mandy and Phil know he was coming, but he'd chucked his phone in his bag along with all the rest of his stuff—well, most of it; Tag still had his pills—and he couldn't seem to summon the energy to fish it out.

He should have taken the pills with him, he thought, then realised that didn't matter. He wouldn't need them now. Jay closed his eyes, waiting for a reaction to that thought. Relief perhaps. After all, he'd barely slept these last few days, relentlessly worrying about opening night, his stomach permanently tight with anxiety, his appetite non-existent. Now, that worry was gone. He was free. No more play, no more fear of freezing on stage. The stress that had been riding him for days should be gone. But he didn't feel any better.

In fact, he felt worse, wounded and dazed from his argument with Tag. When he closed his eyes, he saw Tag again, cold fury in his usually warm, amber gaze. Tag would probably never look at him any other way now. After this, he'd be lucky if Tag so much as spoke two words to him again.

His throat closed at the thought, the corners of his eyes pricking, and he rubbed pointlessly at his forehead with one hand, concealing his distress in case the driver was watching him in the mirror.

Ridiculous to be this cut up over it. He'd known his fling with Tag wasn't going to last forever—Tag had been very clear that he wasn't in this for the long haul, and Jay had accepted that. But it was one thing to contemplate an amicable split at some point and quite another to have that split happen—and for it to be very far from amicable. To have to face up to the fact that, from now on, Tag would see Jay as someone who had let him down. Just… left him to sink or swim.

And he'd be right. That *was* what Jay had done.

Just like Seb had left Jay to sink or swim that night on stage.

He squeezed his eyes closed tighter, biting back a moan of distress. The thought of Tag hating him was awful. Intolerable. Just last night, Tag had been so fucking *tender* with him, caring for him in a way no one else ever had. Lately, Jay had come to realise that he'd never really recovered his confidence after the disaster of his relationship with Seb. Since then, he'd kept his sex life uncomplicated with a string of carefully controlled, but not particularly satisfying, one-night stands—much to the dismay of Katie, his agent. His brief arrangement with Mason had been a godsend from that perspective, giving him someone to be photographed with while avoiding all the dangers of a genuine intimate relationship. But with Tag, for the first time since Seb, he'd found himself letting someone in, allowing himself to be *seen*. The vulnerable parts, the unattractive parts. Trusting Tag enough to ask for what he really wanted. And Tag had given him that.

Now Tag probably felt like Jay had just thrown all that back in his face, walking out on the play without a backwards glance.

Jay swallowed hard. He *had* tried, though. He really had. And he'd been intending to keep on trying, despite knowing he was falling apart. He'd have kept on trying right up to the curtain going up. He'd have taken the meds and forced himself on stage if they hadn't had that awful argument.

If Tag hadn't discovered those pills and confronted him.

If he hadn't demanded that Jay do it without the pills.

If he hadn't… given Jay a way out.

"Mate, I said we're here."

The cab driver's irritable voice made Jay startle. "Right, yeah, sorry. I was miles away. How much do I owe you?"

After settling the fare, he dragged his case out. He should probably ask the cab driver to wait while he buzzed the house —from behind the big front gates, you couldn't tell if anyone was in—but he let him go, dragging his suitcase over to the side gate to press the visitor buzzer.

It took a while, but eventually, there was a crackle on the line, then Phil's voice.

"Jay? Is that you?"

Jay waved at the camera. "Yeah. I was hoping to crash here tonight if that's okay?"

"Of course. Come in." The side gate clicked open, and Jay entered, trudging up the gravel drive to the front door where Phil was waiting in a shabby, faded blue towelling robe over plaid pyjama bottoms and thick slipper socks, his expression concerned. He pulled Jay into a warm, enveloping hug, his burly arms reassuringly firm, and pressed a smacking kiss to the side of Jay's head before releasing him and guiding him inside, closing the door behind them.

"Your mother and Amanda are out at a ladies' dinner at

one of the neighbours. It'll probably be a late night. Do you want me to call them?"

Jay made a face. "No, it's probably for the best that Mother's not here, to be honest. I'm not sure I'm up to facing her yet. She's going to freak out."

Phil merely raised one brow. "Need to talk?"

Jay sighed. "Yeah, and to be honest, I could do with a drink."

"Like that is it? Come on then." Taking the suitcase from him, Phil led him down the hall into their cosy, farmhouse-style kitchen. "Park yourself there," he said, pointing at the big wooden table. "Wine? Beer? Whisky?"

Jay settled into one of the big comfortable wooden chairs. "Whisky." It was Phil who had taught him to appreciate good whisky, often at this very table, and there was a certain comfort in the ritual of drinking it with him.

He watched Phil shuffle round the familiar kitchen, pulling a bottle of single malt out of one of the cabinets and two glasses from another. A lumbering bear of a man with a grey-streaked mop of unruly hair and a lumpy sort of face, Phil was very much the beast to Mandy's beauty. In truth though, she had been the one to pursue him.

"It took a while, but I wore him down," she'd say when people asked how they'd got together, and everyone would laugh, assuming, wrongly, that it was a joke.

Sliding into the chair kitty-cornered to Jay's, Phil poured out two generous measures and raised his own glass in a brief toast before sipping it reverently. Jay raised his glass in turn, but he swallowed the whole measure, wincing a little at the burn that followed.

"Well, that's a waste," Phil said conversationally, not sounding the least put out.

"I'll sip the next one," Jay promised.

Phil topped him up. "Make sure you do," he said. "This stuff's too expensive to waste on getting drunk." Then, leaning forward, he said, "So, do you want to tell me what this is all about?"

Jay stared at his whisky, unsure how to begin. At last he said, baldly, "I've walked out on the play. I just—" He broke off and gave a wet laugh. "I can't do it."

When he lifted his gaze to Phil's, it was to find the man watching him with concern. "Your mother seemed to think it was going well. Did something change?"

Jay shook his head numbly. "The opposite really. Nothing has changed—reality caught up with me, that's all." At Phil's questioning look he added, "I'd almost convinced myself I'd got over my stage fright, or that I could will myself out of it." He met Phil's gaze and added flatly, "You must have guessed that was why I never perform live."

"I had an inkling," Phil admitted. "But you never said anything, and I didn't want to pry."

"Yeah, well, it was kind of taboo to talk about it." Jay shrugged. "Mother wants to believe I'm every bit the stage actor she is. Even right after the *Birthday Party* debacle, she just waved it off, saying every actor has bad nights and to put it behind me. *'Onwards and upwards'*."

Phil sighed. "You know I love your mother dearly, but she does have a tendency to *waft away* problems." He made an airy gesture with one arm that was so characteristically Dame Cordelia that Jay couldn't help but laugh a little. Phil gave him a wry smile. "It can feel dismissive—I know that's how Amanda's felt sometimes—but I think it's Cordelia's way of saying everything will be okay, you know?"

"Yeah," Jay said wearily, "it is, but it *is* dismissive too. The truth is, she doesn't want to recognise problems, or deal with them. She prefers to act like they don't exist, and—well, she's good at acting, isn't she?"

"I'd say it's a bit of a family trait," Phil said pointedly. "I mean, you've been in rehearsals for this production for weeks, and it's only now that you've come to the conclusion you can't go on."

Jay blew out a breath. "True," he said. "I've been burying my worries for a while, refusing to face up to them. I mean, I wasn't *blind* to them—they were always at the back of my mind. But it was only as we got closer to opening night that they began to really surface. And then at the party…" He trailed off, running both hands over his face tiredly. After a pause, he began again. "These last few days have been hard. To be honest, I've barely slept." He shook his head. "Sorry, I must sound like a self-pitying twat. I don't deserve any sympathy when I'm letting Tag down like this. And Henry and Bea, of course—and everyone." His eyes began to smart. "Shit."

"Tag," Phil echoed. "That's the guy playing Wilfred Owen?"

"Yeah. He's—he's amazing. So talented. And this is his first professional leading role, so it's a huge deal for him." Jay closed his eyes. "I'll really be screwing him over."

"Does he know yet?"

Jay felt his cheeks warm. "Yeah, he's been, uh, staying with me."

Phil's gaze flickered to Jay's suitcase and back. "Did you argue?" he asked carefully. "Is that why you need a bed tonight?"

Jay swallowed and nodded. "Yeah," he said. "I kind of decided I was quitting while we were arguing. He found out I'd got some pills—just some anti-anxiety meds, to help me go on, you know? Anyway, he went ballistic and I reacted badly. Before I knew what I was doing, I'd said I was leaving and Rafe—that's the understudy—could take my place."

Phil was silent for a while, his gaze thoughtful. At last he said, "If you don't mind me saying, that sounds like a more-than-friends argument. Are you two…?"

"Yeah," Jay whispered. "We've been, um, *more than friends* for a couple of weeks now."

"And you're serious about him?"

Jay let out a miserable huff of laughter. "Wouldn't matter if I was. He only wanted some fun while we're here in York."

Phil's expression was painfully sympathetic. "Ah," he said. "And you want more."

"Yeah, well, I'm an idiot," Jay said flatly. "Tag was very clear about what he wanted, and what he didn't want, so I was well warned, but I went wading in anyway."

Phil nodded. "Sounds like you've got yourself in a bit of a pickle, son."

Jay could only give another of those helpless, humourless laughs. "That's an understatement," he said. Then he sighed. "I don't know what to do. It's all such a mess. Tag and me, the play, all the people I'm disappointing..." He groaned and buried his head in his hands.

Phil was quiet for a while. Then he said, "Remember what I used to say when you were younger and you'd come and talk to me? About how to think through your problems."

Jay lifted his head. "Yeah," he said with a half smile. "You said, most problems have more than one part and not to try and deal with everything at once, but to look at the parts one by one."

Phil smiled at him approvingly. "So you *were* listening?"

"Of course."

"Okay, let's start with the play then. You said you decided to walk out in the middle of your argument with Tag—were you going to walk out anyway, or was it *because* of the argument?"

Jay made a face. "That's difficult to answer. I *was* intending to go on. I really was. But I was also making damned sure that Rafe was ready to go on in my place. And I know that's not normal." He paused, searching for the truth inside him. "I *wanted* to go on. I wanted to be there for Tag—he's worked so hard. We both have."

Phil nodded, his kind gaze grounding Jay. "And now that you know you won't be going on tomorrow, do you feel relieved?"

Jay blinked. Frowning, he took stock of his feelings, imagining watching the play. Watching as Rafe made that angry, sweet declaration to Owen at the end of the play. And what Jay felt in that moment was *nothing* like relief. He felt jealous —savagely jealous—that Rafe would be sharing those intimate moments with Tag on stage.

"No?" Phil said.

Jay met his gaze, feeling oddly dazed. "I suppose it's not so surprising," he said. "I've worked hard on this play over these last weeks, and it's the first piece of real theatre I've done in years and years—since *The Birthday Party*."

"No, it's not surprising that you'd feel invested after working so hard," Phil agreed mildly.

"It didn't even feel like *work,* though," Jay continued. "The play is really good, and working with Henry—I mean, there's no one like him for getting inside a character. And *Tag*—" He broke off, unable to go on for a moment. Tried again. "Tag is, he's—we had a bond. Acting with him came so naturally. I felt like he brought out the best in me, and it's a long time, a really long time, since I experienced that."

"That sounds pretty special," Phil murmured.

Jay gave an awkward laugh. "It probably wasn't like that for him. He could play Owen just as beautifully with anyone else playing Sassoon." Even as he said that, though, Tag's words of earlier came back to him. *"Yes, Rafe's fine. But he's not you. He's not the Sassoon I want to play opposite."* Jay's throat closed at the memory. And then he remembered what he'd said in return, accusing Tag of just wanting to be the star of the show, of only thinking of his own career. *Christ.* He squeezed his eyes closed and scrubbed at his face with his hands, as though to erase the memory of those unfair words. Tag had been nothing but generous in rehearsals, only interested in what was best for the play, what would best serve the characters, not the least bit grabby or self-seeking. The reason he'd been such a joy to work with was that very generosity, that lack of ego, and now Jay felt ashamed of his petty, shabby accusations. Words he'd thrown as a cover for his own shortcomings, a distraction while he made his cowardly escape.

He had been right about one thing, though: him walking away would probably turn out to be the best thing for Tag.

Quietly, Phil said, "It sounds to me as though you have real feelings for this guy."

Jay's eyes stung and he nodded, swallowing against the lump in his throat. "Yeah," he croaked, and admitting it aloud felt like shucking off a huge weight, an intense, exquisite relief. "I'm—I'm in love with him."

"Does he know?"

Jay shook his head. "I was pretty stupid about recognising it," he said. "We didn't get on when we first met. There was— a lot of friction between us."

"Sometimes friction can be a sign of something else," Phil said, shrugging. "When I first met Amanda, I was convinced I disliked her." He laughed, then gave a rueful smile. "It took me a while to admit to myself that people generally don't spend every waking minute thinking about someone they dislike and finally put that bullshit aside. It sounds like you and Tag did too?"

"Thanks to the play," Jay admitted. "Working so closely, we got to know each other better, and I soon saw how wrong I'd been about him." He shook his head at himself, smiling slightly at the memory of those early days. "I thought he was brash and shallow because he has this jack-the-lad persona. But then I realised he wears that to hide his vulnerable side. He's always cracking jokes and flirting with everyone, and sometimes he's a bit of a hothead…" Jay came to an abrupt stop.

"Like tonight?" Phil suggested gently. When Jay stayed silent, he added, "Maybe he feels the same way as you, Jay?"

Jay shook his head numbly. "Like I said, when we first got together, he was very honest about what he wanted: a quick fling, nothing more."

"Well, maybe he changed his mind. *You* did, after all."

It was a tempting thought, but Jay wasn't about to start fooling himself. "Yeah, well, I changed my mind because I discovered that Tag's a great guy. What he discovered about me was… not so great, you know?"

"Jay, come on—"

But Jay kept going, driven by a painful desire for confession. "I mean it. Now he knows that underneath my confident mask, I'm uptight and inhibited, and needy as fuck, just like Seb always said."

"Sebastian Talbot was an abusive prick," Phil said grimly.

"But he was right about that," Jay said implacably, almost welcoming the stab of pain the admission brought. It was good to remind himself of this. Good and necessary. "Anyway, you didn't see Tag tonight. He's angry and disappointed in me, and he's right to be. I mean, I've just shown him how unreliable and selfish I am. He's better off without me, and now he knows it."

Phil gave a huff of frustration. "Jay, you couldn't be more wrong. You're *loveable*. You're kind-hearted, and you're a good, loyal friend." He shook his head, then gave a rueful smile. "And you're a handsome, young devil. I'll be astonished if Tag doesn't feel just the same as you do, and if I'm wrong—if he really doesn't—he's a bloody idiot."

Jay smiled sadly. "You're biased."

"I am," Phil admitted. "But anyone who knows you would be." He set his hands down on the table in a decisive gesture. "Right, here's the thing, kid. You're knackered.

You've not been sleeping right, and when your sleep's off, everything's off. So here's what you're going to do." He rose from his chair and headed for Jay's suitcase. "You're going straight to bed, and to sleep. No excuses. Everything else —*everything*—can wait till tomorrow. You can give me your phone, too, and I'll deal with any urgent calls." He made a face. "I dare say there'll be one or two."

Despite feeling guilty for the distress he knew he'd be causing Henry and Bea, a powerful wave of relief passed over Jay, and he nodded gratefully, so exhausted he could barely think. Phil was right. He'd deal with their disappointment in the morning. God knew that would be soon enough.

On leaden legs he followed Phil upstairs into one of the guest rooms, dug his phone out of his suitcase and handed it over, then collapsed into bed, falling straight into a deep and, mercifully, dreamless sleep.

CHAPTER TWENTY-FIVE

Tag

Tag woke up, again, for what felt like the tenth time in as many hours.

The flat was filled with the pallid light of early morning, which, at this time of year, was very early. Groping on the floor next to the sofa-bed he found his phone and saw it was 5:15 a.m.

Groaning, he rolled onto his back, phone in hand, and stared up at the ceiling through gritty eyes. He'd hardly slept, spending the night fluctuating between fury, panic, and something that felt painfully like grief. For the play, he'd thought last night, for all it might have been if Jay hadn't thrown his toys out of the pram.

But in that grey dawn light, it was harder to muster his anger. Maybe because he was too tired, or maybe because the cool morning had washed away his hot temper. Now Tag felt … nothing. Flat.

Depressed.

In his palm, his phone buzzed with a notification. Tag's

heart buzzed too, jumping in his chest with hope that—what? Jay had changed his mind? That was hardly likely.

"...that's all you want, isn't it? To be the star of the show, to get all the good notices, to launch your bloody career. Well, now's your chance, Tag. The stage is all yours."

All night, he'd been thinking about what Jay had said—first in irate indignation but later, in the darkest hours, grimly recognising a grain of truth in the accusation. He *was* focused on his career, but he had to be. He'd had to fight twice as hard to have even half a chance at making it.

Not that Jay could ever understand that. And if he really, truly thought that all Tag cared about was being the star of the show, he wouldn't be changing his mind about working with him, not now or ever.

Even so, Tag's fingers were all thumbs as he swiped open his phone, and disappointment flooded him when he confirmed his suspicion that there was nothing from Jay. The notification had been for an email. He opened up his email app anyway, just in case, against the odds, the email was from Jay. But no, it was just spam.

There was another email, though, sent yesterday, which Tag stared at in confusion.

From: Geoff Hall@hallbeaumont.com

Re: Settlement - Rent Refund

Blinking sandy eyes, Tag opened the message. It was short and to the point. The dispute with his former landlady in York had been resolved. His security deposit and rent advance would be returned in full on condition that he did not pursue legal action against her. Hall Beaumont's fees would be taken care of by Mr. Warren. Therefore, if Tag was agreeable to these terms, he should simply forward his bank details to Mr. Hall's secretary and payment would be made forthwith, after which the matter would be considered closed.

It took a second for that to register.

Geoff Hall was Jay's lawyer. With everything that had

happened since they'd moved in together, Tag had forgotten that Jay had asked Geoff to look into getting Tag's rent back. To be honest, he'd hardly even registered the offer at the time because it had seemed like such a throwaway comment, and at that point, they'd barely moved beyond the frenemies stage of their relationship.

Even so, Jay had done that for him, hadn't he? He'd taken the trouble to ask his lawyer—at Jay's own expense—to look into Tag's little problem. And all for a guy who, back then, had been more antagonist than friend.

Why had Jay done it?

It wasn't a difficult question for Tag to answer. Jay had done it because he was a kind, generous man. The sort of man who'd invite you to stay when you were in trouble even though he hardly knew you, the sort of man who'd agree to take a role in a play because it might help you get your break. The sort of man who'd celebrate your little triumphs with balloons and champagne…

Shit. Tag squeezed his eyes shut against that memory, but his heart was squeezing tighter, so tight it hurt.

Everything Tag had learned about Jay over the last six weeks told him that he was a caring and giving man. So why the fuck had he stormed out on the play—on Tag—last night?

Maybe, Tag thought bleakly, *because you were being such a fucking shit to him.*

"I always knew you were a selfish dick!"

Tag winced, the words in his memory sounding crueller in the ruthless light of day. Whatever else Jay might be, he had never been selfish. The total opposite, in fact. Tag had let his temper get the best of him last night, and it had made him mean.

With a groan, he swung his legs off the sofa and sat up. As he did so, his gaze fell on Jay's box of pills sitting on the kitchen counter where Tag had thrown them in disgust. They too looked different this morning. Just an ordinary box of pills with a prescription sticker on the back. Medication prescribed to Jay, presumably by an actual doctor treating an actual mental health condition. Stage fright, Jay had called it, but what was stage fright if not a form of anxiety?

Tag had a sudden flash of memory, not of acting with Jay but of being in bed with him. Jay, tense and self-conscious, riddled with performance anxiety, unable to ask for what he wanted. Christ, Tag should have realised then, shouldn't he? Well, he *had* realised. He'd known right away that someone—Seb, it turned out—had done a number on Jay's sexual confidence. How much bigger impact had that bastard had on Jay's professional confidence? On his personal confidence?

No wonder Jay suffered from stage fright.

And what had Tag done to help? Fuck all, that's what. He'd accused Jay of being a diva, when Tag was the one ranting at Jay for screwing up *his* big break, *his* career, *his* play. Not once last night had Tag considered that Jay had an actual fucking mental health condition, one for which he'd sought help.

Help Tag had stolen, and then blamed Jay for using. No, worse: *banned* Jay from using.

Christ.

Dropping his phone, Tag buried his face in his hands. "Shit," he breathed. "What the fuck have you done?"

A moment later, he was on his feet, pacing backward and forward in the little flat. Jay's flat. There were traces of him everywhere: his sweatshirt on the back of one of the dining chairs, the mug he always used for coffee by the sink, his dog-eared script on the nightstand by his bed—the bed Tag hadn't wanted to sleep in alone last night.

But Jay was gone, and his absence suddenly felt raw, like a hole in Tag's heart, bloody around the edges. Everything about the last few days was unravelling in Tag's memory, reforming to reveal a new picture. Jay's tension at Dame Cordelia's party, his desperate neediness afterwards, his restlessness and refusal to talk about the play all weekend—all of it, Tag saw now, was Jay's way of trying to cope with his anxiety. Asking for Tag's help the only way he knew how. But Tag had been blind to it, too caught up in the glamour and excitement of opening night, unwilling to see what was in front of his nose.

He saw it now, though, and he was ashamed of himself.

What did the bloody play even matter next to Jay's well-being? Next to Tag's feelings for him? And, yes, that was something else he'd been trying to ignore, wasn't it? His *feelings*, the ones that had erupted into hurt fury last night, the same ones that were now churning so painfully inside him that he felt physically sick with guilt, and fear that he'd lost Jay over this. Lost the man he'd maybe—

Oh, fuck it, *not* maybe. Time to stop lying to himself and just fucking own it.

He was in love with Jay. Stupidly, crazily in love with him.

Tag let out a bleak, helpless laugh as he finally admitted it to himself, staring unseeingly out of the apartment window at the river. It wasn't that he hadn't suspected it before, but just like with everything else that he deemed secondary to his ambition, he'd ignored the inconvenient truth because it was difficult, because Jay might not feel the same, and because it was simpler to focus on his career plan and his big fucking break.

Well, he couldn't ignore it now, could he? It was eating him alive.

He was completely, helplessly in love with Jay Warren. Jay, with his posh accent and kind heart, his generous talent, and his unexpectedly sensitive soul.

Tag loved him, and he'd hurt him, and all he wanted now was to make things right again. Not with the play. *Fuck* the play. That came as another shock—realising that he didn't care whether or not Jay performed tonight, or even about his own big break, not if it came at the price of Jay's happiness.

Right now, this minute, all he *did* care about was that Jay was okay, and that maybe, if Tag grovelled enough, he might forgive Tag for being such a selfish, thoughtless shit.

Snatching up his phone from where it had fallen on the floor, he was about to call Jay when he remembered the time. Not even six o'clock. Jay would have got back to London in the small hours of the morning—hopefully he was asleep now. God knew he'd looked exhausted when he left last night. Tag wasn't about to wake him up at the crack of dawn just because he desperately needed to soothe his own guilt.

Instead, he fumbled open his messages, then paused. Not knowing what to say—there was so *much* to say—he went with the most urgent.

I'm sorry. Are you okay?

There was no answer, and he could tell the message hadn't even been read. Which was good, because it probably meant Jay was sleeping. Or ignoring him. He pushed that thought to one side for now. He'd try calling later, and then he'd know.

In the meantime, the question was, what to do next? Mostly he just wanted to jump on a train to London and bang on Jay's front door, but he didn't even have Jay's address. Besides, the play was opening tonight, and Tag knew Jay would want him to go on. That he wouldn't want Tag to let down Bea and Henry.

Okay, so he couldn't leave York, which meant he had to find another way to help Jay. Someone needed to check on him today. Tag didn't know anyone he could ask, but Henry would; he was friends with Dame Cordelia, after all. Not that Tag wanted to confess to Jay's mother what a crap friend he'd been to her son, but he'd suck it up if it meant someone could be there for Jay.

Squirming with discomfort, he checked the time again— almost six—and decided that was late enough for Henry. Pacing again, he dialled.

Henry picked up after a couple of rings, sounding bright

and breezy. "It's completely normal for first-night nerves to strike this early," he said by way of greeting.

"Yeah," Tag said. "Look, have you heard from Jay?"

"No, about what?"

Tag swallowed. *Fuck.* "He's—shit, Henry, he's gone."

A long pause followed.

"Gone home to—" Tag's voice cracked and he cleared his throat. "He said he couldn't handle his stage fright. He's quit. He left last night."

"Oh sodding hell," Henry said, with feeling. "I really hoped this wouldn't happen."

Tag couldn't help saying, "I really wish someone had told me it was a possibility! I could have…" He closed his eyes, squeezing the bridge of his nose. "I could have been less of an arse about it."

Another silence crackled down the line before Henry said, "Does Bea know?"

"Not from me."

"Right. I'll call her and round up the others. We'll meet at the theatre at seven. We've got twelve hours until curtain up."

Tag blinked, staring at Jay's coffee cup by the sink. Curtain up? "Henry," he said, "I have to—we have to speak to Jay and make sure he's okay."

"And we will," Henry soothed. "Don't worry. Just come to the theatre and we'll sort everything out."

Tag nodded, then realised Henry couldn't see him and said, "Okay."

"Oh, and Tag? Don't tell anyone else about this yet."

"Of course not." After fucking up with Austin Coburn, telling anyone Jay's business was the last thing Tag would ever do. "I'll see you at seven."

It was five to seven when he reached the theatre, after forcing himself to take a shower, shave, and pull together everything he needed for the day, and for the evening in case he didn't get home before the performance.

Even so, he wasn't the first to arrive. Bea was already there, pacing outside the locked door, her red hair a wild tangle scraped back into a hasty ponytail, looking like she'd just rolled out of bed. Rafe was with her, and Tag didn't miss his air of suppressed excitement. Couldn't blame him for it either. Any actor would jump at the chance to take over a leading role, even at the expense of another's misfortune. Tag's stomach sank, Jay's absence now a physical ache in his chest. Rafe was a decent actor, but Tag wanted Jay.

He wanted Jay in every part of his life.

"Tag," Bea wailed, reaching in to give him a hug. "I can't fucking believe this." She sniffed, and Tag could see she'd been crying. "Daddy warned me it was a risk, but I can't believe Jay would *do* this!"

"He didn't do it on purpose," Tag said, giving her a brief squeeze and letting go. "It's not his fault he suffers from stage fright."

"I know, but on *opening night*?"

Tag dragged a hand through his hair, aware his temper was short, aware they were all dancing on raw nerves. He didn't blame Bea for being pissed off—it was exactly how he'd felt last night—but that only made him feel worse about how he'd acted. He'd been so self-centred and dismissive. "Everyone's nervous on opening night," he pointed out curtly. Then, to cut the conversation short, he went over and tried the handle to the stage door. "Don't you have a key?"

"Henry does."

"Listen," Rafe said then, resting a hand on Tag's shoulder. When Tag looked around, Rafe was regarding him earnestly, although the gleam of excitement in his eyes wasn't quite doused. "I know this isn't ideal, but I just want to say that I'm going to do my best tonight. It's going to be a good show regardless."

Tag nodded, patting Rafe's hand and subtly dislodging his

grip. "Yeah. And listen, for the record, I think you're great. We'll be fine."

"We will," Rafe said sincerely, turning his attention to Bea. "You can rely on *me*."

Had Tag really heard that subtle emphasis on *me*?

Bea gave a watery smile. "I know I can, Rafe. It's just—" Her eyes filled. "Since it came out that Jay was our star, we've *totally* sold out for every show. And now everyone's going to be *so* disappointed. I'll be a laughing stock."

Irritated, Tag said, "Shame we didn't keep it secret, then."

"Well *I* didn't tell anyone," Bea objected, although her cheeks flushed. "I mean, nobody who mattered."

Soothingly—and without looking at Tag—Rafe said, "I'm sure Tag was talking about himself, giving the scoop to Austin Coburn."

"Oh God," Bea cried, "Austin's going to be there tonight!"

Which, thank fuck, was the moment a cab pulled up and Henry climbed out of the back seat, Freddie getting out on the other side.

"All right, troops," Henry said, striding to the stage door, brandishing the key. "*Stiffen the sinews and summon up the blood.*"

Wryly, in his wake, Freddie muttered, "*Cry 'God for Harry, England, and Saint George'.*" She gave Tag a sympathetic smile. "Well, this is a muddle isn't it?"

"It's my fault," he said. "I was a shit to him."

Stopping, letting Henry and the others head into the theatre first, she squeezed Tag's shoulder and said, "You can stop that right now. I doubt Jay would have stayed this long without you. Anyone who saw you work together can tell you've got a special bond."

"Yeah?" His throat closed again. "Well, if we did, I totally destroyed it last night."

She sighed. "Come on, let's go inside and see what we can do. It's not over till it's over."

They found the others in the Green Room. Henry held his phone while he paced, Bea sat perched on one of the threadbare sofas, her hands clenched between her knees, while Rafe stood by the snack table looking decidedly put out.

"...tried his home number," Henry was saying, "but there's no answer, either."

It sounded like he'd been trying to call Jay, thank God. "It's still early," Tag said. "He'd have got home late. He's probably still sleeping."

"True."

"Is there someone who could go over and check he's okay?" Tag asked. "He must have friends in the area."

Freddie said, "Anyone you can suggest?"

"Me? I don't know his friends. But could we ask Dame Cordelia? You have her number, right?"

She shook her head. "I can tell you right now—Cordy is the *last* person Jay would want to know about his little wobble."

"Wobble? It's hardly—"

Henry interrupted them. "Freddie's right. *We* need to speak to Jay, and quickly, if we're going to get him back before we open."

"Could we go down to London?" Bea said. "Is there time?"

Henry frowned. "Not for Tag. We can't risk neither of our leads being here. But I could—"

"Wait," Tag blurted, struggling to take in what they were saying. "You're going to try to persuade Jay to come *back*?"

They both looked at him. "What else can we do?" Henry said. "He needs to be here."

"But... look, I'm sorry, Jay doesn't *want* to do the play. He told me so last night."

Henry gave him a very direct look. "Do you really believe that?"

"Yes!" He shifted, feeling all their eyes on him. "I think he knows himself better than anyone, and if he says he can't go on, we should respect that."

Freddie lowered herself into a shabby armchair with a huff, depositing her huge folder on the small round table in front of her. "Not being *able* to do something is different to not *wanting* to do something."

"Maybe so, but it's still Jay's choice. We shouldn't fucking guilt him into it."

"Nobody's suggesting that," Henry said sharply. "I just need to speak to him. As the director, that's my right as well as my duty." He sighed, lifted his phone again and dialled. Obviously, there was no answer because he lowered it with a frustrated sigh. "I don't think we've got a choice. I'll have to high-tail it down to London and speak to him in person. The longer we dither, the less time we'll have to get him back here."

"I'll get you train tickets," Freddie said, already swiping her phone.

"All right," Henry clapped his hands. "Bea—you start working with Tag and Rafe. Focus on anything Rafe's not comfortable with."

"Oh, I'm comfortable with all of it," Rafe said eagerly.

Henry grunted. "I suggest you start with Act Two, Scene Four."

"Right," Freddie said, tucking her phone away, "I've got you on a train at 8:13 to King's Cross. It's an open return, so you'd better be walking in this bloody door by six."

"I will, and hopefully sooner." Henry looked at Tag again, skewering him with those bright eyes of his. "I know this is unsettling, Tag, but try to keep your head in the game. Whatever happens today, *Let Us Go Back* will open tonight. This is your moment, and I have absolute confidence in you."

Tag nodded, part of him gratified by Henry's belief in him and part of him wishing he could be heading to London in Henry's stead. Whatever Henry might say, Tag knew that he would try to pressure Jay into going on tonight, and he hated that. Bad enough that Tag had been so fucking cruel last night; he couldn't stand the idea of Henry doing the same thing. He might be more polite about it, more reasonable, but the message would be the same: you can do it, we need you to do it, don't let us down.

And that all might be true, but even if it was, it didn't matter. This was Jay's choice, and he'd chosen not to perform tonight. Like it or not, the rest of them had to accept it.

Clearly, though, Tag wasn't going to change Henry's mind, and so he said nothing more as he left, the door to the Green Room swinging shut behind him.

"Well, fuck-a-doodle," Freddie said, "I need a coffee. A good one." She pushed out of her chair. "Let's give ourselves half an hour to clear our heads and get back here for eight. Sound good?"

"Yeah," Bea said shortly.

Rafe tossed his head moodily. "This is *very* stressful, not knowing if I'll even be going on!"

"Welcome to live theatre, sweetie," Freddie said with a wolfish grin. "This is how it is."

Tag might have smiled at Rafe's expression of wounded dignity, but his spirits were too low for smiling. Besides, he had a mission.

When they left the theatre, he headed in the opposite direction from the others, saying he needed a walk to calm down. He didn't really think about where he was going, but he found himself walking towards the deli—his and Jay's favourite lunch spot. With a pang, he remembered waking up on Sunday morning to the sight of Jay coming back from his run with Tag's favourite deli breakfast sandwich. It had felt so… perfect. He'd never really been a couply guy—or rather, he'd never had time to be a couply guy—but with Jay, those little moments of togetherness, of simple companionship, had somehow filled a hole Tag hadn't known was empty.

The thought that he'd thrown all that away was unbearable.

He stopped outside the deli, not remotely hungry, and pulled out his phone. He felt a little guilty, but he couldn't let Jay be ambushed by Henry. Tag might not be able to stop Henry going, but he sure as hell could warn Jay he was on his way.

As soon as he looked at his phone, he noticed that his previous message to Jay had been read. In fact, it showed that Jay was currently active online. Stupidly, Tag's heart began to thump. No sign that Jay was typing, though, but he was certainly awake. Probably Henry's calls had woken him up.

Tag started typing, then stopped, deleted. Started again.

Fuck, he didn't want to send a message. He wanted to talk to Jay. He wanted to hear his voice, to apologise, and to find out whether Jay was okay. Probably Jay wouldn't answer, but Tag had to try.

Blowing out a breath, he attempted to calm himself, but, fuck, this was worse than an audition. Giving up, he just stabbed Jay's number, pressed the phone to his ear, and squeezed his eyes shut.

It rang once, twice, three times.

On the fourth ring, Jay picked up.

"Hello, Tag," said a voice that wasn't Jay's, "this is Phil. I'm looking after Jay's phone at the moment."

Tag's eyes popped open. Who the fuck was Phil? "Er, okay. Is Jay there…?"

"I'm afraid he's unavailable."

"Right."

Phil went on. "Jay's had quite a few messages this morning, mostly from Bea and Henry. I was interested to see that yours was the only one that asked whether he was okay."

"Oh." Tag wasn't sure what to say to that. "Um, *is* he okay?"

"Yes, I think so." Phil's voice, which sounded mature and

kindly, brightened with humour. "Although he's currently being monopolised by his mother in the kitchen, so you never know…"

Tag's head was starting to spin. Dame Cordelia was there? At Jay's home? He'd thought she was staying in York for tonight's performance. He rubbed his forehead. "Listen, I was phoning to give Jay a heads-up. Henry's on the way down to London to see him. Jay might want to be out when he shows up because Henry thinks he can push him into going on tonight. And I think that's the last thing Jay needs right now."

Phil made a disapproving sound. "I agree, but I can't say I'm surprised—it's all this 'the show must go on' nonsense, isn't it? Sometimes, I think they forget actors are just human beings. Mind you, Mandy was just as bad in her day, dragging herself around the stage with a migraine, lamenting as if the world was ending when anyone dared suggest she just take the bloody night off."

Mandy…? "Wait, do you mean Amanda Fyffe?"

"That's right. I'm her husband."

Tag could hardly breathe. "Then… is Jay at your house? Is he still in York?"

After a moment's pause, Phil said, "I take it you thought he'd gone back to Chalfont St. Giles."

"He told me he was going home."

"And so he did, in a way." Phil sounded pleased by the idea. "He turned up at about eleven last night, quite upset. We talked, drank whisky, and I put him to bed."

Tag let out a huge breath of relief. "Oh thank God. I was afraid he'd been on his own all night."

"Were you?" There was a smile in Phil's voice when he added, "It sounds like you're rather fond of him."

Stupidly, Tag felt himself flush. "I am, yeah. Very fond of him, actually."

"Well, in that case," Phil said, the smile warming his voice, "I think you know where we live, don't you?"

CHAPTER TWENTY-SIX

Jᴀʏ

Despite everything, Jay slept the whole night through, from the moment his head hit the pillow until the next morning. Perhaps it was because the looming stress of opening night had been lifted, or perhaps it was that the bed in Phil and Mandy's guest room was amazingly comfortable—or perhaps it was just that he was so damned exhausted by then he couldn't have stayed awake another moment. Whatever the reason, he slept long and deeply and woke feeling refreshed for the first time in days.

Automatically, he pawed at the bedside table, searching for his phone to check the time, only to remember—when he encountered nothing but smooth, bare wood—that Phil had taken it away with him last night. And why he had done so.

Sighing, Jay sat up, rubbing at his face with both hands. Today was not going to be easy. There was music to be faced, starting with his mother. He wondered if she knew yet—if she and Mandy had spoken with Phil last night when they got home, or perhaps this morning over breakfast. Of course, by now she might have already had a call from Henry or Freddie begging her to stage an intervention.

And he thought he knew whose side she'd be on in that fight...

With a groan, he levered himself out of bed and headed for the en suite bathroom where he took a quick shower and brushed his teeth. Then, pulling on clean jeans and t-shirt, he headed downstairs to the kitchen, where he found his mother.

She was sitting alone in her pyjamas at the big, wooden table, nursing a mug of coffee between her hands. As soon as she glanced up at him, he knew she knew. Her expression was tragic, and he had to stifle the urge to sigh.

"I presume you've heard my news?" he said lightly, making a beeline for the extra-large pot of coffee which Phil made first thing every morning. Pouring himself a large mug, he stuck a bagel in the toaster, more to occupy himself than because he was hungry.

"I have," she said heavily. "Mandy told me this morning." After a pause, she added, "I feel awful that I was out when you got here last night. You must have been frantic when you learned I wasn't in."

Somehow, Jay managed not to roll his eyes. "Actually, I came here last night because I needed a bed for the night, not because I was desperate for maternal advice."

"Julius," she remonstrated gently, but he didn't reply, staring steadily at the toaster which finally, obligingly popped.

She managed to stay quiet as he buttered the hot bagel, then brought it to the table, but as soon as he sat down, she blurted, "I was *so* upset when I heard what had happened. It's awful. I can't—"

"I know, I know," he interrupted. "You don't need to say it, all right?"

"Say *what*?" she retorted, a note of offence in her voice.

"You're not even giving me a chance to speak! What is it you *think* I'm going to say, Julius?"

He shook his head wearily. "That I've let everyone down. Bea, Henry, Tag, *myself*." He paused, then added flatly, "You."

"*Me!* Why would you say that?"

"Oh, come on, Mother," he scoffed. "I know how mortifying this'll be for you. Me failing at this *again*. Letting down the family name—"

"You haven't let anyone down!" she cried. "And certainly not me. Never think that."

"*Never think that?*" he echoed in disbelief. "Of course I think that. You never stop going on about how live theatre is the be-all and end-all. How any actor worth their salt should honing their craft on stage. What else would I think?"

"Well, yes," she spluttered, "but I realise you're a successful, busy television actor and—"

"You despise television actors," he interrupted. "Even more than movie actors. You think we're hacks."

"I do not!" she said hotly.

"Yes, you do. At least be honest."

She gave an anguished gasp at that, her expression beautifully wounded—which was usually Jay's cue to apologise, but instead he lifted the bagel and took a huge bite. It might as well have been sawdust, but he chewed manfully away, leaving it to her to break the silence.

Eventually, she did. "Look," she said. "I adore the theatre —it's the great love of my life, after your father, of course, so yes, perhaps I sometimes denigrate other fields of acting and talk up my favourite. I don't *mean* to be judgmental." After a pause, she added, "I've never wanted to *upset* you, darling." She offered him a watery, hopeful smile, but he couldn't bring himself to smile back.

Dropping the bagel onto the plate, he gave a long sigh and rubbed at his temples. The last thing he wanted right now was to get into this with his mother, but for once, he didn't want to walk away and pretend everything was fine, like he'd done so often before. And really, there was never going to be a more appropriate time for this conversation.

"I believe that, Mother, but the truth is, you *have* upset me."

Her face fell. "When?"

"When I had that *Birthday Party* disaster, you wouldn't even talk to me about it—or even acknowledge it had happened."

Dame Cordelia's face pinkened. "Perhaps you don't remember," she said. "But I wasn't actually here when that happened. I was rehearsing in Vancouver."

"I do remember," Jay said. "I spoke to you on the phone the next day, and several times after that, but you always played it down, like I was making a big deal out of nothing." He shrugged. "I get why. You were embarrassed that I'd failed so publicly and—"

"*Embarrassed?*" his mother said furiously, her colour high now, her eyes sparking with outrage. "I was not, and I will never be, embarrassed by you! I am ridiculously, insanely *proud* of you, you absurd boy! I admit I thought that putting that debacle—and that bloody awful Sebastian Talbot—behind you was the best thing to do. I hated the idea of you wallowing in regret and '*what ifs*'—especially over *him*. Maybe that was wrong. Maybe I *should* have talked to you, and commiserated with you. But right or wrong, I most certainly was not embarrassed. I was trying to *help* you, the best way I knew how."

"Help me by constantly telling me I needed to ignore my fears and force myself back on stage?" Jay said incredulously. "You know, it didn't really *help* that you kept reminding me of exactly how it was that I was failing as an actor, telling me that I wasn't *stretching myself* by sticking to television. At least be honest—you were desperate for me to go back on stage."

"*Yes!*" she cried. "Of course I was. I wanted you to try

again, but not because I thought you were failing or because I was ashamed of you. I thought it was the best thing for you to do because it was what had worked for me!" She gave a harsh laugh then, and he realised he probably looked like a stunned mullet at this revelation. "What, you think I've never had a disastrous performance?" she continued. "I can assure you, I have. More than a few, and once or twice so badly I thought I might as well throw in the towel."

Jay stared at her, taken aback. She had never admitted to messing up before. "I find that… quite difficult to imagine."

"We all have to learn. The difference between you and me was that I got to be an unknown when I started out. I got to learn my craft slowly, making my mistakes in small roles before I finally took a leading part." She smiled at him sadly. "That was something you never had. You were born famous, so you were handed opportunities on a plate. And some-times… they were things you weren't ready for."

Jay swallowed. "Poor little nepo baby, that's me," he said, trying for a light tone and failing miserably.

She gave a rueful smile. "No, you're a talented actor, Julius. I know I'm your mother and inclined to be biased, but I've heard that confirmed by plenty of others who I trust to tell me the truth. Henry Walker included."

Just a few weeks ago, Jay would probably have made some self-deprecating comment at this point. But for once he didn't feel the urge to do that, and it struck him, quite suddenly, that that was because of the work he'd been doing on *Let Us Go Back*. Challenging, satisfying work, with people he respected and liked, and who had helped him build his confidence back up.

"I don't know if you remember," his mother went on, "but before I flew to Canada, I advised you not to take the part in *The Birthday Party*. I was worried you didn't have the experi-ence to carry off a character so much older than you were."

Jay frowned. He'd forgotten that, but yes, now he remembered that conversation. He'd been so excited to call her and tell her about landing the part, and at the time, her unenthusiastic response had crushed him. *"I don't think it's really you, darling. Perhaps you should pass on this one?"* Now he saw her tentative comments in a very different light.

"You were right," Jay confessed. "Obviously. It was only later I realised that I'd got the part because of Seb. At the time I was too excited to question it, but it was embarrassingly obvious. He'd pulled a lot of strings, quite hard, to get me a last-minute audition, then leaned on them to offer me the part. The truth was, nobody else really wanted me. The director was pissed off from the start, and Clive—the understudy—hated me. He was probably lined up for the part before I came along. The lead's new boyfriend waltzing in and stealing it from under his nose." He grimaced.

His mother sighed. "I should have made the point more forcefully."

Jay smiled wryly. "I probably wouldn't have listened anyway. I was so starry-eyed about Seb and my big break. I thought it would be wonderful, being in the same cast, working together every night." He gave a short huff of laughter. "And then it all fell apart on opening night."

"Oh, darling!" his mother said, reaching for his hand. "I never liked Sebastian Talbot. Such a dreadful, *selfish* actor. I'll never forget the way he undermined darling Sissy when they appeared together in *Streetcar*—Cecily Carruthers, you remember her? Dear, dear friend of mine from rep days. *Complete* nymphomaniac." Waspishly, she added, "And Talbot wasn't anywhere near butch enough to play Stanley."

Jay gave a croak of laughter. Even his mother's moral intuitions were shaped by her profession, but for once, rather than feeling irritated by her tendency to see everything through the acting lens, it occurred to him that this was her way of showing her loyalty.

"You're right about that too," he admitted. "Seb wasn't

exactly easy to work with. It was always all about him. When anyone else had lines, he'd do these distracting things, as though he couldn't bear the audience's attention to be off him for even one second." Embarrassing to remember that Jay had once thought this was the mark of a deeply committed performer, inhabiting his character fully. Now he compared Seb's self-absorbed behaviour to Tag's generous, collaborative approach and felt like an idiot for ever thinking that.

In that instant, he remembered the words he'd thrown at Tag last night.

"…that's all you want, isn't it? To be the star of the show…"

He cringed at the memory. How could he have said that? It was so untrue. So *unfair*.

When he glanced at his mother again, it was to find her eyeing him curiously.

"Do you mind if I ask," she said tentatively, "what actually happened that night? When you froze, I mean? I realise I'm a little late with this, but I'd like to know what it was you wanted to tell me."

Jay blinked, surprised. *Did* he want to talk about it now, after so long? In truth, he wasn't sure, but at last he shrugged. "We didn't get off to a very good start—Seb and I had argued the night before, and he was barely speaking to me when we got to the theatre." Jay grimaced at the memory of that argument—it had been another fight about their sex life, with Seb, who was an uncompromising top with little patience for foreplay, accusing Jay of being uptight and impossible to please because he couldn't orgasm within five minutes of them getting naked. It had been the last thing he'd needed when he was already eaten alive with nerves at the thought of his first big opening night.

"What a shit," Dame Cordelia said feelingly.

Jay gave her hand a comforting pat. "He was a shit," he agreed. "And I was terrible at sticking up for myself. It's embarrassing to look back on." He paused, then went on.

"The moment I stumbled was quite near the start of Act Two —there was just the two of us in the scene, and there was this one line—when we'd done it in rehearsal, Seb would always walk to the front of the stage, looking out at the audience. He'd have his back to me, but I was looking at him as I delivered the line." He paused, taking a shaky breath, a little surprised by how emotional he felt even now, after all this time. "But on the night, he didn't do what we'd rehearsed. Instead, he walked behind me and sat down on a chair, completely out of my line of sight, so I'd have to turn away from the audience to look at him." Jay swallowed hard, embarrassed by the constriction in his throat. "I got completely flustered. I remember thinking, *Should I do what we rehearsed? Should I improvise?* And then I became aware of the silence—too many beats passing since Seb had spoken—and then the words were just… gone and my mind was racing with complete panic. I remember I turned to look at him and tried to catch his eye to get him to give me a prompt, but he wouldn't"—Jay's voice broke—"he wouldn't even *look* at me."

It was even worse than that in fact, though he found he couldn't bring himself to share every single humiliating detail with his mother, who was already looking furiously angry. Seb had been doing little things to put Jay off from the moment the curtain had gone up that night, and when he'd finally managed to throw Jay off his game, there had been a nasty little gleam in his eye. He'd been pleased that Jay was struggling, and that was the thing that had really winded Jay. That this man, who had professed to be in love with him, seemed to be relishing his humiliation. It had been a punishment for the fight. At the time, that was what had finished him off, the pain of that betrayal stealing the very air from his lungs.

"That's fucking *appalling*," his mother said grimly. "And the director said nothing?"

Jay shook his head. "He couldn't get me off the stage—and Clive on—quick enough."

Dame Cordelia pressed her lips together. "I'm going to need a list of names, you know."

"Don't be silly," Jay said. "It was a long time ago. I'm long past the revenge fantasy stage."

"Well, I'm bloody not!" She shook her head then. "I'm sorry, darling. I should have talked to you about this before. I've always lived by my old mentor's advice that dwelling on things that go wrong in performance is a mistake—he used to say that the best thing was to put it behind you and get back on the horse as quickly as possible. But that's all very well when the mistake is your own fault. This was— Darling, I hadn't realised what actually happened to you!" Her eyes filled with tears and she gave a noisy sniff. "I shouldn't have assumed it was all down to your inexperience."

Jay shrugged. "You weren't the only one. Everyone thought that. To their eyes, I'd just forgotten my lines—which, in fairness, I *had*. It *was* me who fucked up. Seb just—"

"Seb is an irredeemable, abusive shit!" his mother snapped. "He plainly put you off deliberately because he was annoyed with you—and he was probably jealous of you too. His talent is *vastly* overrated. And now I feel *awful* for all those times I pressured you to get back on stage." She dashed tears from her eyes. "God, I'm a horrible, *horrible* bitch!"

Jay gave a rueful laugh. "You're not a horrible bitch, Mother. You're actually very nice." He leaned forward and kissed her cheek. "Do you want some more coffee?"

She sniffed again, and nodded, and he got up to refill both their mugs.

When he returned to the table a few minutes later, she was looking calmer.

He set her mug down in front of her, and she sipped at it thoughtfully. After a bit, she said, "Can I ask you something about *Let Us Go Back*?"

"Okay," he said warily.

Meeting his gaze, she said simply, "Do you think Tag is capable of doing to you what Seb did?"

Jay jerked back in astonishment. "*No!* He would never do something like that!"

She nodded slowly. "Then, can I ask… what *is* it that you fear might happen?"

Jay opened his mouth to answer her, but nothing came out. He just sat there, staring at her open-mouthed as he tried and failed to come up with an answer to that simple question. But there was no answer to it. He knew with absolute conviction that Tag would never turn away from him as Seb had, that he would never leave him isolated and floundering, much less deliberately make him feel that way. Hell, Tag would break character in a heartbeat to give Jay a prompt if he needed it, even if it compromised his own performance. Even if they'd fought the night before.

Jay knew it. He knew it with a solid, unmovable certainly that made his chest ache.

"It's about trust, you see," Dame Cordelia went on. "Trusting the other person to have your back. Trusting them enough to be vulnerable with them. It's always difficult, never easy, but if you have that trust, it's… very possible." She smiled fondly at him, her eyes damp.

"Are you still talking about acting?" Jay said huskily.

"I'm talking about all of it. Acting, yes. But also living. And loving."

He narrowed his eyes at her. "Have you been talking to Phil?"

"I don't need Phil to tell me what's going on," she said, rolling her eyes. "It was obvious at the party that Tag's absolutely besotted with you."

"Yes, well, as much as I'd like to believe that—"

But Jay didn't get to finish that sentence, because just then, the kitchen door opened and Phil stuck his head inside.

"Are you up for a visitor, Jay? Your friend Tag is here—I've left him kicking his heels in the orangery. Do you want me to chuck him out, or are you happy to see him?"

Tag was here? Jay's heart leapt with a sudden and undeniable gladness that took his breath away. Clumsily, he got to his feet, nearly tripping over his chair in his eagerness. "Yeah, I'll see him."

Phil looked mildly amused. "Righto," he said cheerfully, stepping fully into the kitchen and opening the door wide to let Jay pass through. "You know the way, son."

CHAPTER TWENTY-SEVEN

Tag

Last time Tag had visited Amanda Fyffe's house, for the party, he hadn't really noticed how grand it was. Probably because he'd been so caught up in Jay that night.

Today, though, on his own and in the bright, unforgiving light of day, it was impossible to miss. He passed through electronic gates bristling with CCTV cameras, walked up a vast, sweeping drive through beautiful grounds, and was faced with a gorgeous mansion house complete with an honest-to-god *turret*... not to mention its own orangery. That's where Phil, Amanda's husband who had met him at the front door, was now leaving him.

"Grab a seat," Phil said with an easy smile. "I'll just get Jay. Cordy's had him cornered in the kitchen for the last forty minutes."

"Oh," Tag said, dismayed. "I don't want to interrupt them. I can wait till they're done."

But Phil just twinkled at him—a neat trick that, since he didn't actually change his expression—and said, "Oh, I think he'll be happy enough to be interrupted."

Whether Phil thought Jay would be glad because it was Tag, or because Jay would want to escape his mother, Tag never got a chance to ask—the man was already heading out the door.

Tentatively, Tag lowered himself onto a small rattan sofa with off-white cushions, but when he couldn't stop his knees bouncing nervously, he got back up and began pacing around. The sun was out today, and though it wasn't especially warm outside, the glass roof and doors of the orangery trapped the heat. Feeling uncomfortably warm and sweaty, Tag yanked his hoodie off over his head. The movement took his t-shirt with it, baring his chest—which was of course the exact moment that the door opened and someone walked in.

"Um, Tag?"

Jay's voice.

Flustered, Tag fought to shove his t-shirt back down before wrestling the hoodie off. "Hi! Hi. Sorry about that," he babbled as he freed himself. "It's so warm in here and I was just—" He broke off as his gaze tangled with Jay's.

Neither of them spoke and the silence felt heavy, full of last night's argument and this morning's regrets.

"Are you okay?" Tag managed, at last.

Jay *looked* good, perfect somehow, even in simple jeans and a t-shirt, and those horn-rimmed glasses that Tag liked so much. Jay was always hot, of course, but today? Well, it was impossible not to notice how much less tense he looked than he had these last few days. And thank God for that; Tag had been afraid Jay might be... Well, he'd been afraid.

"You look good," he croaked. "Better, I mean. Not that you looked bad! Just stressed and—shit, I'm messing this up already, aren't I?"

Jay smiled. "It's okay. I probably do look a lot better. I just slept the whole night through for the first time all week. I didn't realise how exhausted I was." He gave an awkward laugh and shoved his hands in his back pockets.

Why was he standing so far away, Tag thought helplessly. Not that the physical distance really mattered. A different sort of gap had opened up between them since their argument that felt totally unbridgeable, regardless of how far apart they stood.

"How about you?" Jay prompted. "Are *you* okay?"

Tag gave a short laugh. "I don't think I slept as well as you." He offered a wry smile. "My own fault. Guilty conscience, I suppose."

Jay's gaze was direct, his expression difficult to read. "Guilty conscience?"

Tag swallowed, then forced himself to pull the bandage right off. "Yeah," he husked. "I was a shit last night, Jay, and I'm *so* sorry. You know I can be hot-headed sometimes, but that's no excuse. I wish I could take it back."

"Which part?"

"All of it. You were suffering and all I could talk about was how your situation would affect me, and the play." He shook his head, ashamed. "I was so selfish. I should have been trying to help you, not putting pressure on you to ignore how you felt and just soldier on. Fuck, I even took your meds off of you." He closed his eyes, disgusted with himself. "I wouldn't blame you if you never talked to me again."

Jay didn't say anything right away, just stood there, searching Tag's face. Then he sighed. "You're not the only one who said things they regret. I did too. That crap about you only wanting good reviews and to be recognised as the star? That's bullshit, and even when I said it, I knew it."

"I don't blame you for thinking that."

"Well, you should," Jay said shortly. "Because it's not true. You've been amazing to work with. Rehearsing this play has probably been the best experience of my professional life." He gave a soft, wondering laugh and added, "It's been like being back at drama school—excited for every day, completely focused on the work."

Tag could only stare at him, genuinely taken aback. He'd felt that way too, of course, but somehow he hadn't imagined the experience would be as profound for Jay.

"It's not just the acting," Jay went on. "Getting to know you has been pretty awesome too." He huffed a laugh. "Which is not something I'd imagined myself saying before we started rehearsals. Me and my sworn enemy, Tag O'Rourke, becoming…" He trailed off, his gaze still holding Tag's.

Lovers. That was what Tag wanted to say, but he didn't.

He wanted to say other things too. *Let's go back to that, Jay.* Christ—*Let Us Go Back*—could it be more apt? But he didn't say that either. He bit the words back because he couldn't allow himself to put another ounce of pressure on Jay. Not to return to him *or* to the play. Jay was too vulnerable to that sort of pressure. His instinct was to give, to be generous, to help whenever he could. Tag had learned that about him over these last weeks. It was why Tag felt so ashamed of how he'd behaved last night. The very least he could do now was give Jay the room he needed to work out what *he* wanted and make his own decisions.

Realising he hadn't said anything for a while, Tag said huskily, "I—I've loved getting to know you too." He tried for his trademark grin, though he suspected it was a weak attempt. "Turns out you're a pretty great guy. Who knew?"

Jay smiled back, but it was a little strained now, and disappointed somehow. In that moment, Tag felt like he'd made a mistake, or maybe missed an opportunity. Urgently, he said, "Jay, listen—"

But right then, there was a sharp knock at the door, and Dame Cordelia's unmistakable voice said, "Julius, it's me. Can I bother you for just a moment?"

Tag met Jay's gaze. A part of him wanted to ask Jay to tell her to go away, but that was ridiculous, and when he stayed silent, Jay called out, "Sure, come in."

The door opened, and Dame Cordelia's head appeared around it. "You um, have another visitor, darling. It's Bea."

"How did she know Jay was here?" Tag blurted, frowning. "I didn't tell her."

Dame Cordelia sighed. "She didn't, actually. She came to talk to me, to find out if I could help track Julius down. But when Mandy was showing her into the kitchen, she overheard me and Phil talking about him." She glanced back at Jay and added in a small voice, "Sorry."

"You don't have to talk to her," Tag said urgently, turning back to Jay.

Jay looked startled, probably by Tag's vehemence. "I know," he said, "but I want to see her. It's the least I can do after walking out on her play."

Dame Cordelia gave a little nod of satisfaction and disappeared, presumably to fetch Bea.

Concerned, Tag took a couple of steps closer to Jay. "She's going to try to guilt you into going on tonight," he warned. "But ignore her. You don't have to do anything you don't want."

Jay ran a hand through his hair, and when he let go, the strands fell in silky disarray—no hair product, Tag thought. Why that particular detail should make his chest ache, he couldn't say, except that it somehow made Jay seem less polished, more vulnerable. "What I *don't* want is to let her down," he said ruefully. His eyes lifted to Tag's. "Or you."

"You're not." Tag covered another couple of feet between them, fighting the urge to reach for Jay. "Christ, don't even think like that. You have to do what's best for *you*."

Jay's eyes held Tag's, his gaze searching. "What if I don't know what's best for me?"

Then listen to me, Tag thought, but who the fuck was he to tell Jay what was best for him?

Their intense, silent look was broken when Bea burst into

the room, dramatic as a heroine in a Gothic romance, her cloud of red hair escaping her ponytail and her face distraught. "Jay! Thank *God* I found you in time. I've phoned Henry—he only got as far as Doncaster—and he's on his way back. There's still time to save this."

Behind her came Dame Cordelia, Phil following them both into the room. What Phil thought, Tag wasn't sure, but everything Jay had told him about his mother suggested that Dame Cordelia would be firmly on Bea's side. *The show must go on, darling!*

Well, not if Tag had anything to say about it.

Stepping between Bea and Jay, Tag folded his arms over his chest and said, "Jay's not going on tonight, Bea. You need to accept that, and we both need to get back to the theatre and make sure Rafe's ready."

Her eyes widened, chin lifting. "I think that's up to Jay, don't you?"

"I do, yeah, and he's already given us his decision."

But then Jay's hand touched Tag's shoulder, warm and so familiar that Tag's heart gave a pang of want as Jay stepped around him to face Bea. "I'm so sorry for all this trouble," he told her. "I'm afraid you'll have to get used to dealing with flaky actors as your career goes on."

"For fuck's sake," Tag muttered. "Protecting your mental health doesn't make you *flaky*."

Ignoring him, speaking directly to Jay, Bea said, "But you'll be *fantastic*. I know you will. You've been so good in rehearsal. And we have a full house every night of the run, thanks to you! They're *your* fans, Jay. They want to see *you*." She pressed her hands together in front of her chest, eyes filling. Christ, she should be on stage herself. "Please don't let them down."

"None of that matters," Tag objected quickly, moving to put himself in front of Jay again. "Honestly, Jay, it doesn't.

Your wellbeing is more important than anyone's night out." His throat thickened, and he added, *"You're* more important."

More important to me.

Jay's eyes held his, clear and grey as the dawn. His voice was a little rough, though, as he said, "You think so?"

"Yeah, I do." Keenly aware that this was a public performance, that Dame Cordelia, Bea, and Phil were all watching them, Tag restrained his impulse to just…kiss some sense into Jay. Instead, he said, "I'm sorry I made you doubt that."

After another long look, Jay said, "I *don't* doubt it. I… I trust you, Tag."

"Yeah?" Tag's pulse rushed in his ears, the world narrowing to the space between himself and Jay. "That's good, because you *can* trust me. I'll always have your back."

"Yeah, I know that."

From behind Tag came a dramatic intake of breath. Bea? Dame Cordelia? It didn't matter; this was between him and Jay.

"The thing is," Jay went on, never breaking eye contact, "I think I might…"

Tag's breath stopped when Jay hesitated. Might *what*? A sudden wild surge of hope made him giddy.

"I might want to… try, tonight."

"Try…?" It took Tag a moment to understand, and then to swallow his surprise and—yes—disappointment. "You mean try *performing*?"

Jay nodded. "I think I might be able to." He swallowed, visibly. "For you."

"No, Jay," Tag said, alarmed. "No, you don't have to do anything for me."

"Not *for* you," Jay corrected, his clear-eyed gaze still fixed on Tag. "*Because* of you." His attention flickered then, darting over Tag's shoulder and back. "Because I *do* trust you, Tag. I know you won't leave me out there alone, the way Seb did."

"No, of course I fucking won't, but—" He tried to read the truth in Jay's expression. "Are you sure? You don't need to do this for *anyone* but yourself."

Jay smiled, a slight tilt of his lips. "I *would* be doing it for myself, but for you, too. And for Bea, and Henry—and the audience. No man is an island, right? I want to do this play, Tag; I admit that I'm still afraid that I can't. But I think, with you, I could at least give it a shot." He made a face. "No guarantees, though."

Behind him, Bea squealed. "Oh my God, I'm phoning Henry…!" Her footsteps hurried off across the orangery.

Tag didn't drop Jay's gaze. "If it's really what you want, then I'm there for you one hundred per cent." He pulled Jay's meds from his back pocket and held them out. "Here, I should never have taken these from you. I'm really sorry."

Jay took the box, carefully. "Thank you."

"Oh darling!" Apparently unable to contain herself any longer, Dame Cordelia swept in to envelop Jay in a hug, and Tag was ridiculously envious that she got to do that—but that was his fault, not hers. "I'm so proud of you, Julius," Dame Cordelia was saying, "but are you absolutely *sure*? Nobody will think any less of you if you pass. And if they do, fuck them!"

Tag couldn't keep the surprise from his face as he raised his eyebrows in Jay's direction. Jay gave a little smile. "I *am* sure, Mother. I want to try, and there won't be a better time than this."

"No," she said, suddenly serious. "No, I don't think there will be." She turned to Tag then and pulled him into an equally enthusiastic embrace. "Darling, Tag, I *know* you'll take care of him out there. You simply *must*."

"Mother!" Jay objected, sounding fondly mortified. "You make me sound like a lost dog."

"I will take care of him," Tag promised, laughing a little.

When his eyes met Jay's again, he added, "We'll take care of each other, right?"

Jay's answering expression was complex, difficult to read, but he nodded. His gaze skittered away from Tag's, though, when he said, "There's no actor I'd trust more."

No actor…

Tag didn't miss that careful wording, but this wasn't the time to delve into the future of their personal relationship. Definitely not with Phil and Dame Cordelia urging them into the kitchen for brunch, and Bea on the phone at the far side of the orangery in animated discussion with Henry. Besides, a deep conversation about their future—if they even had a future—was the last thing Jay needed right now. Or Tag, for that matter. What they both needed was some quiet time to focus and prepare for tonight.

Everything else would have to wait until after the show.

Nine hours later, there was plenty of quiet and focus in the dressing room where Tag sat, waiting to go on. Maybe too much.

Ness, from the theatre's hair and make-up team, had just left, and Tag was gazing at himself—at Wilfred Owen—in the mirror, at his hair, slicked back and down, at his neatly pressed khaki uniform, and at the little pencil moustache glued onto his top lip.

Fifteen minutes until curtain up.

His nerves were jangling, adrenaline buzzing in his finger-tips and toes. Fizzing in his stomach. He'd been to the loo three times in the last twenty minutes. If *he* felt this nervous, how the hell was Jay managing?

Tag had barely seen him since early that afternoon. They'd ended up spending the rest of the morning at Mandy and Phil's. Christ, 'Mandy and Phil's'? Listen to him name-dropping like a fucking pro. Anyway, it had been clear that Jay wanted to stay. He'd looked relaxed there and was obviously fond of them, and his mother had been there too, of course. Tag couldn't help worrying that Jay had maybe also wanted to avoid having an awkward conversation with him. They'd done a lot of cautious smiling across the big wooden table, and talked a little about the play, but Jay had made no attempt to speak to Tag alone. And Tag hadn't pushed it.

Then, at one o'clock, Tag's mum had messaged from the train to tell him that she and his dad were almost in York. So, he'd left to meet them at the station and help get their luggage to the Travelodge they'd booked for the night. Just as he was leaving, Jay had looked up and Tag had smiled. A little part of him had hoped Jay might offer to come along. He was pretty sure that a day ago, Jay would have jumped at the chance to meet Tag's mum and dad. But this afternoon, he'd only smiled and said, "I'll see you at the theatre, then."

Tag had spent the afternoon showing his parents the sights of York, letting his mum fuss over him, and treating them to afternoon tea at Betty's. It was only when he was paying the bill, thankful that he'd soon be getting his rent money back, that he realised he'd forgotten to thank Jay for sorting that out.

Which had made him feel like an ungrateful idiot all over again.

Leaving his parents at their hotel, Tag had headed into the theatre early. After the turmoil of the previous twenty-four hours, he'd wanted time alone to get his head back into the game. Jay had arrived an hour later, looking tense and pale, but calm, with Henry sticking to his side as if afraid he might do a runner.

Tag *had* managed to grab a couple of moments alone with Jay in the Green Room while Henry went to speak to Freddie. It hadn't exactly been awkward between them, but it hadn't been what it was before their stupid argument. Tag felt as though they were both treading on eggshells. When he'd asked Jay how he was doing, though, Jay had given a nervous laugh and held out a trembling hand.

Taking it, Tag had gripped it in both his own and fixed Jay with a firm look. "I'll be with you the whole time. If you forget a line, I'll prompt you. If it's all too much, we stop. Okay?"

Nodding, gazing right into Tag's eyes, Jay had looked like he wanted to say something more, but in the end all he'd managed was a heartfelt, "Thank you." Then he'd squeezed Tag's hand, let go, and disappeared with Henry.

Tag hadn't seen him since.

A loud knock startled him from his thoughts, and he turned to see Freddie poking her head around the dressing room door. "Five minutes!"

Tag said, "How's Jay doing?"

"Coping. You worry about getting yourself where you're meant to be on time." She flashed him a quick smile before she left. "Break a leg, kiddo."

Standing, he took a final sip of water to moisten his dry mouth, closed his eyes, and spent a full minute doing his favourite breathing exercise. Then he picked up his cap, note-book, and pen, and headed up to the wings.

The curtain was metaphorical in this theatre, but the stage was in darkness and the house lights were up. From the audi-ence came an expectant babble of laughter and chatter, washing across the stage towards him, and Tag felt a rush of excitement as it reached him. Magically, his nerves trans-formed into anticipation and he found himself bouncing on his toes, eager to get out there. Eager to begin. Christ, but he fucking *loved* this.

The play's first lines were Jay's, which was unfortunate. But Tag would be on stage with him, hidden in the darkness, sitting at a table in the officers' bar. Jay would walk across the stage, his appearance morphing from old man to soldier before the scene came to life around him.

If he froze, if he forgot that crucial opening line…

Tag tamped down a spike of alarm on Jay's behalf. If that happened, Tag would handle it, that's all. Whatever happened, he'd make sure Jay was okay.

In the wings on the far side of the stage, Tag glimpsed Jay waiting, too. He was shaking out his hands nervously, and Henry stood with him holding the rifle Jay would carry.

Sensing Tag's gaze, perhaps, Jay looked over and, for an instant, their eyes met.

Then the house lights went down, the audience quieted, and Freddie touched Tag's shoulder. His signal to get into position.

Silently, he moved across the dark stage to sit at the table, setting his cap down, opening his notebook, and setting his pen to the paper. His heart hammered, a flood of adrenaline sharpening his focus, bringing everything they'd rehearsed over the past six weeks to bear on this single moment in time. This was *it*.

And then the spot came on, and Jay was walking on stage. *Jay was walking on stage.*

Bent over, using his rifle as a stick, he shuffled towards Tag, gradually straightening, shifting into the posture and gait of a young man. A soldier.

Quietly at first, then louder, a piano started to play, the muffled grumble of the guns not quite masked by its cheerful plink-plonk. Tag drew a breath, and the lights went up around him. His eyes were on the notebook he was writing in, but all his focus was on Jay in his peripheral vision, willing him on, willing him to speak.

The wait felt eternal.

"Owen?" Jay said at last, in the clipped upper-class accent he used for Sassoon. "I can't believe it. What are you doing here, old boy?"

Tag lifted his eyes to Jay's and saw his tension, saw his courage, but, above all, he saw Sassoon. And his heart soared. "*I* never left," he said. "You're the one who got lost, remember?" He offered one of Owen's shy smiles. "But I'm glad you're back, Sassoon. I've missed you…"

CHAPTER TWENTY-EIGHT

JAY

"I never got the chance," Jay said. "You died too soon."

The audience's silence was a kind of presence, a watchful, breath-stopped hush that filled the darkness of the theatre. From what sounded like a long way away, a single flute began playing *Hanging on the Old Barbed Wire*.

Owen—Tag—lifted his head, and his gaze was bleak. "Millions did. I'm nothing special, just another dead soldier."

"Not to me." Jay stepped forward, taking Tag's hand. Lifting it, he held it between both of his own and gazed into Tag's eyes. "Never to me. I grieved you. I wanted you back."

"Why? You already had my poetry."

Jay shook his head. "*Damn* the poetry! I wanted *you* back —not your poems."

Tag stared at him with naked emotion in his eyes, and for an instant, Jay felt like they were entirely alone in the theatre, just him and Tag, on this curious, frightening, *wonderful* adventure they'd embarked upon. They'd rehearsed this scene dozens of times and it was always intense, but this, tonight, was something else. Jay was brimming with love for the man standing in front of him. He'd already realised he loved Tag, but in that moment, he *knew* it. Knew it without fear. With the brakes off. And as he absorbed that knowledge, he'd never felt stronger or braver—or freer—in all his life.

The single, distant flute was joined by more flutes, then a drum, the music rising, growing more urgent. Tag shot a devastated look over his shoulder. "I have to go back," he said, his voice breaking on the words.

"Then I'm coming with you," Jay said, resolute.

Tag turned back to him, his expression all painful hope. "You can't."

"Of course I can. I'll take death with you, Owen, over a life forgotten and alone."

Tag closed his eyes, as though in prayer. When he opened them again, they were shining with tears. He held out his hand. "All right then, Sassoon. *Since you and I are one, Let us go back. Let us undo what's done.*"

The music rose further, as though growing closer. Jay set his hand in Tag's—and the lights went down.

When the music ended, a brief silence hovered. Then the audience broke out in wild, thunderous applause.

In the darkness, Tag pulled Jay roughly into his arms. "Fucking *hell*, Jay. You were amazing! I'm so fucking proud of you!" And Jay started laughing, partly in abject relief that he'd *done it*, and partly because Tag's was such an absurdly generous reaction. This should be far more his triumph than Jay's—his first leading stage role, his big break—but Jay couldn't seem to get a single word out. And then he realised that the lights had come back on and he was standing there in Tag's arms, his face wet with tears. They both laughed and turned to the audience, and it was like being drenched in love.

The next few minutes were a blur of bows and applause. At one point, Tag dashed off-stage and returned dragging Henry and Bea, who was also in tears, after him. Eventually, though, the noise died down and Henry shepherded them all firmly back into the wings. After that, the audience began to slowly dissipate, leaving only a few friends and family hanging around for the backstage party that Freddie had organised.

Jay felt like he was walking on air, too giddy even to formulate coherent thoughts. He realised he'd lost sight of Tag but relaxed when he turned to look for him and saw him being hugged to death by a beaming Freddie. No sooner had she released Tag than she fell on Jay, treating him to a similarly fierce embrace and incoherent words of congratulation.

They were all caught up in the same feverish joy—the joy of a performance gone well, and for Jay something even more than that: the slaying of his own personal dragon.

"Right, let's celebrate!" Freddie cried when she let him go. "We've set everything up in the Green Room—I sent Rafe to get the champagne open so you lot can go through. I'll go and round up the others and bring them along."

"Thank God, I bloody need a drink!" Henry cried, clapping his hands together. He led the way, Bea following eagerly in his wake.

Jay turned to look at Tag, blinking, still feeling a little out of it, his cheeks achy from smiling. Tag's expression was affectionate, and Jay's heart squeezed at the sight.

"Shall we go?" Tag said and held out his hand. After a moment, Jay took it, and let Tag lead him towards the party, grateful for the warmth of Tag's strong fingers tangled with his own, grounding him.

Perhaps he shouldn't be allowing this—letting Tag look after him again, when Tag should be celebrating his own success—but he was still caught up in that astonishing feeling, *knowledge* really, that he'd experienced on stage. Of fully loving Tag and being loved in return. And anyway, Tag looked pretty happy with his lot, and it felt good to hold his hand as he led Jay down the corridor to the party.

The Green Room had been cleared up, and there were trestle tables set up against the wall for the drinks—a ridiculous number of champagne bottles, courtesy of Mandy—and nibbles. Rafe was already busy pouring glasses of champagne, but when he saw them, he gave a blinding smile and bounded over.

"Oh my *God*, that was *incredible!*" he babbled, hugging them in turn. "I was seriously blown away." Tag looked as surprised as Jay felt at his enthusiasm, but they didn't have time to compare notes because now Dame Cordelia was sweeping into the room with Mandy and Phil following like a pair of bridesmaids in her wake.

"Darling!" she called out as she trotted towards him, her arms held out wide. "That was wonderful—simply *wonderful!* I was crying like a baby during the final scene. I hope I didn't put you off with my sobbing!"

She hugged him hard, and he hugged her back, whispering, "Thank you, for today." She'd spent hours with him after Tag left to meet his parents, talking him through preparatory exercises and breathing techniques. Stuff he'd stubbornly refused to let her show him when he was younger. And it had helped. It really had.

After that there were more hugs with Mandy and Phil, then Bea's parents, Timon and Rosie. And then Tag was shepherding two unfamiliar faces towards him.

"Jay, meet my parents, Bridget and Sean."

Sean was like an older version of Tag, at least in his height, build and facial features. Tag clearly got his colouring from his mother, though. She had the same dark hair and pale skin, though her hair was shot with grey.

"It's nice to meet you, love," Bridget said, beaming. "Tag never stops talking about you when he phones."

Jay glanced at Tag, raising his brows, and was amused to see colour flood Tag's face.

"As if I ever get a word in when I phone you," he grumbled, but he shifted awkwardly as he said it, rubbing at the back of his neck with one hand.

"Well, of course he talks about him," Sean said. "He's his boyfriend, isn't he?"

Tag, Jay, and Bridget all turned as one to look at Sean. Jay wondered if he looked as shocked at the other two.

"Well, aren't you?" Sean said.

Tag cleared his throat. "Well, um—"

"For God's sake, Sean! Will you keep your nose out of their business?" Bridget scolded. Then she turned to Jay and laid her hand on his arm, saying, "If you are together, though, we'd be pleased as punch. You seem like a very nice fella and we love that television programme you're in, about the vampires. Oh, our Caitlin's just daft about Skye and Faolàn, isn't she, Tag? She reads all that fanfiction, you know."

Tag's face was scarlet now. He mumbled his agreement, but looked very relieved when Jay's mother joined them. She introduced herself to Bridget and Sean with her usual panache, then announced that Tag had revealed that Sean was a fan of *Foxy PI* and would they like to meet Amanda Ffyffe?

Unsurprisingly, the answer to that question was an enthusiastic yes, and moments later, Jay and Tag were finally alone.

"Hi," Jay said softly, feeling unaccountably shy all of a sudden.

"Hi." Tag's smile was sweet, but it wavered when he spotted something over Jay's shoulder. "Wait, what the *hell*?"

Jay turned to look—a new, unfamiliar group of people had just arrived backstage, led by none other than Giles Cox. Jay recognised Orange-sack-dress-woman from his mother's party, though tonight's equally shapeless dress was royal blue. And yes, that was her strange, nautical husband with her, in baggy boat shorts, deck shoes with no socks, and a denim sailing cap. What were their names again? The man gave Jay a jaunty little salute, and Jay smiled wanly back— until they moved aside and Jay spotted who was lurking behind them: none other than Austin Coburn, who immediately made a beeline for Rafe and the champagne.

"Fucking hell!" Tag hissed. "What are *they* doing here?"

Clearly, he wasn't the only one thinking that because Freddie was already beating a furious path towards Giles, muttering, "Cast, crew and family only!"

"Coburn's got a bloody nerve!" Tag said angrily, hands fisting by his sides. "I'm not having this." And with that, he stalked off in Austin's direction too, leaving Jay standing paralysed behind him.

Fuck. Jay was resigned to getting the usual hatchet job from Austin about his performance, but the last thing he wanted was for Tag to make himself a target as well, so he hurried after him, desperately trying to come up with a damage control strategy.

Rafe was in the process of opening another bottle of champagne as they approached, and Austin was speaking, his expression smug and sneering. Jay could only imagine what he was saying. But before he and Tag reached them, and with the towering presence of a natural-born prima donna, Rafe reared back from Austin, fixed him with a look of utter disgust, and said loudly, *"Really?* I think we must have been watching different productions, Austin. I thought Jay was *incredible* tonight!"

Everyone in the room must have heard that because all other conversation came to an abrupt, screeching halt, and every single head turned to stare at Austin and Rafe. Austin's expression morphed in an instant from supercilious to hunted.

Never one to be upstaged, Dame Cordelia pronounced, in her hit-the-back-of-the-stalls voice, "Are you talking about Julius? Who's saying he wasn't incredible tonight?"

"Oh, it's only *Coburn*—that tabloid critic?" Rafe replied, still very loudly, his voice dripping with contempt. "And to be perfectly frank, if that's how he feels, I can't for the life of me understand what he's doing here, can you?"

"Not at all. Perhaps he got lost." Dame Cordelia sent Giles a withering look before fixing her attention on the now cowering Austin. "This is a *celebration*, darling, and I'm fairly sure you're not invited."

"Besides," Rafe said acidly, "don't you have a column, or something, to scribble? You'll want to make sure you get it right. I suggest you give your words some *very* careful thought. I've already told Grandy all about the show, and you know how he loves his theatre."

Austin's face, which had flushed a deep red, went suddenly very white. He opened his mouth to say something but Rafe had already turned away, champagne bottle in hand, and was approaching Jay and Tag, standing just a few feet away now. "More bubbly?" he trilled, as though he hadn't just made a lifelong enemy of one of the country's nastier critics.

Automatically, Jay and Tag lifted their glasses, and Rafe calmly topped them up while, behind him, Austin slinked towards the door and made a hasty and very quiet exit.

"Bloody hell," Tag breathed.

"Is he gone?" Rafe asked, seeming unconcerned. "God, what a prick!"

Jay made a face. "Unfortunately, he's a prick with a big audience. I'm afraid he won't forget that, Rafe. He's a vindictive bastard. I should know. He's been writing crap about me for years."

Rafe chuckled. "Oh, I'm not worried about him."

"You're... not?"

"No, of course not. Grandy owns the rag he writes for—the whole media group, actually. And whatever he was planning to write won't be what appears now, I can assure you of that."

Tag blinked. "Oh, is that what you meant when you said he should think about what he puts in his column?"

"Well… yes." Rafe gave a rueful pout. "I know I shouldn't flex my connections, but in this case, I don't care. You were awesome tonight, Jay, and I'm not going to let that slimy little prick attack our play just because he had a grudge against you at school."

Now it was Jay's turn to blink. "You know about that?"

Rafe made a face. "I was talking to him at your mother's party. He can *really* get going on the topic of you and the sodding drama club, can't he? It's very obsessive and weird." Rafe looked a little shamefaced then. "I may have got a bit drunk that night, and, well, I *may* have been bitching about being the understudy. So I suppose it's *possible* I gave him the impression I was a sympathetic ear." Flushing, he added, "Sorry about that. I can be a bit of dick when I drink too much."

But Jay couldn't bring himself to mind about that now—hell, Rafe had just slain another of his dragons, at least for now. "It's okay," he said. "I get your frustration—you just want a chance to perform. We all do."

Rafe's smile in response was a bit more genuine than all the stagey ones he'd been doing up till now. Almost shy, in fact. "Yeah, well, it looks like I am going to get my chance. Bea told me that if the play's a hit, there's going to be a regional tour—and since most of the dates will be when you're filming the next season of *Leeches*…" He trailed off, sending Jay an almost apologetic look.

Jay grinned and clapped him on the shoulder. "That's great news. And you'll be fantastic."

Rafe looked quietly pleased at that. "Thanks," he said. Then, sounding more like his usual self, "Guess I'd better go and top up some more glasses. This champagne isn't going to drink itself!"

"Well," Tag said once he was gone, lifting his glass in a

toast. "Here's to you, Mr. Warren, and a truly triumphant night. Even Austin Coburn's been sorted out." He grinned, his eyes warm with affection.

And somehow, that was when the words that had been hovering on the tip of Jay's tongue for so long came tumbling out.

"God, I love you."

Tag had already raised his glass to take a drink. In fact, he was tipping champagne into his mouth at the exact moment Jay said the critical words. His eyes went wide over the rim of his glass, and the next second he was choking and spluttering on the wine, and all Jay could do was relieve him of his glass, then gently thump his back a couple of times.

"Cool reaction," Jay said mildly, as Tag gasped in several big breaths, making Tag choke again, this time on a laugh.

When he finally got his breath back, Tag said, "I can't *believe* you said that when I've been such a—" He broke off. "*Fuck*, come with me, will you?" Grabbing Jay's hand, he towed him towards the door.

"Where are you two going?" Freddie demanded as they passed her and Henry.

"We won't be long," Tag said, without looking at her or slowing his pace.

Jay suddenly felt elated, buoyant even. All his anxiety over his feelings and whether Tag would share them seemed ridiculous. For these last few weeks, Tag had been telling Jay through his actions how much he cared about him. Jay had never had a partner who had been so concerned about his happiness and comfort. Even if this *was* just a fling, even if Tag didn't fully return his feelings, even if he preferred them to go their separate ways when the festival was over, it wouldn't change the fact that Jay loved him, and he wanted to own that truth, and to say it aloud. He wanted Tag to know it.

Tag didn't stop walking even once they were out in the corridor.

"Where are we going?" Jay asked, a hint of laughter in his voice.

"The stage—we'll be tripping over people going to the bloody loo out here," Tag said firmly. "I want to do this properly, in private."

Jay refrained from pointing out that a theatre stage was a pretty weird place for a private conversation because, yes, it probably *was* the most private area of the building right now.

When they got there, Tag turned around so that they were facing one another. "Now, can you say that again? Because I need to know I didn't imagine it."

"You didn't imagine it," Jay said, smiling, "but fine. I love you, Tag. I'm hopelessly in love with you—have been for a while, if I'm honest."

"Fuck," Tag swallowed, his throat bobbing hard. After a moment, he added, "I mean, I love you too—and now I feel like a dick for not saying it first. Shit, I should have said it first!"

Jay laughed softly. "*Still* so competitive?"

Tag looked adorably rueful. "More like, you deserved to hear it first. It's just that I've been scared shitless you wouldn't feel the same way. Especially after I made such a big deal about keeping our relationship quiet. Which has backfired on me, by the way, since I find myself wanting to tell every guy who so much as glances at you that you're mine."

"I was afraid you just wanted something casual."

"I was afraid you only *did* casual," Tag replied, his gaze very direct. After a beat, he added, "If I'm honest, you're the first guy I've gone to bed with that I've *never* felt the least bit casual about."

"Yeah?" Jay whispered.

"Yeah," Tag breathed. "Right from that first time, after the awards dinner."

Jay raised a brow. "You could have fooled me—what was it you said? About never having had to work so hard for a blowj—"

"*Please* don't remind me," Tag begged. "I was such a dick that night. All I can say is that I was freaking out over how perfect you were."

"Perfect, huh?" Jay teased.

But Tag just smiled. "Yeah," he said, sliding a hand around Jay's neck and pulling him closer, murmuring, "Perfect for me," a second before his mouth covered Jay's.

Jay closed his eyes, loving the gentle, persuasive pressure of Tag's lips, the tentative stroke of his tongue over the seam of Jay's mouth, his deepening of the kiss when Jay opened to him. Loving the perfection of it, here, on the stage where, tonight, everything had gone so wonderfully, unexpectedly... right.

When they finally broke apart, Tag said, "I'm not sure what happens next. Does this mean...?" He let the words hover, his eyes searching Jay's face.

"What do you want to happen next?" Jay asked. "I've not thought about it beyond telling you how I feel."

"Well," Tag said carefully, "I'm not really sure what I'll be doing over the next year or two, but"—he took a deep breath —"I want us to be together. And I'd prefer to be out in the open about it. I want to tell my family about us, and my friends. I've discovered that I don't like hiding stuff."

"You're not worried about what people might say about how you got cast?"

Tag shrugged. "If there's one thing I've learned over the last couple of days, it's that you can't run scared of arseholes like Coburn. Fuck them. They can say what they want. I'm very proud to be with you, and I want everyone to know it." He paused, then added, "Does that sound... okay?"

Jay's smile felt huge. "It sounds very okay. In fact, it sounds pretty damned perfect."

Leaning in, Tag kissed him again, warm and affectionate but full of promise. When he pulled back, he held out his hand in invitation. "Come on then. Let's go back to the party and make this official."

Taking Tag's hand in his, threading their fingers together, Jay let Tag lead him off-stage and back to a world he'd thought lost to him forever. A world of drama, theatre, and passion. A world that Tag's love and loyalty had helped him rediscover.

Tag might not have realised it yet, but as they walked together into the darkness of the wings Jay knew that he'd be sharing that world with Tag for the rest of their lives. And he couldn't wait.

ENCORE

Tag

Four months later
Hallowe'en

"Ta-da!" Tag sang, as he burst into the living room, where Jay was waiting for him.

"Well now," Jay said slowly, his eyes not moving from Tag as he got up from the sofa. "Don't you look sexy?"

Tag did a little twirl, the long leather coat flaring out round his shins. "I do rock the Skye Jäger look," he admitted, "but I'm not sure this tops last year's costume for sexiness—remember my zombie barista?"

Jay slid his arms around Tag's waist and pulled him in for a kiss. "The memory of you in those silver shorts is burned into my memory forever. But this is sexy too, in a very different way. Mmm, major bad boy vibes. I think you'll need to fuck me after the party. Or maybe *at* the party…"

Tag's cock hardened on cue. "Or maybe right now," he growled, then groaned when Jay's phone pinged. "Tell me that's not our cab," he whined.

Jay checked his phone. "It's our cab," he sighed. "Come

on. We'll have fun, and there'll be plenty of time for shagging like rabbits later. We have three whole days together after this."

Three whole days. Tag grinned, leaned in, and kissed Jay quickly on the lips. *Bliss.*

"I must say, you're looking pretty damn sexy tonight yourself, *Bishop*," Tag said as they left Jay's house and headed for the waiting cab. They'd decided to go to the RPP Hallowe'en party as each other's characters this year, so Tag was vamping it up as Skye, while Jay was looking adorably butch as an eighteenth-century street lout.

"At least I'm in a costume this year," Jay said, modest as always.

It was a fifty-minute drive to the hotel where the party was happening—longer if the traffic was bad—and Tag found himself wishing there was some sort of privacy screen they could put up because he really wanted to suck Jay off. His breeches had a very convenient little flap that you could unbutton and uncover everything, and Tag's mouth was watering just looking at it. It had been a long three weeks, and those historical outfits really got him hot.

"We should have hired a limousine," he said absently, and Jay looked at him like he had a screw loose.

"A limousine?"

Tag cleared his throat. "Doesn't matter. So—who else will we see there tonight? Everyone from *Leeches*, I assume."

"Yup—we all tend to come to this party given it usually happens shortly after we start filming. And at least some of your lot should be there." He smiled. "You must be looking forward to seeing them again?"

"Yeah, I am," Tag said, grinning nervously.

Tag hadn't seen the *Bow Street* cast or crew since filming the pilot, but shortly after the pilot was shown, it was announced that the show had been picked up for a full season. Aaron's writing team was working hard on the scripts—including a much bigger and more significant role for Tag's character, Bishop—and filming was due to start in the new year. In the meantime, he was touring *Let Us Go Back* with Rafe playing Sassoon. Thankfully, they had a short break just now, but on Tuesday, he would have to head for Reading, where they were playing two nights before moving on to Nottingham. Touring a play was, he had discovered, a gruelling business—fun and satisfying, but definitely gruelling. And he missed Jay like mad. He'd been on the road for three weeks solid before this short break, and he'd have five more weeks to go after it. But then he'd be moving in with Jay, and they'd get two glorious weeks off over Christmas before they started filming their respective shows in the new year. And living together.

Life was pretty damn good.

Tag gazed at the fine, beautiful lines of Jay's profile in the dark interior of the cab. Jay Warren, his *boyfriend*—God, sometimes, the reality of that hit him and he couldn't quite believe how lucky he was. Because of all the good things that had happened to him this year, Jay was the very best of them.

Feeling his gaze, Jay turned to Tag, his eyes gleaming in the darkness. "The timing could be better," he said, "I was hoping to spend our first night together alone. But I suppose we don't have to stay all night. Pity it's another hour's cab ride to get home."

"Yes, about that," Tag said. "I was going to keep this as a surprise but… I might have booked us a suite at the hotel?"

"A suite?" Jay echoed. "You did?" His grin was huge.

"Yup, so we can put in an appearance at the party for a while and then disappear upstairs for reunion sex whenever we want!"

Jay chuckled even as he cast an embarrassed look in the driver's direction. God, he was adorable. Clearing his throat, Jay said, "That review in the Birmingham Mail was really good—I bet Rafe was loving the bit about him *delivering a poignant performance*?"

That was a blatant change of subject but undeniably effective. "Oh, I haven't seen that one," Tag replied, excited. "Show me."

Jay pulled out his phone. "I've got a message from Ronnie," he murmured. "Probably about Mother's birthday. Give me a sec."

He swiped at the screen a couple of times, then blinked and started to scroll intently.

"Is something wrong?" Tag asked, noticing with concern the frown forming between Jay's brows.

"You could say that," Jay said and glanced up with an incredulous look. "But not for us. Check this out... Ronnie just sent me the link."

He turned his phone towards Tag.

The screen displayed an article from one of the tabloid sites, a big splashy piece under the headline 'My Gay Marriage Hell' accompanied by a pouting picture of a pretty young man perched on the lap of Sebastian Talbot, both of whom were dressed in white robes and wreathed in flower garlands. Presumably a wedding photo?

"That's Seb's husband?"

"Soon to be ex, apparently." Still intently reading, Jay gave a soft laugh. "Wow, listen to this—'*almost as soon as we'd exchanged vows, Seb became controlling and abusive,' says Niccolò, Talbot's estranged husband. 'In bed, he was selfish and very dull. He made love like a man late for work—bored with the drive and only interested in reaching the destination as fast as possible.'*"

Tag grimaced. "Ouch."

"Accurate," Jay said with an amused snort. Then his expression changed, growing more serious. "Oh shit. This is even worse. Listen. '*Obsessed with being upstaged by younger actors, Niccolò claims that Seb would frequently trade juicy theatre*" *gossip with a prominent critic in exchange for favourable notices in his column.'"*

"Jesus," Tag said, horrified. "Do people really do that?"

"Seb does, apparently." Jay looked thoughtful, his frown deepening. "I knew he deliberately tripped me up in *The Birthday Party*, but I'd always assumed it was because he was pissed off at me. But what if…?" His eyes met Tag's.

Grimly, Tag said, "I suppose it did make a good story."

"It did, yeah. For Austin Coburn."

For a moment, they just stared at each other.

"In which case," Tag said, turning his gaze back to the screen. "This looks like karmic justice."

The party was in full flow when they arrived, and they spent a good hour just circulating and saying hello to a million people before Tag dragged Jay up onto the very crowded dance floor. When they finally stumbled off, sweaty and thirsty, and desperate for something to drink, Tag spotted Aaron and Lewis. He elbowed Jay. "Look who it is!"

"Wow! Lewis turning up for the second year in a row." Jay grabbed Tag's hand and towed him towards them, calling out, "Hey, you two!"

Aaron was working a sexy devil look in a long, dark red coat over tight black trousers and shirt, a neat pair of black horns, and a painted-on moustache and goatee. Lewis, however, just seemed to be wearing his usual shirt and trousers, though he had a bunched-up wad of white fabric under his arm.

"What are you meant to be?" Tag asked him.

"He forgot to pick up his costume," Aaron said placidly, "so we improvised a ghost outfit for him, but he's taken it off, as you can see."

"A... sheet with eyeholes?" Tag said, raising his brows. "Classy."

Lewis sent him a flat look. "Boo."

Tag bit back his grin, but Jay laughed out loud, slinging an arm over Lewis's shoulder and saying, "Come on, grumpy. I'll buy you a drink."

They headed to the bar, leaving Tag and Aaron to follow.

"I'm surprised you didn't pick his costume up for him," Tag said. "You're normally the organised one, aren't you?"

"I'm actually just back from the States today," Aaron said. "Had to go over for some meetings about *Bloodsuckers.*" *Bloodsuckers* was the US version of *Leeches,* and Aaron had taken on some fan liaison role or something. Tag wasn't very clear what it was all about, but it seemed to involve lots of high-powered meetings and calls with big executives in between his *Bow Street* work.

"I've been away for a week," Aaron continued, "so, to be honest, we could have done without a party tonight, but I persuaded Lewis that we needed to put in an appearance. It's only once a year, and it's always good fun, right?"

Tag grinned, remembering last year's party. It had been pretty eventful, but he would always think of it as the night he'd met Jay for the first time.

As though reading his thoughts, Aaron said, "So, you and Jay?"

Tag flashed a grin at him, but he felt his cheeks warm too. "Yeah. It's a thing. We're a thing!"

"I'd say I didn't see that one coming," Aaron said drily. "Except I did. From a mile off."

"Easy to say, after the event," Tag said, threading his arm though Aaron's as they strolled after their boyfriends. "But I don't remember you mentioning it before now."

Aaron raised a brow. "All I'm saying is that there was a *lot* of Unresolved Sexual Tension going on at that awards dinner you came to with Owen."

"Yeah, well, it didn't stay Unresolved for long that night," Tag shot Aaron a look. "After Mason and Owen left, Jay took me back to his hotel room."

"Oh my God! You shagged him *that night*?" Aaron's face was comically astonished. "You've been together since then?"

"Not exactly," Tag hedged. "That was… kind of a one-night stand. But once we got to York and started rehearsing, we… Well, let's just say we eventually got our shit together. And now here we are. All loved up, just like you and Lewis, which, speaking of, seems to be going well?"

Aaron's whole face softened, the soppy git. "Yeah," he said. "It's going *really* well. I mean, he *must* love me because he actually came to this party, and he even wore a costume!" He made a face. "Well, sort of."

"He fucking adores you," Tag said, squeezing his arm. By this time, they had caught up with Jay and Lewis, who already had drinks ordered. Aaron sequestered a table for them, and over the next hour, they caught up on all the other RPP gossip. Lewis even unbent enough to laugh at Tag's jokes, which was quite something given that, a year ago, he'd been giving Tag death glares—admittedly while Tag hung all over Aaron in nothing but his notorious silver shorts. Hell, a year ago, Jay and Tag had been butting heads in this very bar.

A lot could change in a year.

"Oh, hey," Aaron said then, grabbing Lewis's arm, "you'll like this. You know that critic you hate?"

Lewis frowned, clearly drawing a blank. "I hate all critics."

"True," Aaron conceded, "but I mean the one you *really* hate, the one who's always calling *Leeches* a melodramatic angst-fest?"

"Austin Coburn," Jay supplied, giving Lewis an apologetic smile. "Mostly, that's because he hates *me*, not *Leeches*."

"The feeling is *very* mutual," Tag added. "He's a total dick."

Aaron chuckled in agreement. "In that case, you'll all enjoy this. Apparently, Coburn's been outed as giving good reviews in exchange for gossip for his '*Little Bird*' column. His paper couldn't cancel him fast enough."

"Oh my God," Tag said, turning to Jay.

Jay's eyes were wide. "Outed how?"

"Sebastian Talbot ratted on him," Aaron said. "Or, rather, he claimed Coburn had been threatening to trash his productions if he didn't hand over backstage gossip. Apparently, it all came out after Talbot's ex did some kind of kiss-and-tell piece."

"We saw that," Tag said, casting another look at Jay. "Sounds like Seb's trying to cover his arse."

Jay nodded. "And throwing Austin under the bus to do it is totally on brand for him." He added with laughing disbelief, "Christ, what a pair of shits."

"Good to see them get flushed together," Tag said, relieved by Jay's laughter. "And good riddance."

Lewis snorted. "Well it's the best fucking news I've had all day."

"The best news except for me coming home?" Aaron said, with a blatant flutter of his lashes.

Lewis gave him a direct look. "Speaking of, I think it's time we headed off."

"Is your socialising well full up?" Aaron asked, grinning affectionately at him.

Lewis cleared his throat. "Um, not really, but we do have those… *plans*?" And then he blushed. Yes, Lewis fucking Hunter actually *blushed*. Tag stared at him, fascinated. He hadn't thought blunt-to-the-point-of-rudeness Lewis was capable of such a thing, but here he was, face as red as a tomato.

"Oh. *Oh!*" Aaron said, recognition dawning, and then he was blushing too. "Yes, right, we do, don't we?" He bit his lip, then mouthed a *Sorry* at Lewis.

Tag opened his mouth to make a crack about reunion sex but closed it again when Jay nudged him.

"We need to head off too, actually," Jay said, twisting his fingers with Tag's. "Right?"

Oh. Right.

"Yeah," Tag said. "We've got plans too. A big bed-shaped plan two floors up to be specific." He waggled his eyebrows.

Subtle, he was not, but even Lewis laughed at that.

Once Lewis and Aaron had said goodnight, Tag pulled Jay into a quick, hard kiss, then gasped melodramatically, "Take me to bed, Julius, or lose me forever!"

Jay laughed and got up. "Come on, you nut. I've got plans for you too."

"Intriguing… Care to share?"

Jay just pulled him to his feet and towed him out of the party, waving at a few people as they passed, but not halting to speak to anyone. *Man on a mission*, Tag thought approvingly.

The suite was pretty small and not nearly as fancy as the last one, but then this hotel wasn't as fancy. The bed looked good, though. Huge and comfortable, with a cloud of pristine, white bedding, and there on the sideboard was a bucket with a bottle of champagne in it, a platter of sliced fruit, and yes… a box of After Eights tied up in a big red bow.

Tag glanced at Jay, to see his reaction. He knew he'd be pleased—he was always incredibly touched by even the smallest of romantic gestures—but he was still surprised to see the tears glimmering in Jay's storm cloud eyes.

"Hey," Tag said softly, pulling him into his arms. "You okay?"

Jay sniffed and nodded, blinking the tears away. *"Very* okay," he said, before covering Tag's mouth with his own.

Tag had intended to strip Jay out of his historically accurate garments slowly, but somehow they ended up ripping off their clothes and tumbling into the big white bed absurdly quickly, and then it was just their mouths and hands moving, their bodies sliding together, Jay slipping his fingers inside Tag, stretching him carefully before Tag climbed on top and took Jay's hard, solid cock into his body. Jay was beautiful beneath him, all dark hair and golden skin against the white sheets, his expression nakedly adoring as he watched Tag moving above him, his hands hard on Tag's hips. When they came, together, it was in a rolling, undulating wave of pleasure that seemed to connect every part of Tag: his happy, spurting cock, his very full heart, and his deliciously fuddled mind.

"Love you," he mumbled, sprawled on top of Jay like a blanket.

Jay stroked Tag's sweaty hair back from his forehead and murmured, "Love you too."

As he lay there, Tag thought about life before Jay. He'd had no time then for more than the occasional hook-up with hot, nameless guys. No time for anything that wouldn't either earn quick money or boost his acting career. It had been tough, but it had been necessary. Without those years, that focus, he might never have forced the door open wide enough to land the role in *Bow Street* that had led to everything else. To Jay.

Yeah, those years had been important. But *this,* with Jay? This was something else—something so much *more.*

Tag knew now that whatever the future had in store for him, be it stardom or obscurity, it wouldn't matter because he'd have Jay at his side. And finding Jay, loving Jay—being loved by Jay—was the luckiest break of Tag's life.

The End

THANK YOU, DEAR READER

Thank you for reading this book, the third and final book in the Creative Types series. We hope you enjoyed spending time with Lewis & Aaron, Owen & Mason and Tag & Jay as much as we did.

We love hearing from our readers. You can find all the different ways to connect with each (or both!) of us below.

If you have time, we'd be very grateful if you'd consider leaving a review on an online review site.
Reviews are so helpful for book visibility and we appreciate every one.

Joanna & Sally x

∾

CREATIVE TYPES, BOOKS 1 AND 2

Want to find out how Lewis and Aaron got together? Check out **Total Creative Control**. And for Mason and Owen's story, check out **Home Grown Talent**.

~

Total Creative Control *(Creative Types 1)*

Sunshine PA, meet Grumpy Boss...

When fanfic writer Aaron Page landed a temp job with the creator of hit TV show, *Leeches*, it was only meant to last a week. Three years later, Aaron's still there...

It could be because he loves the creative challenge. It could be because he's a huge *Leeches* fanboy. It's definitely *not* because of Lewis Hunter, his extremely demanding, staggeringly rude...and breathtakingly gorgeous boss.

Is it?

Lewis Hunter grew up the hard way and fought for everything he's got. His priority is the show, and personal relationships come a distant second. Besides, who needs romance when you have a steady stream of hot men hopping in and out of your bed?

His only meaningful relationship is with Aaron, his chief confidante and indispensable assistant. And no matter how appealing he finds Aaron's cute boy-next-door charms, Lewis would never risk their professional partnership just to scratch an itch.

But when Lewis finds himself trapped at a hilariously awful corporate retreat, Aaron is his only friend and ally. As the professional lines between them begin to blur, their simmering attraction starts to sizzle

… And they're both about to get *burned*.

∿

Home Grown Talent (*Creative Types 2*)

Are you for real?

From the outside, it looks like model and influencer Mason Nash has it all—beauty, fame, and fortune. With his star rapidly rising, and a big contract up for grabs, Mason's on the verge of hitting the big time.

When an opportunity arises to co-host a gardening slot on daytime TV with his ex's brother, Owen Hunter, Mason is definitely on-board. And he intends to use every trick in the book to make the show a hit—including agreeing to his ruthless producer's demand to fake a 'will-they/won't-they' romance with his co-host…

Owen Hunter is a gardener with a huge heart and both feet planted firmly on the well-tilled ground. He's proud of the life he's built and has absolutely no desire to be on TV—yet somehow he finds himself agreeing to do the show.

It's definitely *not* because he's interested in Mason Nash. The guy might be beautiful—and yeah, his spoiled brat routine presses all Owen's buttons in the bedroom—but Owen has no interest in a short-term fling with a fame-hungry model.

As the two men get closer, though, Owen starts to believe there's more to Mason than his beautiful appearance and carefully-curated online persona—that beneath the glitz and glamour is a sweet, sensitive man longing to be loved.

A man Owen might be falling for. A man who might even feel the same.

But in a world of media spin and half-truths, Owen is dangerously out of his depth. And when a ridiculous scandal explodes online, with Owen at its heart, it starts to look as though everything he thought was real is built on lies—including his budding romance with Mason…

CONNECT WITH JOANNA

Email: authorjoannachambers@gmail.com

Website: www.joannachambers.com

Newsletter: subscribe at my website for up to date
information about my books, freebies
and special deals.

All new subscribers get a free novella and two exclusive
bonus stories from the Enlightenment series.

Joanna

CONNECT WITH SALLY

Email: sally@stargatenovels.com

Website: www.sallymalcolm.com

Newsletter: subscribe at my website for news, book recs, and giveaways. All new subscribers get a free copy of *Rebel: An Outlawed Story*.

Sally

ALSO BY SALLY MALCOLM

* free for newsletter subscribers

THE LAST KISS

When Captain Ashleigh Dalton went to war in 1914, he never expected to fall in love. Yet, over three long years at the front, his dashing batman, Private West, became his reason for fighting—and his reason for living.

For Harry West, an ostler from London's East End, it was love at first sight when he met complex, compassionate Captain Dalton. Harry knew their friendship wouldn't survive in the class-bound world back home, but in the trenches, there was no point in worrying about tomorrow…

Now, gravely wounded, Ash has been evacuated home to Highcliffe House, his father's Hampshire estate. Bereft of Harry, angry and alone, Ash struggles to fit into the unchanging world he left behind. Meanwhile, Harry, broken-hearted, doubts he'll ever see his beloved captain again.

But when the guns fall silent and Harry finds himself adrift in London, a desperate hope carries him to Highcliffe House in search of work—and of the officer he can't forget…

∾

EXCERPT FROM THE LAST KISS

12th October 1917, Flanders, Belgium

"Captain Dalton." He was woken by West's hand on his arm, a gentle shake. "Sorry, sir, but it's time."

West sat next to him still, but the book was put away and Ash could see first light creeping around the edges of the gas curtain. His stomach clenched, his heart racing sharply. Morning had arrived, cold and cruel.

West's hand tightened on his arm. "We'll have to finish that chapter later, sir."

Later. It felt as longed for and unreachable as home.

"I'm afraid I dropped off. We might have to repeat some of it." Their gazes tangled and locked, too raw for bravado now. Ash's faux bonhomie fell away. "Good luck today, West."

West's throat moved as he swallowed. "You too, Captain."

Above them, the barrage continued unrelenting, their guns firing five miles west, towards the village they were attempting to take. Had been attempting to take since July. What the hell could be left of it now?

"It's six-thirty, sir." Less than an hour to go. It was past time he was outside with the men. Ash rose and West helped him on with his trench coat, buttoning it like a London valet before handing him his tin hat. Another pause followed. Then Ash said, "I don't want to...to let the men down today."

"You, Captain? Not a chance." West squeezed his shoulder. "We'll get through it, don't you worry. We'll get through it together."

How to explain that it wasn't for himself that he worried, that there was something he feared more than his own death? Impossible, of course. The best he could do was grip West's forearm. "Together."

There was no more to be said. Ash led the way out into the miserable morning where his men watched him from drawn, frightened faces. None of them had slept, counting down the hours until the attack, and he felt guiltily grateful for his short reprieve with West.

"Taff," he greeted the dark-eyed Welshman sitting smoking on the fire step.

Taff's fingers shook as he lifted the gasper to his lips. "Captain Dalton." His guarded gaze moved to the dugout and back, aware as all the men were—as Ash was—of the unearned privileges his rank enjoyed. "Get some kip?"

"Hardly, with this racket." Ash forced levity into his voice. "I dare say there'll be post waiting when we get back to the relief trench. It feels like an age since you've had a letter. All of two days, I should think."

Taff gave a reluctant smile. "My missus does like to write, sir."

"And we all want to know what happened about...what was his name? Your neighbour's story about the vicar and the missing pig."

A flash of teeth. "Mrs. Evans. Terrible gossip, she is, sir. I don't believe half of what she says."

And so it went on, the excruciating duty of finding a word here and there for each of the men while they endured these last dreadful minutes of waiting, a grotesque noblesse oblige that Ash probably resented as much as his sullen, frightened men. His rank gave him no special insight when staring death in the eye and nobody knew that better than himself. But Little Bill looked rough, scared almost out of his wits, and Ash spared him a firm hand on the shoulder as he passed. "You'll have a story to tell your sweetheart when you're home, eh?" The boy nodded, eyes wide and glassy. Ash resisted the urge to hug him. Instead, he had the rum passed around and let Little Bill drink liberally.

He checked his watch. Six forty-five. Half an hour to go.

His head felt woolly, blood pounding in his ears. Fear did that, he'd learned. Scattered your wits, broke your nerve. He looked up into the sky, fading remorselessly to grey, and made out the tangle of wire above them. A scrap of uniform fluttered there, dank in the dank morning. Some poor sod, dead. Him, maybe, in a matter of minutes.

Terror closed his throat, accelerated his racing heartbeat. He felt clammy and sick. God, he hoped he didn't lose his nerve, not in front of the men. Men? Boys, some of them.

Beautiful and full of life when they were laughing together behind the lines, kicking about a football or telling off-colour jokes. Grey-faced now, they looked even younger than their too-few years.

An odd thought struck him: at least Tilney had been spared this dreadful bloody wait. His drowning had been sudden, unanticipated. The thought almost made him laugh, but he swallowed the terrifying bubble of hysteria. Dangerous, that. Rum lingered in the back of his throat and his watery guts squirmed. If he survived this damned war, he'd never touch the stuff again.

Carefully, he set one foot on the ladder that would take him over. How far would he make it before he was cut down? Ten yards, a hundred? Would it be a shell or machine gun fire that did for him? If he made it to the German lines, maybe a bayonet to the belly. Or would he get stuck on the wire? His fingers, of their own accord, drummed out a tune on the ladder as if playing a mute piano.

If you want to find the private, I know where he is,
I know where he is, I know where he is.
If you want to find the private, I know where he is,
He's hanging on the old barbed wire...

He felt for his whistle, secure on its leather lanyard. His mouth was dry. From along the line came a rumpus, someone shouting and quickly stifled. It took men like that sometimes, the long wait. It broke their nerve. And who could blame them? This was tortuous.

He checked his watch. Six fifty-nine.

Time was crawling, he'd never known it to move so slowly. And yet too fast. Their lives were measured in moments now. He cleared his throat. "Fifteen-minutes," he told the men.

Behind him, feet shuffled as the men moved about, making whatever peace they could, bracing themselves to meet their fate. It would be easier to be one of them. The weight of giving the order, of leading men to their ends, felt heavy as iron.

A shoulder brushed his, solid and steady. He glanced sideways and found West watching him. In the growing daylight, he could see the warm hazel of his eyes and the curl of his golden hair beneath his tin hat. West's friendship was everything to him here. He'd made the last three years bearable, even pleasurable at times. It wasn't right, of course, for a man like Captain Ashleigh Arthur Dalton, son of Sir Arthur, to be friends with plain old Private Harry West. But friends they were, closer than brothers. How many nights had they spent in conversation or in reading aloud to each other, playing cards with the men or in Ash's quarters? How many nights had they hunkered down, side-by-side in the support trench, sharing warmth and the comfort of each other's presence?

And if anything happened to West today, Ash didn't know how he'd bear it. Well, he couldn't bear it. Simple as that.

He'd rather die himself than lose Harry West.

～

ALSO BY JOANNA CHAMBERS

You can start the ***Winterbourne series*** for **free** today by signing up to my newsletter

GENTLEMAN WOLF, BOOK ONE IN THE CAPITAL WOLVES DUET

He must master the wolf within...

Edinburgh, 1820.

Thirty years after leaving Scotland, Drew Nicol is forced to return when the skeleton of a monster is found. The skeleton is evidence of werewolves—evidence that Marguerite de Carcassonne, the leader of Drew's pack, is determined to suppress.

Marguerite insists that Drew accompany her to Edinburgh. There they will try to acquire the skeleton while searching for wolf-hunters—wolf hunters who may be holding one of their pack prisoner.

But Drew has reason to be wary about returning to Edinburgh —Lindsay Somerville now lives there.

Lindsay who taught Drew about desire and obsession.

Lindsay who Drew has never been able to forgive for turning him.

Lindsay who vowed to stay away from Drew twelve years ago... and who has since taken drastic steps to sever the bond between them.

Marguerite's plan will throw Drew and Lindsay together again—and into a deadly confrontation with Lindsay's enemy, Duncan MacCormaic. They will be tested to their limits and forced to confront both their past mistakes and their true feelings.

But it may be too late for them to repair the damage of the past. The consequences of Lindsay's choices are catching up with him, and he's just about out of time…

~

READ ON FOR A TASTER OF GENTLEMAN WOLF…

MacCormaic's Keep, Achinvaig, Scotland March 1682

Awareness returned to Lindsay one sensation at a time. First, the dank, rough stone beneath his cheek. Then the stale, chill air of the dungeon.

The pain came last—when he tried to move his thin and wasted body. The agony of movement forced an inhuman noise from him, like the whimper of a dog.

A cur.

Swallowing, he tasted blood, sharp and metallic on his tongue. He tried to open his eyes but only managed the right one. The left stayed stubbornly closed. Not that there was anything to see down here.

The thick, soupy darkness of the dungeon was all too familiar to him. He'd lost track of how many years—or decades—he'd spent being thrown into and plucked out of this putrid hole, over and over. A plaything to be used for his master's entertainment.

For all that time, his life had been nothing but shadows and madness and pain. And the pain was very far from being the worst of those things. Sometimes he even welcomed it. At least pain anchored him in the here and now. When it faded, there was nothing. Endless, immeasurable nothing, and no way of counting the hours or days or weeks.

An ordinary man would have perished long ago from

such treatment, but Lindsay was no longer an ordinary man. Though what he now was, he did not fully understand.

When first he'd come to the Keep, he'd been a handsome, vain young officer, so fine in his uniform. So proud of his looks. He could scarcely remember that laughing, beautiful boy anymore. Over the decades of incarceration, his uniform had turned to rags and fallen from his wasted form. Now he was a sorry, naked creature, pale from lack of sun, his once shining dark hair grown matted and filthy.

He was physically stronger though. Many times' stronger than the innocent mortal he'd once been. Now he was a two-natured creature, a man with a powerful beast inside him that the moon could draw out. A man who did not age, and whose physical wounds healed virtually overnight.

Lindsay sometimes fantasised about death. It was possible for his kind to die—a blow powerful enough to sever the spine in two would do it. But even if such a blow could be self-inflicted, part of his curse was a burning and irrepressible desire for survival, an instinct that prevented him seeking out his own end, no matter how wretched his circumstances might be.

In the end, the physical strength his new nature gave him was for nothing. He was as weak as a babe in all the ways that counted. Slave to a master he had no power to disobey, and slave to his own fierce drive to live. Unable to choose death, he was bound to his fate as surely as Prometheus to his rock with no escaping the endless, repeated torment.

Groaning, Lindsay shifted his body and began to inventory his hurts. His ribs ached on both sides. His upper back and shoulders were raw and stinging. His left hand was agony—he cradled it against his chest, the right one cupped around it. What else hurt? Oh yes, his closed left eye. And every muscle, without exception.

He slowly moved his aching body into a sitting position, his chains stirring sluggishly. Once up, he raised both hands to his face, the injured one and the good one together, tentatively probing the area around his closed left eye with shaking fingers. The surrounding flesh was puffy, his eyelashes gummed together with something sticky.

His fingers crept to his throat next, his gut twisting sickly when he felt the cold silver band there, sleek and smooth against his fingertips.

He remembered Duncan's parting words of the night before, as Mercer had half-carried, half-dragged Lindsay's exhausted body off to the dungeon.

"Collar him. That'll give the cur something to think about till we get back."

As much as Lindsay hated his beast nature, being unable to shift into that form was even worse. That was what the collar did, imprisoning the animal inside him. Until the silver collar was removed, he would be stuck in his human form. The realisation made him raise his head and howl with desperation and grief, his human voice a sad imitation of his beast's. Bad enough to be imprisoned in this dungeon. Being collared was a second, more horrible incarceration. One that deprived him of the full healing power of his shift, leaving him to mend his hurts in the slow human way.

Anguish overwhelmed him as he thought of the long misery-laden days and nights ahead of him. Dropping his head to his chest, he let the tears fall, not attempting to hold them back. He was glad of them, in truth. They would bathe his injured eye, and he needed all the help he could get to heal while his master was gone.

He wondered how long Duncan would be away. Had he mentioned that last night? Lindsay raked through the ashes of his memories, trying to recall some detail that might give him a clue. He hated probing his memory even more than he hated probing his injured body—couldn't bear to recall the long hours of humiliation and agony. Duncan was never satisfied till he brought out *the cur* in Lindsay. The pathetic, cowardly, shrinking part of him that lurked deep inside. The part that would do anything to live, to be spared pain... to please his master.

"Ah, now see, Mercer. We have coaxed him out at last. Come here, cur—"

Lindsay closed his eyes tightly but still he saw Duncan's hand, lazily beckoning him as he belly-crawled forward. Mercer's hot stare as he stood at Duncan's side, watching hungrily. Duncan's laughter, soft and delighted. A cruel curl to his lips.

No. No. No.

Sickened, Lindsay shook his head fiercely from side to side, as though to dislodge the hateful pictures. Squeezing his eyes closed even tighter, he forced them away, pushing the images into the dark place he'd made for them in his mind. Unwilling to probe his memory further, he locked the door on that place up tight and told himself he'd just have to wait as long as it took for Duncan's return.

It was then that he heard it... a skitter of tiny stones on the dungeon steps. The brush of leather sole on stone. Not the heavy clump of the guards, but a tread that was secret and careful.

Someone was descending the winding stone staircase down into the dark, cold belly of the Keep...

Printed in Great Britain
by Amazon

35819427R00235